DEVILS IN EXILE

A NOVEL

CHUCK HOGAN

SCRIBNER

New York   London   Toronto   Sydney

SCRIBNER
A Division of Simon & Schuster, Inc.
1230 Avenue of the Americas
New York, NY 10020

First Scribner hardcover edition February 2010

SCRIBNER and design are registered trademarks of The Gale Group, Inc., used under license by Simon & Schuster, Inc., the publisher of this work.

For information about special discounts for bulk purchases, please contact Simon & Schuster Special Sales at 1-866-506-1949 or business@simonandschuster.com.

The Simon & Schuster Speakers Bureau can bring authors to your live event. For more information or to book an event contact the Simon & Schuster Speakers Bureau at 1-866-248-3049 or visit our website at www.simonspeakers.com.

Designed by Carla Jayne Jones

Manufactured in the United States of America

10 9 8 7 6 5 4 3 2 1

Library of Congress Control Number: 2009043459

ISBN 978-1-4165-5886-6
ISBN 978-1-4165-5923-8 (ebook)

Author's Note

Homes for Our Troops is a nonprofit, nonpartisan, national organization committed to building specially adapted, barrier-free homes for severely injured servicemen and -women in all branches of the military—at no cost to the veterans they serve. A portion of the author's proceeds from the sale of this novel will go directly to this top-rated veterans' charity.

www.homesforourtroops.org

The Lot

A COLD SATURDAY NIGHT IN NOVEMBER.

Neal Maven stood on the edge of the parking lot, looking up at the buildings of downtown Boston. He was wondering about the lights left shining in the windows of the top-floor offices—who does that, and why—when a thumping bass line made him turn.

A silver limousine eased around the corner. Its long side windows were mirrored so that the less fortunate could see themselves watching the American dream pass them by. Maven stuffed his hands deep inside the pouch pockets of his blanket-thick hoodie, stamping his boots on the blacktop to keep warm.

Nine months now. Nine months he'd been back. Nine months since demobilization and discharge, like nine months of gestation, waiting to be reborn back into the peacetime world. Nine months of transition and nothing going right.

He had already pissed through most of his duty pay. The things you tell the other guys you're going to do once you get back home—grow a beard, drink all night, sleep all day—those things he had done. Those goals he had achieved. The things the army recommends doing before discharge, to ease your transition—preparing a résumé, lining up housing, securing employment—those things he had let slide.

A lot of businesses still stuck yellow SUPPORT OUR TROOPS ribbons in their front windows, but when you actually showed up fresh from Iraq, looking for work, scratching your name and address on an application pad, they saw not a battle-tested hero but a potential Travis Bickle. Hiring a guy with more confirmed kills than college credits was a tough sell. Maven could feel civilians' discomfort around him, their unease. As if they heard a *tick, tick, tick* going inside his head. Probably the same one he heard.

Barroom conversations took on subtext.

"Let me buy you a drink, soldier" meant *If you wig out and decide to start shooting up the room, spare me, I'm one of the good guys.*

"You know, I came close to enlisting myself" meant *Yeah, September eleventh made me piss my pants, but I somehow pulled myself together and haven't missed an episode of* American Idol *since.*

"I supported you boys one hundred percent" meant *Just because I have a ribbon magnet on my car doesn't mean you can look at my daughter.*

"Great to have you back" meant *Now please go away again.*

He finally did drop by the VA for some career guidance, and a short-armed woman with a shrub of salt-and-pepper hair and everyday compassion sat down and banged out that magical résumé, omitting any reference to combat experience. What he considered to be his proudest accomplishment in life, aside from not getting maimed or killed in action—namely, passing the six-phase Qualification Course at Fort Bragg, earning his Special Forces tab in the run-up to the Iraq invasion—was shrunken to a bullet point on the "Skill Sets" section of his résumé. "Proficient at team-building and leadership skills." Not "Mud-hungry, man-killing son of a bitch." So much of his life since coming back had been about writing off what had happened.

The resulting document was a skimpy little thing that whimpered, "Please hire me." He had fifty of them printed on twenty-four-pound paper at Kinko's and seeded another seventy-five around the city via e-mail, to a great and profound silence.

The parking-lot-guard job—6 p.m. to 2 a.m., three nights a week—came via a posting on craigslist. The owner of the parking lot was a builder looking to jab another diamond pin in the cushion of downtown Boston. The property manager who hired Maven, a square-shouldered navy vet of two Vietnam tours, clapped him on the back fraternally and then explained that he would break Maven's thumbs if he stole so much as a penny.

After a week or two of long hours stamping his feet out in the bitterly cold night, warding street people away from soft-top Benzes and Lexus SUVs, this threat took the form of a challenge. Every shift now, Maven showed up thinking he wouldn't steal, only to soften after long hours soaking in the lonesome marinade of night. $36.75 FLAT FEE, ENTER AFTER 6 P.M., NO BLOCKING, EASY-IN/EASY-OUT. He kept it to one or two cars a shift, nothing serious. Latecomers always, inebriates pulling in after midnight, addressing Maven as "my man" or "dude," and never requesting a receipt, never even noticing him lifting the gate by hand. All they cared about was tucking their silver Saab in near the downtown action, wanting nothing to disrupt the momentum of their weekend night.

It was funny money, the $73.50 he skimmed. He wasted it accordingly, opening the gate at quarter to two and walking a few blocks south to Centerfold's in the old Combat Zone, dropping his dollars on a couple of quick beers and a table dance before lights-up at two. He was in a bad way. Any money he had left over, he would take two blocks over to Chinatown, ordering a pot of "cold tea" along with the club zombies and the Leather District poseurs and the college seniors too cool for Boston's puritanical 2 a.m. closing time. Maven sat alone at a cloth-covered table, the piped-in Asian music trickling into his beer buzz like sweet rain as he drank the teapot of draft Bud, throwing back pork dumplings like soft, greasy aspirins. Then he overtipped the rest, tightened up his boot laces, and strapped on his shoulder pack for the long run home.

Home was Quincy, 8.2 miles away.

Running was a purge and a meditation. His thick boots clumped over the cracked streets of rough neighborhoods, along dormant Conrail tracks, and under expressway bridges. Past dark playgrounds and suspicious cars idling at corners, traffic lights blinking yellow overhead, people calling out from porches and stoops, "Who's chasin' you, man?"

Quincy is home to beautiful ocean-view properties, seven-figure marina condos, and is the original homestead of this country's first father-son presidents, the Adamses.

Maven's converted attic apartment was nowhere near any of these. It had sloped ceilings in every room, a stand-up shower with almost zero water pressure, and stood directly under the approach path into Logan.

This was where he lived now. This was who he was.

Sometimes, during his run, he remembered the dancers and the way they eyed themselves in the strip club's mirrored walls as they worked the stage: so unashamed and even bored by their public nudity, as though they considered themselves just part of the spectacle, and not in fact its focus.

This was Maven's attitude toward himself and his own life now. He felt as though he were watching a man slowly slipping over the edge of a deep chasm, not at all concerned that this man was him.

SIX NIGHTS BEFORE, HE HAD NEARLY KILLED A MAN.

The rain had been coming down hard that shift, hard enough to wash away the usual symphony of the downtown weekend: no laughter from passing couples; no Emerson students gloating in packs; no snatches of discussion from scarf-wearing theatergoers; no club-hoppers tripping over sidewalk cracks and laughing off their ass.

The gate had a small booth, but with the rain banging on the tin roof like gunshots, it was easier just to stand outside, letting the rain rap his poncho hood and shoulders, blowing down in sheets from the high security lamps like the rippling sails of a storm-battered ship. He imagined himself a rock beneath a waterfall, and the sensation, as such, was not unpleasant; this was the kind of mind game he had taught himself in the Arabian desert.

People think it never rains over there, but it does: rarely and suddenly, as out of place as applause inside a church. Desert rain tastes silty and runs in dirty black tears down your face. Boston rain, on the other hand, thanks to recycled industrial emissions, tastes and smells as sweet as a soft drink.

Since returning to the States, Maven had battled reimmersion issues common among discharged Iraq veterans. A heightened startle reflex; avoidance of crowded places; sudden, overwhelming anxiety attacks. Discarded food containers, dead animals on the roadside, a man walking alone into traffic: in Iraq, the appearance of these things portended death. Any of them had the potential to detonate fatally without notice. His time over there had been one of unremitting suspense, which he had met with unrelenting vigilance, one of many habits he was still having trouble unlearning.

Two things conspired to distract him from his usual psychotic vigilance that night. The insulating rain was one of them. The other was a gleaming black Cadillac Escalade that pulled in around ten.

The Escalade was a big SUV, the driver sitting at about Maven's eye level. Nothing about him jumped out at Maven: black hair, a no-nonsense face, perfectly shaped shirt collar, jutting chin. The dash was loaded with electronics, more sophisticated than anything in Maven's entire apartment.

As the driver went poking into the sun visor for cash, a woman leaned forward in the passenger seat. She threw a brief glance Maven's way—nothing more than a peek around a blind corner—just curious to put a face to the dark figure working in the rain. The liquid crystal display of the navigation screen lit her green and blue like some beautiful android. Maven glimpsed a flawless neck, a delicately pointed chin, and a tantalizingly thick line of cleavage.

All in an instant. She eased back again—no spark in her eyes, no recognition, nothing.

"Messy night, huh?"

The guy was talking to him, a neatly creased fifty clipped between his fingers. The windshield wipers flicked rain into Maven's face.

"Yeah," said Maven, slow to recover, his hands disappearing inside his pants pockets within the poncho, making change.

The guy accepted the damp bills and coins and spilled them into his cupholder. "Stay dry, man."

He pulled in and parked, exiting with a wide black umbrella, and Maven watched them walk away arm in arm, focusing on the woman's bare shins beneath the cut of her dress, her heels picking at the sidewalk, the sound fading into the rain.

Maven knew her. Knew *of* her, anyway. A girl from his high school. Older than him by three years, a senior when he was a freshman, but as clear and as fixed in his memory as the bikini model who used to smile down at him from the poster on his bedroom wall. Smiled knowingly, with one crooked thumb hooked in the side string of her pink bikini bottom, drawing it an inch away from her cocked hip. That kind of memory.

Her name came back to him with the slap and sting of a snowball to the face: Danielle Vetti.

He said it aloud a few times in the rain. "Danielle Vetti, Danielle Vetti, Danielle Vetti." Watching it steam and disappear. He was amazed to have seen her again, marveling at the gyrations the paths of their lives had to have taken in order to intersect once again, momentarily, that rainy night. The mere memory of her, and this one-second encounter—even the *taste* of her name in his mouth, after all those years—all put a charge into him the likes of which he hadn't felt in a long, long time.

Danielle Vetti had been *the* girl in high school. Passing her in the hall was the highlight of your day, something you'd brag about to your seatmate in the next class. Guys at their lockers—guys in the bathroom you didn't even know—would spread the word: *Check out Danielle Vetti today.* They just didn't make people like that in Gridley, Massachusetts.

Danielle Vetti.

"Hey, man, you see a little, wet dog come through here?"

A guy coming off the street. The Latino accent didn't jibe with what Maven glimpsed of his face beneath the hood of an oily anorak. But this detail didn't jump out at Maven—not until the second guy did.

The blow came from behind, Maven going down and rolling in a puddle. They pulled him up, his head throbbing, and a thick strap was fitted around his chest like the kind used to cinch down loads in a flatbed truck. It was ratcheted fast from behind, pinning Maven's arms against him inside the poncho.

The first guy showed a knife, low and silver, turning it so that it caught the overhead light. A fat, three-inch blade. Maven's focus went in and out.

The guy behind him tugged Maven back between two cars, out of sight from the street.

"The money, man," said the first one, the one holding the knife. "I might just cut you anyway, so give it up fast."

Steam from the mouth of the guy behind Maven smelled sour and chemical. Maven couldn't clear his mind, couldn't get any thoughts started. A cold automobile engine that wouldn't turn over.

They pulled him toward the booth. The knife guy backed inside, Maven getting a better look at his face, his smile sharp and hungry, breath squeezing through widely spaced teeth like fog through a broken fence. He pecked at the register keys, hitting the big button, the drawer shooting open.

Empty.

The knife guy's smile faded. He came back outside, the knife low at his waist. He was set on using it; Maven could see that much. This guy wasn't going away until his blade was bloodied.

"Search him."

Maven set his teeth hard, his tongue pressing against his gums—feeling the notch in the right front quadrant. This recognition relaxed him. A kind of deadness crept in, which was the prelude to combat readiness, a feeling he had once known so well.

EVERYONE WHO COMES BACK HAS HIS ONE STORY.

Even if you come back with a lot of stories, there's still always that one.

Maven's was about a girl. Young, maybe fourteen, her head wrapped in a kaffiyeh of caramel-gold cotton. Maven was working a sneak-and-peek at a house in Samarra with his fire team. Young Iraqi girls often detoured past American soldiers, looking to draw a reaction they could ignore. The concept of America and the freedoms it represented frightened and attracted them, and so to be fancied by a Westerner was like having your forbidden dream beckon to you.

Maven, posted outside the house, didn't see her until she was maybe twenty meters away. She wore a smile, but even at that distance Maven could tell that something was behind it. Her breathing was quick and shallow, and she walked with her arms raised from her sides.

His first thought was that she was in trouble, looking for help, and Maven actually took a step or two toward her, moving into her kill range. She reached inside the loose sleeve of her robe and yanked down, shivering, expecting to die.

Her hand came out holding a broken wire.

She looked at Maven with sweaty panic, then reached back inside her sleeve fast.

Maven brought up his M16. He could have cut her down right there, a chest-pattern, three-round burst. *Brr-rrr-rrp.*

She bent over, working hard, reaching up into her armpit. Maven spun behind a parked Humvee just as she exploded. Shattering car windows sprayed his armor-plated vest, and he was thrown through a thin wooden fence. His fire team found him on all fours, spitting blood, and thought he'd been hit. A warmth spread over his gums, pooling in the right pocket of his cheek. He choked on something wedged in his throat, swallowing it down.

He had bitten off a chunk of his own tongue.

He saw many things during his tours there—many worse things—but it was always this girl who appeared in his dreams. Ended them usually, waking him up. Why she came at him, why she chose him, was a question for which there was no answer. Insurrectionists had been hiring head cases to do pay-and-sprays on American troops, even locking IEDs to noncoms against their will. He wondered if the near-death experience of the first misfire had made her change her mind. Maybe, in those last frantic moments, she was actually trying to get the device off her.

But in the end, what did it matter? The brutality of war, the random nature of man's existence: she represented none of those things to him. All Maven got out of it was a few weeks of speech therapy, and a reminder of something he already knew: trouble had a way of finding him. Always had, always would.

As THE STRAP CREAKED TIGHTER BEHIND HIM, THE NOW SMOOTH tongue notch pushed against the inside of Maven's bite. The second guy's free hand came around to pat Maven's chest and gut through the wet poncho. He felt each side of Maven's waist, pausing at his pants pockets, gripping a mobile phone, then continuing, the guy stooping now, his hand at the cargo pocket along the lower left thigh of Maven's camo fatigues.

The guy's molesting hand squeezed excitedly, closing around the wad of bills inside, his grip on the strap easing just a bit.

Maven shoved backward, driving the guy off-balance. He kicked back with the heel of his left boot and got lucky—catching the guy's nose, a crunch and a dull pop, like the bursting of the glass tube inside an old-fashioned fire alarm.

The knife came thrusting at him, Maven seeing only the blade, pivoting away from it and kicking out, catching the first guy's front left knee. His leg wouldn't bend that way, the guy going down face-first onto the slick pavement.

The guy behind Maven had released the strap, doubled over now, holding his gushing face with both hands.

Maven watched the first guy up on all fours, looking at his knife, the blade edge tipped in blood. He had landed on it when he fell. Maven gave him no time to find the wound, punting him in the ribs, the knife skittering loose.

Maven dropped and rolled over the knife, feeling for the handle with his hands still trapped against his sides, beneath the poncho. He grasped it and sawed at the strap, cutting his arms free—just as a blow from the side knocked the knife from his grip, sending Maven tumbling.

He sprang up fast into a fighter's crouch. He faced the second guy, who still had both hands up protecting his busted nose and bleeding face. Maven threw two low jabs, quick-quick, cracking ribs on either side of the guy's midsection. He tried to go down but Maven shoved him backward, up against the rear of an SUV, driving the heel of his boot into the guy's crotch as if he were squashing a tarantula there. The guy's hands sprang open off his bloody face, a wail escaping his mouth like that of a drunk thrown through saloon doors.

The other one was back on his feet behind Maven, retrieving the knife. Maven saw him reflected in the SUV's rear window, and when Maven turned hard, the knife guy seized up, thinking Maven's powers of perception were beyond human. He reset himself, holding the bloody slash in his side, and led with the blade, Maven sidestepping the clumsy thrust almost before it started.

Behind him, Maven heard the scuffing of the other guy's footsteps as he hobbled off the lot, making his escape.

The knife guy came in with a wild, diagonal slashing move, its tip catching the nylon of Maven's poncho beneath his raised arms, slicing it as Maven pulled away. The knife guy's face sharpened as though he had drawn blood, and not just ruined a $7 surplus poncho.

This sneer of victory made Maven snap.

The knife came at him again and Maven stepped into it this time, catching the guy's hand and twisting, rotating the entire arm. He peeled two fingers back off the knife handle, all the way down, fracturing both. He wrenched the man's wrist like the cap on a stubborn jar, cracking bones. The guy was screaming and trying to fall but Maven would not let him go. Maven gripped the knife in the guy's own broken hand and stabbed down into his leg just above the knee, slicing upward, opening the guy's thigh. Then Maven bent the guy's arm back upward, ignoring his cries as he forced the trembling knife toward the strained muscles of his screaming throat.

Another arm hooked Maven's. Not the guy who had run away; this was a good pro grip locking his arm, keeping him from slicing the guy's throat. Maven's legs were pushed out from behind, putting him off-balance, taking away his leverage.

Maven never saw the third man's face. Only the woman a few cars down, a man's black jacket draped over her shoulders, her silver dress shimmering like rain within the rain.

It was Danielle Vetti, watching him, her hand covering her mouth.

Maven released the knife guy, who had already fainted. The man behind him released Maven, and Maven backed away from Danielle Vetti's eyes, walking, then running full out, so hard that even the rain couldn't catch him.

SEE, ONCE UPON A TIME, THERE WAS THIS KID.

A lonely kid from a wrecked family, no father, barely a mother. A kid who didn't know how to be liked, never mind loved. Growing up, this kid never guessed hundreds, if not thousands, of other kids out there were just like him: teenagers spurned by their parents and peers, outwardly quiet but inwardly raging.

It turned out he was one of an entire subset generation of would-be terrorists, adolescent time bombs sitting alone at the foots of unmade beds, managing their misery by drawing up scenarios of violence, vengeance, and immortality.

But he didn't know this at the time. No one did.

These were kids for whom simple self-destruction wasn't enough. Suicide would only have confirmed other people's view of them as a nothing, a no one, a defeated outcast.

So why go out as a question mark when you can go out as an exclamation point instead?

But for this kid, as for most, the flip-switching bully's punch or crushing social slight or failing grade never quite came to pass, at least not with the annihilative force he had imagined. Fantasy, in the form of death lists, detailed school maps, and first-person-shooter visualizations, appeased his teenage longing for mayhem in the same way that masturbation alleviated his longing for sex.

When the Columbine school shooting occurred in the spring of his graduating year, he was more appalled than fascinated. He saw his own dark shadow there, in the cafeteria video of the two trench-coat-clad shooters, and knew then, more than ever, that he needed to get the hell out of Gridley, Massachusetts.

So he visited his local army recruiter before graduation, stayed off pot all summer to pass the drug screen, and returned on his eighteenth birthday to sign on the dotted line and swear to uphold the Constitution against enemies foreign and domestic.

That was two Septembers before 9/11.

Before Afghanistan.

Before Iraq.

Many speak of the fog of war, but for this kid, war brought clarity. It gave him a mission, clearly defined. Rules of Engagement. A six-article Code of Conduct. He experienced the fellowship of men in combat and learned to give and to earn respect. He was commended, awarded, promoted. Honor, Discipline, Integrity: all those formerly bullshit, silver-plated words came to mean something to him. He was recommended for the six-month Q Course training and even learned passable Korean to earn his Special Forces tab.

He wore the Green Beret. He was accepted, even esteemed, if never totally understood. For the first time in his life, Neal Maven belonged.

And that vengeful, damaged kid, the one everyone tried to piss on? He was gone forever.

Or so Maven had thought.

IT HAPPENED TOO LATE FOR ANYTHING TO BE IN THE NEXT DAY'S papers. Maven spent the morning walking around in a daze, waiting for a call from . . . who? The police? His boss?

He returned to work that night without any idea what he might be walking into. The rain had cleared, the night mild and almost meek in comparison. The day guy had nothing for him. Maven had stashed the previous night's take under the counter and would make a double deposit that evening; with banks closed for the weekend, his boss would never be the wiser.

He went over to where the fight had happened, the rain having washed away any blood. Cars started pulling in, and bit by bit the tension in his chest began to go away.

The Boston police detective stopped by around eight thirty. A black guy, he pulled his unmarked Sable over onto the curb, came out with a badge and a quick handshake. Smelled of Italian food, tomato sauce and oregano. He belched softly into his fist and excused himself. He wanted to know about a guy they had found earlier that morning, unconscious and bleeding a block down the street. Two fingers broken, a fractured wrist, his right thigh sliced open like a Sunday roast. Maven told him that he hadn't seen anything, and the detective pointed out that a guy cut like that tends to make noise. Maven shrugged, reminding him of last night's rain.

"You a veteran?" asked the detective.

Maven looked at him, bewildered.

"It's the boots," said the detective.

Maven noticed the cop eyeing his hands. Looking for cuts, for bruises.

"Between you, me, and the butcher," noted the detective, "said victim has a rap sheet this long. Not exactly the innocent-bystander type, know what I mean? The blade he got cut with was his own. I'm thinking maybe he tried to roll the wrong person last night. What do you think?"

Maven shrugged and had no idea.

The detective took down Maven's address and his digits before thanking him and heading home for the evening.

That was it. Maven played his misshapen tongue against his lower gums, a ruminative habit. Funny how large the tongue feels inside your head. The wound was not much bigger than a nick, but inside Maven's mouth it felt like a major deformity.

He stood like that until a passing girl caught his eye. Over an expensive top and a tight skirt, she wore a clinging wrap that detailed rather than concealed her figure. She was hugging it to herself for warmth, her hair flowing behind her like a black satin scarf. She turned at the gate, stepping onto the lot in dagger heels. She didn't mince in them, but strode sure-footedly with the confidence of a woman used to walking on knives.

Then Maven recognized her face. Danielle Vetti. In the flesh.

"Huh," she said, close enough to speak, looking disappointed. "I bet him a hundy you wouldn't be here."

Her body was like the fulfillment of her high school promise. She moved with assurance, hugging the night to herself as she did her crocheted wrap.

"Do you talk?" she said.

"Yeah. Sometimes."

She kept a few yards between them, appraising him as she

might an unfamiliar dog. "You were going to kill that guy, weren't you?"

Maven tried to shake his head. It wouldn't move.

"Is that why you ran off?"

Maven did not have an answer for her.

"He dragged the guy away from here. So you wouldn't get in trouble. Ruined a two-hundred-dollar shirt. I waited in the car."

A breeze came up, cartwheeling a flattened drink cup across the pavement, stirring her hair. She hugged herself a little tighter.

"Why didn't you just give them the money?"

Maven shrugged. "I never even thought about the money."

She shook away the hair strands blowing across her face and opened a tiny clip purse. She stepped to Maven, presenting him with a card, blank but for a handwritten phone number.

"His number, not mine. He wants to meet you."

"Meet me?"

"I think he wants to offer you a job."

Maven looked at the numbers on the card again. "A job? But why would he . . . ?"

"Want to hire someone he stopped from killing another man in a parking lot in the middle of the night?" She shrugged. "He collects people like you. If you ask me."

The alarm chirped on a silver BMW, and she sat inside, starting it up and pulling around to the gate. Maven raised the orange-striped arm, watching her profile for something more, anything— but she pulled out without another glance his way.

Ricky

MAVEN CRACKED OPEN HIS SECOND ROCKSTAR ENERGY DRINK AT
the 3 a.m. mark, drinking half of it before setting down the
tall can behind the lottery machine. He had already restocked
magazines and candy, cleaned and refilled the coffee and Slush
dispensers. Soon the news carriers would arrive in their open-
doored trucks, dumping off bundles of newspapers. Skimming
the *Herald* and the *Globe* would take him through to the first-
shifters stopping in for Merits and City Oasis java. At some point
he would sell his first scratch ticket of the day, and then dawn
wouldn't be far behind.

The City Oasis was a four-pump gas station and convenience
store on Hancock Street in downtown Quincy. The owner's name
over the door was Iranian, which was ironic, or *Iraq*-ic, as Ricky
once said, Maven now employed by a Middle Eastern man selling
gasoline to Americans. But the guy was totally hands-off, letting
Maven and Ricky eat their fill of corn chips and Yodels so long as
the store was kept clean and secure.

The buzzer went off, Ricky checking the pump cameras, a white F-250 awaiting a fill-up on pump two. Overnight drive-aways were a problem in the down economy.

Ricky switched on the pump after the debit card was approved, saying, "We should put a sign up out there, apologizing."

"For?" said Maven.

"The fifty-dollar fill-up. I feel like we went out and liberated Iraq, and somehow the cost of a barrel of light sweet crude doubled. Somebody fucked up somewhere. Must have been us, right?"

"Yeah. Me and you." Maven tapped the $3.99 GOD BLESS OUR TROOPS yellow-ribbon magnets for sale on the counter. "What happens when the price of gas goes higher than the price of a ribbon?"

Ricky reached for the bathroom key and pulled a copy of *Hot Rod* off the magazine rack and headed to the john in back. "Then we cross out the word *troops* and write in *cars* instead."

Maven guzzled more caffeine, looking out at the lit island of gasoline pumps. A white Mazda pulled into the handicapped space, three kids walking to the door, the chime sounding as they filed inside. Not much younger than Maven, but looking like kids to him, decked out club-casual for a night of let's-get-lucky, which, evidently, they had not. Maven could smell the failed evening on them, the booze, the endgame before last call, the flop sweat. He could hear it in their husky voices. Half-in-the-bag and light-in-the-pocket, yet happy. Upbeat. Too wound up to do the sensible thing and call it a night already.

One pulled a quart bottle of chocolate milk from the wall cooler and uncapped it and started chugging. Another snagged a bag of Cool Ranch Doritos and a bottle of phosphorescent green AMP. The third wax-bagged two stale Boston cream donuts from the pastry cabinet and a flavored Diet Pepsi. They reconvened at the front counter and pooled their bar-dampened dollars, one of them plucking a *Maxim* from the display underneath the mints. He flipped through it with a practiced hand, pointing out the good parts to the others, one laughing, the other sighing, the magazine holder sticking his nose into the fold and inhaling deep.

In a moment of woozy solidarity with the working stiff behind the counter, the kid with the magazine turned it around toward Maven. It was an actress peeling the back of a white lace thong off her ass crack, lips pursed. "You see this, dude?" the kid said with a grin.

Maven looked. "That's not a dude."

The other two chuckled at their horndog buddy, who pushed the wrinkled magazine to the counter, adding it to their tally. "My goal in life, man? Seriously? Two chicks at once."

Maven said, "My advice would be, start with one."

The other two hooted, grabbing their bellies to keep from choking, while the third guy grinned good-naturedly, proud to have discovered a clerk with character.

Then the laughter died away and their smiles flattened. Ricky had returned from the back of the store, standing to the side. Maven wondered what exactly about Ricky spooked them. The dent in his head? His left arm, the way it hung stiff and crooked at his side? Or the fact that Ricky was their age, his eyes looking out at them from a place they had never been.

All three, Maven figured, watching them collect their purchases and change and pushing back through the chiming door to the Mazda.

Ricky, if he was even aware of his effect on them, said nothing, coming around to return the bathroom key and finding his patrol cap where he had left it, the one he always wore, popping it back onto his head. "Lightbulb out over dairy."

"Magnificent," said Maven, finishing his soda. "This oughta chew up a good ten minutes."

THE TOP OF THE STEP LADDER AFFORDED MAVEN A GOD'S-EYE VIEW of the store and its overbright, machine-cooled aisles of candy-colored packaging. Ricky once said that others could keep their clouds of dead relatives playing harps; his idea of heaven was an immaculate convenience store.

"You know what we need?" said Ricky, sipping a blue raspberry Slush Puppie below.

"College educations?" said Maven.

"Our own lightbulb joke. Example. How many Vietnam vets does it take to screw in a lightbulb?"

"I don't know."

"You don't know because *you weren't there, man.*"

"Okay," said Maven. "That's actually pretty good."

"Now we have ourselves a project, see?" Ricky nodded excitedly, sipping more blue. "Now the rest of the night's gonna fly."

People assumed that Ricky Blye had gotten his screws knocked loose in the war, but Maven suspected he had always been a little off. Skinny, gawky, not so smart, and not so good at sports either. One day the D student at Gridley High School walked into a recruiting office in Brockton, Massachusetts. One year later, he was driving a diesel supply truck across the Fertile Crescent between the Euphrates and Tigris rivers, known in ancient times as Mesopotamia, the reputed site of the Garden of Eden.

He had been driving down a trash-strewn road outside Al Gharraf when his front left tire rolled over a discarded U.S. army humrat—the humanitarian rations distributed to civilians, distinguishable from military meals-ready-to-eat by its bright yellow packaging—rigged as an improvised explosive device. The blast drove Ricky's head into the ceiling of the cab with such force that it pushed the dent in his helmet down into his skull, the truck flipping onto its side, leaking fuel. While Ricky lay unconscious in the burning cab, another soldier from his convoy braved the heat to haul him out, just before the truck fireballed. That soldier smothered the flames on Ricky's arm and waited with him until medics arrived.

No, that hero soldier's name was not Neal David Maven. Maven's role in Ricky's military career was a little different. After basic training at Fort Campbell, the army sends its newly minted soldiers back home to spread the word about how fantastic and rewarding military life can be. Maven walked the length of the Westgate Mall wearing his Class A uniform, looking sharp, a clipboard under his arm. His quota was five phone numbers a day.

He vaguely recognized the small-headed kid sucking on an Orange Julius. Three years behind him in high school, they had shared one mixed-grade study hall. A kid in a RUSH T-shirt, copying out the lyrics to "Red Barchetta" on the back of his paper-bag-covered textbook.

Ricky reminded him of this when he caught up with Maven again, two months ago, at Maven's sister's funeral. His half sister, three years his senior, Alexis Maven, dead of a drug overdose at age twenty-nine. She and Maven had never been anything other than sworn enemies, but in the absence of his AWOL mother, Maven had been forced to return, ever so briefly, to his hometown, to go through the motions of a graveside observance.

Ricky had seen the notice in the *Patriot Ledger*. He showed up in a short-sleeved shirt and tie, his left arm hairless and mottled, creased along the underside and withered looking, thinner than his right. He wore his old patrol cap—flat-topped, digital camouflage, his last name on the back—cocked at an angle to hide the bare patch over his left ear where hair no longer grew.

Ricky had gotten him the City Oasis job. Occasionally the headaches were bad enough to keep Ricky away from the store, dropping out of sight for a day or two, but otherwise he lived for their shifts together, for the camaraderie he had been denied when his tour was cut short. One minute he was living in the Green Zone with his asshole buddies, bitching about sandstorms, crap food, the heat; the next he was waking up in a hospital in Germany, looking at his bandaged arm, wondering *What the fuck?* Mobility restrictions in his left hand, wrist, and elbow earned him a disability retirement he didn't want, and a one-way ticket home. Ricky appealed, requesting a desk job, anything that would get him back in uniform and back in Iraq. But the medical board denied him, and now he found himself, at twenty-five, a disabled American veteran.

THE NEW BULB CAME ON BRIGHT, LIKE A HOT IDEA. MAVEN CLIMBED down and collapsed the ladder. He felt the emptiness of the store and must have had a funny look on his face because Ricky said, "You still thinking about going back?"

Maven had made the mistake of allowing as much a few weeks earlier. "Not really."

Ricky trailed him back to the front counter. "Sick part is, you can earn more killin' and chillin' over there than you can here. I wouldn't blame you. I'd go back if I could."

"I know you would." Maven poured himself a blue one from the Slush machine and turned to drink with Ricky.

Ricky said, "Here's to the best job I ever hand. Second best, after this one."

They tapped puppy-labeled paper cups, and Maven drank until he got that forehead pain. He was thinking about Danielle Vetti, about the card she had given him, nestled in his wallet like a lottery ticket. Wondering about that job.

The door chimed again, and a blue uniform entered. A Quincy cop, a regular, standing in the doorway a moment, sizing up the place. "How ya doin' tonight?" he barked, and strode off down the center aisle.

Maven and Ricky looked at each other, then Maven went up to take the counter.

The cop came back with a Muscle Milk and one of those meal bars that taste like Sheetrock. "Quiet one, huh?"

"Average," said Maven. "You?"

"Not bad, not bad."

The cop was in his early thirties, decent build, cocksure eyes. He had a swagger, even when standing still. Here in Quincy, with a silver shield pin and a fifteen-load nine-millimeter snapped to his belt, this guy was the shit. In Eden, he'd be just another walking pouch of entrails.

"And whyn't you gimme a *Cheri,* there," he said, peeling a few more bills off his roll.

Maven reached into the magazine rack, between *Barely Legal* and *Celebrity Skin,* and slid the publication into a flat brown paper bag, sending him on his way.

Ricky came up opening a pack of Sour Patch Kids. "Dickhead brings home sixty K a year, plus details at forty bucks an hour. One-*tenth* our training. Wonder how he'd stand up if any real shit ever came his way."

The cop had never got to Maven before, but Ricky was right: how had they come to be stuck here selling candy and cigarettes?

He turned to Ricky. "You ever hear of Danielle Vetti?"

"Vetti?" said Ricky. "Sounds familiar. Gridley High?"

"Before your time. A senior when I was a freshman."

"That puts me in middle school. Why?"

"Thought I saw her somewhere."

"Yeah? She used to be something?"

"Still is," said Maven, staring out the window in the direction the cop cruiser went. "Still is."

He felt something then, something he hadn't felt in a long time. Hope, it turned out, was a very real thing for a convenience-store clerk at three in the morning—as potent an impulse as hunger, or lust.

He was going to call this guy in the morning. As soon as he got off work, first thing.

Ricky broke into his reverie. "I got it. Check this out. How many Iraq War veterans does it take to screw in a lightbulb?"

Maven said, "I give up."

"Only just one."

Maven looked at him, shrugged.

Ricky continued, "But, hey, we got over one hundred thousand applications, we'll give you a call."

ROYCE

MAVEN. I LIKE THAT. WHAT'S IT MEAN, 'EXPERT'?"

Maven patted down his napkin. "It means 'one who is experienced or knowledgeable.'"

"And is that accurate?"

"About some things. I guess."

Brad Royce appraised him, and Maven felt something in the scrutiny, something he wanted to measure up to. Going in, he didn't think he'd take to this guy at all, but Royce had won him over early by doing nothing more than talking and listening, and Maven wanted to impress him right back. This guy had a way. The way he wore his jacket. The way he folded his napkin across his leg. The way he sat at the corner table, surveying the restaurant as though it had been constructed to his precise specifications. His easy rapport with the server. His easy rapport with his utensils, with his food—with everything. Maven admired that immediately. Admired that which he himself lacked.

Authority without arrogance. Royce wasn't putting on a show

here. He talked to Maven not as an equal but as someone who one day could be. Royce had ten years on Maven, Maven wondering if it had taken him all that time to grow into himself. And thinking that he would like someday to achieve the same.

No idea what Royce's game was here, but Maven was content to sit and listen. Danielle Vetti was not in attendance, and Maven tried to stop himself from wondering about them as a couple.

"So what I'm guessing is, based on what I saw in that parking lot, you've got some experience and knowledge that is, say, highly specialized. That doesn't translate all that well to the States. To the here and the now."

"That's one way to put it."

"You're overqualified for peaceful living. Overqualified and undercompensated. Sitting here in this restaurant with your back angled to the door, you can't relax. You're waiting for someone to come inside and start something."

Maven eased back a little, feeling some tension go out of his shoulders.

Royce grinned. "And that's not a bad thing. In fact, that's a good thing. There's not enough of that around. I'm talking about readiness. Readiness is all."

Maven felt he was being too passive, too quiet. He said, "So what's this about a job?"

Royce waved his hand as if he were clearing away a puff of smoke. Dismissive, but not rude. The gesture said, *We have a ways to go before getting to that.*

Chastened, Maven settled back even more. The restaurant, named Sonsie, was fronted with door-size windows that opened out onto Newbury Street and the midday shoppers, art-gallery owners, and day models parading past. He glanced at the mahogany bar, this grand old masterpiece that made you want to order a drink whether you were thirsty or not. Maven had asked for a Coke, like a kid. Royce drank premium water from a green bottle with a picture of Italy on it. Maven had ordered pizza because it was the only thing he recognized on the menu, but when his meal arrived, it looked like no pizza he had ever seen. Royce was eating a spicy noodle dish called Mee Krob. He had started with an Asian Mizuna Salad with Tempura Shiitake Nori Rolls, and iced market oysters ordered for the both of them. Maven had never eaten oysters before. They were an acquired taste he had yet to acquire.

Royce said, "I spent the bulk of my tour in Germany. We ramped up for the first Gulf War, but, as you know, that was all foreplay and no happy ending. I got over to Kuwait for about five months, just long enough to take friendly fire from some shithead alligator farmer from Florida, and to be surrendered to by three thirsty Iraqis. So I don't pretend to know exactly what you feel. But at the same time—I know, you know? How long since you rotated out?"

"Nine months now."

"Shows." Royce forked some more Thai noodles into his mouth. "No offense, but you're wearing it pretty heavy."

Maven had on Old Navy khakis and the collared shirt he had worn to Alex's funeral. Royce wore a charcoal jacket over dark pants, casual but put-together. Maven could see himself copping this guy's style. He was on the lookout for somebody to model himself after.

Royce said, "That one-year demob anniversary, that's the kicker. That's when you take a long, hard look at where you used to be and where you are now. That's when you have to decide if you are hacking it away from the discipline. A lot of guys, one year out, all they want to do is re-up. Crawl back inside a tank for three more years. You're nodding."

Maven said, "Guys I served with bet me I'd be back in Eden inside of a year."

"And you'd like to prove them wrong. Send them a fuck-you postcard from Maui or New Zealand or something. From the Playboy Mansion. But here you are. Working in a parking lot."

Maven sat up a little. "It's not that bad."

"No, because you're on your own, because there's no boss to fuck with you, and because you're not some hamster in an office somewhere, scratching at the walls. And maybe there's a little skim off the top every now and then. When the timing's right, of course."

Maven blinked, said nothing.

"It's only natural." Royce's smile said that he was humoring Maven, but also that it was okay: he humored everybody. "I'm not looking for saints. We've all got crime in our hearts." He pointed at Maven's chest with his fork. "It's how you manage that, where you channel it, that counts."

Maven nodded, after a moment. This lunch had a rhythm, and Maven could feel himself falling into it.

Royce said, "You considering reenlisting?"

"Not seriously."

"That's a yes. What's your current living situation? Apartment, right? Let me guess. Outside the city?"

"Over in Quincy."

"Uh-huh. Nice building? Doorman? Bowl of mints in the lobby?"

"Not quite. A converted two-family."

"Illegal apartment, you're probably in the attic. Three-flight walk-up, galley kitchen, closet-sized bathroom. Split the utilities with the freaks downstairs, stoners growing marijuana in a spare closet, heat lamps threatening to burn the old place to the ground. What you pay, three fifty a month?"

Maven squinted. "Three ninety."

"To answer what you're thinking, yes, I am in real estate, but only tangentially. And, no, that is not what this"—indicating the lunch, the meeting, the interview—"is about. High school graduate, equivalent?"

"Graduate."

"Grew up around here?"

"In Gridley."

"South of here, right?"

"About thirty minutes."

"Any family?"

"No."

"Nobody?"

Maven shook his head.

Royce liked that answer. "What about friends, roommates?"

Maven shrugged. "I got a buddy I work with at my other job."

"That's it?"

"That's it right now."

"No girlfriend?"

"Not really."

"Not surprised. Belt should match the shoes, by the way. At least look like you want to get lucky."

Maven checked: woven black leather belt, brown boots.

"You're too alone," said Royce, patting the table. "Gotta get some people around you, keep your head straight. You're what, twenty-seven? No infirmities?"

"No."

"Not a scratch?"

Maven shrugged. "I got scratched. I was lucky overall."

"Good. Good to be lucky. Honorable discharge, of course."

"Sure."

"You'd had it?"

"I don't know. Seemed like I needed to try something else."

"They let you go?"

"My contract was up. I could be recalled."

"You *will* be recalled, don't kid yourself. Hell, I'm twelve years out, they better not come back for me. You got a short window here, maybe real short, you should make the most of it. Post-traumatic stress?"

"I don't think so."

"Loud noises? Crowds?"

"Getting better now."

Royce set down his fork and pushed back his plate to lean closer to Maven. "So. Let me ask you this then. Why'd you run off?"

Royce's scrutiny made an already uncomfortable question even more uncomfortable. "I don't really know."

"You want me to tell you?" Royce waited patiently for permission. "You ran off because you almost killed that guy. Because you *wanted* to kill him, and you were going to kill him." Royce swiped his mouth gently with his linen napkin before laying it down next to his plate. "And that scared you."

Maven didn't answer. He didn't move.

"Muscle memory is all that is. Doesn't mean anything. You're not some twitchy Vietnam vet. It's your training. You were attacked. You responded."

Maven nodded.

"What you are now, you're like a guy who doesn't know his own strength anymore. Like an astronaut back from the moon, dealing with gravity again. You know how when you go into the refrigerator for a gallon of milk sometimes, and you pick it up expecting it to be full, and you hit the ceiling of the fridge with it because it's basically empty? Your hands are too big for your arms. Am I right?"

"You're right."

"It's clear you've had Special Forces training. And I don't care where you served, what battalion, who with. Because it doesn't apply here at home, and because fuck you what you did, everybody did something. Guys who think they're owed something, those guys are the ones fucked from the jump." Royce shook his head. "This isn't about any of that. This is about now." He scanned the other diners, checking for eavesdroppers. "So. Being honest now. You miss the action?"

"I don't know." Maven exhaled. "Maybe."

"Meaning you do, but you wish you didn't. Because you think it's taboo to admit it." The contradiction made Royce grin. "So admit it."

Royce's grin pulled one out of Maven. "I miss the action."

"You're damn right you miss it."

Royce pulled back, scanning the other diners yet again. This time his gaze settled upon one in particular. Maven glanced over his shoulder at a man sitting alone, bald with an immaculately clean scalp, a little smudge of sandy hair beneath his lower lip, wearing a sage green jacket and thumbing through messages on a BlackBerry. The man's napkin rested next to an empty pasta bowl.

"So," said Royce, pulling Maven's attention back to their table. "You're home now, you made it in one piece—no small feat. Big question is, now what? What are you going to do with the rest of your life? A cliché for everyone else, but for you, right now, a critical question. Looking ahead. What is it you want out of life?"

Maven knew he should have an answer. "I don't really know."

"What's your passion? Obviously it isn't food." Royce pointed to the basil pesto pizza sitting left on the round warming stone. "A goal. In the distance. Gotta be something."

Maven said, in order to say something, "A house."

"A house."

"Yeah. Nothing big, just . . . something not rented. An actual house on actual land. Ownership."

Royce finished his glass of Italian water. "Good. That's good. It's tangible. Most guys, nine months out—I'm serious—they say, 'Rock star,' you know? 'I just wanna get my raps heard . . .' " Royce drew a neat wad of U.S. currency from his pants pocket, peeling off two fresh fifties and a twenty, tucking them into the leather booklet without even looking at the check. "U.S. military is putting out more Eminem wannabes than firemen and cops."

Maven pulled his eyes off the cash roll, playing a hunch, glancing back at the guy in the green cashmere jacket.

He was laying a credit card faceup into his leather booklet.

Royce said, "You done?"

Maven looked at his pizza. It was rude not to eat more. "I guess I should . . ."

Royce pushed back from the table, nudging Maven's arm as he stood. "You're done."

Maven watched Royce start away from the tables, wondering what was happening. Had he flunked the test?

He stood after a moment and followed Royce out, catching him on the sidewalk outside. Royce was feeding his ticket to a black-vested valet, who took off jogging toward Mass. Ave.

"Look around you, Maven," said Royce, putting on a sleek pair of sunglasses.

It was a sunny November afternoon, a break from the late-year chill, probably the last warm day until early spring. The fashionable street crowd milled past carrying oversize shopping bags and grande lattes.

Royce said, "You look at these people, and you think, 'This is who I went over there to protect?' "

A heavy woman in a too tight business suit passed them, spooning candy-studded ice cream into her mouth.

"Grazing on sweets, wandering around a major city like kids inside a resort hotel. This guy."

A dumpy man in his thirties exited a shoe store across the street, dressed in a T-shirt, loose shorts, and flip-flops, mobile phone wedged against his ear.

"Out-of-shape guys in the prime years of their lives. I see someone walking around town in flip-flops, you know what I think? Gazelle sunning itself on the plain. Who's he going to outrun in those things? Who's he going to take in a fight? That's a willing victim right there. I think to myself, 'I could take your wife, your kids.' " Royce snapped his fingers. "You saw it, right? Iraqis whose families were taken from them? This guy would say, 'But this isn't Iraq.' And I say, 'Neither was New Orleans.' " Royce passed behind Maven like a breeze. "Nobody's fucking ready. None of them. Take away their mobile phones, and you've all but cut their throats. When the shit goes down, you might as well scratch 'nine one one' in the dirt with a stick, the good it's going to do you. They think big-daddy government is going to protect them? Think the police can keep them safe?"

Maven said, surprising himself, "Cops are out jerking off to *Cheri* magazine in their cruisers."

Royce shot Maven an approving glance. "Damn right they

are. I'm telling you things you already thought of but never put words to. You've been to the other side. You've seen what happens when the strings get cut. These people, the fight has been programmed out of them. These poor fucks actually believe they are *entitled* to peace and security. That war thing in the newspaper? It's a message that's not getting through. A warning they just don't want to hear. They'd rather trust, and be lied to. It's easier that way. But you, you're ready. You've got that good tension just below the surface. These fucking sleepwalkers—they have no idea. You've come back to a dream world, Maven. A world of virgins. They don't know."

Maven did look around. He looked with fresh eyes.

The neat brick-front stores. The self-absorbed consumers. The smokeless blue sky. Everything moving in slow motion for him, like a trick revealed.

"You ever wish sometimes," said Royce, so quietly it was as though he were talking in Maven's ear, "that you could have brought a bit of war back home? Just a taste? Enough to wake them up, show them what it's really like?"

Maven experienced a vision then, of Newbury Street under siege. Mortar impacts zapping the air pressure, exploding parked cars, and cratering the street . . . smoke grenades billowing, swirling green as Cobra helicopters thumped overhead, opening up 20 mm machine guns . . . rocket volleys painting the sky with white burn trails . . . armor-penetrating SLAP rounds collapsing the brickstones, rubble and dust cascading into the street . . . and shoppers fleeing with bleeding eardrums, while Maven, in full armor, M4 in hand, was cleared hot for Newbury Street . . .

Maven turned back, smiling, until he saw the man in the sage cashmere jacket again. Standing on the sidewalk now, his phone in one hand, a smart leather grip with long, buckled straps in the other. He looked bigger and harder up close, like a rugby player dressed for a business meeting. He handed his ticket to a second valet, who ran off.

Royce remained at Maven's side, seemingly ignoring the other guy, and yet—Maven was sure—completely aware of the man's presence.

"What I'm looking for," said Royce, low and quiet, "is somebody reliable. Somebody who can keep it tight. Somebody who's good in a pinch. Somebody who likes the action, but isn't a cowboy, who isn't going to light up a room just for the fuck of it. Somebody smart, or who can pass for same. And, yes—somebody who's lucky, and interested in staying that way."

The car arrived without Maven's noticing. A shiny black Audi with a cream interior. Royce went around to the driver's side and duked the valet, who then jogged over to open the passenger door for Maven.

Maven hesitated. The purring car, so smooth and sexy that the valet should have tipped Royce just for the privilege, woke Maven up a little.

"What?" said Royce, seeing him waiting.

"What happened to the Escalade?"

"Gave it back. In case anyone saw it in the parking lot that night."

Maven looked down at the soft leather seat, a marshmallow waiting to suck him in, maybe hold him there. Royce's rap was seductive. Maybe too much so. Maven's faulty trouble sensor was giving him fits. He was torn.

"You know . . ." He tried to wriggle away gracefully. "Thanks for lunch, and the food for thought. I think maybe I'm gonna go walk it all off and digest."

Royce's arm remained relaxed on his open door, his head and shoulders visible over the roof of the car. "What are you talking about, what?"

"It's just that, I'm not really . . . it's not my scene, I don't think. With all due respect."

"Not what scene? What? What do you think this is? Speak in sentences."

The street was busy enough that Maven could speak over the

roof and not be heard by anyone else. He framed his words with a forgive-me wince. "You're a drug dealer."

Royce smiled. He smiled wide, and he laughed, with something knowing in the laugh, something that told Maven there was so much more to this world than he knew.

Maven said, "Aren't you?"

The laugh faded. "Maven, get the fuck in."

The Tingle

ROYCE TRIED TO SETTLE IN, BUT SOMETHING WAS WRONG. "They always adjust the seat. They're in here three fucking minutes." He pushed a button and the driver's seat whirred, automatically readjusting to his comfort.

The dashboard readouts glowed cockpit red. Maven saw that the odometer was under two thousand miles. The new-car smell hit him. "How do you give cars back?"

"A place by the airport, rents luxury vehicles." Royce fiddled with the air, generating a gentle breeze. "My only beef with your homeownership idea, by the way. The American dream is just another scam. A trap. You haven't figured that out yet. The shit you own does wind up owning you, and not in some Zen bullshit kind of way. Giving you something to lose if you don't play by the rules." Royce put them up on his fingers. "Houses. Cars. Women. These are pearls I'm dropping, scoop them up. You got to stay liquid in order to stay alive."

Maven said, "Got it," though now he wondered again about Royce and Danielle Vetti.

Royce pulled into traffic, Maven using his side mirror to look back.

The guy in the sage green jacket was still at the curb, waiting for his vehicle.

So they were leaving him behind. Maven wondered what the hell all that had been about.

They stopped three cars back from the red light at the Mass. Ave. intersection, art students and Berklee College musicians winding between the cars, a guy with a folding table selling incense sticks out in front of the futon store across the way.

"Where we headed?" asked Maven.

The light turned green and Royce turned left, crossing over the turnpike. He slowed in the left lane, as though waiting to turn onto Boylston, against the traffic.

Maven said, "You're not supposed to turn here—"

Royce took it, peeling across two lanes of traffic, horns blaring in his wake.

"See, here's what the U.S. military does," Royce said. "It takes boys and turns them into men—but while still preserving that adolescent sense of invulnerability. Without that innocence, all they've got is a bunch of nineteen-year-olds standing in a puddle of piss. *Everybody* goes in thinking they're going to be the hero. The guy on your left will take a round in the head, and the guy on your right will turn chickenshit, but you, you will stand and fire. You will slaughter the enemy and pink-mist the suicide bomber and save the fucking day. Because it's your own personal movie, right? And the hero in the movie never gets his leg blown off, or his face, or his cock. Following me?"

"Uh-huh," said Maven.

"Now here's the other thing. What you see, what you experience, the things you learn in this quest for glory, are way beyond what other noncombatant twenty-seven-year-olds know. More life and more death have been burned into your young brain than you know what to do with. Like in *The Matrix,* when they upload kung fu and Drunken Boxing into Neo's head? Even the laziest-ass, PlayStation-playing reservist got more animal knowledge by pure osmosis over there than anyone here with the same number years of college.

"So—now you're out, and here's where you're stuck. Socially, developmentally, you're really not much older than the teenager you were when you first went in. But, *mentally,* experience-wise, you're at least a decade older than your calendar age. It's like those body-switching movies. There's a progression of life that every human being goes through, and for you it's been messed up. You've been taken out of life, dropped onto a desert battlefield half a world away, then taken out of that again and dropped back into peace. You're off by ten years from where you should be, going each way, backward and forward. You feel ten years younger and think ten years older. And it fractures you. What I'm saying makes sense?"

"Yeah," said Maven, borderline amazed. "Yeah, it does."

The car stopped under the carport overhang outside the big Sheraton hotel on Dalton Street. Royce stepped out and instructed the valet to keep it close, he wouldn't be long.

Maven followed Royce inside the busy lobby. It was wide and deep but not grand, flanked on both ends by escalators ferrying pedestrians up to the connected Prudential Center shops and the Copley Place Mall. Royce found two high-backed chairs together and sat in one, Maven taking the other, both of them half-facing the rotating doors at the entrance.

Maven's head was buzzing. This wasn't a job interview, this was like a life *over*view, and a lot to take in. Maven waited for more.

Royce checked his watch—thick-faced, the size of an Oreo cookie—then crossed one leg over the other, folding his hands in his lap. "Now I'm gonna drop my theory on adaptive mental health on you."

Maven said, "Your what?"

"The Tomorrow Man theory. It's pretty basic. Today, right here, you are who you are. Tomorrow, you will be who you *will* be. Each and every night, we lie down to die, and each morning we arise, reborn. Now, those who are in good spirits, with strong mental health, they look out for their Tomorrow Man. They eat right today, they drink right today, they go to sleep early today—all so that Tomorrow Man, when he awakes in his bed reborn as Today Man, thanks Yesterday Man. He looks upon him fondly as a child might a good parent. He knows that someone—himself—was looking out for him. He feels cared for, and respected. Loved, in a word. And now he has a legacy to pass on to his subsequent selves."

Royce glanced at the hotel entrance before returning to the subject at hand.

"But those who are in a bad way, with poor mental health, they constantly leave these messes for Tomorrow Man to clean up. They eat whatever the hell they want, drink like the night will never end, and then fall asleep to forget. They don't respect Tomorrow Man because they don't think through the fact that Tomorrow Man will be them. So then they wake up, new Today Man, groaning at the disrespect Yesterday Man showed them. Wondering why does that guy—myself—keep punishing me? But they never learn and instead come to settle for that behavior, eventually learning to ask and expect nothing of themselves. They pass along these same bad habits tomorrow and tomorrow and tomorrow, and it becomes psychologically genetic, like a curse.

"Looking at you now, Maven, I can see exactly where you fall on this spectrum. You are a man constantly trying to fix today what Yesterday Man did to you. You make up your bed, you clean those dirty dishes from the night before, and pledge not to start drinking until six, thinking that's the way to keep an even keel. But in reality you're always playing catch-up. I know this because I've been there. The thing is—you can't fix the mistakes of Yesterday. Yesterday Man is dead, he's gone forever, and blame and atonement aren't worth a damn. What you *can* do is help yourself today. Eat a vegetable. Read a book. Cut that hair of yours. Leave Tomorrow Man something more than a headache and a jam-packed colon. Do for

Tomorrow Man what you would have wanted Yesterday Man to do for you. Does that sound like an action plan?"

Maven nodded. This was like watching a magician shuffle and reshuffle the deck, pulling Maven's card again every time.

"Is this a program you think you could get with?"

"Probably, yeah," said Maven. "I should."

Royce uncrossed his legs and sat forward, again glancing at the revolving doors. "You're earnest, Maven. A rare quality these days." Three guys in business wear walked past towing golf bags and carry-ons. "Those guys are about your age, right? Doing all right for themselves, looking to get eighteen holes in before dinner. See, me, I rotated out in the midnineties. Boom time. The Internet boom, the dot-com boom. Boom, boom, *boom*. In the NASDAQ nineties, there was money everywhere. I mean, I struggled at first, sure. But there were opportunities. But now you come back, you rotate out of this bitch-mother of a war, and they drop a recession over your head like a black hood. Now everyone's ahead of you. Everybody your age either has a college degree or else years invested in the job market. They have employment equity, because they've been enjoying the fruits of *your* labor, working here in this nice safe bubble of Fortress America. Now you come back, and it's like, 'Thanks, kid. Let me shake your hand. Damn proud of ya. Now take a place at the back of the line.' "

Maven watched the golfers with a mixture of anger and envy.

Royce said, "Why, after all you've done, would you ever want to wait in a line?"

Maven looked back. He wanted to hear more. But Royce's eyes were trained on the hotel entrance now, and not looking away.

Maven turned and looked in the same direction as Royce.

The man in the sage green jacket entered the lobby, grip in hand.

Maven instinctually turned away. Royce produced a slim mobile phone, one-touch dialed it, and brought it to his ear. "Ready-up," he said, then closed the phone again.

The man in the sage green jacket walked to the elevators behind the registration desk. Royce stood, and Maven rose and followed him around the opposite corner, past restroom doors, into the stairwell.

Royce said, "Let's see how your wind is, soldier."

They ran up each floor, half-flight by half-flight, Maven sucking air after eight, feeling pain after twenty, going totally out of breath at the top. He stood doubled over before a fire door numbered 29, Royce blowing air too, but upright and smiling.

A small window looked into the carpeted hallway. Maven straightened behind Royce, watching as the man in the sage green jacket turned the far corner, reading room numbers as he went.

"What . . . the . . . hell?" whispered Maven, between breaths.

Royce shushed him. "What do you think about the jacket?"

Maven swallowed. "The jacket?"

"A Zegna. Cashmere, retails about two grand. The briefcase?"

"Yeah?"

"A thirteen-hundred-dollar Mulberry. Now, what's that tell you?"

"The guy overpaid."

"You say that because you've never touched anything of real quality." Royce said this without insult, a simple declaration. "What you should realize is that the stuff he's used to carrying inside that case must be worth considerably more than the case itself."

The guy slowed before a room halfway down the hall. Both Royce and Maven ducked away from the window, in case the guy looked left and right before going inside.

Maven said, "What does this matter to you?"

He heard faint knocking. Maven edged back to the window just in time to see the door open and the guy step inside.

Royce pulled open their door and went silently down the carpeted hallway. At first, Maven thought they were moving to the same door, only to stop behind Royce at the one before it.

A DO NOT DISTURB card hung on the handle. Maven heard a television playing inside.

Royce produced a key card from his jacket pocket, fed it into the slot, and when the light turned green, he eased the door open with barely a click, moving inside.

Maven lingered where he was. Another moment of hesitation. He felt strangely exposed, standing alone in the hallway. The door was closing and he stopped it with his fingertips just as the lock was about to catch.

He entered and shut it quietly behind him. Past a closet and large bathroom on his right, the room opened into a wide suite. Two men, both of them close to Maven's age, stood between a writing table and the loud boxing match on television. A laptop was on the table, and one of the men, a blue-eyed Latino, watched the screen intently, listening through headphones, not even looking up at Maven. The other one, a spike-haired, blond, all-American type, wore a gun in a shoulder holster, and didn't take his eyes off Maven until Royce gave him a nod.

A third man, closer in age to Royce, his skin dark brown, reclined on the high, made bed with his fingers laced behind his head. The television remote was nestled in his crotch, a handgun on the comforter at his side. The guy sized up Maven without expression before returning to the roaring of the Ali-Holmes fight being rebroadcast on ESPN Classic.

The room smelled of coffee and last night's Chinese food. The curtains opened on west-facing windows, looking out over Fenway Park and the city limits to neighboring Brookline beyond.

A thin, firm cable ran from an intermediate box plugged into a USB port on the laptop, leading under the locked door between the adjoining rooms. Royce plucked one of the earphones off the Latino's head and joined him, listening.

Maven saw a video playing full-screen, good quality from a low, Dutch angle, as though from a camera dropped on the floor. The side of a bed, the top of a closet, the ceiling.

The Latino tapped the keyboard arrows, and the cable under the door quivered the slightest bit, the camera view twitch-panning incrementally.

On-screen, the man in the sage green jacket walked into view.

The cable under the door was a scope camera snooping into the adjoining room.

The Latino guy looked at Maven for the first time. "This the new man?" he said softly.

Royce, watching the laptop feed, nodded.

Maven opened his mouth to speak, but Royce silenced him with an open hand. On the screen, two other men appeared, just heads and shoulders, but Maven could see that they were heavy-set, both wearing New England Patriots team jerseys. They looked like brothers. The man in the sage green jacket opened the straps of his briefcase on the bed and handed them a paper packet. The brothers opened the packet and emptied the powdery contents into a hotel drinking glass. One brother then produced a vial from a small, zippered pouch and squirted it into the glass, swishing the solution around until it turned blue.

There was more conversation then, and Maven lost focus, what with the TV fight blaring, armed men in the room with him, and the edge of the city spread out twenty-nine stories below.

The Latino guy looked over at Royce and nodded. "Same Bat-time," he said quietly. "Same Bat-channel."

Royce pulled down his ear wire and said, "Pack up, check out, then reregister under a different credit card. A regular room, a few floors down."

He started toward the door, making his exit without any formalities. Maven started after him, glancing back at the man on the bed, whose fingers were still laced behind his head, watching Maven go.

Royce turned right out of the room, walking boldly past the door to the adjoining room and continuing to the corner. He pushed the button to summon the elevator, and they waited in silence until the doors opened. Inside, Royce pressed the starred button for the lobby, and the doors closed. The car started to descend.

At about the twelfth floor, Maven said, "You're a cop."

Royce smiled, checking the fit of his jacket in the mirrored wall, brushing some lint off his lapel. He said, "That's strike two."

They walked through the lobby and the revolving doors to the circular driveway outside. Royce passed the ticket to the same valet as before, who jogged off.

Maven stood next to Royce, near an ash can, trying to figure out which question to ask first.

Royce said, "Why did you rotate out, Maven?"

Maven's mind felt wobbly, like a table with one short leg, which Royce kept leaning on with his elbow. "Because my contract was up."

"You could have stayed. They offered a bonus to retain you. Sure, it sucked over there, but for someone with your level of training, it took a lot to walk away. What was the real reason?"

Maven shook his head. He was waiting for Royce to tell him.

Royce said, "Maybe you were worried you weren't cut out for anything else."

Maven stared at Royce, in the way you watch a magician up close to see that his talent really is sleight of hand and not some mystical power.

Royce said, "Maybe you were afraid that was all you were. A soldier. A killer. So you opted out. You wanted to see what life was like back home. To see if it's for you. The job, the car, the house, the wife, the kids."

Maven said, "What was that up there?"

Royce ignored him, taking out the room card and jamming it into the ash can. "Every fear reveals a wish. You know what that means? The reason you fear something is because part of you secretly desires it. Or desires what it could get you. Or what it might turn you into."

"I don't desire to reenlist."

Royce smiled to let Maven know that he was missing the point. "You come back home looking to find your way in this world, to stake your claim. That's what warriors have done for centuries. But you can't figure out how to take these military skills you have and use them to get ahead. You can't find a way back into the peacetime world."

Maven stared at him. "Those guys up there, in your room."

"Associates of mine. All ex-military, like yourself."

"And the guy in the two-thousand-dollar jacket? The one we saw at lunch?"

"An importer, wouldn't you say?"

"A drug dealer. We just watched them do a deal."

"The prelude to a deal, a meet and greet. A taste test. The Venezuelan with the Mulberry briefcase, he is a courier, but at the highest level. This is no mules-shitting-balloons operation. The two mooks in the Patriots shirts, they are the Maracone brothers out of East Saugus. Someone's fronting them the financing to take a giant step forward in the local powder trade. The substance they were testing in there is pure, uncut, top-quality cocaine, no more than one week removed from processing plants in the eastern jungles of Colombia. Tomorrow, cash and drugs will change hands. The Maracones will transport their purchase to a safe house on the North Shore, where they will lock themselves inside a strong room, and after setting aside an ounce or two of pure for themselves, will use pastry scrapers to chop up the caked kilos on a large, glass worktable. They will then sweeten the product—most likely with mannitol, a baby laxative with anticaking properties—increasing their volume, in turn increasing their profit, growing two kilograms into three. Using electronic jewelry scales, they will repackage the new weight into half-kilo bricks for distribution by their lieutenants, who will further trample on the product, now with pure lactose or actual flour or ground plaster or whatever the fuck else they can get their hands on that's white and granular. Much of it will be cut with baking soda, that mixture then heated to remove moisture, forming into small, crystal-like rocks known as crack. The end product will be out on the streets by noon Friday." Royce unfolded his sunglasses and slid them on. "What do you think about that?"

"I think it sucks."

Royce put a finger in Maven's chest, as though injecting this idea straight into his heart. "What if somebody were to step in unexpectedly, say tomorrow, at this hotel, at this same time—and interrupt this transaction? Stop the flow of drugs into the community."

Maven was starting to get it now. Royce radiated confidence like heat. Maven felt electricity in his own hands.

"I'm on a crusade here, Maven. There's a war on in this town, only you can't see it. Turf battles everywhere, victims dying slow-motion deaths every day. There's blood in the streets—but you can't fucking see it, and you know why? Because junkie blood is too thin to stick to the pavement. It hoses off too easily, washing right down into the gutter."

Maven was nodding, even feeling that same old precombat testicular tingle.

"This is what you were trained for. Sneak-and-peeks. Hit squads and house raids. You *know* the drill. Now, what if you could do some good in this world—some real good, for a change—and at the same time profit handsomely from it? I mean, how often does a clear moral imperative come complete with a get-rich-quick scheme? The fucking win-win situation of all time. You feeling me now, Maven?"

Royce's conviction was an intoxicant. "I think so," Maven answered, feeling the edge of his bitten tongue against his teeth.

"'Think so,' nothing. You're feeling me. I see it in your eyes." The valet reappeared, Royce's car pulled curbside. Royce tipped the kid and sent him on his way. As Royce climbed into the driver's seat, he said to Maven, "I'm your ticket out of that parking lot and into one of these cars."

Overnight

"WHERE YOU AT TONIGHT?" ASKED RICKY, CHEWING SOUR PATCH Kids.

"Huh?" said Maven, zoning out on a stool before the wall of cigarettes behind the counter, ruminatively working his deformed tongue against his gums. "Nowhere. Tired maybe."

"Two a.m." Ricky flipped on the small television between the cash register and the pump monitors, tuning in a re-airing of that afternoon's *The Tyra Banks Show.* "Time for my girl."

When Ricky was still stateside in Kentucky during the ramp-up to Iraq, Tyra Banks visited Fort Campbell as part of a post–9/11 USO thing. Ricky lucked out, drawing the assignment to escort her vehicle back to the airport. Before they left the base, Ricky was sneaking a Snapple out of the hospitality tent when Tyra and her entourage breezed past him, as close to him as Maven was now.

"And it wasn't even her body, you know, which is, by the way, ka-*pow*! No, it was her skin. No lie. She has this perfect, like, creamy cocoa complexion that you've never even seen in your life.

And her hair—she had on a patrol cap with her name on the back, BANKS—her hair had a life all its own, like a fifth limb. And the way she moved . . . I mean, *lust* just demeans it. It was true love. I seriously understand now why kings and shit launched entire wars over just one woman—risked their countries, their fortunes, gave away everything they had. I understand chivalry now, dude. She is Tyra of Troy. Just look at her."

She came out to applause, turning on her big Tyra smile, playing surprise at the warmth of the reception, putting a flat hand to her breathless, voluptuous chest, then pursing her lips in a kiss.

"There. The air kiss. That's our little signal."

Maven looked at skinny Ricky hunched over before the small screen. "Your signal?"

"This cruel world keeps us apart. Experts say there are three events that could trigger a worldwide cataclysm. One—the sun burns out. Two—an asteroid impact destroys the atmosphere. Three—Tyra Banks marries a white man."

Maven thought about it, and agreed. "I think three would cause the most typhoons."

Ricky watched his goddess on a flickering four-inch screen. "She should wear stretchier tops."

A pickup stopped outside, the driver bald, leather-jacketed, with the extremity of a tattoo—something dull, blue, penal—visible at the sides of his neck. He left the pickup running with a pit bull sitting in the front seat, came in, paid cash for a box of Phillies Blunts and some beef jerky, then drove off feeding the jerky to the dog.

The prison tat jumped out at Maven, got him feeling that nervous energy again. Beyond all his qualms, beyond all the questions he still had, beyond the voice in his head telling him, *Don't,* he was undeniably excited. He couldn't wait for his shift to be over. For the new day to begin.

He had gone into this thing wanting to know more about Danielle Vetti, and instead found himself beguiled by Brad Royce.

Ricky said, his mouth full of Sour Patch Kids, "You're not eating tonight?"

Maven shook his head. *Tomorrow Man.* "I'm thinking about trying to get back into shape."

That straightened Ricky. "You're going to reenlist," he said, as though it were something he had been dreading all along.

Maven smiled and shook his head, looking out the window again, searching the sky for signs of dawn.

Rats Dance

THE SIGHT OF HANDGUNS ON THE HOTEL ROOM BED JOLTED MAVEN. He hadn't seen a plain-view hot weapon since returning to the States. In Eden, they were standard-issue, like bottles of water. Here in a Back Bay hotel room, a pistol loaded with live rounds looked like a bomb waiting to go off.

He geared up with the others. Royce provided him with soft tactical body armor that fit all right, except for riding up into his throat when he wanted to sit down. The vest had full-wrap protection, critical for close-quarter engagements, when an arms-out gun stance left the sides of the torso vulnerable. Because soft body armor did a decent job of fragmenting pistol bullets but repelled rifle fire about as effectively as a wool sweater, Maven was used to wearing ceramic plates in the front and back pockets. So the vest felt light and almost silly, like wearing a life preserver indoors.

A patch was Velcro'ed onto the vest front, wide and rectangular. Maven started to pull on it when Royce's hand touched his arm. "Later," he said, handing Maven shooting gloves made of neoprene and synthetic leather, and a police-blue windbreaker long enough to hide his belt holster.

Maven stepped to the corner and drew his sidearm, a Sig Sauer 225. He was familiar with the weapon, knowing, for example, that the 225 was manufactured without a safety. He pressed the side button and caught the magazine as it ejected from the grip. He racked the slide and found the firing chamber empty, then racked it a few more times, trusting that it wouldn't stick if he needed it. He then thumbed the rounds out of the magazine, counting eight, a full load for the 225. He fed them back inside the magazine, one by one against the spring, and slid the magazine home into the Sig's grip. The weapon felt comfortable in his hand, but without his having fired it, nothing really mattered. Borrowing a handgun is like borrowing a parachute. And the first rule of jump school is, always pack your own kit.

Royce said there shouldn't be any shooting. "Not if we do this thing right. You think you can do this thing right?"

Maven racked one round into the firing chamber, then decocked, releasing the magazine again, now one short of a full load, and thumbed an extra round from one of the two backup mags in the nylon pouch on his belt, then inserted it into the current mag and thrust it back inside the grip. Now he had nine, a full wad. He holstered the weapon and zipped up his blue jacket to cover it.

The Latino's left cheek egged out from a fat dip of chewing tobacco, another thing Maven hadn't seen much of since Eden, where everyone dipped. Royce and the others looped ZipCuffs onto their chest straps, but Maven wasn't issued any restraints. They pulled black balaclavas down over their faces, fixing the stitched holes so they sat over their eyes, then rolled the masks up to sit on the tops of their heads like knit caps. Maven did the same.

He appreciated the seriousness in the room. These were men dressing for work.

Royce's phone buzzed. The blond guy had left the room a while ago. Maven realized that he had gone down to the lobby, to eyeball the Venezuelan as he entered the hotel.

Royce listened and reported, "He's in. With muscle. One man, rolling an oversized suitcase. Tan jacket, bulge underneath. Waved off a bellboy at the door."

Maven yawned deep. From tiredness, from nerves, from the hormones released by his battle-alert brain, already relaxing his bronchial tubes for deeper breathing. His chest, tight inside the shell of the protective vest, felt like a jar of fireflies. He tore open a foil packet of Nescafé instant coffee crystals—nicked from City Oasis—as he hadn't got any sleep that morning, emptying it into his mouth and dry-crunching it like candy, ramping up on undiluted caffeine.

"Second elevator," reported Royce, hanging up. "Remember the security camera in the elevator panel. First man in body-blocks it."

"That'll be me," said the green-jacketed Latino, spitting his plug and a string of brown drool into the plastic-lined trash can.

The black guy passed Maven on his way to the door, smelling of hotel soap and pistol cleaner, his yellow eyes looking like stones in need of polishing. "Don't don't fuck it up, newbie," he said with a smile.

The Latino followed him into the hallway, quietly singing, "We're gonna have a party . . . ," until the door closed and they were gone.

Then it was just Maven and Royce, alone in the narrow entryway. Royce checked him face-to-face like a man examining a thermostat before leaving the house for the day, making sure it was right. He looked satisfied.

He pointed to the door, and Maven went out first.

THE L-SHAPED HALLWAY ON THE TWENTY-SEVENTH FLOOR WAS EMPTY. At three in the afternoon, all the USA Todays had been claimed, the maid service had come and gone. A couple of room-service trays, set out after lunch, lay next to doors.

The Latino and the black guy waited at the near elevator. The UP button had been pressed, a glowing white eye. The Latino's voice came back faintly—"gonna have a party"—all nervous energy and nicotine.

Maven swished around the last of his soldier's Starbucks. He looked down at a silver-handled room-service tray containing two small jars of marmalade and honey, the congealed remains of an egg-and-pepper omelet and a bowl of hash, a linen napkin, and a side plate of wheat toast. As Royce peered around the corner again, Maven bent down and stuffed a slice of cold, buttered bread into his mouth.

Royce leaned back, checking behind them. "These guys," he said, tugging up his jacket to expose his Beretta, "are fucking scum. You remember that."

Maven nodded, swallowing the toast. The elevator dinged and a red arrow appeared on the overhead panel. Maven followed Royce down the hall, everyone pulling down his balaclava mask and converging on the doors.

They opened, and the first two were inside immediately. Royce advanced with his Beretta out of his holster, aimed low at the floor, ready. Muffled yells and wall-thumps, but no gunshots. Maven couldn't see inside, remaining a few yards back, uncertain whether he should draw. The door tried to close twice, each time Royce stopping it with his foot.

The scuffle ended, and the Latino exited the elevator car with the Venezuelan in front of him, the man's wrists cuffed behind his back. A nylon mouth gag accentuated the wild and stunned look on the Venezuelan's face. The black guy came out second with a bigger guy, identically bound and gagged, but more bent over, perhaps more hurt. He wrenched the man's arms higher and handed him to Maven, who gripped the guy by his elbow.

Royce retrieved the wheeled suitcase, then the black guy stepped back inside the elevator, Maven seeing, reflected in the wall mirror before the door closed, him screwing a tube-shaped suppressor onto his pistol muzzle.

Then they were running, feet thudding heavily on the carpet as they pushed their captives around the corner, rushing to the stairwell. Maven followed the Latino's lead, strong-arming the muscle up the steps, bumping him around a little when he resisted. He saw someone moving floors below them, but it was just the blond coming up the stairs.

At the top floor, Royce squeezed past them to the front, knocking the Venezuelan's head against the wall to get his attention. Royce unzipped his own jacket and pulled down the flap on the front of his vest. White block letters read FBI.

The Venezuelan's gagged grunting echoed inside the deep stairwell.

Royce bounced him off the wall once more for emphasis, and the Venezuelan sagged but the Latino held him up. Royce reached for Maven's jacket and unzipped it, tearing down his FBI patch too. Maven didn't feel good about this.

Royce said to the Venezuelan, "Play along and your lawyer will have you out by midnight. But fuck with us, and you die resisting arrest. *Comprende? Entiende?*"

They went down the twenty-ninth floor hallway, met halfway by the black guy, holding another man doubled over in front of him. His face was bloody and he wheezed into his gag—probably a lookout posted at the elevator.

The blond took the lookout, and the black guy lined up on the hinge side of door 2919. The Latino pushed the Venezuelan's face into the peephole. Royce crouched beside him, his gun pointed at the Venezuelan. He pulled down the man's gag and knocked on the door.

A voice on the other side said, "Yep," and the door started to open, and the Latino drove the Venezuelan forward. The black guy went in solo behind him, long gun out. Then the blond with the bloodied man, then Maven.

Maven's guy tried to kick him and pull free, so Maven shoved him down, hard, the man crashing into a table and falling onto his side. Maven had his gun free and was in a good two-handed crouch—but it was already over.

Nobody moved. Not the goon who had answered the door and was thrown back against the wall. Not the goon by the window, his hand frozen halfway to his holster. Not the fat Maracone brothers, seated at the far table like diners awaiting their meal.

It was the letters FBI. Not one shot was fired.

The Maracones looked at the bound and gagged Venezuelan with disgust. They kept their fat hands visible and their mouths shut. The black guy went over and shouldered each one to the floor, twin silver .25 handguns falling from beneath their fleshy thighs.

Everybody was then cuffed, hands and ankles. Furniture was cleared away so that they could be laid out on the floor, heads in, like a six-petal flower. The Venezuelan's muscle, the heaviest of them all, was left where he had fallen, lying on his side by the wall.

Then a thorough frisking, the Latino throwing mobile phones, wallets, car keys, pistols, and pistol magazines onto the bed.

"I want my lawyer!" barked one Maracone brother, lying red-faced on his big belly. "And a motherfucking receipt!"

"Who here blabbed?" said the other Maracone. *"Who was it?"*

The Venezuelan was trying to protest through his gag.

The *rrriiippp* they heard was the blond tearing off lengths of duct tape.

"What the fu—?" was all the Maracone brother could get out, as the tape wrapped around his mouth to the back of his head. Another strip covered his eyes to his ears. Leaving only his nose.

The same was done to all of them.

A couple thrashed afterward, making a racket on the floor, until the black guy went around kicking each one in the ribs until they stopped.

The blond took the clock radio from the nightstand and placed it on the floor in the center of the ring of taped heads. He found a hip-hop station and turned up the volume.

Maven, fascinated by all the activity, heard a thumping and turned just in time to see the muscle stagger to his feet against the wall. He came at Maven head-down, bull-style. Maven side-stepped him and dropped the heel of his hand down onto the back of his head, flattening the guy, dropping him hard.

The black guy tossed over a roll of silver duct tape with an approving look.

The blond unfolded a medium-size white paper bag and picked up each confiscated weapon from the bed, releasing ammo clips and clearing the firing chambers. He deposited all ammunition in the bag, dropping the empty guns back onto the bed. He then removed each mobile phone battery and dumped both pieces separately into the bag. Then both room phones, including the bathroom extension.

Royce gave a low whistle, summoning Maven to the bathroom. It was spacious, with a separate interior door to the toilet, and one of those bidet things. Royce shoved the complimentary toiletries aside, making counter room for the Venezuelan's suitcase. He ran the zipper along the sides, opening the cover to reveal a layer of plush white towels.

Beneath the towels lay tightly packed parcels wrapped in green-tinted plastic, bound with tape. Royce removed one with his gloved hand, the parcel roughly the size of a hardcover book. With a small folding knife, he opened up a three-inch gash lengthwise in the plastic wrap.

The dope inside was caked and chunky, dull white with a yellowish tinge.

"Cocaine hydrochloride," said Royce, picking at the drug with the tip of the blade. "One metric kilogram. About thirty grand worth, wholesale. Or a ten-to-life stretch, depending on which way you look at it. Five or more kilos means possession with intent to distribute, jumping it up to forty to life. If real cops busted in here right now, our next lunch in the outside world would be in about 2050. A science-fiction stretch. Just to put this into perspective."

He handed over the parcel, slit side up, and Maven was holding a kilo of uncut cocaine. It was lighter than he had imagined, like a flat loaf of unleavened bread.

Royce grabbed a second kilo and slit its green plastic, this time bisecting the sealing tape. He carried it to the open toilet, dumping the coke into the bowl, kneading the clumps until the package was empty.

He pushed the handle, the mixture swirling until it was swallowed down the drain, the bowl refilling with clear water.

Royce said, "The sewer rats dance tonight."

He had Maven dispose of the one in his hand, and they switched off flushing away the rest. The cocaine didn't dissolve well, sinking slowly into the water like cake mix. Maven lost count, but there were fewer than twenty flushes.

When they were done, Royce mashed up the wrappers and brought them out to the white paper bag on the bed. He dumped them in, then his white-dusted gloves.

Maven followed suit. Then they returned to the bathroom and removed their jackets and holsters, patching up their FBI signs and unstrapping the armor vests, stripping off their masks and piling everything into the suitcase, which they then brought back out to the main room. The dealers remained on the floor, music pounding in their ears. The others were all unmasked now too, packing up. Maven was handed the white paper bag full of pistol magazines, coke wrappers, and unpowered mobile phones. Royce grabbed a suitcase roughly the same size as the Venezuelan's, but softer.

BACK INTO THE STAIRWELL, DOWN TWO FLIGHTS TO TWENTY-SEVEN, then along the L-shaped hallway to the elevators and down. They exited at the second floor, the mall level, Royce wheeling his travel bag behind him past the kiosks and upscale stores.

At the edge of the food court, Royce nodded toward a trash container, and Maven dumped the white bag with evident relief.

Past Legal Sea Foods, they rode the long escalator down to revolving doors, exiting onto Boylston Street, where a cold, canyonlike wind cuffed them, street grit spraying their skin as they crossed three lanes of traffic to the shelter of a side street.

"And that," said Royce, "is that."

"Christ," said Maven, running off a string of expletives, the by-product of adrenaline-induced elation.

"Take it easy," said Royce, keeping an even pace.

Maven reined in his manic exhilaration, moving past a mother walking a blanketed newborn. What he was feeling could almost have been a contact high from flushing all that coke. "Now what?"

"Now we walk."

They were already walking. Maven wanted to sprint. "What about them back there?"

Royce crossed Newbury Street, not waiting, traffic stopping for him. "They'll get themselves free eventually. By now they know they got ripped off. I want them to think we took the product too. Double the pain, double the blame."

As they approached Commonwealth Avenue, Maven shoved his hands into his pockets to keep them from flying away. "FBI? Fucking hell."

Royce nodded. "We're breaking all kinds of laws here. Point is to settle them down immediately. Especially in a public place like that, a hotel. Get them under control fast. Thinking it's an orderly raid, something their lawyers can beat. Getting arrested to them is like a dentist appointment. Getting ripped off—that's another thing entirely."

Maven eyed the suitcase, rolling at Royce's heels like a puppy. "How much is in there?"

Royce shrugged, though Maven could tell he knew already. "Dealers can't exactly run to the cops to make up their loss. That's why getting out clean is imperative. No gunplay, no going off and capping anybody if we can help it. Because gunshots bring heat, and dragging the law into this thing defeats our advantage."

Royce slowed to a stop, turning to Maven on the sidewalk in the median pedestrian mall of Commonwealth Avenue.

"I want you to never, ever forget how stupendously fucking dangerous this is, what we just did. Taking big money away from well-funded sadists. We made it look easy back there only because we've been working this thing for weeks, planning it out, training to get it right. One little mistake, one slipup—and we're smoked. Done for. Not that it would end fast. These fuckers would want to get their pound of flesh, you can believe it. Getting jacked makes them punk. Street cred is everything out here. Why retaliation is a motherfucking guarantee—*if* we screw up. Which we will not."

Royce's stare was intense, but nothing at that point, not even the fear of death, could have doused Maven's flame. He nodded, hands squirming in his pockets, anxious to get wherever they were going.

GRIDLEY

THEY TURNED ONTO MARLBOROUGH STREET, NARROWER THAN THE other avenues in the Back Bay, quieter, lined with trees and gas lamps. The formerly Brahmin, currently swanky side of town.

The clicking of the suitcase wheels over the brick sidewalk stopped at a low, black, wrought-iron gate outside a street-level real estate office, listing sheets taped to the window underneath a sign reading ROOF DECK PROPERTIES AND MANAGEMENT.

Royce pushed through the ornamental gate toward the stone steps. Maven looked up at the curved-front Victorian brownstone, then followed.

Inside the unlocked first door, Royce waved to the side office entrance, where a frazzled-looking receptionist on the phone waved back and reached beneath her desk to buzz them inside. The second door in front of them buzzed and Royce pulled it open, revealing a chandelier of violet-tinted glass hanging in a richly paneled lobby. A thin Oriental runner led to the foot of a broad, curving staircase.

"Eleven real estate agents working their asses off," said Royce on the way up the stairs, "hustling student apartments, business sublets, artist lofts. Knocking each other over to land exclusive listings. The business is actually profitable, not that I give a damn. It's a laundry machine to me. A front. Cash goes in dirty and comes out clean. But the workers, they have no idea. So they keep busting their asses for their commissions, trying to keep the office afloat. Poor fucks."

He stopped at the only door on the first-floor landing. His key turned in the lock, and Maven followed him inside to a splendid, modern kitchen with beet red walls, glass-front cabinets, stainless-steel fixtures. A floor-through apartment, running left through an archway to a larger room in the rear, and right down a short hallway to the street-facing front.

Maven closed the door, and the entire city vanished. Royce set the suitcase gently down atop the silver-speckled countertop. He opened a panel on the island unit and a gasp of freezer steam escaped, and he withdrew two chilled pint glasses. He opened the door to a giant silver refrigerator, a bank vault of food, and pulled out two bright red, bottle-shaped aluminum cans of Budweiser. "They only drink American. I'm betting you won't mind."

"Who's they?" said Maven, still back on his heels. "You don't live here?"

"Me? I live upstairs," said Royce, pointing. He opened the bottle and poured for Maven, the golden yellow beer sliding down the frosted side of the glass, then poured his own. He handed Maven his glass and clinked it.

"To gay sex," Royce said, watching Maven almost choke. "I got you."

Maven grinned, then drank down about half, as much as he could handle until the coldness started to close his throat. The suitcase was just sitting there on the counter. He forced himself to look away. Through the short hallway to the front, he saw a large pool table. *"Damn,"* he sighed, moving to it.

The table had tassels on the sides and soft, ropy purses for pockets. Massive mahogany legs. A real Victorian-type piece set out on a plush Oriental rug, the entire room given over to it.

Maven ran his fingers over its crimson cloth playing surface. A cue-stick rack hung on the wall between two enormous World War II–era propaganda posters. AVENGE DECEMBER 7 rallied the first, an angry man raising his massive fist into the air. BOOKS ARE WEAPONS IN THE WAR OF IDEAS proclaimed the second, a giant book burning in vivid color. The opposite wall was dominated by a stone-manteled fireplace.

"They had to bring this thing up from the outside, like a piano," said Royce, coming along behind him.

Maven went to the far, curved wall, the centered window offering a view across Marlborough Street, and, over them, the top of the Prudential building beyond.

Cars lined both sides of the street below, the wind spiriting the last of the fallen tree leaves. From the east, two men came along the brick sidewalk, each carrying a duffel bag. Maven made the Latino and the blond, approaching the front door below.

He stepped back from the window. He felt anxious suddenly, out of place. He needed a moment to get his shit together, and emptied his beer glass. "There a bathroom?"

IT SMELLED CLEAN, SPICED WITH COLOGNE. THE SHOWER CURTAIN was brass-colored and drapes-thick, the walls and floor made of marble tile.

He ran cold water, splashing some on his face, then looked at himself in the mirror over the sink. He wondered again, *How did I get here, exactly?*

The ceiling creaked. Light footsteps along the third floor overhead. Somebody upstairs. Faint music too.

Then voices down the hall. Maven hated being the new guy. The first day of school all over again. He sucked it up and opened the door into the hallway.

The Latino and the blond all-American had dumped their duffels in the kitchen, turning to Maven as he entered.

"We're good?" said the Latino, referring to Maven.

Royce said, "What do you think?"

The Latino then came forward, offered his hand. Maven shook, a good Marine grip. "Name's Suarez. Carlito Suarez."

"Neal Maven."

"Carlito, just like Al Pacino in that movie." Suarez grinned. "Only more badass."

The blond came forward with a similar grip. "Jimmy Glade. How's it goin'? Where'd Royce find you?"

"Pulled him off the scrap heap," said Royce, coming out with more beers, passing them around, no glasses this time. "Same as you."

Glade said to Maven, "You snore, man?"

Carlito said of his big blond friend, "Milkshake here likes his beauty sleep."

Maven shook his head in confusion.

Royce said, "Jimmy's going to be your roommate."

Maven stopped with his bottle at his lips. "My roommate?"

"You're moving in. This is your new place."

Maven stared at him. "I'm doing what?"

Royce stepped over to the suitcase. "Sticking close is how we do. This is your barracks now. Eat together, sleep together."

"Not *together* together," stressed Glade.

"And, rent-free," said Royce, drawing the zipper along the edges of the suitcase. "Except on paper."

"More flow for the tax man," said Carlito.

"You're learning," said Royce, lifting the top of the suitcase as if he were opening the white box cover on a cake.

The cash was laid out in overlapping stacks of elasticized bundles. All Jacksons and Franklins, staring faceup.

A moment of reverence as they all took in the beautiful sight.

Carlito said, "Fuckin' Fourth of July."

He gave Glade some skin. Glade said, "'Lito, you get any chub out there today? What about you, Maven? Get any chub on that lick? A combat rodney?"

Maven said, "Not like I'm getting right now."

Glade nodded in agreement. "Chub factor of three. Just north of flaccid." He finished his beer. "Saving it for tonight, is all."

A key scratched in the lock. Royce dropped the cover on the money bag, but it was purely precautionary and nobody was really concerned.

In walked the black guy, the fifth member of the crew. Royce said, "What took so long?"

"Settling up at the front desk," he said, laying down a tan garment bag. "Who the fuck cleared out the wet bar?"

Glade smiled, pulling a handful of vodka nips from his pockets.

"That fucking nine-dollar Snickers, that's coming out of your kick too." The black guy sized up Maven, standing on the side of the island, and still didn't smile. "So what's the verdict on the FNG?" FNG: fucking new guy. "We going to deep-six this motherfucker, or what?"

When the others laughed, Maven smiled. The black guy kept his snarl, but some play came into his yellowed eyes.

"Just shittin'," he said, offering Maven his hand.

Royce did the introduction: "Neal Maven, meet Lewis Termino."

They shook, Maven hearing something in the name.

Termino said, "You look like you heard of me before. You grow up in Brockton?"

"Near there."

"Lewis 'the Dynamo' Termino." He dropped his chin and assumed a loose-fisted fighter's stance. "Rocky Marciano, he was the pride of Brockton. But Dynamo was its soooul."

"I do remember," said Maven.

"He had all the tools," said Royce. "Fast hands, granite jaw. All class. Only problem? Feet of fucking clay."

"I'd rather stay and take a beating than retreat. Turns out that ain't good for judges' cards, or a long-term career."

Glade uncapped all four nips, sliding them around the island.

Royce watched everyone drink together. "Now we've got trust. We've got a foundation. We sealed the deal with a crime. Better than a contract inked in blood. Maven—you're one of us now."

Glade said, "Soldiers of fortune."

"You got something on us," said Carlito, swallowing, "and we got something on you."

Royce said, "It's the doctrine of mutually assured destruction. The best possible basis for a secure and honest partnership."

Termino nodded and opened the suitcase lid on the cash. "Nobody pushes the button on anyone else without everyone going *ka-plooey*."

MAVEN DID NOT FEEL THE VODKA BURN UNTIL HE WAS IN THE POOL-table room with Glade and Carlito. Royce and Termino remained behind in the kitchen to handle the split. The bluster and the buddy talk was easy to fall back into, caught up in the crosscurrent of a waning adrenaline charge and his burgeoning buzz. The cold beer warmed Maven's tongue magically, and he had questions, lots of them.

He learned that, whether he rented or owned it, the building belonged to Royce. Neither of the other two had any idea how he had made his wad in the first place.

Maven learned that they had not been at this long. "Not long enough" was Carlito's answer, as he banked the eight ball into a corner pocket.

Maven learned that the hotel jump was maybe 5 percent of the total effort expended on this job. Most of it was van surveillance and telephone traps.

He learned that Royce was the one who put them on the Venezuelan. They did not know how he originated the information, nor did they care.

"When Royce found me," said Glade, "I was detailing cars in a mall parking garage. Pocketing fucking nickels and dimes found

under the seat cushions. I'm out running this half-triathlon to get
my ass back into fighting shape, and this guy comes up to me on
the last leg, running beside me, gets me talking. Half out of breath,
we're shooting the shit like we're at a cocktail party or something.
And he lays all this broad shit out on me, smart stuff, where I'm at,
where I'm going."

"Yeah," said Maven. "Exactly."

"Fearless leader, you know?" said Glade. "So I don't ask."

Carlito nudged Maven, looking down the short hallway into
the kitchen, Royce and Termino stacking cash on the kitchen
island. "Mad money, dude. It's sick."

Glade said, "Royce takes a double share off the top, and all I
know about that is, he earns it, for sure."

Maven sank a ball, then attempted a touch shot and missed
completely. "What about Termino?"

Carlito said, "He's older. An acquired taste, but tough as
fuck."

Glade said, "He and Royce served together in Germany."
He paused to chalk up. "What about you? Royce said Special
Forces."

"Yeah," Maven allowed.

"Where'd you get dirty over there?"

"All over," said Maven. "Mostly north of Baghdad. Samarra."

"I was in Samarra," said Carlito. "Late '04. Samarra, Fallujah.
Every fucking resistance base. Just my good luck."

Glade said, "You did the job."

"Yeah, I did the fucking job." Carlito smacked the cue ball
down into a cluster of solids and stripes, not aiming anywhere in
particular, just breaking them up as hard as he could. "And what
fun we had. That was the asshole of all assholes." Carlito straightened and said to Maven, with a thumb toward Glade, "Milkshake
here still believes in the war."

"Fuck, yeah, I do. I didn't waste five years of my prime for nothing. Maven here stands with me, don't you, New Guy?"

"Enough," said Royce, coming into the room. "Fucking boring." Termino followed with the open suitcase, setting it down on the pool table. "It's payday, boys."

They gathered around.

Royce said, "It was sixteen keys, total. I know, we were hoping for twenty or more. The Maracones were getting them for a nice round thirty each, either a sweetheart deal or the price per key is falling again. Thirty times sixteen is what, Carlito?"

Carlito answered, "A lot of dough."

"Four hundred and eighty thousand."

Royce separated big stacks of cash. Maven moved his hand off the felt bumper so that he would not leave a sweat mark.

"Divide by six, that's eighty grand each. Six being two shares for me, one each for you three." He pushed piles toward each man like casino winnings. "And one for the new guy, Maven." Maven's came last, smaller than the others, but still a lot of green. "Maven gets a half share. Consider it a gift."

"A generous fucking one at that," said Termino.

"Start-up money. Our investment in you. You could park cars for a full year and never see that much." Royce looked to the others. "Maven's other half, the forty, was cut in fourths, so ten more on top for each. Bringing your total to ninety. Not too shabby."

"Well goddamned done," said Glade, getting skin from Carlito and vice versa.

Termino said, "If only this shit had been brown and not white."

The others nodded. Royce explained, for Maven's benefit, "What Lew is whining about here is the fact that heroin is worth more than twice as much per kilo as cocaine. Scag has the biggest upside, but we can't always pick our poisons, can we?"

Termino said, "I'm not sayin', I'm just sayin'."

"Let me give you some perspective, Maven. Jimmy here *still* doesn't understand why every kilo isn't worth millions automatically, but it's simple economics. Wholesale versus retail. The per kilo cost of cocaine in Bolivia or Colombia is about fifteen hundred dollars. That's its export value. As soon as it crosses the border into the United States, the price jumps two hundred per-

cent. Actual price varies from region to region, but thirty g's is
the average Boston area wholesale price right about now. The
buyer, the Maracones in this case, then break these kilos into
more affordable ounce lots. Ounces are again broken down into
grams by midsize shops, and grams into powder bags and crack
caps by street crews. Two things happen at each step. One, the
purity gets cut. Two, the price goes up. For scag, the basic rule is
seven to one. For every one wholesale kilo, seven kilos of product
eventually hits the streets. It's like black magic. Cocaine purity
runs a bit higher, but consider this. Step down one kilo to say
three-quarters purity, and you've just turned one thousand grams
of product into one thousand three hundred and thirty-three
grams total."

Glade said, "This is where my head starts to hurt."

"Staying conservative, say that every one-thousand-three-
hundred-and-thirty-three-gram magic kilo was broken up into
one thousand grams of crack and three hundred thirty-three
grams of powder. For simplicity's sake. Say two hundred dollars
per crack gram, one hundred dollars per gram of powder. Carlito,
compute that?"

"I'd run out of fingers and toes pretty quick."

"About a quarter mil. That's retail gross earnings, per original
wholesale kilo. So, sixteen kilos? Four million dollars' worth of
action we took off the street today. Four mil. That's a shitload of
ten-dollar street-corner deals. One number I don't have for you is
how many lives we just saved. Overdoses, drug crime. Think on
that."

Maven tried to. He thought of the money changing hands all
across metro Boston.

Royce said, "The others, they've heard this before, but my
bunkmate, back in Germany, he died of an overdose. I was the
one who found him. He was my best buddy out there, and I never
even saw it coming. And that still fucking haunts me to this day.
The waste of it. Why I'm a little psycho about this, understand?
A little fucking evangelical. My tolerance for this shit is zero. In

case you were wondering how I came to this unusual line of work. It's taken me a long time to put this thing together, and now it's starting to flower, starting to bear some serious fucking fruit." He nodded to the table. "So, Maven, consider yourself lucky. Even thankful."

Maven nodded. A big pile of cash sat out in front of him. "I do."

As the others celebrated, Royce walked Maven back into the kitchen. "You have questions."

Maven said, "I have a lot of fucking questions."

"Save them. We'll go over things step-by-step these next couple of days. Starting tomorrow morning, when we go out and rent you a safe-deposit box. A big one. A bank account won't do."

"But . . . how is all this possible?"

"Drug dealers are a paranoid lot. You have to be either fucking crazy or fucking hard-core to think about crossing them. We happen to be both. I didn't bring you in for your personality, I brought you in because no one else can do what we do. The equipment, the training. The work is hard and it can be tedious, but now you see it more than pays off in the end."

"But how do you know—"

"I have some connections. And that, right there, is the sum total of how forthcoming I am going to be on this matter. I will tell you nothing more, and you will ask me nothing more from this day forward. Can you live with that?"

Royce's entire demeanor had changed. Looking at him, Maven felt ungrateful. "Sure."

Royce shook his head. "Not 'sure.' I want it clear. I want it absolutely rock solid, right here, right now. Your pledge."

Maven nodded. "Okay. Yes."

"All right." Royce backed off a bit, but kept his tone serious. "We're doing good here. Every fucking crumb of that shit that goes down the drain—we've made a difference. And the best part of it is, nobody else will ever know."

A knock at the front door interrupted their talk. Royce turned to answer it, then looked back to Maven. "Oh, and one more thing. Danny doesn't know anything. And that's how it stays. For your safety, for everyone's safety. Understood?"

"Sure. No problem. Just one question."

"What's that?"

"Who's Danny?"

Royce smiled and opened the door. Danielle Vetti stepped inside. "Are we still going out tonight?"

Royce turned and said, "Danny, this is Neal Maven, the guy from the parking lot. He's with us now."

She showed Maven a flat smile of supreme disinterest, then went right back to Royce. "I need a new dress."

"Of course you do. The ones in your closet upstairs, it would be ridiculous of me to even consider suggesting you wear one of those twice."

She wore a fitted shirt that was very fitted, a snug, military-style jacket over it, and shimmery black slacks. "Maybe, if we went to a different club for a change, then I could wear the same dress more than once. But since we always go to the same club, and sit in the same exact booth, and do the exact same fucking thing, I need something new." She drew a nail across his cheek. "I have to look good for you, don't I?"

"Ah. It's for me you do this."

"Always, baby."

"Tell you what." Royce thumbed over at Maven. "Maven here's recently come into some money. He'll need some fresh duds for tonight also, but if I turn him loose on his own, he'll go raid the military surplus store. Why don't you let him accompany you over to Newbury Street, help him pick out something competent to wear, and as a thank-you, I'm sure Maven will buy you your dress."

Royce looked over at Maven.

Maven said, "Uh . . . sure."

Danielle looked at Royce doubtfully, then over at Maven. "Any dress?"

Maven shrugged. "Why not?"

"Fine," she decided, turning to leave. "Come on."

HE WASN'T EVEN SURE THE STORE THEY WERE IN WAS A STORE. IT WAS more like walking around some stranger's huge, dramatically lit walk-in closet.

No circular racks. The clothes hung on angled rails or else lay folded on white shelves. Nothing had a price tag.

Danielle went around feeling fabrics with a practiced hand. She eased a striped jacket off a padded mannequin and held it to his chest. She had been quiet and a little sulky on the way over, but moving around the store seemed to lift her mood.

She grabbed two pairs of pants for him and led Maven to the back.

"So," she said, "you're getting into the real estate game?"

She said this with a smile, as though she knew more, or perhaps wanted him to believe she did.

Maven was in way over his head, and the adrenaline fizzle coupled with the beer-and-vodka buzz didn't help.

"I guess I am," he said.

The fitting rooms were open stalls, no doors, facing a carpeted walkway ending at a three-paneled mirror. Maven stepped into the farthest stall and pulled off his jeans, a wad of twenties and hundreds bulging the left front pocket. He came out to the mirror in the first pair of pants, and Danielle hated them immediately, pinching the fabric at his thigh, then tugging on the crotch.

"No. Off. I'll be back."

He was standing in his underwear when she reappeared. She held two more pairs up to his waist, then took away one and waited outside for him to pull on the other.

Now he was getting chub. Wouldn't be good if she came yanking down on his inseam again. He needed to distract himself. *Start talking.*

"Uh, so you grew up around here, right?"

"I guess," came her voice.

"You went to Gridley High School, right?"

He received no answer. He zipped up, figuring she had walked off to find a matching belt or something. He pulled on the shirt and jacket and stepped out, and there she was, standing in front of the mirror, facing her three selves. She looked at him in the reflection. "I don't recognize you."

"Oh, you wouldn't," said Maven. "I was a couple of years behind you. My sister, she was in your grade."

Danielle squinted, unsure of this whole thing now.

"Alexis. Alexis Maven. My half sister, actually."

"Alex Maven?" said Danielle, her squint relaxing just a bit. "Holy shit. We used to smoke together sometimes. Out at the 'lounge.' The woods behind the north wing?"

Maven nodded as though he had ever been there.

Danielle turned, looking Maven up and down. She hadn't really looked at him since they'd arrived, only his clothes. "So you're Alex's younger brother."

He nodded. "Half brother."

"Small world." She stepped behind him, plucking at the shoulders of his jacket. "She was a party girl, wasn't she? What's Alex doing now?"

"She's dead."

The tugging stopped. Danielle's eyes flared as though he'd said something embarrassing, not her. "Sorry."

"She never left town," he said. "Kind of dug her own grave there. I remember, I saw you once, after you graduated. At the South Shore Plaza, spraying perfume on women walking into Filene's."

Danielle hissed out a laugh. "I was saving up. For New York. Modeling."

Maven nodded. "That figures."

She resumed with his jacket, feeling it under his arms, ignoring what he had intended as a compliment. "I had everything but the height, they said."

He nodded. "So how'd you wind up back . . . ?"

"Here? Long, boring story." She came around in front of him. "You getting all this down, or what?" She got out of his way, and Maven looked at himself in the three-way mirror. "So what do you think?"

He barely recognized himself.

"You feel good, right?" she said. "You feel different, don't you?"

He turned to one side, then the other. "Actually, I kind of do, yeah."

"Bolder. Sexier. Isn't that what you want, Gridley?"

She was studying the fit of his clothes, while he was studying her.

"Yeah," he said.

FOUR MONTHS LATER

THE THAW

A PROLONGED COLD SNAP HAD ICED THE SURFACE OF THE Charles River, the body of water separating Cambridge from Boston, since before the first of the year. Beneath the Boston University Bridge, and the lower Grand Junction Railroad bridge that ran below it, a northward bend narrowed the river, and well-worn paths in the snow showed where pedestrians, mostly students, had exploited this seasonal quirk by crossing the frozen moat on foot.

Not until mid-March did a few consecutive afternoons of sunshine start melting the snow. At noontime one day, a life-sciences major crossing the river toward MIT noticed something in the ice beneath her feet. It was a body, curled up and facedown, as though embarrassed by its own mortality. The student plucked out her earbuds and dialed 911, standing there in the middle of the Charles. State police answered the mobile call, and after a few moments working out her exact location—the geographical middle of the river was the borderline between Suffolk and Middlesex counties—determined that she was closer to the north and so transferred her call to Cambridge PD.

A patrolman met her there, leaving his car and his spinning blues blocking one inbound lane on Memorial Drive as he made his way down to the bank. She couldn't stay, she had a class to get to, an exam to take, but she left her name and number with the officer and directed him to the body. When the patrolman walked out to look, the ice gave way and he dropped right through.

Other students crossing the bridge whipped out their phones, and multiple videos of the soaking cop crawling out of the river were uploaded to YouTube within minutes.

His fall cracked out the ice chunk containing the body, and backup patrolmen used long poles from a sculling shed down the river to pull in the corpsicle. They saw that his hands had been removed at the wrists, and left the deceased out to thaw in the sun while awaiting the arrival of homicide detectives.

The left flap of his sage green jacket defrosted quickly. Tucked inside the breast pocket was a wallet of expensive lambskin, the oversize passport-style favored by international business travelers. The issuing country was Venezuela. His name was listed as Señor Gilberto Vasco.

Running the name tripped a Homeland Security watch-list alert, which routed a bulletin to the Drug Enforcement Administration's New England Field Division, headquartered in the JFK Federal Building on Sudbury Street alongside Boston City Hall and the Government Center plaza. The DEA's NEFD then notified the agent who had flagged Señor Vasco's card via Immigration and Customs in the first place.

That agent, Marcus Lash, had been lunching on a tuna melt at the Busy Bee on Beacon Street near the St. Mary's T stop, just minutes from the BU Bridge. That was how he came to be squatting down on the Cambridge side of the river, next to a young medical examiner from the coroner's office, before homicide arrived and the meat wagon took Señor Vasco away.

"DEA?" said the ME, eyeing Lash's credentials.

The ME was a young kid, brown-skinned like Lash, wearing a fur-hooded L.L. Bean parka over evidence-preserving Tyvek overalls and bootees.

"Possible drug-related homicide," said Lash.

"Drugs? Because the decedent's a well-dressed foreigner?"

Lash gave the kid another look. A fellow brother, but Lash didn't get the confrere vibe. No shorthand, no soul-brother discount on a fast friendship. No love. Kid must have got all that affirmative-action shit drummed out of him in med school.

"Because he's a KA. A known associate."

"Is cutting off hands a drug thing?"

"It is when you steal." Lash looked at the kid. He had kind of a natural antipathy toward lighter-skinned intellectuals that he was trying hard to overcome. Mostly because that was the same track his own college-age son was on. "How about we switch this around and you start telling me things now."

The ME leaned forward to take a second look at the defrosting wrist stumps. "Nice clean cut. People think wrist joints, flexible, easy to cut. The reverse is true. This was done with a table saw, looks like. Postmortem for sure. No fish bites." The ME looked closely at the fleshy sleeve. "Or very few, anyway. Body is well preserved on the whole. Essentially mummified. But as he continues to thaw, he'll decompose faster than usual." He looked up to the road where his white ME van was parked. "Guy's going to drip all over my wagon."

"You can't keep him cold somehow?"

"Pack him in dry ice? Great if we had the budget. And the time. If he was chopped up into cooler-sized pieces, I could get him home that way."

Lash thinking, *Home?*

The ME shuffled forward on his haunches, noticing something. The dead man's face was half-emerged from the ice, glistening. "Chunk missing from his lower lip, see there? Could be a fish bite. Or . . ."

He worked his gloved fingers inside the dead Venezuelan's

parted teeth. With some effort, he slid out a wedge of melting river ice—meaning the body had gone into the water with its mouth open—then produced a small flashlight from his overalls pocket.

"Tongue's cut off too."

Lash looked in. The cut had been made at a slight angle, maybe an inch from the base at the back of the throat.

The ME mimed the procedure on the corpse. "They went in probably with garden shears or maybe butcher's scissors, one snip. But as they did so, rubbing the lip over this lower canine here, it cut the lip. See? Can't get a clean angle like that." He pulled back, flicking his gloved fingers toward the river to get the wetness off. "So what does that mean?"

Lash sat back from the melting corpse. "Traditionally, you get your hands cut off for stealing, and your tongue cut out for squealing."

"Uh-oh. Mixed messages."

Lash stood, looking across the river at the Back Bay apartments and the Citgo sign. "He did something to piss off the wrong people. Not a lot of second chances in this game."

A growing rumble became a train of six cars barreling across the Grand Junction Railroad bridge, shaking the crumbling stone struts of the overhead road as it passed into the rail yards on the Boston side.

"Did you know," the ME said, once the train was clear, "that this is the only spot in the world where a boat can sail underneath a train running under a car driving underneath an airplane?"

"No, I didn't," said Lash, unable to figure out this kid. He reached into his coat pocket for a business card. "You won't learn much, I don't think. They dumped him here to be found. But here's my card with my e-mail on the bottom there. If you could, cc me your autopsy report."

"Sure, yeah." The ME looked at the card, the embossed DEA seal in the corner. He was a little more interested now. "You got it."

Lash turned to make his way back up the embankment.

"Hey," said the ME. "So what does this mean anyway? Is this the start of a gang war or something?"

Lash stopped, turned back. "You know how they say, for every one dead rat you see, there are a hundred more living in the walls around you?"

The ME nodded. "Okay, I see what you're saying."

This kid had come in with hackles up, for whatever reason, but he was basically all right. Lash wanted to leave him with something, to appeal to their shared heritage, such as it was. "My grand-pops used to have this thing. He was a big tea drinker. Smoked tea too, but that's a different story. Back in the day, tea bags were for fancy folks. Tea came loose, and you made a pot and you strained out the leaves. He'd serve me some, wait until I drank it down to the bottom. 'Gimme here,' he'd say, motioning for the cup. 'I'm 'on read your tea leaves for you.' It was a way of fortune-telling, by the pattern they left. He'd take it and look at it this way and that, swirl it around a little and squint hard, then nod and make his pronouncement. 'You're going to take a piss soon.'"

The ME loosed a grudging smile.

Lash nodded. "That's what I get off this. Somebody's going to be taking a piss soon. All I really know is, it won't be me."

LASH HATED NARCOTICS THE WAY SOCIAL WORKERS HATE POVERTY, the way epidemiologists hate disease. Not an active, festering hatred, but as something to push against. A battle he didn't expect to win, only to wage honorably.

He had thirty-three years in the DEA. A third of a century. *Where did it all go?* is what people always say, as though they hadn't been paying attention, or else somehow imagined it was all going to come back around again.

But Lash knew where it went. It went into this job.

He had been with the DEA almost since its inception. People would ask him sometimes, *Why drug enforcement?* as though it had to be a calling, because who else but a fool would devote himself full-time to a losing cause? Or maybe some personal tragedy in his background had propelled him into this unforgiving line of work.

There was none. He came out of the service in 1975 with a helicopter license, a 'fro he was itching to grow, and a fuck-it-all attitude. The two-year-old DEA was a good fit. It was small and underfunded, and the agency needed a black guy with combat pilot experience more than he needed it. In the late seventies and eighties, narc work bloomed with the diversification of the drug trade. Undercover was where the action was, and for a time he lived the lifestyle, like the mirror image of a dealer. And he excelled. A black fed working UC in the early eighties was a lot less makeable than a gregarious white dude showing up in town with two days' worth of beard growth and a spray-on tan, carrying a briefcase full of cash and looking to front some snow.

The job had cost Lash his marriage, and any shot at a normal American life, which was never really what he'd wanted anyway. Vietnam had pretty well cured him of that. He liked action. He was used to action. He had never sought a desk job, and a street agent's pay grade could rise only so high. But what he did get was more pull. He got some sway. That was his reward for longevity. That was how he came to head up Windfall.

Windfall was a multiagency task force set up under his command. Cartels and drug rings had a unique problem, one Lash.had come to appreciate over his career: they made too much money. Too much cash, specifically, which they then had to devise ingenious ways of getting out of the United States, requiring almost as much energy as did importing their contraband. If the average wholesale price of a kilo of cocaine equaled $30,000, that's three hundred Benjamins going the other way, taking up as much volume as the drug, if not quite as much mass. With heroin, it's double the dough, so now you're moving two to one exports to imports. With the drug cartels each grossing tens of billions every year, and the United States far and away their largest market, that meant $100 billion a year in cash flowing out of this country.

Some of this they accomplished with shell corporations and paper transactions. Some of the money they "smurf" out. Smurfing means breaking down large sums into smaller chunks of less than $10,000, to avoid federal Currency Transaction Report filings. Smurfs are locals who move from bank to bank, depositing cartel money in accounts opened under various aliases, or else converting it into cashier's checks and post office money orders under the CTR limit. For this, they earn one or two cents on the dollar.

Eighteen months ago, Lash and his team—which included rotating agents on loan from the U.S. Treasury (IRS and FinCEN, the Financial Crimes Enforcement Network), U.S. Customs and Border Protection, Department of Homeland Security (U.S. Citizenship and Immigration Services), U.S. Secret Service (Investigative Support for Money Laundering), Massachusetts State Police, Rhode Island State Police, and Boston and Providence police departments—stopped a husband and wife outside their Methuen home. They were in their fifties, which trended old, but otherwise they fit the profile: neatly dressed, inconspicuous, law-abiding foreign nationals from Mexico, Central America, or northern South America (in this case, Guatemalans), with good language skills, established in the community (their daughter was enrolled in a Catholic high school, and they had a one-year renter's agreement on their house). Smurfs are rarely armed, notably compliant, and never see or handle the powder: the money cells and the drug cells are kept entirely separate, for security reasons.

The woman carried a large Vera Bradley knockoff—the fashion among New England–area smurfs that year, thanks to its convenient interior pockets—so full of money, she had to remove banded stacks of cash to dig out her identification. Inside their home, in oversize blue cotton laundry bags next to the basement washer-dryer, Lash had discovered another three hundred K.

No law, federal or local, prohibits people from keeping $300,000 in the laundry area of their home. Because of this, Windfall's arrest rate—their total "clearance" of successfully prosecuted cases—was relatively low. To prefer federal charges, Lash had to prove that a suspect was "structuring"—laundering illegal profits into unre-portable sums—which required a significant paper trail, the lack of which was the whole idea of smurfing in the first place. The smurfs who were arrested almost never cooperated with the government, knowing that family members in their native country would suffer for their betrayal. (This was also why smurfs could be trusted never to skim profits from their cartel employers.)

But large sums of money suspected to be the fruit of illegal activity could lawfully be confiscated by the federal government and held until such time as the possessor could prove it was legiti-mately received or earned. The couple in this case offered no objection to the cash seizure, only requesting a receipt for the full amount, certified by an agent of the IRS: a piece of paper citing proof of law enforcement confiscation, the one thing that ensured they and their loved ones would remain alive.

Such moneys are never claimed, the bulk of the funds turned over to the Treasury's forfeiture fund to be applied toward reduc-ing the federal deficit—with 10 percent recycled back into financ-ing Windfall. Over the past two years, Windfall had confiscated over $31 million in cash and assets in the six New England states. Because Windfall was self-funded and, in this way, self-perpetuating, Lash and his team enjoyed relative autonomy.

Going after the drugs themselves was a failure. It meant agents had to hustle harder than street dealers to make a bust, only to see the bad guys cycle through the criminal justice system as easily as the dollars they laundered. Street money was chump change, because once the product was out on the streets, the source money, the real money, had already been made.

Disrupt the Flow. That was Lash's mantra. Get in Their Shit. The money Windfall had seized wasn't enough to shake the foundations of the cartels—not yet—and admittedly, drugs weren't physically being taken off the street. But Windfall's diligence was beginning to exact a real toll on the suppliers, Lash was sure. They could always manufacture more product, but confiscated profits were gone for-ever. He was hacking away at their bottom line. Getting Windfall implemented nationwide, which was his goal, might even change the face of the American drug problem—not defeat it, never defeat it, but weaken it, break it down, make it more manageable.

LASH PULLED INTO A SPACE ON THE THIRD LEVEL OF THE PARKING garage. He exchanged his overcoat and coffee-and-cream scarf for a San Antonio Spurs hoodie. He used to wear a Celtics hoodie, but too many whites came up asking if he was Robert Parish.

He crossed into the adjacent Museum of Science, paid the entrance fee, and headed over to the blue wing, second level, past the "Seeing Is Deceiving" exhibit. He slowed a moment there, recognizing two M. C. Escher works: the hand drawing the hand, and the stairs that went around in a perpetual up-or-down circle. Prints of these works adorned the office of his boss, the special agent in charge of the New England DEA, was really all one needed to know about the current state of conventional drug enforcement.

At the far end of the wing was the entrance to a separate exhibit named "Butterfly Garden." A bunch of little kids were attacking a coatrack there like locusts denuding a tree. Padded parkas of pastel vinyl, blues and reds and pinks, getting their last few wears of the season. Lash barely remembered his children from those days because he had barely been around. Rosey, his boy—Roseland Douglass Lash, named by his mother in a pregnancy-induced hormonal rush of heritage pride—was a junior at Tufts now. Lash had set up Windfall in Boston in order to be with Rosey, an engineering major and lacrosse midfielder, before the boy was out of his grasp for good. To that end, he had offered Rosey a deal with the devil: Lash had agreed to take on his full tuition if the boy agreed to share a house with his old man. They lived together on the bottom floor of an old triple on Rogers Avenue in Somerville, two bachelors at opposite ends of the spectrum. The tuition was breaking him, but this was Lash's last chance to connect with Rosey, and he was not going to mess it up.

The "Butterfly Garden" was a narrow, glass-walled conservatory full of exotic plants, overlooking the greater basin of the Charles River: the wide, lakelike head of the Charles that fed off Boston Harbor, before it narrowed to the icy glut that had coughed up Vasco. A twenty-person occupancy limit meant they had to stagger entrances like in the VIP section in a club. A good, small room for monitoring ins and outs. No one could tail you inside without getting made.

Inside the door, a perfect monarch settled on Lash's shoulder, fluttering its stained-glass wings. Butterflies were everywhere, drinking nectar out of feeders, courting among the exotic foliage, basking in the early-spring sun.

There was a bench for sitting, and on it, hunched forward from the back slats, hands folded over his splayed knees, was a black man in his late twenties. Oversize Phat Farm T, wide-legged, many-pocketed carps, thick chains visible around the back of his neck. He was pondering a tiny, purple-winged butterfly perched on the base knuckle of the top thumb of his folded hands.

Lash settled next to him and the butterfly lifted away.

The man gave Lash some skin, rough-palmed and hard-nailed, and said, "M.L."

"Tricky-Trey," said Lash. The man's name was Patrique Molondre, but on the street he went by Tricky. "I'm digging the spot."

"Bro of mine from the inside hipped me to it. I need more of this peace in my life."

Some dudes get their minds shaped more by prison than by the chaos of their childhood. The Zen of the pen. The Tao of the dungeon. Time in isolation opens some up to concepts of harmony within a culture of violence. The hidden garden deep within the fortress under siege.

Lash picked at his collar, billowing out his sweatshirt. "Hot-house."

"Yeah," said Tricky. "They should be growing weed up in this mo-mo."

Lash smiled, Tricky having him on. Nice and loose.

They watched two elderly women shuffle past, each with a death grip on her purse. A sign at the exit reminded visitors to check themselves for butterflies in the mirrors before leaving, and when the door opened, a blower came on, keeping the residents inside.

"Minimum security," said Tricky. "Nobody trying to bust out of this paradise." He reached over, plucking a reddish orange number off Lash's shoulder. Held it pinched by its wings. "Brother here got six to ten for unlawful pollination."

"Butterflies are the white-collar criminals of nature."

"This boy, he goes out, drinks himself some nectar, has himself a time, right? People say, 'Oh, well. He don't know no better, he's a butterfly.' But when some fucking big-ass bumblebee buzzes over, sticks his stinger in—look out. Larceny. Shut that mo-mo up in the bee house, give him twenty years, throw away the key. *Cage* his black-and-yellow ass."

Lash nodded. "Ain't no justice for a bumblebee."

Tricky watched the critter try to fly, then opened his fingers and let him go. "I guess you hearing me now?"

"I heard you before, Trick." Lash sat back. "I just didn't know. Wasn't seeing it."

"Won't never see nothing till it bleeds out onto the street." Tricky stayed forward, talking over his hands like a man in church. "They been hitting it hard. I don't mean ambushing street-corner buys. These ain't stickups. I mean high-line, pro licks. Takedowns. Inside baseball."

Tricky let that last part hang out there with the sound of the trickling water.

Lash said, "I'm listening."

"Nobody knows who, or what. No one I hear from anyway. I sure don't. But they're tight. Laying dudes out, rodeo-wrappin' them, pulling phones and straps."

"Who they hitting?"

"It's all vague. Nobody wants to bark about getting punked.

What I do know is, peeps are gearing up. Strapping it on. All that peacetime, turf-respecting shit—that shit is *done*."

Lash had no real problem with upper-echelon dealers being taken down, per se, but instability concerned him. Innocents and the day players might suddenly find themselves in the cross fire.

"These guys," said Lash, "these sugar bandits. Are we talking shooters?"

"Naw. Pros. Heavy-hitting pros."

"Heavy?"

Tricky nodded big, up and down. When he stopped, a little sulfur-yellow butterfly landed on his back. "This dude in the drink. You knew him?"

"Knew *of* him," said Lash. "You?"

Tricky shrugged.

"A Venezuelan named Vasco."

Tricky shook his head. The butterfly stayed put. "He don't shop my side of the street."

"Chopped off his hands and his tongue."

"Dude's tongue?" Tricky clucked his own. "His dick?"

"You know, I didn't think to check."

"Everything I hear says these guys are pros. That shit there sounds collateral. The people he got ripped off with, needing to vent some, save face. You got a line on them?"

"I have a few ideas."

"Then, shizz, you don't even *need* me."

Lash smiled. Tricky had grown up in Mattapan, the wild, fully Americanized son of Cape Verdean immigrants, street-running at twelve, enforcing at fifteen, doing drive-bys at seventeen. Lash had never even laid eyes on him before the night he saved his life. Lash was speaking at a "Mattapan Strong!" community meeting, competing with sirens out in the street, when he heard the distinctive *crack-crack* of a gun outside. Everybody in the audience hit the floor as Lash ran out, following the police lights to a lanky kid in long Girbaud shorts lying half off a curb, blood gurgling out of his neck like water out of a playground bubbler. One uniformed and two plainclothes cops stood around the kid dumbfounded, so Lash badged them and moved in, gripping the kid's neck tight, closing the circuit, feeling the pumping action against his fingers like someone knocking to get out. Tricky made it through that night, and the next. Lash dropped in on him at the hospital, later showed up at his arraignment, and went on to visit him inside Cedar Junction. Something formed between them as naturally as the scooped pink scar on the side of Tricky's neck. At one point, Lash even thought he had him hooked, he believed he could pop him free of the street life after his release. But the battle mark on his neck and his time served inside only raised his status, and soon Tricky fell back in with Broadhouse and his crew.

Still, Lash managed to exert some influence over him, prevailing upon Tricky to keep dealers away from schools, away from methadone clinics. Most of all, Lash kept him talking.

Lash folded out a guide he had picked up at the door, about the life of a butterfly. "Nice if people had stages, huh?"

"What now?"

"Four stages, like a butterfly. Says here. Egg, caterpillar, chrysalis, adult. If we grew in these stages—if there was some door you walked through, saying NOW ENTERING MANHOOD. If we were caterpillars before we were butterflies. Learn a little humility. A little self-respect."

"I know you talking to me."

"Look at you up in here. Your soul wants this. It wants peace. You could make it work, fool."

"Always preaching."

"Pull your shit together. Get some love in your life, boy."

Tricky turned his head a fraction. "And if I told you, 'Yo, Lash. Listen up, fool. Get out of the DEA, get into, I don't know—selling cars. Something regular. Make a change,' you'd be like, 'Sho 'nuff. Easy. Here I go.'"

"I hear you, but—"

"Solutions always look good on paper. I got to *make* paper. To sur*vive*."

"You can cut the movie talk. I saved your black ass once. I can save it again."

Tricky scowled at the floor as if Lash were a fool. Somehow sensing the butterfly on his back, Tricky shook it away, agitated. "Here's the thing. They don't take no powder."

"You lost me."

"Cash only, these bandits. No weight." Tricky was talking out of the side of his mouth. "All's they take is the green."

"Hold up, hold up." Lash watched Tricky's profile, not getting this. "They're leaving half the score on the table?"

"Naw. Worse. They *flushing* it, yo. Spoiling it. Queering it up with bleach."

"What are you saying? Like vigilantes?"

"Like vigilantes getting *paid*," said Tricky, mashing one hand into the other. "Robin Hoods, robbin' *hoods*."

"Flushing away half their score? You sure about that?"

"This is what I'm saying. This is a different breed of cat. Not needy or greedy. Maybe it's simple smarts—'cause that shit can be traced. You put somebody else's product on the street, you be *found*, and quick. All I know's, they taking game off the street. Got me thinking maybe it was you."

The only downside to running a program like Windfall was sheer temptation. Millions of dollars of untraceable cash. The majority of organized sugar bandits out there were dirty cops. This was why Lash cycled manpower in and out of the task force every nine to twelve months. Still, people talked. The enticement was strong. And Lash was ultimately responsible.

Lash said, "I can take care of my own guys."

"So can I. To a point."

Lash already knew he wouldn't go to anyone else in Windfall about this. He'd have to be his own internal affairs—just in case.

"Where's Broadhouse on this whole thing?" asked Lash.

"Pissed, man. What you think?"

"Gonna be a summit?"

"I don't have much ear right now, the shit that's been going down. Too much fucking distrust going around. To the point where, I fucking don't *want* to know shit, because everybody's all looking for leaks. Jumpy. Everybody sniffing out everybody else."

Three Pins, or drug kingpins, currently stood atop the ever-fluid Greater Boston drug game. Other little players operated at their own discretion and danger, but generally for the past year or two, most of the flow in and around town had to go through three top guys. Broadhouse, based out of Mattapan, Dorchester, and the projects on Mission Hill. Lockerty, out of East Boston and points north. And Crassion, everywhere in between.

"I just want this cleared up," said Tricky. "These bandits, they got to be *got*."

Lash squinted. "You trying to get me to do Broadhouse's work for him now? Are you my inside man, or am I yours?"

Tricky leaned close. "I'm saying this shit's going to explode. Escalating like the fucking stairs at Macy's. These mo-mos, you don't need to make 'em any more paranoid."

Lash nodded. "On that, we agree."

Tricky looked him over. "But you say it ain't you."

Lash sat on that, surprised. "You really thought so?"

Tricky pulled back, shrugged. "It would be a good play, that's all. Couldn't put it past you." He palmed his knees. "We good here?"

Lash nodded. "We're good."

Tricky stood, hiking up his baggy carps. "Stay black, M.L."

"You stay breathing, Tricky-Trey."

LASH SHRUGGED OFF HIS OVERCOAT AS HE ENTERED THE VISITING room at MCI Concord, laying it and his scarf across the back of the cleanest-looking chair before sitting down to wait. Monday was the only day they didn't offer visiting hours, but he had arranged this exception.

Peter Maracone was brought to him from the Special Housing Unit. He wore an extra-large, orange T-shirt over prison jeans, looking like a double orange Popsicle on two blue sticks. He studied Lash as he sat across the table from him, keeping his eyes beady and putting up a tough front. His hair was stiff and pushed all around as if he were afraid to take a shower.

"Who're you?"

"Me?" Lash said. "I am the Ghost of Drug Deals Past."

The guy frown-smiled. "Thought ghosts were white."

"The good ghosts are. I'm a bad spirit."

"Why ain't I scared?"

"Maybe you got an alibi for last November?"

"Last November? Let me check. The whole month?" Maracone thought about what that question might mean to him. "I suppose I could get one."

"How much you get taken for?"

Maracone did the exaggerated head tilt, suddenly hard of hearing. "What's that?"

"A lot, huh? Too bad. They tie you up? You must have pissed yourself."

Maracone's eyes stayed narrow but receded farther into his skull. "Was it you, you piece of shit?"

"Me? Huh." That got Lash thinking. "Were all of them black, or just some?"

"Fuck you."

"Okay. Not all then. More than one?"

"Who the hell are you?"

"Just one. Got it."

"You don't know what you're talking about. I'm in here for a domestic dispute."

"Whipping your girlfriend with an extension cord. You're all class, Petey."

Maracone folded his pudgy fingers on the scratched-up table, going quiet, tired of getting outtalked.

Lash said, "You used a table saw on his hands, huh?"

Maracone smiled. Just a little one, his clownish fat face. "I'll let you know when what you're saying starts making sense to me."

That smile was exactly what Lash had come for. Confirmation. Assholes can never help but congratulate themselves.

Lash said, "Your brother, where's he at?"

"Sport fishing in F-L-A."

"Hiding out, in other words. I guess he's the smart one." Lash sat back. "You're obviously very busy here, Petey, trying not to get raped, so I'll just ask you one more question, straight up. You and your brother were looking to become players, buying in big, and fell flat on your face. So you took out the Venezuelan in anger— fine. But you two don't have the juice to jump into the game so big like that. Somebody was fronting you. Who?"

Maracone kept his hands folded, deciding to say nothing.

"Lockerty," said Lash. "Yep. That's what I'll tell people you told me."

"Fuck you. I didn't tell you shit."

"Lockerty. That's what you said."

Maracone almost levitated out of his chair. "You fucking trying to get me killed? What is this?"

Lash smiled. "Petey, reading you is like reading the front page of *USA Today*. Too fucking easy."

"I didn't say nothing."

"Sure you did." Lash stood, grabbed his coat.

"What the fuck was this? Who the fuck are you, anyway?"

Lash smiled, laying his scarf down soft against the late-day roughness of his neck. "That should have been your first question."

"It fucking was!"

Lash walked back outside to his car, needing to find a place to eat with a nice bathroom where he could wash the prison off his hands.

PRECIPICE

TWO DOZEN KILOS OF SCAG AND A FEW POUNDS OF WEED ARRIVED on Cape Cod on a trawler from Florida. It was off-loaded early in the day along with a legit bluefin haul, but the dock wasn't the transaction point. The deal had to be physically consummated. Credit deals were rare, as any misunderstandings or miscommunications quickly led to bloodshed. Banks were almost never involved because the law loved paper trails and electronic records. The hand-to-hand exchange was the point of highest risk for both dealer and buyer.

In this brief moment of vulnerability, this synapse of paper and powder, lived the sugar bandits.

Osterville Grand Island is a circular land mass located just off the triceps of Cape Cod. A private, gated community of 150 homes and an exclusive golf course, accessible only by a two-lane drawbridge, past a guard who takes names.

The wayward fortyish son of an oil-corporation executive owed the wrong people a lot of money. Playing host to a secure-site transaction would not forgive his staggering debt, but would extend the grace period for its repayment. He had e-mailed the gate guard the names of a plumber and of a tile company who he said were coming that night to repair a bathroom-pipe rupture.

Traffickers making adjustments out of fear was the clearest evidence yet of the bandits' influence on the drug trade.

Termino was the point man in Royce's absence. He, Maven, Glade, and Suarez ditched their kayaks on a sandy barrier beach of low dunes named Dead Neck, entering the frigid water in insulated neoprene and dive boots, swimming out into Cotuit Bay under cover of night. A breakwater calmed the surf as they snorkeled around the west end of the island, one hundred meters off the densely wooded shore, each man tugging a watertight bag strung from a gas-filled bob.

They cut in toward the fifth dock from the turn, floating easily and watching the house lights through the oaks, monitoring the shore for any activity. Satisfied with the stillness, they walked out of the water onto beach grass and opened their wet bags, exchanging snorkels and dive masks for light vests, balaclavas, and weapons. Maven made sure his 9 mm MP5 submachine gun was moisture-free, then extended the butt stock of the hybrid handgun-rifle. The others pulled on their masks and started up the dune on either side of the wooden stairway, looking every bit like amphibious commandos.

This drill they had repeated each of the previous four nights. They knew the layout of the property, they knew everything.

The others took entry. Maven went alone through pines to the front of the estate, spotting the lookout halfway down the curling drive of crushed white seashells. He stood on the near side, allowing Maven to come up on him silently over grass, catching the goon on the side of the head just as he started to turn around. Maven relieved him of a handgun and a Nextel mobile, then bound him in ZipCuffs and a gag and loaded him into the back of the tile truck parked before the three-car garage.

A glance through the windows revealed that the dealmakers had been subdued. His all clear was three taps on the glass, masked Termino responding with a nod. Maven then did a full perimeter walk before entering, making double sure there was only one lookout.

Four men lay prone on the floor. The one guy freaking out wore navy blue corduroys, a collared shirt, and a kelly green whale belt: the homeowner's son. Guns and mobiles were set out on a wide coffee table with ammo mags and phone batteries removed. The bags of heroin were piled on the granite counter in the center island of the kitchen, smelling like the seafood section of Stop & Shop. Glade transferred cash into two large backpacks.

Suarez ran the kitchen sink, washing down the scag and chasing it with Drano. The bags of pot they left on the floor. The homeowner's son—receding hairline, the stink of failure all over him like the dead-fish smell—continued to whine under his gag, wanting to register a sternly worded complaint.

Maven made a circuit of the ground floor. Paneled walls, museum-quality lighting, inch-thick rugs. He looked at a large, carefully drafted map of the island, hand-lettered and handsomely mounted, an antique from its legitimate oystering days. The owner's son was a broker who had been "borrowing" from the family money entrusted to his care to fund his own vices and crude interests—money he planned to earn back twofold through risky investments, none of which had yet panned out. The family was down in Hialeah; they didn't know this yet.

Maven was in the front of the house, looking at the old seaman's map that now hung on the wall—one man's tool another man's trophy—when he heard a sound out of place. A creak. A step.

He started toward the intersecting hallways, keeping his dive boots silent on the thick rugs. As he turned the corner toward the shore side of the house, he saw a crouched form emerging from an old servants' set of stairs. He saw a handgun silhouetted against the kitchen light as the body sprang forward.

The gunman got off a single round before Maven plowed him over with a forearm to the back of his head. The man hit the floor with such force that the gun in his hand cracked in two at the wooden grip.

Maven dropped a knee into the man's back, turning to see where the shot had gone.

Suarez was on one knee before the sink, neck arched in pain, one hand gripping his back.

His vest had absorbed the round. Suarez's face went dark when he realized what had happened, and he straightened in pain, pulling his MAC-10 machine pistol off the kitchen counter in a blind rage. He turned to execute the shooter—but Maven collapsed on the unconscious man, shielding him with his own vested back until Glade and Termino intervened.

Maven ZipCuffed the shooter and they finished fast, taking the money, phones, and weapons and leaving the way they had come, down the grassy elevation to the sand at the empty dock. Masks and guns went into wet bags with the cash, snorkel gear coming back out.

Suarez was grunting in pain, still muttering under his breath. The gun report had put a pealing into Maven's ears like a distant alarm. He was knee-deep in the frigid water, towing out the bad guys' guns and phones, when Suarez hooked his arm, hard.

Maven turned fast, responding to the grip. But instead of anger, he saw gratitude.

"Thanks, man," said Suarez.

For knocking out the shooter, and for stopping Suarez from killing him. Maven clapped him on the chest and they pushed out into the water.

Halfway to Dead Neck, Maven sank the bag of guns and phones to the bottom of the bay.

MAVEN CAME UP FROM THE SINK WITH HIS FACE DRIPPING, STARING at himself in the restroom mirror. The water dribbling off his chin, the tightness of his sore muscles, brought him back to that night before, the job on the Cape. Despite two hot showers, he could still smell salt water on his hands. The sick feeling he had got when he saw the shooter emerge from the shadows was still with him.

It could happen that quickly, that easily. One slipup. Game over.

He dried his face, taking a squirt of cologne from the complimentary dispenser on the counter, patting his neck and jaw. Salt water is good for the complexion, it turned out. His neck was smooth and clean, no razor burn, nothing. He looked strong and ridiculously healthy. That was what money did for you.

He accepted a linen towelette from the black-jacketed attendant. "Thanks, brother," said Maven, depositing a finsky into the glass tip bowl.

"Thank *you*, sir," said the attendant, opening the restroom door.

Maven stepped into the swirl of light and sound that was Precipice. Royce said that the best nightclubs maintain just the right mixture of sexy and sinister. Precipice had that: walking through it was like patrolling a dark cloud during a lightning storm. The pulsating lights, the music thumping from the walls, that pheromonal musk of sweat and perfume and alcohol that was pure sexual incense: every club had these things, but here the mix achieved a sort of exotic frenzy.

The VIP room included a catwalk overlooking the downstairs dance floor. Red velvet curtains draped doorways leading to interconnected rooms, some so dark you couldn't guess their dimensions upon entering. As many times as he'd been here, Maven still, at least once each night, lost his way.

The club was located on the edge of the Theater District, before it gave over into Chinatown. The outrageous $60 cover charge weeded out students and barhoppers, who could find what they were looking for on Lansdowne or Boylston Street at one-sixth the price and one-tenth the hassle. Unaccompanied women were admitted free if they looked the part, and judging by the traffic-stopping scrum outside, looking the part was apparently the goal of half the twenty-one-year-olds in town.

Maven circumvented the balcony and ducked off into one of the velvet curtains, searching for a smaller bar. Indigo neon light signaled it, and he made his way to the corner rail, yelling out an order for a Seven and Seven and laying a fifty on the bar.

The music was less pounding in here. To his immediate left stood a Middle Eastern guy in his early twenties. Charcoal suit jacket, red silk shirt. Army age, for sure. Possibly Iranian or even Iraqi, impossible to tell in the cool blue light. Precipice hosted its share of layabout Euro trash and Middle Eastern money. Maven eyed him via the mirror backing the bar. Fate put a cocktail in one man's hands and a rifle in another's. In another room halfway across the world, Maven and this guy might have been enemy combatants. Here they were just two more guys on the make.

Their drinks arrived together, and Maven paid for both. He pulled out his lime wedge and stirrer and left them on the bar napkin, toasting the guy with a quick nod before pushing off from the bar and heading away.

"Mave!"

Just past the curtain at the next doorway, Jimmy Glade stood bookended by two ladies in thigh-length dresses, all bare shoulders and full legs, each with a bit of glitter mixed with the color on their cheeks. One blonde standout and her more eager brunette friend.

Milkshake shouted introductions, Maven shaking each woman's warm little hand.

Realtors, were they, Maven and Glade. Housemates in a condo on Marlborough Street. Glade had already hit all the selling points. "Their first time here!" shouted Glade, showing Maven his *Jackpot!* face.

Milkshake should have been a military recruiter. There wasn't much to Jimmy Glade—he was big and square-headed and more goofy than funny—but he had confidence, and he had a strategy. A few months back, Glade had generously offered to take Maven under his wing. Maven's experience chatting up hot girls in clubs was zilch. For a time he picked up Glade's routine, his patter. Most guys were hesitant to approach girls in pairs, in threes, but that was Glade's comfort zone, that was where he worked best, playing girlfriends off each other. Flattering questions ("What would you say is her most attractive feature?"). Soliciting opinions ("Which do you prefer, somebody who plays the game, or a guy who calls you right away?"). Sparking competition ("So which one of you is the smartest?"). Everything he did worked. That was the insane thing. Granted, sharp clothes and flash money helped too. As did copious amounts of alcohol. Bizarrely, so did borderline insults ("Your hair is getting a little crazy there.") and heavy-handed divisive ploys ("I'm trying to figure out which one of you has the prettier smile."). If you establish a competitive situation, women will compete. That was his secret. Glade was never the object of their desire, merely the facilitator. By challenging them, by provoking jealousies and conflicts—exposing the rivalry inherent in most female friendships—he established a contest wherein he was both referee and grand prize.

Genius. To a point.

Because Glade's play went way beyond game. His thing was steering two or more buzzed girlfriends back to the Marlborough Street pad and, in the wee small hours of the morning, Howard Stern–ing them into consummating their hot-girl friendship. He was into "making" lesbians. But that wasn't the weird part. In fact, for a while, that was the best-roommate-in-the-history-of-the-world part. No, the skeevy thing was that Glade never slept with them himself. He was totally content to play mind games and memorialize the seduction on his handheld Sony, screening his masterwork the next day on the flat screen in the living room for all to enjoy. No saint was Maven—he had spent those heady first few months in a pleasant and near constant state of debauchery—but Glade's Machiavellian zeal, and that he got off on the manipulative aspect of it rather than the girls themselves, cast a shadow of sadism over the entire affair that had ruined it for Maven. Glade's creepy coaching and coercion, and the girls' sloppy tongue kisses, all viewed through the unblinking eye of his camera, got repetitive for everyone but him.

Glade, arms around both young ladies, said to the brunette about the blonde, "Wow, her waist is *small*."

The blonde leaned winningly into Maven, speaking into his lowered ear, something he couldn't quite catch, Maven getting every third word of it. Something about loving dancing ever since doing gymnastics when she was a kid. She squeezed his forearm as she spoke, sending all the signals, but foreseeing her future manipulation at Milkshake's hands killed it for Maven. He made nice and hung around only as long as he needed to, not to step on Glade's game, then excused himself.

"You heading back to the pad?" said Glade.

"Yeah, in a while."

He rubbed both girls' backs. "Maybe we'll see you there."

The blonde reached for Maven, but he pretended not to see it and left her to the night.

He spotted Termino leaning against a bar in one of the back rooms. Termino was probably the least dressed-up guy in the place, wearing a long suede jacket over a white shirt, black pants, black shit-kickers. He usually had something good going, but kept his playmaking skills to himself.

Maven caught his eye, asking, with a shrug, *Where is he?*

Termino gave a little head dip toward the back booths. As he did so, a lady standing next to him turned to see who had claimed his attention, and a hot sigh emptied Maven's lungs. She was a Pam Grier–in-her-prime type with a neckline that plunged like the hopes and dreams of every guy in that room whose name wasn't Lew Termino. Maven saluted her, as the military had trained him to do to any person who clearly outranked him—and that salute was his first indication that maybe the drinks were starting to hit home.

Royce was seated alone at an oval table in back, before a half dozen picked-over platters of food, his face lit by his BlackBerry. Laser lights scribed geometric patterns on every table except Royce's, who'd nixed it as he always did with a quiet word to the floor manager. As Maven slid in over the plush red banquette toward him, Royce clicked his PDA dark. "What say you, Mercutio?"

Maven sat back and stretched out his neck. "Headache."

Royce nodded to Maven's cocktail. "That's not going to help you any. Get some distilled water in you, try some caffeine."

Maven, angling his head around to crack his neck, saw a small silver clutch on the other side of Royce. "Think Danny has anything for it?"

Royce passed him the clutch, going back to his PDA. "All kinds of shit, good luck."

Maven unsnapped the clasp and picked through the contents. A folding brush, mini-hairspray, some hair wax. Lip and eye stuff. Altoids. Her little red phone, an open pack of Camels. A dozen or more twenties and fifties crumpled like tissues. A flat, ornamental pillbox. A small amber vial.

Maven almost pulled out the vial, so struck was he by its appearance. A tiny brown test tube with a silver screw top. He tried to get a better look, but given the darkness of the table, it was impossible. He turned it over and felt some substance shifting inside—then became self-conscious next to Royce and shoved the little vial back down underneath the bills and snap-closed the purse.

"No?" said Royce, clicking off again.

Maven shook his head and slid the bag back to him. Royce plucked a shrimp from one of the platters and swiped it through some sauce on its way to his mouth. "Try this. From Changsho. Salt and Pepper Crispy Shrimp."

Maven passed. Whenever they went to Precipice, which was two or three times each week, Royce ordered several dishes from his favorite high-end eateries, cabbing them in from all across Boston and Cambridge. Maven recognized yellowtail sushi from Oishii, raw Kumamoto oysters from B&G, a hanger steak from Craigie Street Bistrot. He liked the Texas beef ribs with hot sauce from Redbones, and the buffalo wings from Green Street, but didn't see either of those here. Despite all the other traits Maven had cribbed from Royce, the fine-food obsession had yet to take hold.

"Good gig last night."

"Yeah," said Maven. "You should have been there."

In recent weeks, Royce had pulled back from the actual take-downs. He was busier than ever locating targets and initiating surveillance, doing all the advance work, the covert stuff he never let anyone else touch or even ask about. He presented them with a dossier—usually addresses and license plates and some photos—and took them out in a rented van to cruise the players, the locations, the vehicles, then let them take it from there. They were always busy, doing two jobs a month. "That was a good save, you kept your head."

"We fucked up."

Royce shrugged. "Keeps you on your toes. It's a dangerous game, and it's only going to get more difficult. They're aware of us now."

"We've lost the element of surprise."

"But gained the element of intimidation. You're building up quite a nice little treasure chest now. Moved up to a bigger safe-deposit box yet?"

"Soon," Maven said.

"Now I *really* gotta stay on top of you dicks. Keep you motivated. Money makes you lazy. Makes you conservative, makes you scared. What is the one thing worse than having nothing?"

Maven nodded. "Losing something."

Royce shot him with a finger gun. "Why we have to keep pushing ahead. Keep up our energy here. Give no quarter."

"You know what's good about this?" said Maven, getting comfortable in the booth. "What's best about it—besides the money? It's that we're like cops and thieves at the same time. Doing good by doing bad. Taking down dealers and fragging the product . . . it feels like a big 'Fuck you' to someone, I don't even know who."

"To these jackasses," said Royce, dismissing the room. "To everyone in this club, in this city. Anybody you pass in the street who stayed here and played Xbox while you were over there baking in the Arabian sun. Now you're back and you're beating the system—and it's fucking perfect."

"It is."

Royce popped an oyster and chased it with sushi. "Let's just make sure no one else ever finds out how fucking smart we are, huh?"

Maven grinned wide as a six-year-old on his birthday.

"My point, though," continued Royce, "is that this game is all in. You push all your earnings forward every time you head out there—don't ever forget that."

As Royce said this, the crowd before them parted in such a way as to reveal Danielle, dancing alone out on the floor, a high, swirling spotlight writing over her body as though fashioning a female form out of music and darkness. She wore a salsa dress in black and sheer, the asymmetrical hem giving it a shipwrecked flair. She was lost in herself, in the moment, the music and the light.

Maven remembered the vial then, dousing his good mood. The music changed, one beat overlapping into another, and the dance floor closed up again and she was gone.

Maven threw back most of the rest of his drink.

Royce said, "Where's Suarez, you seen him?"

Maven shrugged. "Wherever the Asian ladies are at."

"He does love that wasabi. Know why?"

"Why he only digs Asians?"

"He says that being with a Latina, or even a white girl, would be like being with his own sister."

Maven nearly choked on that, coughing into his fist. "Nice."

"I didn't ask him any more goddamn questions after that."

"I'm not gonna follow it up either," said Maven, shaking off that one. "Termino's doing all right."

They couldn't see the bar from here. "He usually does. What about you? Your action seems to have tailed off a bit."

"Only a bit."

"What's that mean? You were a kid in a candy store for a while there. Too much, too fast?"

Maven grinned. "It's a headache, no big deal."

"Or are you looking for something more regular?"

"I'm just looking, period."

"Tomorrow Man, right?" said Royce. "It's not about who you take to bed, but who you wake up with."

"Exactly."

"Go ahead, Maven—smile a little. Don't forget about that punk back in Iraq, trying to jerk off in the shitter in the middle of a fifty-mile-an-hour shamal. You owe that kid too."

"That's kid's been *paid*. In full."

"Good to hear it." Royce raised his soda water. "Here's to him."

"To him."

"The stupid fuck."

Maven laughed hard and killed his drink.

Come Undone

Maven kept an eye out for Danielle as he navigated the dance floor, heading out through the parted curtain. If nothing else, it gave his wandering around the club a purpose.

He cleared the top-floor rooms without coming across her, then made his way downstairs, patting the VIP bouncer on the back as he passed, emerging onto the main floor. He moved to the main bar and ordered a Budweiser, and while he waited, felt a brushing sensation against his shoulder, a cascade of brunette ringlets.

"Is this all there is?" said a young voice, the owner of the springy hair, jammed up against the bar with her back to him.

"What do you mean?" yelled her friend over the music. She was trying to get served, but the raised finger wasn't drawing any attention. "We made it! We're in!"

"I guess I was expecting gift bags. Or live unicorns or something."

Maven smiled. He saw ankle boots and plenty of leg.

The bartender came back with Maven's beer in an aluminum

can, and Maven directed the barman's attention to the women next to him.

The friend shouted their order, then leaned onto the bar to see Maven and thank him. Her look when she saw Maven—a recognition of something special—got the attention of the woman next to him, who turned. She had a darkly featured face, clever eyes, plum-painted lips, and a beaded choker that crossed her throat like a second smile.

"This is all there is," Maven told her, fighting his eyes' inclination downward. "No unicorns."

"No?" she said with a lingering smile. "Too bad . . ."

Her friend shouted, "What's upstairs?"

"More of the same," said Maven, his eyes going back to the girl with the ringlets. "Only darker and less crowded."

She was smiling at him and he was smiling at her. They were having a moment until two more friends came rushing up, pulling at her arm to go dancing. "Samara, come on!"

She saw the change in his expression, the clouding of his face. Her name was the same as that of the city in northern Iraq—but she had no way of knowing what that meant to him, or why the surprise of hearing it here made him freeze. He watched her—in a denim bustier with a lace-up back and a short, black suede skirt over ankle boots—get absorbed into the undulating mass out on the dance floor.

"Hey. Gridley. Wake up."

It was Danielle, suddenly, next to him.

"Let's get out of here," she said.

"What?" said Maven.

She already had her sunglasses on, her silver clutch under her arm. "I am so done, and not up for driving. He said you had a headache, you could take me."

Maven checked one more time for the girl named Samara, but she was gone.

Danielle looked at him. "Are you drunk, Gridley?"

She still referred to him by the name of their hometown.

"Well, I am," she said, squeezing a numbered plastic tag into his hand. "Now be a fucking gentleman and go fetch my coat."

SHE WAITED AT THE DOOR, AND HE FOLLOWED HER OUTSIDE WITH her coat on his arm—long and black, a light crepe fabric—moving past the queue of hopefuls waiting to get inside. She passed female stares and male sighs and even outright wolf whistles, immune, her arms crossed against the cool night air, or maybe folded in anger against an evening and a city she felt was beneath her.

She moved fast, Maven a step or two behind, watching her calf muscles work, her hemline riding up along her left thigh. That their relationship had formed into a brother-sister thing frustrated him. Calling him Gridley was equal parts affection and put-down.

Maven was still occasionally amazed to be in the orbit of the once unreachable Danielle Vetti. Beyond that, his fealty to Royce superseded all. It was enough just to exist in this alternative reality where he had connected with the girl of his high school dreams. She hadn't demonstrated any true interest in him, and anyway he would never cross that line.

Except in his mind. She once alluded to some questionable photo shoots she had done in pursuit of her New York modeling career, and Maven had spent way too many night hours on the Internet searching for the pictures.

She rounded the corner, not slowing down. Maven said, "Something wrong?"

"Yes, something's wrong. I'm fucking cold."

"How about your coat here?"

She didn't answer. That solution made too much sense.

"Every week, the same goddamn thing," she said. "Week after week after week. How does he not get sick of that place?"

"He likes what he likes."

"Admit it, you're sick of it too. I mean, it wears on you. It's like partying inside a bug zapper in there, those swirling blue lights.

No—they should actually do that. That would be so worthwhile. Every fifteen minutes or so, just randomly zap somebody on the dance floor. Put them out of their misery."

She unfolded her arms to go into her bag, bringing out a cigarette and a butane lighter. Danielle only smoked when she drank.

Maven stayed to her left, out of the smoke stream, ears still ringing from the club.

"He is the control freak of all control freaks." She made a wild gesture with her cigarette before pointing it at Maven. "You want to drive a girl crazy, Gridley? Insist on only tantric sex."

Maven's face widened. Too much information.

"And then—" She smoked. "And *then* there are these tenants of his. The four fucking Musketeers living below us. Running around at his beck and call . . . doing God knows what. I mean, what am I here, a kept woman?"

"A very well-kept woman."

She glared back at him, and Maven realized maybe "a kept woman" wasn't a compliment after all.

"I *work* for what I have," she said. "Believe me—*believe me.*"

She was smoking the hell out of that Camel. It was almost gone.

"*Boston,*" she said, looking at the buildings overhead, enunciating it like a curse. She turned into an open-air parking lot—and Maven stopped.

She realized he was no longer with her and turned.

"Huh," she said, flicking her cigarette away after one last puff, talking smoke. "You haven't been back here?"

Maven stood in his old parking lot. He looked at the cars, and up at the familiar buildings. The acoustics of the lot came back to him, the cars rolling by, the nightlife blaring one street over.

Nothing had changed. Except him.

He looked to the gate booth and saw a new guard sitting on a stool inside, arms crossed, headset buds in his ears.

Danielle tapped her foot. "You *are* drunk, aren't you."

Maven followed her to a black Range Rover with twin chrome

exhaust pipes. Inside, he settled into a seat fleshed in white leather with smooth black pores.

How far he had come was obvious: from the guy checking cars to the guy riding in the Range Rover with Danielle Vetti. More startling to him was how staggeringly fast it had all happened.

He felt elated suddenly and turned to share a revelation with Danielle. "Do you know that life is just a dream?"

She handed him the car keys. "Could have fucking fooled me."

He started up the Rover, the heat vents coming on, and she immediately went to work on the radio.

Maven backed out and rolled to the gate, the attendant stepping out of the booth in jeans, work boots, and an olive-drab field jacket. Hard to tell if the army coat was just warm and fashionable or really his. He raised the gate arm, watching them pull through. Maven checked the guy's face, imagining a moment of solidarity between two guys on opposite ends of the spectrum. But the guard never even looked at Maven. He was too busy trying to sneak a look down Danielle's dress.

Maven pulled away, revving the engine a bit, actually pissed. Danielle squirmed in her seat like someone trying to get comfortable in bed. "Let's not go back yet. What do you say? The night's not over yet. Let's drive around a little."

Maven looked over, her perfect bare knees twinned beneath the dash, her chest swelling against the confines of her dress. At a red light before Tremont Street, he turned and reached across her, past her shoulder, grasping the seat belt there and drawing the strap down across her body, clasping it between the seats. She laughed at his attending to her, then the light turned green and he drove on.

He took them north under the sails of the Zakim Bridge, starting to feel good again. The luxury vehicle at his command, his just right blood-alcohol mix, slinky music on the radio. He didn't mind playing chauffeur because he was with her, she was feeling loose, and for once they were alone.

"So what's with this headache?" she said.

"Nothing. Gone now."

"Really? Been kind of a mope lately."

"I—what?"

"A mope. A drip. A bummer."

"Look who's saying this to me."

"Where were you Musketeers all last week?"

"We were . . . away."

"Cape Cod." Maven looked at her, and she smiled. "Brad said so, on the phone to Termino."

"So?"

"Do anything fun?"

"Not really."

"Little early for beach weather. You guys go antiquing?"

"A little."

"Catch up on your reading?"

"Exactly. Caught up on all my reading."

"See? Sourpuss. What's the matter, poor baby? Has it been a while? I find that hard to believe."

She slipped her left hand over his thigh, faking a grab for his crotch. He kicked up and swerved the Rover, not a good maneuver at seventy miles an hour.

She pulled her hand back, laughing. "The look on your face."

Did she do these things to be funny or provocative? "I'm just saying—don't reach down there unless you mean it."

"Oh? You want me to mean it?"

"I'm just saying."

He didn't need to look over to know that she enjoyed her effect on him. She turned up the radio and went fishing inside her clutch for another cigarette. "Hey, Gridley." She held something toward him. "Gridley," she said again. "What do you say?"

"I don't smoke," he said, still not looking.

"I know that." She pulled it back, holding her hand to her nose as though fighting off a sneeze. "I'm asking if you want to hit up."

Maven turned and saw the silver-capped amber vial in her hand. "What the fuck is that?"

"Artificial sweetener."

"Are you fucking offering me blow?"

"Oka-ay. I guess that's a no."

She hadn't been fighting off a sneeze. She had been snorting a bump off the webbing between her thumb and forefinger.

Maven caught her wrist as she was pulling back the vial. "Who gave this to you?"

"Christ, Gridley, relax. Eyes on the road."

He shook her wrist. "What are you doing with this?"

"What do you mean, what am I doing with this? What's the big fucking—"

"The big deal?" He was incredulous. *The big deal?*

"Mother of Christ, all right, already."

"What about Royce?"

"Royce?" She swung her head around to look. "Gee, I don't know. Is he here now?"

"You know he—"

"I didn't ask *him* if he wanted a bump, I asked *you*. Which was a big mistake, I can see that now." She pulled back but he did not release her. "Christ! Always so concerned about him. It's unmanly. You forget that I'm not his employee. Now will you fucking let go of my wrist, pretty please?"

He shook it again. "Who gave it to you?"

"You don't understand, Gridley. People don't *give* it to you. You have to *buy* it."

"Someone at the club?"

She was glaring at him, and finally he released her wrist. She pulled back angrily and dumped the vial into her clutch and dropped her bag to the floor. "Fine." She leaned an elbow against the window. "Just drive then."

He was going to cut off at the next exit and take her back home, but when the sign came up, he changed his mind, staying on the highway. Because fuck her.

"The way you four tiptoe around him," she said. "Genuflecting. So desperate for somebody to lead you, to tell you how to think and what to do. Like a cult. You're all brainwashed, fucking stars in your eyes. And so secretive. What a joke. Do you really think I don't know what you were doing out there on Cape Cod all week? Do you really think I don't know?"

She couldn't know. She was guessing. She was close enough to Royce to figure some of it out if she cared—though she had never seemed to care before.

"Then again," she said, "maybe he's not exactly who he appears to be either."

Maven drove on, saying nothing, not taking the bait.

"'Realtors.' That's a good one. What's 'real' about any of you?"

"You want me to take you home? Will that make you stop talking?"

"Home." She huffed a laugh. "Home to your boss, you mean. Your master."

She was high, and it was getting ugly, and being alone with her no longer seemed like a good idea. Maven decided to come back to the city on Route 1, giving her time to settle down while returning her to Marlborough Street before Precipice closed.

She rolled down her window after a while and turned up the music, singing along quietly with some of it, her arm outside the window, coasting on the current. Wind roared through the Range Rover, the stereo music like a jukebox playing inside a tornado. At one point he looked over and she was wiping her face, either pushing hair out of her eyes, or maybe crying.

Eventually she put up the window, but remained angled toward her door, watching the night go past. Maven eyed her shoulder beneath the thin strap of her dress, and the underside of her thigh below the slanted hem of her dress—until he realized she could probably see his reflection in the window. He settled back to drive the rest of the way in silence, and a memory returned to him.

Freshman year of high school, the parents of his pot-smoking buddy, Scotty, took them out to J. C. Hillary's in Dedham one night. This was out of character for Scotty's not-interested, never-around parents, and Maven and Scotty were both pretty well baked at the time, two little shits gorging on dinner rolls and giggling at silverware, trying to play it cool while the adults drank manhattans. The sedate, mid-to-upscale restaurant had Maven on sensory overload, compulsively taking little birdlike sips of water to keep from freaking out—but at one point he noticed a girl returning from the ladies' room. After a few confirming blinks, he accepted that it was indeed Danielle Vetti, *the* Danielle Vetti, right there in the restaurant with him. She wore a knee-length skirt and a tight, cherry-red top, and he tracked her to a nearby table where she sat down with her family.

Another girl sat at the Vettis' table, her back to Maven, a pair of crutches stood up against her chair. Not the sprained-ankle kind with the padded underarm bars, but the forearm collar, cerebral-palsy-type walking sticks, the sight of which sobered him. Maven never saw her face—the face of Danielle Vetti's younger sister— nor that of her mother, who sat next to the girl, occasionally reaching over to swipe a cloth napkin across the girl's mouth.

The hottest girl in high school had a handicapped sister. This discovery made a profound impact on him. Looking at Danielle Vetti pushing food around her plate, the rest of her family eating in silence, brought her down to earth for him. She was no more attainable, but at least understandable. She was real.

His school-shooter fantasies changed soon after that. He wasn't the shooter anymore; he was the hero kid who jumped the shooter and knocked him out, saving Danielle Vetti. The one girl in school who secretly understood him.

She captured a song on the satellite radio and played it over and over again, Duran Duran's moody and liquid "Come Undone." As they neared the city, the overnight mist caught the ambient light and created a tangerine aura, a glowing shell of moisture over the city, dawn still hours away.

"He likes you, you know." She said this so quietly, still looking out the window, that he wasn't sure she was talking to him at first. "He talks about you, more than the others."

Maven nodded, pleased, but didn't let on.

She sat forward and turned down the radio. "Maybe I am a kept woman. Everybody pays one way or another. Just look at you."

"What about me?"

"Come on, Gridley. You don't think you're a kept man?"

Maven sat alone inside the Marlborough Street pad, thinking about what Danielle had said. He realized that the bed he was sitting on, the tumbler of water in his hand, the Back Bay address—none of it was his.

What was he exactly? Royce's employee, or his partner? His muscle, or his friend?

Maven shook it off. The best way to kill a good thing was to question it to death. Bottom line, the day he met Brad Royce was the luckiest day of his life.

He looked up at the ceiling, hearing her footsteps cross the floor upstairs. When he let her off at the door before going around to the alley to park the car, she had said to him:

"You're a good soldier, Gridley."

Then she reached over and held his cheek with her hand. A gesture of affection mixed with apology. He leaned into her soft palm, so slightly she could barely have noticed. It ended with her playfully pushing his face away.

He took it from her because he liked it, because he was all tangled up in a swirl of desire and concern. Even now, staring at the ceiling, he could still feel the touch of her hand upon his cheek.

THE ROUND TABLE

THEY KEPT THE RENTED VAN PARKED ACROSS THE STREET FROM THE smoke shop, moving it at least once daily. They took turns wandering inside the cramped shop to play a quiet hour of keno, so that they came to be seen as regulars around the Brockton neighborhood.

This was the grind work. Recon. Days of tedium leading up to ten minutes of action. "Eyes on the prize," they reminded each other when patience wore thin, cooped up in the back of the hot van. They talked about the bikes they were going to buy themselves when this job went down.

Around three-thirty, two bikers pulled up outside the smoke shop on major-league Harleys, the chapter head of the Crossbone Champs motorcycle club and another full-patch member. Their colors—two white bones surrounded by a red circle, forming crosshairs over a small skull—were obscured under black ponchos due to the rain.

Bikers are easy to follow but notoriously tough to get close to.

They are especially easy to follow when you know ahead of time where they're going.

On the floor of the rear cargo area of the van, lined with sound-baffling furniture pads, they sat in gaming chairs. Instead of game controllers in their hands, they worked with five different mobile phones.

One was the work phone, labeled T for "talk," with Termino at the other end. The ex-heavyweight was too well-known from his Brockton fighting days to be of any use here, so he was set up outside the Crossbone Champs clubhouse in Abington, one town over. They never brought personal phones on a job because the location was too easily traced.

Two Samsung phones labeled CL-1 and CL-2 were exact clones of the bikers' own mobile phones, handy for checking voice mail and text messages, as well as accessing their contact lists. The chapter head's clone held photos from bike week in Laconia, New Hampshire, grinning biker babes flashing tats and tits.

The phone labeled W was another work phone. The bikers' phones had not only been cloned, but "ghosted" as well. A clone was an exact copy of the unit's microchip, whereas a ghost modified a phone's chipset with an embedded implant. When dialed from this W phone, the bikers' phones answered without ringing or vibrating, automatically switching on its microphone. Any ambient conversations were then narrowcasted back to the W phone. No need to risk infiltrating the motorcycle club itself, which was a near impossibility anyway: bikers' paranoia topped even drug dealers' paranoia. Modern mobile-phone technology made anyone a potential walking wiretap.

The fifth phone was one of a separate pair of ghost phones, thin, high-end Razr models. These units they kept swapping in and out of the store, stashing them behind the lottery station next to the front counter like a dropped phone. They rotated them out twice a day because ghost phones burned through batteries. If not for this, they could have monitored their marks from the comfort of home, or even a beach two thousand miles away. But burning out the bikers' batteries would raise red flags, so they had to coop out in the van to eyeball their marks so as to know when to call and listen.

The w phone was hooked up to a laptop, recording now. Transmission from the ghosts inside the bikers' leather jackets were too muffled, but the keno plant eavesdropped clear. Three men, the two bikers and the store owner, a Crossbone prospect, were discussing a shipment of "pellets," code for ecstasy pills.

Royce had presented them with all this, the cloned phones, the ghosts, the bikers' mobile numbers, along with photographs and RMV printouts. A bounty of inside information.

"How does he get this stuff?" asked Maven.

They talked about Royce, talked about him a lot, especially on long surveillances, either speculating about his past or cracking on his legend—but tradecraft discussions were for some reason taboo.

"I heard him and Termino talking a couple of days ago," said Glade, pulling one headphone away from his ear. "I think Royce owns a piece of a couple of Verizon store franchises."

Suarez marveled. "The man is a genius."

"Agreed," said Maven. "But how does he get close enough to the marks to get their phones for cloning in the first place?"

The other two shook their heads, shrugging, the question beyond their pay grade.

"You know what I heard?" said Suarez. "I heard that Brad Royce lists his occupation on his tax return as 'Brad Fucking Royce.'"

Glade smiled. Using Royce's full name was the tip-off to the joke. "Yeah?" said Glade. "Know what I heard?"

Suarez said, "What?"

"I heard that the pope once found a potato chip? Looked *exactly* like Brad Royce."

Maven said, "You know that statue, *The Thinker*, the guy sitting like this?" He put his chin on the back of his hand and got pensive. "That guy's thinking about the size of Brad Royce's cock."

Some were old, some were new. Some Glade had stolen off the

Internet. But it was enough to pass the afternoon in the back of the work van.

STARVING WHEN THEY GOT BACK INTO TOWN, MAVEN LANDED A LATE-day space down the block from J. J. Foley's. He went to the bar to order them a couple of pops, and a guy in a patrol cap turned at his voice.

"Neal."

Ricky. Maven was a few full seconds recognizing him. Not because he'd changed, but because it had been so long. The old cap was cocked over his dented head as usual, a long-sleeved henley covering his bad arm. Razor burn reddened his neck, his hair too long over his ears.

"Rick," said Maven.

He had never called him Rick before. Always Ricky. This threw everything off.

Ricky looked at Suarez and Glade on the other side of Maven. Maven did the introductions, and Ricky's buddy, a small guy next to him, nodded with a quick tip of his chin, then looked back at his beer. Maven felt the contrast between them, him and Glade and Suarez, big guys, vital, energized, and Ricky and his friend, slump-shouldered, nearly invisible.

"Long time no see," said Ricky, a Sam Adams tangled in the fingers of his good hand.

"Been busy," said Maven, uncomfortable and showing it, nodding too much. "I'm working real estate now. With these guys."

Ricky looked them over again. "Real estate. Wow."

"Yeah," said Maven. "Funny how things go." Ricky was still sizing up Suarez and Glade, who were paying for the beers. "City Oasis?"

"Still there."

To the others, Maven explained, "We used to work together at this convenience store in Quincy." In this way, he was bringing

Ricky into the fold and at the same time distancing himself from him: *some guy I used to work with.* "That dickhead cop still come in?"

"Still comes in."

"Holy shit. Crank mags?"

Ricky was flat. "And a protein drink."

"Right, crank mag and a protein drink. Christ."

Then came the nodding pause they had both been waiting for. "So, you guys, uh, eating?" asked Maven.

"No," said Ricky. "Just hanging."

"We're gonna . . ." Maven pointed to the rear of the pub, the tables. "You wanna join us?"

"No," said Ricky. "We're cool here."

Both of them going through the motions. "You're sure?"

"Yeah. Sure."

This was his exit slot, but he couldn't leave Ricky like this. Suarez handed Maven his beer, and Maven told him and Glade to go on ahead, he'd catch up.

"Man," said Ricky, once they stepped away, "you really dropped out of sight. Like a stone."

"I know, things happened pretty fast. I'm working a ton. I . . . I should have come by."

"Yeah . . ."

"Said good-bye. I just got really caught up."

Ricky nodded, letting Maven twist.

"What nights you at the Oasis?"

Ricky told him.

"I'll come by. We'll hang out. Still get free Sour Patch Kids?"

"All you can eat."

"You work with anyone else?"

"He didn't hire anybody after you left. Not enough business. On my own now."

"Just you and Tyra."

"Right." Ricky showed the tiniest of smiles. Just enough for Maven to break free.

"I'll come by then."

"You should," said Ricky, lifted. "Definitely."

Maven glanced at Ricky's buddy's back at the bar, getting a weird low-level vibe from him, then walked back to join the other two. He took a chair facing away from the bar so there wouldn't be any awkward cross-glances after the fact. Another ten minutes or so passed before the blushlike heat of the encounter wore off. When Maven got up a little while later to hit the john, Ricky and his buddy were gone.

As their burgers arrived, Suarez's phone rang. It was Termino, letting them know that Royce had made a reservation at the Berkeley Grill for nine o'clock. They looked at each other, each taking a quick bite or two out of his burger, then downing the rest of his beer before heading back home to get cleaned up.

ON FEAST NIGHTS, ROYCE HIRED A TOWN CAR TO DRIVE THEM, INSISTing on traveling in style, even when the restaurant was only a couple of blocks away. The street-level dining room of the Berkeley Grill was once the commodities trading floor of a famous tea company, a room with massive Corinthian columns and mahogany paneling with green marble accents, and Royce favored a round table in the rear corner. They sat there in dress jackets, like gentlemen, even Termino, shoe heels sharp on the polished oak floor, drinking Budweisers and feasting on starters from the raw bar. The headwaiter, Sebastian, knew Royce by name and always sent over some new appetizer for a taste, and the chef emerged from the kitchen for a handshake and a laugh. Royce placed five identical orders—ten-ounce Kobe cap steak, medium rare—then everyone and everything else went away, the entire city retreating as all the energy in the room was sucked toward their round table. For the remainder of the meal, their round table *became* the city, the only place in it that mattered.

Before the steak arrived, Royce slipped off his new wristwatch and passed it around. Not a wristwatch, he informed them, but a

"Big Crown Telemeter Chronograph." Maven took it in his hands and felt the new leather of the strap, the fluted top telemeter ring of the oversize face, then turned it over and viewed the Swiss gears working inside the see-through crystal back. He passed it on to Glade, and it found its way around to Termino, who barely looked it over, returning it to Royce.

"Got one just like it," Termino grumbled, the others laughing at him.

Then Termino pulled back his sleeve. He did have one just like it.

Royce passed out three black boxes labeled ORIS. Three identical timepieces. "I hear any of you call it a *watch,* I'm taking it back."

Maven buckled his, admiring the oversize stainless-steel casing, the solid feel of it on his wrist.

"Retails for two grand, in case you're wondering," said Royce. "I did better than that, of course, but it's the thought that counts. And here is the thought. We are at the top of our game right now. A game no one else could play—not at this level. Look around at these people here. These civilians. They call us heroes, right? But they're afraid of us. You can feel it. They were much more comfortable with us over there, protecting them and their wealth. Not back here looking to get some of that for ourselves. The country-club door is closed. But—we've been to the other side. We've seen it. We know, and they know, that all this civility is a construct. A fantasy, and a pretty thin one at that. Our presence here is a reminder they don't want to get. Because if it all started to go south stateside, who would be running things? We would. This round table right here. Be running *everything.* And I happen to believe that day will come. That the pendulum will swing back, and all the warriors who got civilized out of the power structure will reclaim their glory. But, for now, we have to dwell in the shadows. Like kings in exile. Waiting for the day."

Maven had heard variations on this theme from Royce before, but never so bold a call for revolution. Glade said, "To the exiled kings," and everyone drank.

"They say, 'Work hard,'" continued Royce, "but what they

mean is 'Obey.' They got from us what they needed and now have to find ways of keeping us out. They want us to come back and be good little checkers on their board, plodding along one space at a time. But they forget that the warrior in us got activated. We come in like bona fide chessmen, badass rooks and bishops and knights, breaking all the rules, jumping their kings, and they're like, 'Fuck was that?'"

Maven grinned at Royce miming someone getting ripped off. But Royce wasn't looking for laughs.

"They want us tamed. They want us happy and distracted. To keep us in line. But look at us here. We *defy*." He raised his bottle. "Tomorrow? Who knows what it will bring. But right now—tonight—we are the shit. Far as I'm concerned, this round table right here is running this city. *Salud*."

THEY LEFT THE STEAK HOUSE WITH BELLIES FULL OF MEAT AND BLOOD full of Bud. Royce wanted to go someplace to get a decent cocktail, but he allowed himself to be outvoted and the Town Car took them up to Bukowski Tavern, a narrow bar on Dalton Street dangling over the Massachusetts Turnpike. A no-pretensions, cash-only bar to balance out the clubby steak house.

"Grunts with money," said Royce. "Dangerous fucking combination."

Glade and Suarez cornered up with Termino, making enough noise to clear out a pocket of space at the kitchen end of the bar. Maven settled in at a window overlooking the cars speeding below them. The collar of the bartender's vintage RATT concert T-shirt was cut straight down to the midpoint of her cleavage, and it was worth the price of a draft just to watch her pour it. Royce let the "Wheel o' Beer" spin and ordered a round of whatever came up.

"Glade tells me you're all getting street bikes," he said, sitting alone with Maven.

Maven nodded, swiping the foam off his upper lip. "We all caught the bug, watching these Harleys all day."

"We'll go up to New Hampshire, get them there. No sales tax, and they're used to seeing cash."

Maven nodded again, the matter decided with inebriated certainty. "No Danny tonight?"

Royce threw Maven a close stare that made Maven wonder if his voice had said something other than those three words. Maven didn't know why he had asked in the first place.

"She calls you Gridley."

Maven nodded, eager to elaborate. "Turns out we're from the same town. Couple of years apart."

"I know why she never went back. What about you?"

Maven shrugged. "I did go back, once. My sister's funeral. *Half* sister." His grip on the bottle grew tighter. "Nothing for me there."

Royce saw something in Maven's expression that pulled him closer. A darkness that intrigued him. "What'd you think about that, back at the restaurant?"

"Yeah, it was great, the meal—"

"No, I meant, what we talked about. What I was saying."

"Oh. Yeah, it was interesting."

"I'm not looking for fucking feedback, Maven. I want to know what you *think*."

"About what you were saying?" Maven shrugged, not knowing how to say this. "It's kind of dangerous, I guess."

"Dangerous."

". . . Unless I missed something."

Royce backed up, ready to take another run at it. "Look, the other guys, Glade and Suarez—I know my rap is wasted on them. You're different."

Maven shook his head.

"Sure you are. This, here in the States, it's Candy Land. This is a dream. A fantasy compared to over there, which was reality. Cold reality. But here comes the bitterest irony. Over there, in the real world, you had power. A rifle in your hand, a flag on your shoulder. Over there, you were a king. But back here in fantasyland, you're like anybody else. Only less so, because you've been gone so long, you're a couple of steps behind. See? All backwards. In reality, a king. In fantasy, a peasant. A dangerous fucking peasant. A peasant who knows what it is to be a king." Royce leaned closer again. "That seem right to you?"

Maven tried to inhale a little sobriety, feeling over his head here. "No, but—we're winning, right? We're beating the system."

"Absolutely we are. For now. But what happens next?"

"Next what?"

"It's just common sense. Things can't go on like this forever, right? Things are going to reach a critical mass at some point. Then what? Do we call it a day? Or is there another stage in the evolution?"

Maven turned his head for a different angle of understanding, but it didn't work. He looked down at the new timepiece on his wrist instead, the second-hand needle doing a slow lap around the face. "I don't really want to think about what comes next."

"You're crazy not to. Why?"

Maven shook his head.

Royce made a face. "Tell."

"You'll think I'm a jinx."

"If I ever believed in that sort of thing, I wouldn't be here now."

"I'm just waiting for the worm to turn."

"Go on."

"Look, I'm not being ungrateful. I'm extremely grateful. For the opportunity, for this beer—for fucking everything. But the thing is—trouble has a way of finding me."

Royce sat back, not perplexed, not amused. "That so."

"Historically, yeah."

"You're saying you got the mark on you. So how do you explain all this good fortune in your life now?"

"Exactly. It's all tits and butter. That's what's got me worried."

"That you never had it this good?"

"Never in my life."

Royce finished his beer. He looked disappointed—or maybe that was just Maven's impression, as he felt he was always giving Royce wrong answers. "Who knows, Maven?" said Royce, standing up with his empty bottle. "Maybe your luck has changed."

ANALOG GROOVES

LASH RECOGNIZED THE FAMILIAR MUSK OF STUPIDITY UPON ENTER-
ing the Barnstable County lockup and decided he had been
spending entirely too much time in jails. He feared becoming
like a career garbageman whose nose can no longer discriminate
between sweet and sour.

This, he thought, as he looked at the faces of the men doubled
up in the cells, is the side of the Cape that few people see. Turns
out it's not all sand dunes and ice cream shops. He was buzzed
through another door and found the Harleton cat's cell wide-open.
Overweight, white, the executive type, dumping toiletries off the
wall shelf into a plastic bag.

Lash said, "Hi, there."

The guy turned, startled, seeing Lash filling the open door. A
man walking freely inside the lockup. Harleton looked behind
Lash, expecting others. "Who are you?"

"I'm Boston Celtics legend Bill Russell, how you doing?"

The guy shrank back, a dry toothbrush in his hand. He was on the verge of walking out of this place, and now here was a black man in his cell messing with him. "They said my lawyer is coming."

Lash looked around. "Not here yet."

Harleton appeared pained, waiting to be let in on the joke. "I don't know who you are."

"Let's just say that I'm an agent of the Drug Enforcement Administration. And let's just say that you were found three days ago all trussed up in your family's home on some island-sized golf course, along with three known heroin dealers and eleven pounds of weed."

Harleton's mouth flinched, his eyes cheating around the room in anticipation of a beating. "My lawyer is on his way."

"You said that. I guess your family popped for bail. Very considerate, in light of the circumstances. Very forgiving. I gotta tell you, my son played host to a drug deal in my house while I was away in Florida? He'd be coming up with his own damn bail money."

"I'm sure you don't know anything about my family—"

"But I know about you, Mr. Harleton. You're the fuckup son, a grown man still taking help from parents he doesn't respect. But I'm not here to scold you. I wouldn't waste my motherfucking breath." Lash cursed because Harleton expected it from him. Lash had no problem being his scary stereotype. "I don't even care about your case. Someone else will handle it, and they will be left holding the bag when you screw. Now, don't give me that shocked look—you think I don't know you're going to run?"

Harleton was over his initial fear, his mind-set back to *A man like me doesn't belong in a place like this.* Lawyers had been consulted, bail had been posted. The world he knew was righting itself like a good ship in a storm. "Run where?"

"Like I said, somebody else's problem. Two days is a good long time to be tied up, isn't it?"

"I guess so."

"Your parents know you better than you think. Two days without hearing from you, and they call the police, ask that their house be checked. Osterville cops find you bound up with a bunch of felons and weed. One of the felons was beat-up. They recovered a casing and a round on the floor—and yet no firearms anywhere in the house. The round was scored and mashed, meaning it had been fired and impacted with something—and no bullet holes in the house. They found heroin movers and heroin buyers—and yet no money and no heroin. See a pattern here?"

Harleton kept mum.

"I'm not here about you. I'm here about the guys who ripped you off."

Harleton's eyes, accustomed to a lifetime of blinking and prevarication, held firm.

"These other shits you were with, they'll deny anything occurred. *Especially* after going to such lengths *not* to get taken. The island. This gated little golf sanctuary. Only to be made fools of. Which is where you come in. One bridge connects to the mainland, and the guy at the gate, he checks names. So your guests, they had reason to feel pretty secure. But they didn't pay enough attention to the beach, huh?"

Lash started to pace inside the small cell. He wasn't even looking at Harleton now, Lash putting all this together in front of him. Harleton's role in Lash's ratiocination was that of the finger around which a knot was being tied.

"Coming in by water. That shows skills. Were there four or five of them?"

Lash didn't need straight-out answers. Just being near the guy allowed him to see. In the way a psychic worries a possession of the recently disappeared, or a bloodhound pokes his nose in a shirt. This was why Lash had come all the way out to Cape Cod.

"I'm betting the shot came from your side. Because the round was blunted, like it hit Kevlar and bounced away. That explains the guy getting smacked around. He got a shot off . . . and yet he wasn't killed in retaliation. That's enormous restraint, isn't it? Heat of the moment? These guys are disciplined, they're patient, they're prepared. And plenty well equipped. A lot of which says cops. But the amphibious stuff—no. Maybe federal . . . ?" Lash played this out in his mind. "Maybe some rogue tactical team, freelancing. Or *ex*-agents. But how do they *know*? Field intel. That's the fucking weak link here, that's the key. If I can find any agency, local or federal, that was onto you"—Lash pointed to Harleton, still standing with his back against the far wall—"or those others . . . a snitch somewhere . . . somebody undercover . . ."

Harleton relaxed a little more. Now he'd had some time to think. "Cops?"

Lash looked up at him. "That surprises you. They didn't seem like cops? Do cop shit?"

Harleton clamped up again.

Lash returned to his pacing. "That's the one part that doesn't play, isn't it? Cops who turn like this, they hide behind the badge. Who wouldn't? You're gonna go dirty, why play fair? You're gonna use the golden key that opens every door in town. And there's a big difference between taking a shot at some guy trying to rip you off, versus capping a fed. About a life's sentence difference."

Lash looked back at Harleton, the man wearing a funny, distant-looking smile on his face.

Lash said, "You're wondering about cops. Thinking this could help you, help your case. Only thing is—I'm not even going to bother talking to your known associates. So if you go blabbing any of this to your lawyer, they'll know you were the source, and they'll think you were talking to us feds." Lash made a *snick* noise with his cheek. "I don't know. Maybe they'll kill you anyway. For knowing they got taken—for *seeing* it. They don't like that. Maybe you lost money too, maybe you financed some of this hijacked cake. Though I doubt it. These aren't your people. This is more like you owe them something. Like you've been living out on the wild side. That it, tubby?"

The guy was getting pissed. Lash should have stopped there but he couldn't pull back. This guy in front of him was the embodiment of his own nightmare about raising a son.

"Vengeful little kid cutting up Mommy's dresses. When you screw out of here, jumping bail and fleeing the country, who's going to pay? As always, your beautiful, loving parents. Only this time, they're going to pay in bullets. I'm sure the last thing they'll be thinking about is their son, whose fat finger is practically pulling the trigger. Thinking that maybe they should have handled you differently. That maybe getting you out of trouble isn't the same as raising you right."

Harleton looked as if a stopper in his throat had been pulled, the crust of recalcitrance and malfeasance that clogged his head beginning to drain down. He looked as contrite as he'd ever been in his entire life. And yet Lash knew it wouldn't last. He'd still go off running with his parents' lives in his pockets like the gold from their teeth, and crying all the way.

Lash said, as he turned to leave, "Thanks, you've been a help."

CURTIZ KNOCKED ON LASH'S DOOR, CARRYING IN HIS BACKGROUND work on Vasco, the Venezuelan they had pulled out of the thawed Charles River. They called this a digital profile, outlining the last days of a dead man via his electronic echo.

Curtiz focused on Vasco's credit card purchases and mobile phone records.

"We never found the phone," said Lash.

"Tracked his number via his e-mail account. It was a U.S. phone. GPS triangulation puts the phone at the Sheraton Boston on Dalton Street when it went dead."

"He was registered at the Boston Harbor Hotel." Lash turned his Zippo over and over in his hand. The map of Vietnam inscribed on the back had all but worn smooth. "I don't suppose GPS can give us a room number?"

"Only reads horizontally. But I went in and had them go back through the register for that day, they gave me this printout. See there?"

Curtiz had highlighted the name *Maracone*, a two-night registration in a junior suite on the twenty-ninth floor.

"No complaints from the hotel that day, nothing logged any-way. But there was a housekeeping note saying that the telephone was gone from the room and had to be replaced. The charge was added to the bill." Curtiz handed Lash a copy of Maracone's room bill. "Maybe they cut the room phone and disabled all the mobiles, including Vasco's. Makes sense, right?"

"Perfect sense," said Lash.

"Here's the other peculiar thing. See his call log? It's summa-rized there on the first page. His minutes don't add up. More air-time used than total logged calls."

Lash flipped through the pages. "Phone company mistake?"

"Could be. They never made a mistake on my bill though. You want to leave it at that?"

Lash shook his head. "I guess I don't."

HE WAS LOOKING FOR A MAN NAMED SCHRAMM WHO SOLD GOTHIC and Celtic jewelry out of a cart set up near the *Cheers* bar repro-duction at Faneuil Hall. Lash poked around, eating a soft-serve ice cream cone, while Schramm flirted with two truant teens shop-ping for pewter pendants and sterling-silver belly rings.

The waiting allowed Schramm to make Lash as a cop. Once the girls moved along, Schramm went up to him and said, "Look, man, I'm out of it. I did my bid."

"I have only come here seeking knowledge. Somebody gave me your name."

Schramm wore a winged-reaper ring on his middle finger, a death's-head pin sewn into the skin over his right temple. "Can I see the shield?"

Lash obliged.

"So we're talking casually here, then?"

"So casual." Lash showed him the printout with the airtime discrepancy. "What am I looking at, a cloned phone?"

"Nobody clones phones, not anymore. Too traceable now that

carriers do radio fingerprinting. It catches clones by picking up the unique rise time signature—"

"If you could," said Lash, putting up the stop sign, "just put it in layman's terms, and then maybe step it down another couple of notches. I'm moving through this digital world at thirty-three and a third revolutions per minute."

Schramm made a forget-that motion with his hands. "For the minute numbers to be off, that means somebody had to mess with the internal chip. You do that, you can change a device made for transmitting into an actual broadcaster. A RAT phone, or remote access tool. You control it remotely, usually by sending an SMS—I mean, a text message. You can intercept calls, but more to the point, you can turn a phone into a microphone. Like a bug. You can listen in. Takes a little know-how, but the most important thing is access. Setting up the target phone. You either need to give your mark a tampered phone, or else physically get your hands on theirs for a certain amount of time."

"Okay, so—somebody close."

"Somebody close. Or else a real good thief."

Lash chewed on that. "They use this in law enforcement?"

"You don't know?"

"Told you, I'm made of vinyl. These lines you see in my face are analog grooves."

Schramm patted his pocket to show that it was empty. "I don't carry a phone no more. Such a thing as too much convenience. Too much reliability. Too easy to exploit."

Lash nodded, wondering what it meant that some of the best advice he'd received in his life, he'd got from thieves.

DAMSEL

THEY BROKE EARLY FROM THE CLUB, GETTING BACK TO THE MARL-borough Street pad a little after one. Royce was still at Preci-pice, but no Danielle. Maven realized he hadn't seen her in a few days. Termino stayed out on a midnight rendezvous; Suarez drank too many vodkas and not enough Red Bulls and passed out snor-ing on the sofa with his hand down his pants; Glade was doing his Glade thing with two legal secretaries, holed up in his and Maven's room. Glade's ministrations generally took him into the wee small hours, plying these girls with Midori, getting them used to the camera. The first ten, fifteen, twenty times Maven had watched the resulting video, it was great. Now it was like a porn he'd seen over and over. It had got so that he was blaming the victims for their pliability, rather than his sociopathic roommate, in the same way Maven used to get pissed off at Iraqis for making him shoot at them.

So he was shit out of luck and would have to bunk out here on the opposite end of the sectional from snoring Suarez. Maven wandered to the other end of the apartment, fishing a Red Stripe out of the beverage refrigerator and racking up balls on the pool table. He broke hard, scattering the balls, suspended in the leftover buzz of another lost night. He lined up a few shots, then set down his cue. Even the pool table had lost its allure.

Maven heard creaking above him. He looked up at the high ceiling. Footsteps overhead. Could have been Royce back home, but he didn't think so. The footsteps moved toward the street, and he moved with them, to the French doors opening onto Marlborough.

He stood out in the night air, knowing she was above him. He was with her and not with her, the story of his life. Across the way, in a large, angled picture window, he saw Danielle's reflection. Standing out on the top-floor balcony with a drink in her hand, wearing a short robe and not much else. She looked out into the night like a woman in a high castle. A damsel, only not in distress. Just a damsel.

A breeze came up, a whiff of ocean air brushing his cheek at the same time it shifted the hem of her robe around her thighs, and Maven had to turn away. Had to go back inside, and then, once there, had to get out of that place. He took off downstairs, moving to the sidewalk, hitting the chill and not knowing where he was going. He reached the corner before looking back, and when he did, the top-floor balcony was vacant.

He walked away from the river, toward Commonwealth Avenue, needing to move, working off the alcohol and the discontent. City Convenience at the corner of Massachusetts and Commonwealth avenues was a bright storefront in an otherwise darkened city. He went inside.

Similar to his convenience store in Quincy, only with prices higher by 30 percent. The guy working a laptop behind the counter gave Maven an unsmiling nod, checking him over for stickup potential, and Maven thought of Ricky and felt even worse.

He walked down the hospital-bright aisles, not wanting anything. So he was still smitten with Danielle—fine. He could live with that. In fact, it wasn't so bad. Having his ultimate girl right there, yet out of reach—up on that balcony—freed him to be a little more reckless with other girls.

This was how he was feeling when a group of young women walked in, weaving and husky-voiced from talking over loud music all night. They wanted bottled water, Maven standing near the drink cooler. He glanced over without too much optimism—then took a second look at the one in front.

Brunette ringlets. A beaded choker around her neck.

She drifted near, choosing between flavored waters, her friends still farther back. Aware of him, yet sober enough to avoid eye contact.

"Unicorns and gift bags," he said.

She shot him a so-not-interested squint—followed by a glimmer of recognition.

"That club," she said. "Precipice. That awful place."

"It is, isn't it?" he said, smiling. "But this guy I work with, these people I know, it's like their spot, so . . ."

She nodded. "You didn't look like everyone else there. So thrilled with themselves."

"It's Samara, right?"

Her friends appeared, protectively backing her up. "How did you remember my name?"

"Well, it's unusual."

"So I'm told."

"It's also the name of this city in Iraq."

She nodded. "I've heard it mentioned on NPR once or twice."

"Once or twice," he said, smiling to himself.

"So, were you . . . um . . . ?"

"I was."

"Ah." She smiled uncomfortably. "Wow. What was that like?"

"Less awful than Precipice."

She smiled again, aware that she had asked a dumb question. Her friends looked him over, not making this easy. Samara was Indian by heritage, and American by voice, but something about her—her name, and maybe her exoticism, but also something more—put him in the mind of that rarely glimpsed, peaceful side of Eden, during the war.

She was still smiling at him and not looking away.

Maven said, "I believe it was Nietzsche who once said that the most difficult thing a man can do in this life is to ask a girl out in front of her friends."

Two of the girls laughed, while the other one, whom Maven recognized from Precipice, gave him a corny scowl.

"Okay," said Samara.

They got out their phones, exchanging numbers side by side.

"One *r*," Samara corrected him.

"One *r*." He thumbed OK to save her contact info. "Okay. So I'll call you."

"Okay," she said, closing her phone.

OUTSIDE, TURNING THE CORNER BACK ONTO COMM. AVE., THE WALK back to Marlborough Street made him remember the balcony.

He found her number in his phone and pressed SEND.

She answered, "Hi?"

"Hey. I tried waiting that two-day thing before calling you, but it just wasn't working out . . ."

ANESTHETIC

MAVEN LAY ON HIS BACK IN FULL CAMO ON A BED OF DIRT IN A wetlands field, holding a cold carbine flat against his chest, his finger along the magazine feed outside the pistol grip. A warm, still Sunday morning, clouds drifting across the sky. Kids used to find shapes in them, but he never could. Every cloud he saw looked just like a cloud.

He checked his timepiece, then glanced over at the building through the waving weeds. A warehouse at the swampy end of a Raynham industrial park, a granite and marble wholesaler with a storefront named TAKE FOR GRANITE. One of the Crossbone Champs did some part-time stonecutting for the guy who owned the business.

Eighteen thousand ecstasy pellets at $11.40 per. The price had risen sharply, due to recent scarcity. More demand than supply, thanks in large part to the sugar bandits.

That was $205,200. Plus another $40 K or so in uncut cocaine. A quarter mil on the table.

Maven eyed the advance men waiting near a Chevy, their inked arms crossed. One wore a wild gray beard, the other a brown, braided pony, both in jeans and boots and leather vests. But no club markings: the Crossbone Champs were not flying their colors this morning.

The rest of them showed up in a convoy of three cars—cages, as they called them—looking like the road crew for .38 Special. The buyers arrived less than a minute later, an enterprising concern of younger men led by the nephew of a former capo of the Providence, Rhode Island, Mafia, looking to reestablish the family's influence in that region.

Both factions went inside. Maven touched the TALK button on his Bluetooth. "Go time."

"Let's bring it," answered Termino, little more than a hiss in Maven's ear. Termino and Glade and Suarez were already in position inside the warehouse.

The advance bikers and two mafiosi lingered outside, the bikers sneering over at the buyers, everything a macho trip with these guys. One biker chuckled and said something to the other, then the one with the ponytail tossed away the cigarette he'd been smoking and walked in Maven's direction. He stopped just off the blacktop, unzipping his fly and taking a long leak into the weeds.

His stream stopped as he saw Maven sit up just a few yards away. He saw the camo and the carbine pointed at him, and the crow's-feet at his narrowing eyes tightened.

Maven said, "Don't zip up. Don't do anything."

The biker's urine stream resumed.

Shrubs and thorny overgrowth provided Maven with good cover from the others. In his ear, he heard Termino shouting commands inside, taking control of the room.

Maven saw the other biker look over at his not-moving buddy. The mafiosi stood near their cars, not paying much attention.

Then things started to go bad in his ear.

Glade's voice now. "Hey—you stay down—*stay down!*— don't—"

The yelling was cut short by a *brraapp* of gunfire so loud, Maven flung the device from his ear.

The other biker drew a pistol from the back of his jeans and started for the door.

Maven's biker tried to zip up before drawing his piece. Big mistake. Maven was up too fast, throating the biker with the butt of his carbine, the big man dropping hard.

More gunfire from inside as Maven ran across the blacktop.

The other biker fired at the stunned mafiosi, who took cover behind the cars, now firing back. The biker was hit in the gut but kept going.

Maven reached the rear corner, taking cover there. A bay door near him started to rise, opening a few feet, and Maven took a knee, carbine aimed.

It was Glade. He scrambled out fast, Suarez spilling out after him, but heavily, dropping to the blacktop. Maven saw blood on Suarez's leg.

Termino followed, sliding out and turning, firing behind him. Maven stepped up, in a good crouch, sighting inside the warehouse over the top handle of the carbine. He saw rows of granite slabs stood up on long edges. A spit of flame lashed out from the left, and he answered, the carbine rattling, kicking back hard at his shoulder. Glade hauled out two cases of Olde English 800, glass bottles clanking inside, as Maven held them off. Glade dragged out a vinyl Puma duffel bag, a few shots rapping off the inside of the half-raised bay door.

Maven saw the strap hanging off the bottom of the bay-door handle and took a chance. He launched himself up off one of the rubber truck bumpers built into the exterior of the bay, grasping the strap and firing into the warehouse as his weight rode the door down and closed.

More rounds rapped the inside of the door. Maven spun to

the corner, leaning around it. No gunfire there. He sighted on the vehicles, squeezing the trigger, tires bursting air and moisture, the bodies of the cars sinking.

He spun back to the others, grabbing the Olde English case Glade couldn't handle, and following them into the wetlands, jogging backward, his muzzle on the rear bay door.

THEY GOT DEEP INTO THE WEED GROWTH, PUTTING SOME TREES between them and the warehouse. Suarez was biting down on the neck of his armored vest, screaming into it as Termino carried him on his shoulder.

"What the fuck?" said Maven.

"Fucking bikers," said Glade, breathing hard on the run. "Fucking rather be shot than ripped off."

One of Suarez's screams escaped his vest.

"Pass out already," grumbled Termino.

"How bad?" said Maven.

"Thigh," said Glade.

Outer thigh, okay, just muscle damage. Inner thigh could mean the femoral artery, bleeding out, death within two minutes. Termino would be drenched in Suarez's blood if it were the artery.

They hustled through a swampy field of dead, denuded trees, a clearing that had seen a fire. Termino stopped near a drainpipe, close to the cars, parked in the parking lot of an out-of-business windshield-replacement shop. He dumped Suarez onto a bed of grass, and Maven saw the leg wound, blood pulsing down his pants. Termino fished a telephone out from his vest and tossed it to Maven before ripping open Suarez's jeans around the wound.

Maven opened up the phone; only one number was listed. He pressed SEND and waited, watching Glade open up a case of

Olde English. The forty-ounce bottles were filled with tan pills stamped with the image of a smoking eyeball. Glade dumped the ecstasy pills into water streaming out of the basin.

Royce answered, "What is it?"

"Suarez is hit," said Maven, adrenaline surging with those words.

"How bad?"

"How bad?" Maven asked Termino.

"A round ricocheted off stone," said Termino, over Suarez's groaning. "Sliced him deep, but through-and-through."

"You hear that?" said Maven.

Royce said, "I heard. You get the product?"

Maven looked at Glade starting in on case number two. "We're dumping it now. He's hurting bad."

"Stop. Get the powder."

Glade had the bag of white in his hand. Maven told him to stop.

Royce said, "Sprinkle some over the wound."

Maven looked at the cocaine. "You said what?"

"Cocaine started out as a topical anesthetic. Sprinkle it over the wound. And don't make me fucking repeat myself again."

Maven seized the bag from Glade and put down the phone. He went to Suarez, whose eyes were closed. Maven dusted Suarez's bloody leg wound with cocaine the way good restaurants sprinkle sugar over dessert. The white mixed with the blood and adhered to the edges of the gash.

The other two looked at Maven as though he were insane.

Maven picked up the phone again. "Done."

"Dump the rest, ditch the armor and weapons as planned, and get him back here pronto."

Maven hung up. "We move," he said, stripping off his armor.

By the time they got to Suarez, his tension had broken, and they were able to remove his gear. Suarez sat up, examining his wound, touching it gently around the edges.

"Did you coke up my leg?" he said.

*   *   *

They wrapped his leg in a chamois towel from the boot of the switch car and carried him in the rear-alley basement entrance of the Marlborough Street building. Royce was waiting inside their pad with an olive green medical kit full of field surgical tools, syringes, and vials of anesthetic. He had towels laid out and a pitcher of water. He washed the wound and the coke residue, then pumped Suarez's thigh full of lidocaine before breaking out a suture kit and going to work.

"Who fucked up?" Royce said.

Glade said, "They started shooting—"

"Who fucked up!"

All three of them kneeling around Royce and Suarez, no one said anything. Maven still didn't know what had happened, he wasn't there. But even he felt the tension in the room turning toward Glade. And nobody rising to his defense.

Glade said, "Fuck you, guys. I'm going to let them draw on me?"

Royce said, "You haven't learned anything this whole time?" The gash was so deep, Royce had to sew the inside of the leg first. "They're bikers, professional psychos. You gave them what they want. You had control of the situation, and you fucked it up. And left some of your buddy's DNA at the scene of the crime." Royce tied off the inside and irrigated the wound again. "From now on, Maven, you're inside with Termino. You handle the approach."

Glade soured as if he'd been punched. He stood and walked away, and Royce kept working over Suarez as though he didn't notice.

"How's the pain now, 'Lito?"

Suarez said, "My leg wants to go to a disco."

Maven felt cold. Part of it was the fading adrenaline, but mostly it was the realization that the untouchables had finally got touched. Their winning streak hadn't ended, but it could have. The dynamics within the crew were changing.

Royce prepared another needle for sewing. "Always fucking fun until somebody gets hurt."

Maven turned to stand, and then saw Danielle behind them, at the open door, looking down at Royce sewing up Suarez's leg.

No disgust. No surprise. No expression at all.

She said nothing and backed out into the hallway, gone before anyone else saw her.

POISON SWEET

TIA'S WAS A SEASONAL BAR SET UNDER AN AWNING AGAINST THE high brick wall of the waterfront Marriott Long Wharf. It was that moment when the sun goes down and the city lights start to come up, and everything feels balanced and good. Young professionals crowded the rail, waiting for patio tables to open up. Guys wearing sandals with dress pants, girls in flip-flops and short skirts. All of them drinking candy-colored booze. Jolly Ranchers and Jager Bombs, Midori and Cointreau. Shots called Quick Fuck and Juicy Pussy. Red Bull and whatever. Kids like their poison sweet.

"I went to a peace rally once," said Samara Bahaar, sipping a Bacardi and Diet through two cocktail straws. "On the Common."

"Yeah?" he said.

She wore a top with two stringy shoulder straps over tanned, smooth skin. "Banners, chants, the whole thing. It was packed."

Maven nodded. "Sounds like fun."

"I mean, we knew it wasn't the sixties anymore. But it was good. We got tapas after." Her nose wrinkled a little as she played with the ice in her drink and thought. "All I hear about nowadays is soldiers returning and having problems."

"You know what it's like? Being over there, it was just like going on a trip. Picking up souvenirs and whatnot, weird stuff. But you're so busy looking over your shoulder all the time, you just throw them in your suitcase. Then you get home. You're tired, unpacking sucks. So the suitcase sits for a while. Easier to walk around it than open it. When you finally get to unpacking, you start pulling out all this crazy shit you forgot you put in there, and it's, like—you're home now, and there's absolutely no place for it here. But it's, like, yours, you can't throw it out. So?"

"You're stuck with it."

"Got to find a place. I found a place. Maybe I'm just lucky."

"So could you, like, kick anybody's ass in this joint?"

Maven looked around. "Go ahead. Pick somebody out."

"Can I sic you on some old boyfriends?"

"That's already been taken care of. You won't be running into those clowns anymore."

She smiled, then tapped at the enamel of her front teeth with her fingernail. Probably feeling a little numb from the drinks.

"Here's a question you'll love," said Maven. "What are you going to do now that you are out of school?"

"Ha." She shook out her hair. "With my incredibly valuable double major in psychology and communications, you mean? The sky's the limit. My parents want me to move back to Jersey. Which I'm not. I really want to stay here, but my lease is up September first, and . . . I guess basically I'm putting off what I need to do. Which is—decide."

"You're waiting for something to happen. Hoping that something will decide things for you."

She pointed to him. "You've been there."

"I have." He downed a little more Ketel One. "I told you I work for a Realtor, right?"

"I was going to ask about that. So do you, like, have your pick of great apartments?"

"Something like that."

"Where do you live now?"

"On Marlborough."

"You live on Marlborough Street?"

"Right."

"No, you don't."

"I think I do."

"How do you afford that?"

He enjoyed her astonishment. "How about we give this table to some of these braying donkeys over here, and I'll take you over. I live above the office, we can go down and check some listings, then get a bite to eat."

She pulled out the two purple stirrers and finished off her drink. "Sounds great."

"One more question. Have you ever been on the back of a motorcycle?"

It was a Harley Night Train, done out in sinister black and chrome, low and lean, barely a week old. He handed her the extra helmet. She said, "Maybe I should have had another drink."

He stood astride the seat, standing the bike off the kick. "You'll be fine."

"Okay." She took a breath. She pulled the helmet down over her ringlets. "Killing my hair." She climbed on behind him, putting her hands first on his shoulders, then around his waist.

He started it up, and she gripped him harder, pressing her front into his back as he eased away from the curb. Heads turned as they rode through the city, guys wanting the bike, girls wanting the ride. Once they got into the Back Bay, he could feel her starting to have fun. He turned into the brick alley between Marlborough and Beacon, pulling in at the carriage-house garage behind their building. He parked next to Suarez's and Glade's identical Harleys.

"Was there a special?" she asked, pulling off her helmet, trying to resuscitate her hair.

Inside, climbing the stairs to the second floor, Maven felt a tinge of concern. He had had plenty of girls back to the pad, of course, but always late at night, and rarely half-sober.

Glade was in the kitchen, standing at the counter in his underwear, eating Thai food out of a carton with chopsticks and a fork. After the requisite introductions, Glade said, "This is nice, Maven, you dating girls for a change."

Maven shed his motorcycle jacket. "You putting on weight, Glades?"

Glade smiled a *Fuck you,* shoveling more *rad na* into his mouth.

Samara was bemused by Glade's showmanship, but more impressed with the pad. "*Wow,* that's a lot of phones."

Their work phones lay in the corner next to the refrigerator, twelve units charging, a thicket of wires feeding into the bank of outlets in the tile backsplash.

"Yeah, well, Realtors, you know," said Maven, ignoring Glade's taunting stare.

Suarez came hobbling in on crutches, wearing shorts underneath an open bathrobe, his thigh wrapped in tape and gauze.

"Motorcycle accident?" Samara guessed.

Maven said, "Cut himself shaving."

Suarez said, "Maven ever offers to show you his knife-throwing trick—say hell no."

Maven felt a little looser. "Fixing to go out?"

The front door opened then, Termino walking inside. "You fucking dinks not dressed yet?"

Royce entered behind him. He immediately zoned in on Samara's presence, putting her together with Maven.

"Milkshake here had to eat," said Suarez. "And we have a guest."

Maven rushed the introductions. Royce smiled and took her hand. "A pleasure."

Maven found a key labeled OFFICE on the peg rack by the wall phone. He regretted bringing her up now, his words coming fast. "We were on our way downstairs. Samara's lease is up at the end of August, and I said I'd show her some listings."

Royce said, still with a careful look behind his eyes, "College student?"

"Just graduated," said Samara.

"Congratulations. Don't let us hold you up." He looked at Maven with nothing hard in his eyes, leaving it to Maven to read his displeasure. "Perhaps you can even talk Maven into giving up his finder's fee."

Still gracious, still smooth. Maven felt that he was getting away easy as he steered Samara to the door—and walked right into Danielle.

Danielle wore a smoking-hot dress, black and dangerous, topped by a perfect groove of cleavage.

Danielle took in Samara at a glance, then turned a funny little smile on Maven, seeing right through him. Knowing that this was why he had brought Samara around. He had wanted Danielle to see him with someone else.

Royce said, "Danny, this is Maven's friend. Samara, isn't it?"

Danielle smiled at Samara with too much levity, her dagger heels giving her a few extra inches of condescension. "How perfectly strange to meet you," Danielle said, and Maven closed his eyes a moment, swallowing his defeat.

MAVEN WENT FROM DESK TO DESK SEARCHING FOR A PRINTOUT OF recent market listings, trying to head off any discussion of what had just occurred upstairs.

Samara watched him, still bothered, pretending not to be. "Which desk is yours?"

"Me?" said Maven, finding what he thought he was looking for, then realizing it wasn't. "Oh, I just float around."

Samara became quiet again as footsteps descended the main stairs, past the wall behind them. Glade's voice was loudest, telling jokes no one laughed at, the talk fading as they exited through the back basement to the garage.

"Who was she?" said Samara.

"Who?"

"There was only one 'she' up there."

"You mean Danielle?"

Samara didn't respond.

"She's with Royce."

"Royce is your boss."

"Right."

"She's his wife? Girlfriend?"

"Girlfriend." Maven looked up, confronting it rather than doing a dance. "Why?"

Samara backed off, shaking her head, looking out the window to the street. "Just curious."

GETTING BY

MAVEN WASN'T GETTING FULL VALUE OUT OF HIS NEW BIKE, RIDING stop-and-go around the city. So he took off one afternoon on his own, heading west on Route 2, losing the helmet for a while, putting his face in the wind. He returned to the city that evening and was idling near Charles Street, thinking about dinner, when he saw a woman who looked a lot like Danielle exit a restaurant. She had her back to him, her head down—Maven was across the traffic lane, two cars in back of the light—but the more he looked, the more he became convinced it was her. Strolling under the gas lamps, arm in arm with some other guy. Maven knew her form anywhere, her gait, her calves. He also knew that the guy wasn't Royce, though Maven barely looked at him, he was so tunneled in on the mystery that was Danielle.

They walked to the curb and ducked into an SUV with livery tags before he could see her face. The SUV pulled away, and Maven jumped the small median, rolling after it, remaining a safe couple of car lengths back, his heart pounding more than it did during a takedown.

The black SUV pulled over outside the Omni Parker House across from One Beacon. The driver got out and opened the door for the woman, and Maven made Danielle's profile as he rolled on past. He nearly swerved into the oncoming lane, correcting and then turning around as soon as he could, but by the time he did, the SUV was gone.

MAVEN HADN'T BEEN RIGHT SINCE. HE HADN'T CROSSED PATHS WITH her again—she'd been scarce the past few days—but now he saw her coming toward him from the restrooms. Precipice again, late on a Sunday night, Maven's least favorite crowd. Only the idle rich could afford to party into early Monday morning, but Maven was running out of excuses not to come.

Danielle looked phenomenal in a midriff-baring halter top, but he didn't respond to it the way he used to. It was the betrayal—the assumed betrayal—of Royce, and of him. She and Maven had had their own little thing going for some time now—low voltage, never to be consummated, but always there. Or—had they? Maybe she was that way with everybody. Maybe nothing at all was special about her relationship with Maven, and she was completely off on her own.

"No girlie-friend tonight?" she said, stopping before him, looking up.

Her usual condescension-slash-playfulness only soured him. "Not here."

"Trouble in paradise?"

"She's home for the weekend."

"She's young."

"I guess."

"I didn't know you went for the exotic type."

"You mean, girls from Jersey?"

"Come on." Danielle squeezed his hand. "Dance with me."

"No, I think I'm good."

"Pouting now?" She squinted up at him, getting a new perspective on a faraway object. "New look for you."

In his mind, he was punishing her. "I'm good."

"Fine." She dropped his hand. "Fuck you. Bunch of wallflowers."

She went out to the dance floor alone, and Maven didn't feel any better.

Before long, Danielle found a partner. The guy's shirt matched his tie exactly, cut from the same shimmery fabric, and this pissed off Maven for some reason. Danielle shimmied with him, but locked eyes with Maven, letting him know she was dancing for and without him. He finished his beer and made a point of looking away.

Everything was going to piss. Danielle, the crew. This place. Maven missed Samara.

But did he really miss her, or was he just looking to fill this void that was Danielle?

It was more than that. Samara Bahaar was the one clean, uncomplicated thing he had going.

He brought out his phone, texting her, *Thinking of you, what's up?*

When he looked back out on the dance floor, the guy had Danielle by the arm. She tried to walk away, but he wanted more. Maven watched Danielle smile, trying to charm her way out of his grip, but all the guy saw was the smile. He pulled her closer, wrapping his arm across her bare waist, lights running all over them. He spoke into Danielle's ear, his nose and mouth up in her hair. Danielle smiled in response, reaching up to his neck, then pinching a hunk of skin and twisting. The guy reared back, Danielle almost getting free, but he caught her arm again and shook her.

Then he looked up. Maven was standing in front of him.

"Fuck you want?" the guy yelled over the music.

Dance-floor lights spun between them. Maven said, "Just waiting for you to let her go."

The guy pushed Danielle away, but stood his ground.

Danielle came up next to Maven. "Kick his fucking ass, Gridley."

The guy reached out to shove him, and Maven hooked his right arm, driving a punch into his ribs, his kidney, then holding back on the knockout blow, laying him out without breaking his face.

The guy had friends, who came jumping out of the flashing lights and dance-floor screams, descending on Maven.

Fights are never about what they are about. It's always some guy who got his heart stomped on earlier in the day, or who got shit on at work last week, who decides he doesn't care about his face anymore. The incident that ignites the fight is just an excuse to start swinging.

This fight was Maven whaling on Danielle, her wayward behavior, her sluttiness and her partying, her desirability.

They were all separated in a blur, voices and arms and whatever. Somebody led him away, and Maven looked around for Glade or Suarez, but saw nobody he knew. He checked his face and found no blood, felt no real soreness. He was practically untouched. Then he discovered a tear in the underarm seam of his $350 Varvatos shirt, and he wished he'd fucking murdered the lot of them.

He was taken into the manager's office through the mirrored door behind the DJ booth. Maven knew the manager, but the manager wasn't there. He recognized the bouncer, who nodded to him, and Maven smiled, all set.

The dancer guy Maven had beat up was led inside, but not his friends. He had blood all over his matching tie and shirt.

One more guy stood inside the office, coming off the manager's desk, a black guy Maven had never seen before. He was older, long-armed and tall, wearing a linen blazer and a buttoned shirt with no tie. Chewing gum, his long jaw masticating. A thin brown scarf hung around his neck. He pulled two soft silicone plugs out of his ears and set them down on the corner of the desk.

"Loud as a motherfucker up in this joint," he said. "You reach a certain age, you stop going out to clubs. It's a lot easier and a hell of a lot cheaper to sit at home and stab yourself in the ears."

The dancer guy said, with some kind of European accent, "Who the fuck are you?"

The black guy slowly crossed the small office. The dancer guy backed up to the wall. The gum-chewing black guy opened the dancer guy's jacket carefully, avoiding the bloodstains, and reached inside his breast pocket, coming out with a wallet.

The black guy then looked at Maven, Maven trying to figure out what an undercover cop would be doing in Club Precipice on a Sunday night. Maven raised his arms in a gesture of compliance and fished out his wallet, handing it over.

The black guy looked at the dancer guy's ID, then Maven's, comparing photographs to faces.

"My name is Lash. Federal agent. Drug Enforcement Administration."

He said this while watching both their faces. Maven rode out the reverb of the revelation, fighting hard not to show any expression. It was like stepping down barefoot on a nail and not flinching from the pain, but he did it.

"What was the fight about?"

"What fight?" the dancer guy said.

"'What fight?' is exactly right. You'd do well to forget what a shit sloppy brawler you are. Though I bet tomorrow this story has a different ending, no?"

The dancer guy said, "You are police? I press charges. This man." He pointed at Maven. "I sue!"

"You what?" said Lash.

"I sue!"

Lash lobbed his wallet back at him. "Get the fuck out of here, Sue."

The dancer guy didn't move at first. The bouncer opened the door, scowling, and he went.

Lash backed off, looking around the office. "No security cameras inside, huh?" he said to the bouncer.

"Inside?" said the bouncer. "No. People don't like to think they're being filmed."

"All right, you can let yourself out too. We won't be a minute."

The bouncer hesitated a moment, then went out. Leaving Maven alone in the office with a DEA agent.

Lash tipped his ear to one side, trying to get a fix on Maven. "Who was the girl you two were fighting over?"

Maven shook his head. "I just saw her tonight."

"Really."

"Didn't like the way he was treating her."

"I see. Sir Galahad."

Maven shrugged. "Just common sense."

"So you're a bystander."

Maven shrugged again, not overselling it. "Why—who is she?"

Lash didn't answer, didn't give anything away. "Too bad she didn't stick around, say thank you. She beat it out of here pretty quick. Kind of ungrateful, don't you think?"

"You should ask her."

Lash's eyes narrowed, looking him over. "You a vet?"

Maven was surprised. "I am."

"Back how long?"

"Little over a year now."

Lash nodded. "I'm out since '75, longer than you've been alive. And I can still spot a brother-in-arms. Something about the discipline, standing for questioning. Always thinking you can put one over on your CO."

Maven shook his head. "No, sir."

"You look like you're doing pretty good for yourself."

"I'm getting by."

"Those aren't exactly 'getting by' threads. But you don't know nothin' 'bout the girl, right?"

"That's right."

On a folded piece of paper, Lash was copying down Maven's name and address from his driver's license. Maven's ID still had his old Quincy address. On Royce's advice, he had never registered his move with the post office, never forwarded his mail.

Maven heard the opening beats of the Ultramagnetic MC's

"Traveling at the Speed of Thought" and reached for his mobile. It was gone from his jacket pocket.

Lash drew Maven's old-school-rap-playing phone out of his jacket pocket. "Oh, is this yours?" He opened the flip top. "I found it on the floor out there." He opened the text message. "Who's Samara?"

He tossed the phone to Maven. "My girlfriend," said Maven, reading the text: *I'm asleep—y r'nt u???*

Lash said, "The girl you were fighting over know that?"

Maven put his phone away. "I told you, she wasn't my girl-friend."

"You sure fought like she was."

AFTER LETTING MAVEN GO, LASH UNFOLDED THE PAPER ON WHICH he had scribbled down Maven's vitals. It was a photo printout from an ATM surveillance camera, date-stamped November 9 of last year. The dead Venezuelan, Vasco, back in his walking and talk-ing days, withdrawing cash while a woman waited just inside the door. A tough angle, high and from the side—but it was her. The woman this Maven kid had been fighting over. A lot of fucking clubs he'd hit over the weekend, but sometimes, late on a Sunday night, you get lucky.

Lash pocketed the photo and the address, thinking about Mr. I'm Getting By.

MAVEN ROUNDED THE CORNER AND POPPED THE BATTERY FROM HIS phone, slipping both into a trash can. Outside the Tam across from the dark marquee of the Cutler Majestic Theatre, the door to an idling taxi van opened. Maven ducked inside, sitting next to Royce and across from Danielle.

Royce said, "What the fuck happened?"

Maven glanced at Danielle, just a half second, enough to read that she had been playing dumb.

"Nothing. There was a cop in the manager's office."

"A cop?"

"Random thing. Couple of questions."

"Well? Was it nothing, or was it nothing?"

"It was nothing."

Royce sat back with a frown. He knocked on the partition and the driver pulled away.

"I guess we're done at Precipice for a while." Royce turned, watching Maven. "Fighting on the dance floor? That's something I expect out of Glade, not you. What the fuck happened to staying out of trouble? What's wrong with you?"

Maven looked at Danielle. She was looking out the window.

Maven said, "I don't know."

CIPHER

SAMARA WANTED TO BUY HIM A SWEATER. "I DON'T KNOW WHY, I just think it's going to be a cold fall."

They were walking through the Center Court of the Prudential Center in shorts and T-shirts. "No girl has ever bought me anything before."

"Something nice. So you have to *promise* me you like it. No politeness." She was going through her bag for something, but instead came upon a crumpled envelope and pulled it out. "Oh—and having mail sent to my place?"

It was from the Massachusetts Registry of Motor Vehicles. His motorcycle registration. He didn't want the Marlborough Street addy linked to him on paper, and needed a street address for the bike.

"I meant to mention this," he told her. "The insurance is much higher if I garage this in the Back Bay than in Allston."

"Really? I would think it's the other way around."

"Insurance fraud is a year upstate, tops. I know you'll take the fall rather than rat me out."

A passing voice said, "Is that fucking Cipher?"

Maven didn't stop right away. His first impulse was to keep on walking.

The suit threw him off. As did the haircut, parted on the side, a few inches longer than regulation.

"You fucking pussy," said the guy. Big smile on his face. "Ho-lee shit. Cipher in the flesh."

"Clearwater," said Maven. "Jesus Christ."

They hugged in the middle of the shopping arcade, the older man in the pin-striped suit, Maven in cargo shorts. The backslaps came hard and loud until Clearwater shoved him off. "What the fuck are you doing here?"

"Fucking minding my own business. What about you? You were supposed to be a lifer."

"My twenty was up. I work in the Pru tower. Forty-fourth floor. Investments."

Maven said, "What, you have a career or something?"

"Or something. Jesus, you got fat."

Maven smiled. Clearwater was in good shape for a twice-divorced vet in his forties. Maven remembered Samara and introduced her.

"Apologies for the profanities," said Clearwater. "Army buddies."

"I figured," she said.

"It's just that I can't believe I'm back in civilization standing here with fucking Cipher."

"Cipher?" said Samara.

Clearwater said, "This kid. So fucking quiet when he came in. Borderline *challenged,* you know what I'm saying? We took bets on him, either this kid would be a total washout, crying into his pillow at night, or else the ultimate killing machine. I lost money on his ass, but he did us proud. Did us goddamned proud."

Maven shook his head, wanting Clearwater to shut up.

"Fifteen minutes," said Clearwater. He turned to Samara. "Gimme fifteen minutes with him, to catch up. You come too. I got stories that'll straighten your hair."

She smiled and shook her head. "I'm going to go cruise Saks. You guys catch up without me."

"Twenty minutes," said Clearwater.

"Fifteen," she said, blowing Maven a kiss and walking off.

Legal Sea Foods was nearest, the S-shaped bar empty at three o'clock, overlooking Boylston Street at the end of the arcade. Three quick shots of Hangar One led to a lot of shoulder squeezing and many more *fucks*.

"I looked up to you, man," said Maven. "We all did. You had it fucking figured out. You knew your shit. Mr. Been There, Fucked That."

"It was the uniform, boy. I put it on, I became that guy. Look at this fucking uniform now."

"Still getting it done though. Forty-fourth floor?"

"I'm just starting out. My brother-in-law, he brought me in."

"Whoa, hold up. Fucking married *again*?"

"Why the fuck you think I'm here clinging to you now?" Clearwater pushed away their glasses, loosened his necktie, ordered two more. "So what about you? No work on a weekday afternoon?"

"Flexible hours." The vodkas came, Maven's swimming pleasantly in his view. "Working for another vet now. Reminds me a little of you."

"Handsome feller, hm? What's his name, maybe I know him."

"Royce."

"Royce. Like a Rolls? That's his first name?"

"Brad."

"Brad Royce. Brad Royce." Clearwater brought his drink to his lips, then pulled it away before drinking. "I knew a Brad Royce in Germany."

Maven nodded. "Germany, yeah. Early nineties?"

"He looks like?"

Maven dithered. "Dark hair. I don't know."

"Royce. Roycey. Yeah. There fucking *was* a guy."

"A medic?"

"Nonononono. The Roycey I knew was an MP. Fucking ran that base. Shifty motherfuckers, the military police. Like fucking Newkirk, remember him, that RAF chap on *Hogan's Heroes*? You know, the *Family Feud* guy . . ."

"Richard Dawson."

"The same. Richard Dawson. Cool bloke. He's missed. Here's to Richard Dawson." Clearwater downed his drink.

Maven sipped his. "I think he's still alive."

"Hope so, we need more like him." Clearwater exhaled and set his shot glass down on the bar. "Where was I? Right—MPs. Fucking black marketeer, this little snake. Never trusted him. Supply battalion, he had it all sewed up. Porn. Electronics. Contraband."

Maven had a clogged feeling in his chest. "No. Not the same guy. Different Brad Royce."

"You fucking hope so. Fucking Roycey. I think about him sometimes, wonder where he's at. Guy like that. I wonder about a lot of guys. But not Cipher. Not no more."

Maven stared at his drink, then swallowed it, grimacing through the hurt.

"One more," said Clearwater.

"No," said Maven, putting out his hand.

Samara arrived with a Barneys New York shopping bag. "I've been calling you."

"Uh-oh," said Clearwater.

Maven fumbled out his phone. "I had it set to vibrate."

"You didn't feel it?"

"Not really feeling much of anything right now."

"Blame me," said Clearwater, trying to pay.

Maven refused, laying out the cash himself.

"Look at you," said Clearwater.

Outside, at the escalator leading down, Clearwater had a big hug for both Maven and Samara. His jacket was crumpled over his arm and his shirt was puffed out of the waist of his pants. "You're a sweetheart," he said to Samara, then punched Maven in the chest. "You too."

Clearwater stepped onto the escalator, riding it down to street level.

Samara turned to Maven, more scandalized than angry. "Are you drunk?"

Maven shook his head. "Just out of practice."

"Still up for the movie?"

"Absolutely."

He didn't stop thinking about Clearwater's Royce until ten minutes after the opening credits, when he fell asleep.

Maven rode out to Quincy following the same route he used to jog on his runs home from the parking lot. Now he was on a Harley Softail, the late-night air rippling his leather jacket.

He cut the engine at the pumps outside City Oasis, rolling silently to the front window. Through the phone-plan ads and milk prices stuck to the glass, he saw Ricky slumped on a stool behind the counter, patrol cap atop his head. Maven watched him for a long minute, Ricky kind of staring off, mumbling to himself.

Ricky saw him then, and his smile went ear-wide before he could contain it. He came around the counter, out through the bell-rigged doors.

Ricky was skinnier and shorter than Maven recalled, or maybe it was Maven's bootheels.

"I told you I'd be by."

Ricky wiped his dry mouth with the back of his hand, trying to squash his giddy grin. He was taking a good look at the bike. "Holy shit."

"Take her for a spin."

Ricky shook his head. "I don't want to ride it. I want to make out with it."

Maven got him to sit on the seat. Ricky tried out the handlebars, then shook his head, giggling a little. "Fuck you."

"I know it."

"You fuckin' dick."

They were both all smiles.

Ricky said, "Check out my ride."

Parked near the 75-cent air dispenser was a twenty-year-old, pea green Pontiac Parisienne. "Seriously?" said Maven.

Ricky stood by it with pride. It was a sweet sled in its own retro way: gas tank cap behind the pull-down rear license plate; original velour upholstery; original radio. The kind of lean four-door sedan an undercover 1980s TV detective would drive.

"This is the tits," said Maven, relieved not to have to bullshit him.

"Needs some transmission work. Suspension. Brakes. But I like it."

Inside, Ricky treated Maven to a blue raspberry Slush, poured with a shaky hand. "Store's the same, huh? I tried to pick up some day shifts, but the sun fucks with me. Needling headaches."

They caught up a bit, interrupted by two paramedics coming in for cigarettes and junk food, who failed to see the irony. Ricky was brisk with them, borderline rude, throwing their change so he could get back to Maven, as though he were afraid Maven would disappear again.

"How's your thing?" Ricky asked. "Going good?"

"It's going. You know."

"If it doesn't work out, you can always . . ."

"Yeah. Good to know." They smiled.

"I'm checking in the newspapers now. He's got me doing the candy order once a week, though I always screw it up." Ricky pulled off his cap, rubbing at his eye with the heel of his hand, swiping sweat off his brow. Giving Maven a good look at the ding in his head, where his hair would never grow back.

The door chimed, a transvestite walking in with his head held high. Maven remembered the guy. He went straight to the customer bathroom, as always.

"Nothing really changes in my world," said Ricky.

They talked more about his car until the tranny came out of the bathroom and brought some Schick Quattro blades to the counter.

"Fuck," sighed Ricky.

"It's cool," said Maven, settling him down. He pointed to the EMPLOYEES ONLY door. "I'm gonna . . ."

"Sure."

Maven saw his blue tongue and lips in the lopsided mirror over the employee toilet. He was a different guy from the one who used to stand here taking a leak. He flushed, splashed some water on his hands, looked around for a roll of paper towels. He didn't find any, instead seeing a leather pouch tucked up on the sill of the high, frosted window.

He dried his hands on the thighs of his jeans, staring at this thing. He reached up and pulled it down. He unzipped it.

Inside was a glass-barreled needle and a length of rubber tubing, and a glass ampoule of clear fluid. The white manufacturer's label read, "2 ml Fentanyl Citrate—WARNING: May Be Habit Forming."

Maven knew fentanyl. A prescription drug for cancer patients or long-term pain management. Like OxyContin but more powerful. Something like eighty times more potent than heroin.

Maven went cool and shaky, as though he'd hit up on the stuff just by holding the kit in his hands. He zipped it shut and set it back on the sill. He stood there a long time, immobilized, until he realized that the longer he waited, the better the chance Ricky would know he'd been found out.

Ricky was tearing open a pack of Sour Patch Kids when Maven returned. Ricky was smiling, but everything had slowed down for Maven. He fixed on Ricky's froth-white skin and raccoon-mask eyes. The sweat stain around his collar.

"Tyra's coming on soon," said Ricky. "You gonna hang out, watch with me?"

Maven couldn't remember what he said, or how he did it, but he got away soon after that and took the long way home.

BOUNTY

LASH MET TRICKY AT DAWN ON THE BEACH AT COLUMBIA POINT.
They crossed Day Boulevard into the park, walking wide around
some citizens doing a daybreak boot-camp exercise class, running
up bleachers and frog-walking across the field while instructors
barked at them.

"Here's two hundred bones, please kick my ass," said Trick,
the scar on his neck tightening as he chuckled within his hoodie.
He had been about Rosey's age when Lash saved his life on that
Mattapan sidewalk. Rosey was still laid out in bed, snoring like
a bear when Lash decamped, having stumbled in a few hours
earlier. He'd been going with a girl recently. He had a lot of
friends.

They crossed Old Colony near the JFK/UMass station, staying
wide of the commuters, drifting underneath a bridge.

"Fuckers staying busy," said Tricky. "I ain't heard all that much,
past couple a weeks, but I don't hear everything neither."

Lash said, "Street prices going up."

"Up, up, up. Cost of doing business. Supply drying up all over. Seller's market out here."

No economic system was as pure and elastic as street economy. Tricky showed Lash what he had brought him here for, the tag on the stanchion beneath the bridge, painted red and fresh: BANDITS 25/PER D-O-A.

"A street bounty," said Tricky. "Twenty-five g's each. Dead or alive."

"That's a lot of bones."

"Four bandits is six figs. Tol' you this serious. Somebody gonna get *popped*."

Lash foresaw dead-enders banding together, bandits hunting the Bandits, turning Boston into the Wild West. "Who put it out?"

"We in Broadhouse turf, but I'd put it on L or C." Lockerty or Crassion, the other two Pins. "Probably Lockerty. It's his house getting hurt the most."

"You know this?"

"Who knows anything? It's what I hear."

"You wouldn't just be protecting your own boss?"

"My boss of bosses. That'd be like you hustling to protect your top man in D.C. Broads can take care hisself."

Lash unfolded the ATM surveillance photo, another copy, this one without Maven's vitals on the back. Showed it to Tricky.

Tricky pointed to Vasco. "That Bob?"

"Who's Bob?"

"What you call a guy, cut off his arms and legs, throw him in the river."

Lash nodded. "That's Bob. Vasco, the Venezuelan. What about the woman?"

"Shit. I remember blondes much better." An ambulance siren went screaming past them, down the Southeast Expressway. "You got my attention though."

"It could be coincidence, a blind alley, nothing."

"Not if you're showing it to me." Tricky one-eyed the photo, working through it. "A girl, huh? Part of the outfit? What you think?"

Lash didn't tell Tricky about the phantom minutes on Vasco's mobile, and the bum numbers to a temp phone. Or what Schramm said about needing somebody close to get access to Vasco's phone. The Venezuelan's credit card indicated a bunch of restaurant charges in the weeks leading up to his death, the amounts indicating dinners for two.

The sun was coming up over the first buildings, oranging the bridge. Lash folded up the photo printout. "Let me hear from you. Anything. I want to be the one to settle this, not leave it to the streets. And, hey—if I hear you cashing in these mo-mos yourself, we don't have a pleasant relationship no more, you feel me?"

Tricky flat-smiled him from within his heavyweight hoodie cowl. "I'll take that under consideration."

Painted Rock

T ERMINO MUST HAVE TIPPED ROYCE, BECAUSE ROYCE WAS IN THE kitchen pouring himself a glass of FIJI water when they got back from the surveillance.

Glade started speaking as soon as the door was closed. "So now there's a fucking price on our heads."

They had overheard their name during a ghost-phone snoop. Bad guys talking about a bounty on the Sugar Bandits, making plans accordingly.

Royce said, "That scares you."

Glade rocked back as though Royce had swung a pillow at him. "It doesn't make me feel good."

"It's a mark of honor. A sign of respect."

Glade smiled sideways, looking at Royce as if he were being put on. "Okay, I gotta call bullshit on that one."

Termino, laying his keys on the counter, said, "What'd you expect? We'd steal from these kingpins, and they'd like it?"

Royce said, "We stay tight, stay alert—we're solid. Nothing has changed."

Suarez said, "Nobody expected us before. We swooped in like ghosts. Now they're looking for us. Waiting for us—expecting us."

Maven said, "These guys are hiring cops now. That's right—real cops. Dirty cops."

Royce keyed in on that. "More."

Maven said, "They got on to a BPD cop out of Hyde Park, and his partner."

"You get names?"

Maven nodded.

"They're paying protection?"

"For an escort. Sellers and buyers going in fifty-fifty."

"How much?"

"Five hundy a key."

Royce nodded, wheels turning. "That's a good piece. What's the load?"

"Between eighty and a hundred twenty keys."

Royce smiled after a moment. "The tougher it gets to move the goods, the more they have to try to shove through at once. The more we take down, the bigger the scores that come to us."

Glade said, "Did you miss the part about the cops?"

"So what?" said Royce. "As long as it's not a surprise. We still have all the advantages. Anything we see coming we can neutralize."

Suarez sat down on one of the padded stools, taking weight off his healing leg. "People coming at us now, instead of the other way around—that changes the game."

"So we change with it. Come on. You've all dealt with insurgents before. This is the fun part. Unless you guys want to tail off, feel you have enough money . . ."

Maven grinned. Royce challenging them and enticing them at the same time. Playing Glade and Suarez like puppies.

Royce said, "How much you all worth anyway? Maybe I'll turn you in myself."

Begrudging smiles. Termino went to get himself a beer.

Royce said, "Step back and see this for what it is. This says we are making a significant impact. It says we are now the Man in town. Not the fuzz. Not the kingpins. Us, right here. And nobody knows anything about us, and nobody's gonna know anything about us. So long as we stay razor sharp, as always."

After silent nods, Glade said, "So, what, do we drop these guys? Wait for the next gig?"

"Are you high? Eighty to one hundred twenty keys?"

Termino returned with his beer. "Hell, fifty keys would be a major score."

"But," said Glade, "how're we gonna work around cops?"

Royce looked at Termino. A thinking look, not a knowing look. Maven was still trying to read Royce. This turn of events had the side effect of revealing Royce and Termino's partnership within the crew. Termino was Royce's eyes and ears with the rest of them—which meant what? Was Royce being careful? Or concerned about something else?

Roycey.

Maven had all but ruled out Clearwater's characterization. There had to be many Brad Royces out there. Plus, Clearwater's memory had been a little squishy about other things.

Royce said, "All we've been through, and sometimes I think you haven't learned a goddamn thing. Who's got the most to lose in this whole thing? Not us, no. Hiding behind a badge—that makes a dirty cop supervulnerable. If we play it right."

Suarez sat forward. "And how is that?"

Royce started to speak as the door opened. Danielle stepped inside, the five of them clustered around the granite countertop like players over a Stratego board. She wore tight jeans and a long, hippie-type blouse of thin, white linen, cinched up and bow-tied halfway down her waist, making a shelf for her chest.

She said, "You forgot to put up the NO GIRLS ALLOWED sign."

Royce said, "What is it, darling?"

"I need to borrow Maven." She turned to Maven. "I need a ride."

Maven felt the others stir. He had become her unofficial chauffeur, and that had been all right with him in the beginning, when he was getting to know her. Now she expected him to come when she snapped. Now it made him look different in their eyes.

Maven said, "We're right in the middle of something here."

She rolled her eyes. "What do you want? Me to say 'please'?"

Maven nodded. "Yeah."

"Fine. Please."

Something in her eyes showed him that her "please" was real. She needed him, not just as a driver. He checked with Royce, who gave his permission with a hand wave.

Maven stood and caught the car keys she tossed him.

MAVEN PULLED OUT OF THE ALLEY AT THE WHEEL OF ROYCE'S LATEST ride, a Mercedes-Benz Black Series two-seater. "Why couldn't your boyfriend drive you?"

"I wanted you."

"Why is that?"

Her head was turned toward the window, the radio playing so low that only the bass notes were audible. "I have to go back to Gridley, that's why."

"Gridley? What in God's name for?"

"Just drive. Please."

Another please. He waited for her to say something more, but she just sat there. "Fine," said Maven, plucking Royce's sunglasses from the visor, pushing the car into gear, and rolling out toward Storrow Drive.

She was quiet most of the way. Little pieces of the town had changed since his youth, but not so that it mattered. She directed him to a street he had never been down before, a 1980s-era development. It had an Indian name then, one he couldn't recall now. The sign that had announced it was gone.

"Pull over on the street."

He set the parking brake outside a house of dark brown wood, set back behind trees, its roof coated with green needles. A curtain flickered in a downstairs window.

"Christ, there they go," said Danielle, picking up her clutch off the floor. "Freaking out about who's parked outside their house. So fucking frightened in their small world, God."

Maven made out silhouettes behind the sheer curtain. People looking out without realizing they themselves could be seen. "Is this your parents' house?"

Danielle pulled out a small vial and poured a bump of cocaine onto the webbing of her left hand.

Maven said, "Hey—what the fuck do you think you're—"

"Oh, fucking relax *please.*"

She upped it, trying to improve her mood. Maven's dropped halfway between sickened and pissed off. "Where are you getting this shit?"

"What do you care? You don't want any."

"I care because I'm in the car with you, driving you around . . ."

"Oh, grow up. Jesus."

"You have a problem."

"No, what I have here is a solution." She did another bump, delicately, in a practiced way.

"Jesus, Danny."

She stuffed the vial inside the front left pocket of her jeans. "Just—shut up and come inside with me and be my friend, okay? For fifteen minutes. Okay?"

Maven got out of the Mercedes and followed her down the long driveway to the door. The shadows behind the window didn't answer the bell until the second ring.

Danielle Vetti's father was tall but without much bearing, a thin, gray mustache topping his mouth, a long, brown cardigan sloping off his shoulders over corduroy pants and slipper shoes. Danielle's mother appeared behind him, wearing a heavier sweater, looking stern and concerned. They both had napkins tucked into their collars. The smell of broiled poultry and stewed vegetables passed through the screen.

"You remembered," said Mr. Vetti.

Danielle nodded. "So can I come in?" Challenging him, as though the answer might be no.

She pulled open the screen door, and Maven followed her inside. She made no introductions, so he mumbled, "Hello," and the Vettis nodded back with suspicion.

Danielle rounded the corner to a formal dining room. The long table was set for three, a chair at either end, and a special high-backed wheelchair in the middle. Maven remembered the Vetti family at that restaurant so long ago, the day he discovered—as though it were a scandal—that the hottest senior girl in high school had a handicapped sister.

Danielle leaned around the chair, whispering to its occupant, rubbing her sister's forearm. Maven could not see around the chair back. He was acutely aware of the parents standing near him, ready to leap to intervene.

"I've already served the meal," announced Mrs. Vetti.

Danielle stiffened, then finished what she was saying to her sister, and turned. "Call us down when it's time for cake."

She walked to the stairs, leaving Maven to step past her parents and follow her. He passed two school portraits of Danielle's sister—heavily filtered, her face the center of a cloud, her eyes focused on something way beyond the camera—but none of Danielle.

Upstairs, Danielle entered a room with a stripped-down bed and a bare bureau and sealed boxes. She looked around, then stepped to the window and looked out onto the back slope of a lower section of roof, and the yard below.

"This is the window I used to sneak out of."

She slid open the closet door, revealing plastic storage tubs, garbage bags full of old clothes, and more boxes. From the top shelf she pulled down an oversize book with a hard, black cardboard cover. She set it on the bed, opened it, and returned to the closet.

A modeling portfolio. Maven was struck by the way she set it out for him, with no explanation, no indication that it might be important to her that he see it.

Full-color headshots and swimsuit shots. Various advertisements, some torn right out of magazines, others bordered with product and model info. A few studio shots featuring different, outdated hairdos, of the kind you might have seen hanging on a wall at Supercuts in the late 1990s. Danielle smiling; Danielle pouting; Danielle tossing back her head in laughter. A jeans ad featuring her twirling a lasso and wearing dusty chaps. A Ralph Lauren–style shot of her playing croquet with a shirtless, unmuscled boy. And an underwear ad, a moody, soft-core Calvin Klein knockoff of Danielle sitting on a closed toilet seat in a scooped bra and lace panties, staring out at him from a decade ago, calling to him to come back in time.

He looked up. She had the vial out of her pocket again. She didn't want to answer any questions from him, didn't want to explain herself. Intimacy on her terms alone.

"You know the first time I did coke? Out in the woods during sixth-period study hall, junior year. One of the funnest days in my life. You know who gave it to me? Alex. Your sister."

"What makes you think I want to know this?"

She dumped another lump onto her fist and hit up again. "One of the funnest days ever."

Her mother's voice called up from downstairs. "Danielle?"

Downstairs Danielle refused a chair, crouching instead at her sister's side. Her name was Doreen. Her mouth sagged under red-rimmed eyes, her tremulous arms pale and swollen. Her fingernails were long, responsible for the scratches on her neck and face. Her hair was the same shade as Danielle's, but short, home-cut.

A cake sat before her. One layer, frosted purple. Two candles in the center.

Mrs. Vetti sang "Happy Birthday," and Mr. Vetti quietly joined in. Danielle just stared at the cake, not opening her mouth, not even faking it.

When they finished the song, Danielle blew out the twin candles for her sister.

Mrs. Vetti lifted two wrapped boxes to the table, and Doreen's eyes found them immediately. Her downturned lips straightened into something like excitement, her tongue moving within her mouth.

"Here, Dory," said Danielle, digging into her jeans pocket. For an insane moment, Maven thought she was going to pull out the vial of coke. She drew out a soft blue velvet jewelry pouch. "Open mine first."

Danielle opened it for her, lifting out a stunning bracelet of platinum hearts spaced with purple amethyst gemstones. She held it out for her to see, then fixed the clasp around her younger sister's trembling wrist.

"It looks pretty," said Danielle.

"Pre-tty," repeated Doreen. Though she seemed more taken with the velvet pouch it had come in.

Mrs. Vetti said, "That is much too fine for her."

Danielle responded with a long, uncomfortable stare.

Mrs. Vetti pretended not to notice, picking up one of the wrapped presents. "Look, Doreen." She ripped it open. "A pillow. A new pillow. Hypoallergenic."

Maven stared at Danielle, wondering what she might do. Danielle was touching the bracelet on her sister's wrist, petting it with one finger.

Mr. Vetti, oblivious to the gift giving, asked her, "Where are you living now?"

Danielle did not answer. She never even turned to acknowledge the question. She looked at her sister's face, then hugged her in her seat, pressing her cheek against Doreen's cheek, whispering, "I love you," then standing and walking out to the foyer.

Doreen touched her cheek with her long-nailed hand, finding it wet from Danielle's tears. She wiped hard, nearly slapping herself, wanting the wetness off her.

The screen door slammed, and Maven realized that Danielle had left.

*   *   *

SHE HAD HIM PULL OVER IN FRONT OF BEANO'S PACKIE, UNDER AN arrow sign made up of flashing red, white, and blue bulbs. "You wanna get us a sixer?" she said.

"Look, Danny, you don't want to—"

"Fine," she said, throwing open the door and getting out. "Jesus."

THEY LEFT THE MERCEDES IN AN OLD OFFICE PARK AND WALKED past large mounds of excavated earth left over from the office park's construction decades before. Danielle led the way into the adjoining lot of undeveloped land, bordering the commuter rail tracks.

The Pits, as the area was known to Gridley teenagers, over-lapped Gridley and neighboring Avon. Shared police jurisdic-tion—and being accessible only on foot—meant essentially no police jurisdiction, and so into this no-man's-land came the party kids looking for a weekend place to drink and hang.

Danielle set down the bag of beer, pulling out a quart of Mount Gay rum. "Fuck, look at this wasteland." The low areas were littered with cans, bottles, and rotting tires. "And this was it. This was the place. Our Club Precipice. This shithole."

Maven pulled a Red Stripe out of the bag. She of course bought beer that required a bottle opener. Maven had been in a similar fix many times in Eden. He hooked one of his lower inci-sors under the serrated edge of the cap, biting down, using his teeth for an opener. He spit out the cap and drank half at a gulp.

"I have to see that again," said Danielle.

He opened one for her.

"I'm gonna clip you on my key chain," she said, turning and wandering, double-fisted, toward the unfenced tracks.

Maven drank again. Now he was her babysitter. He went to a

big rock slathered with years of graffiti, that the kids used to call Painted Rock, and leaned against it, facing the tracks.

He had been here once in high school, taken by a friend who straddled the line between outcast and in-crowd. They took turns drinking one bottle of horribly sour white wine while nobody talked to them. After a while he and his friend went off exploring, thinking maybe they could spy into some bedroom windows from atop the high dunes. When they came back, some kid who was popular but not tough asked if they were gay, which got everyone laughing because it was so hilarious to pick on losers. So Maven went back along the paths to a dead raccoon they had seen, picking it up by its tail and coming back to drop it into the comedian's lap while he sat talking to some girl. The kid totally lost his shit and went running off screaming across the train tracks, slapping at himself as though his clothes were on fire, and Maven and his friend split, having had not such a bad night after all.

Someone had erected a cairn of stones from the track bed, and Danielle was dismantling it, hurling the stones into the trees, one by one. Maven watched her, wondering why that DEA cop would be asking questions about her and not Royce.

"Hey!" he said. "Come off of there."

She turned and flipped him off. "What, you think I'm going to jump in front of an oncoming train or something? Trains jump in front of *me*, fuck." She yelled it loud, both ways down the tracks: "*Fuck!*" The echoes carried off like escaping footsteps.

Maven smashed his bottle and opened another with his teeth. Everything smelled the same as it had those interminable summers, growing up. Wildflowers and berries, everything baking in the sun.

Danielle tossed her beer bottle, which landed in the bushes and did not shatter. She turned to walk off the tracks and stumbled on the stones, falling onto her ass. She kicked at the offending stones, smiling at herself, but didn't get up. She sat there staring at Maven.

"What?" he said.

"You. Either you hate me right now, or you love me."

Maven felt a cool tingle. "What are you talking about?"

"Nobody else puts up with me. Nobody bothers. You waste soooo much time on your boss's girlfriend."

"It's true."

"Okay. That's not hate."

Maven was annoyed enough to be truthful. "Then I guess I'm just another idiot in a long line of idiots."

"I wonder who has the lower opinion of themselves, you or me?"

"It's me."

"But you don't act out." She took another drink, squinting up and down the sunny tracks. "Birthdays suck, you know that?"

She tossed the open quart of rum over to him. He caught it without spilling any and took a drink.

She got to her feet, still looking down the line at the train tracks heading into the city. "I was going to get magazine covers. I was going to make a million dollars and Doreen was going to come to New York with me, and I was going to take care of her." She looked back at Maven with a smile that was pure pain. "And look how that turned out. Look how *I* turned out."

Maven didn't know what to say, or how to say it. She came over and took the rum back from him and drank.

"What else can you do with your teeth?" she asked, looking at him. "I had a friend who could do that thing where you knot a cherry stem with your tongue. She tried to teach me, but I sucked at it." She was squinting, her face angled up toward the sun. "I want to see your tattoo."

"I don't have any tattoos."

"The one that says BORN TO LOSE, where is it?" She raised his shirt, revealing his torso, halfheartedly trying to turn him around. "On your shoulders?"

"Hey," he said, not persuasively.

Her hands stayed on his hard chest, flat but tender, a cross between a tickle and a caress. "This thing you have for me, Gridley. It's not just a freshman hard-on, is it?"

"What thing?"

She grinned and pressed up against him, hands sliding down to his hips, just above the waistband of his cargo shorts. "You still think I'm something, don't you?"

"I . . . Jesus . . . I know you are."

His shirt was still up around his armpits, and she was brushing her clothed chest against his bare torso. He was getting hard against her hip. "What about your girlfriend? What would she say if she saw—"

"Don't talk about her."

Danielle's mouth came up to his neck. She nuzzled his throat, whispering, "You ever think about me when you're with her?"

He hadn't done anything yet. His hands were still down at his sides. He was trying to think about Royce. Trying to remind himself of all the things the man had done for him. But it wasn't going well.

He said into her ear, "You know I do."

She kissed him on the mouth. Firm, yet yielding. Tasting, wanting to be tasted.

He was right up at that line. That line he would not cross. Because once across it, he was all in.

She tugged on the front of his shorts. She was undoing his belt. Unbuttoning the top button.

He touched her arms. Didn't grab or hold them. A halfhearted protest at best.

"What?" She had his shorts open. She wasn't stopping.

"Just . . . not here . . . not this way."

She said, "Don't you know by now that nothing ever happens the way you think it will?"

She untied her blouse and pulled it off her shoulders, hooking her thumbs into the straps of her bra and bringing them down so that her breasts fell over the band.

He was on overload. He was so hard, he could barely feel her hand gripping him.

"Jesus," she said.

If only he had known, he would have jerked off that morning. He told her, "We might have to go twice."

At some point, a midafternoon train raced past, Maven vaguely aware of the warning horn, the boulder vibrating beneath them. The rest was all a collision of past and present, of desire and attainment.

THEN THE DRIVE HOME.

Maven started twenty different conversations in his head, none of which made it out of his mouth. Danielle sat with her eyes closed, probably not sleeping. Dreaming, maybe, but not sleeping.

Her smell was all over him. He didn't regret this yet, if he would at all. He only wanted to know, what next? What do we do now? Will this ever happen again?

He backed into the alley garage, killed the engine, pressed the steering-wheel button to lower the garage door.

She turned to him and kissed him before he could speak, long but not deep. A shut-up kiss. She got out of the car, and he did the same.

Royce was coming downstairs with Termino as they went up. Maven was a few steps behind Danielle.

"Everything okay?" Royce asked, stopping.

Danielle shrugged and said, "Ask Gridley," walking past him to the third floor.

Royce watched her go a moment, then turned to Maven. Maven gripped the handrail tightly, transferring all his panic there, so that the rest of him looked relaxed.

Royce said, "That bad, huh? You look like you've been through the wringer."

Maven felt Termino eyeing him more than Royce. "She, uh . . . we split a six-pack."

Royce nodded and continued down the stairs, patting Maven lightly on the shoulder. "You could have said no, you know."

Maven didn't like the grin Termino gave him as he went past.

GYROSCOPE

MAVEN HEARD THE BLOW-DRYER TURN OFF. HE ROLLED OVER, sunlight slanting across the rumpled white comforter. The bathroom door opened and Samara came out dressed in a tan and brown suit.

Maven pushed up a bit, his bare shoulders and his head visible. "Another interview?"

"For a job I don't even really want. With a company that probably won't hire me. My career counselor suggested a few test interviews to warm up." She found her wristwatch on the nightstand, next to his. "Wish I had your life."

"No." Maven picked up the toy gyroscope next to the alarm clock. A physics course requirement her sophomore year. "Just my hours."

He wound the string through the eyehole and got it spinning on the pad of his finger, the rotor tumbling inside the whirring gimbals while the exterior remained fixed.

She put in earrings. "Trouble at home?"

"Huh?" he said, unable to look up from the inner workings of the device.

"I like you spending time here, don't get me wrong. I just can't tell if it's me or that you need a place to chill."

He transferred the gyroscope to the middle finger of his opposite hand so that he could reach for her leg where her skirt stopped below her knee. "Why don't you stay awhile if the interview is a nothing?"

She batted away his hand. "You're a bad influence." She walked away into the kitchen. "Now—out of my bed."

She was gone by the time he emerged from the shower. He tossed his things into his backpack, finding his MP3 player on her laptop—Samara was a Freestyle music freak, late-1980s and early-1990s dance tunes, which she loaded onto his player while he slept—and headed out the door with his pack slung over one shoulder, munching toast.

As he turned off the stoop toward Cambridge Street, a body exited a parked car across the street. Maven did not turn to look. He kept on walking toward the busy intersection, listening to the shoes scuffing the sidewalk behind him. If it was a gunman, this was going to be bad. He made ready to throw off his backpack, stopping and turning fast.

"Easy there, tiger." It was the DEA agent, Lash, wearing a long, asphalt-colored raincoat, a pen and a small notebook in his hand like a reporter.

Maven looked around for more agents. Lash was alone.

"You should really go down to the registry, update your license. Seems you no longer live in Quincy. In fact, it seems you have no known address. Got your motorcycle regged here, yet you're not on the lease and the landlord doesn't know you."

Maven nodded, but inside he was cursing himself. Still—better to do this here than outside Marlborough Street.

"I got some bill collectors on me, I'm saving up to pay them off."

"Must be some heavy bills. You're living here now?"

"Kind of bouncing around with friends. Getting back on my feet."

Lash smiled. "You look pretty solid on your feet, you ask me." Lash put away the pen and notebook. "I wonder what it is you're up to."

Maven gave him his best shrug. "Just trying to live my life, man."

"I was going to ask your girlfriend when she came out, but I thought I'd give you a shot at explaining yourself first."

Maven bristled at the thought of Samara being buttonholed by a federal agent.

"Now, I did you a solid there," said Lash. "Least you can do is answer a couple of questions."

Maven turned his hands up in a gesture of *Go ahead*.

"Had any more time to think about that girl you were fighting over?"

Danielle again. "When do I get to know what the hell this is about? You said you were from the Drug Enforcement Agency?"

"Administration."

"What?"

"It's the Drug Enforcement Administration. Common mistake."

"Okay. What does anything have to do with me?"

"That's what I'm here about."

"Nothing, is what this has to do with me. I stay far away from that shit. Would a piss test get you off my back?"

"Probably not."

"Okay . . ."

"I don't waste my time with end users. That's like picking crumbs out of the carpet. They got vacuum cleaners for that shit. I'm about where these crumbs break off from. The big cookie, shall we say."

Maven shook his head. "No idea what the hell you're talking about."

Lash smiled, having trouble reading Maven. "See, there's this gang of thieves going around, ripping off players. High-level players. Six-figure deals, not street-corner shakedown. They hit the transaction itself, knocking out both sides, buyers and sellers, pocketing the cash but trashing the stash."

Maven put forward a shrug. "Sounds good to me. I don't see the problem."

"Problem is, that's my job they're doing. And not doing it well. Busting up sales without jailing any dealers just ramps things up out on the street. Makes bad people paranoid, and paranoid people crazy."

Maven said nothing, waiting.

"This spring, I had this importer, name of Gilberto Vasco, a Venezuelan, highly placed, thaw out dead in the Charles, his hands and tongue cut off. Seems he'd been taken off by these guys a few months before. Now you say, 'What's one less drug dealer?' And you're right. No argument from me. But dig this. These bandits who maybe think they're on their way to becoming folk heroes— this murder could just as easily get pinned on them. So there's that."

Lash was looking for a reaction. Maven tried hard not to give him one.

"Here's another funny thing I figured out. All the drugs being junked and the money being stolen—as much as I can guesstimate, anyway—source from two of the three kingpins in the Greater Boston area. Three pipelines of product, two of which keep getting blown up, while the third—it just keeps flowing. Untouched."

Maven didn't know how much of this was true. Maybe Lash was trying to trick him. "Again, I don't know what—"

"Somebody's taking drug profits off the table. Upsetting the balance of things. Now this shit is starting to boil over, it's coming to a head. I'm telling you this vet to vet. Something's gotta give. The bottom line, if you need one, is that all this bullshit makes my job harder. And I don't need the competition, or the aggravation. I'm gonna put a stop to it, one way or another."

Lash fished around inside his pocket for something, a business card. He scribbled his mobile number on the back, then tucked the card into Maven's jacket pocket with a generous smile.

"See you around."

Unstoppable Ninjas

MAVEN STILL CONSIDERED HIMSELF FAITHFUL AND LOYAL TO Royce. He did this by confecting a clear rationale for his actions: he was not hooking up with the girlfriend of the man who made him; he was hooking up with a girl about whom he used to fantasize. It was a separate thing, a special thing. Danielle was like a dream he could slip into at will.

This druglike high of sexual attraction made bearable the drug-sick lows, the yearning, the worry. They had hooked up twice since, once in a Marriott in Natick, once at a Hilton in Dedham. Maven tried to avoid Royce, without seeming to avoid him, a plan that could last only so long. He tried to avoid Danielle too, at least when in the others' eyes. The subterfuge wore on him.

He heard his own paranoia echo back at him in the voices of the marks they were snooping on. The dealers were consumed with security measures. The Sugar Bandits were deep inside their heads, haunting every move. They had their cop running criminal checks on any passing car deemed suspicious, which made them tricky to eyeball. Maven didn't like the resulting lack of physical sur-veillance. It didn't feel complete, leaning so heavily on telephone intercepts and ghost-phone spooking. Like listening to a movie on radio. Getting maybe 40 percent of the details and having to intuit the rest.

The cop: he was the key to all this. Instead of making their job harder, he actually made it a little bit easier because, as the dealers' perceived ace in the hole, they took few other special precautions. The cop boasted of his knowledge of security measures and hinted at some special insight into the inner workings of the bandits. The exchange was to be a standard meet, consummated at a Hyde Park auto repair shop owned by one of the cop's friends. A transport truck would rendezvous with them at the Sturbridge rest area of the Massachusetts Turnpike and be tailed on the highway by the cop in his personal vehicle. He would provide a similar pickup for the sellers. This hours-long prelude to the deal only spoke to the cop's ignorance: the bandits could strike only at the point of transfer. Every other precaution was a waste of effort and time.

In puffing up his value to the dealers, the cop made out the bandits to be unstoppable ninjas with supernatural powers. They heard rumors about "Soviet-issued Uzis" and "government squads," someone even floating the scenario of "a crew of renegade cops." The cop insisted that the bandits had to have contacts inside the Boston Police Department drug unit, the "secret squirrels," which he would neutralize by monitoring them on his police radio's scrambled channels. He also warned the dealers to keep a keen eye out for helicopters.

The one thing the cop did right was to pick up a half dozen new "throwaway" push-to-talk phones to distribute to the principals on the morning of the gig. The sellers, however, still carried their per-sonal mobiles, one of which had been ghosted into a broadcaster. So Maven gleaned enough from one-way conversations to be able to time their arrivals.

The auto repair garage looked like a barn, with two drive-in bays and a small, windowed second floor set around the corner from the street. A large and incongruous tree shaded one side, an old factory behind it having been turned into warehouses, only one-third occupied but empty at night. The nearest residence was a good thirty-second walk down the street. Steady automobile traffic out on that end of Hyde Park Avenue provided decent noise cover.

Glade had set two getaway vehicles, each within an eighth of a mile of the job. Additionally, he had dropped off a stolen Subaru Outback that afternoon for an overnight brake-pad and oil change, now parked in the lot adjacent to the garage.

They approached on foot, after dark, Maven wearing armor underneath his jacket, blackout clothes, a face-hiding balaclava. He wore a Glock 17 handgun in the rear waistband of his pants, a "Mexican carry." He'd downed an iced-coffee drink outside the Rite Aid down the street earlier and wasn't sure now whether he felt actual dread now or just too much caffeine and sugar.

The transport was a box truck labeled EMPIRE MOVERS, a work vehicle from a legit moving company carrying actual cargo: discount patio furniture for delivery to an Ocean State Job Lot in New Hampshire. Fourteen hollow umbrella bases were packed with four-kilo bundles of ninety-plus-grade cocaine.

The cop circled the area once, then left to collect the buyers at an IHOP on Soldiers Field Road, with a quick stop to switch into his marked cruiser. After he was gone, Maven worked his way behind some shrubs at the corner of a tile warehouse diagonally across the side street.

The shop was quiet inside, a dim light visible through the blacked-out garage-door windows. He could not see the others, posted at varying distances from the shop, and came to feel that he was waiting an inordinate amount of time. Long enough for paranoia to seep in. He checked his timepiece—the one Royce had given him—then pulled the Glock, done over in dull gray matte and a nonglare finish, invisible in the night. He remembered Royce taking him aside the day before, telling him, "You handle this cop."

Maven said, "I thought you wanted me inside."

"I want you wherever the job is on the line. Wherever a fuckup can do us the most damage. Tomorrow, that's outside. I want the cop handled right. Unless you're afraid of him too?"

Maven shook his head.

"Milkshake and Suarez look at the uniform and still think, 'Daddy.' This guy is a piece of shit, nothing more. You understand that. So do it right."

Before, Maven had appreciated any special attention from Royce, never having been the first-in-the-class type. Now, in the grip of deceit, he analyzed every special request for signs of duplicity, always with the fear that Royce had found out about him and Danielle.

Headlights pulled into the side street. They swept the thick shrubs, Maven not moving. A conversion van, white and windowless in back. One garage door opened and Maven saw the corner of the box truck in the next service bay as the van backed inside. The cruiser did another creeping circle, the cop working his prowler light on the surrounding buildings. Fingers of light pierced the bushes, but died against Maven's blacked-out self.

The cruiser came back and parked in front of the garage. The cop then called in a report of suspicious activity on Factory Street. That gave him clearance on the active list with the dispatcher, and an excuse to light up his blue strobes.

Maven put his head down again as the blues cycled over the surrounding surfaces. He felt like a bar code that wouldn't scan. He switched off the safety on his Glock, switching off his own interior safety at the same time.

From his vest pocket he pulled the key fob to the Subaru Glade had dropped off earlier. Maven pressed the button on the remote starter. The automobile engine turned over, the car coming to life, automatic headlights flashing on, twin beams illuminating the side lot and part of the garage wall.

The cop popped out of his cruiser, leaving his door open as he drew his sidearm and flashlight and went to investigate. He came up on the rear left quarter of the Subaru wagon as though doing a traffic stop. He found the vehicle unoccupied, windows closed and doors locked. He ran his beam around the side lot but didn't see anyone. Then he backed off from the idling car. He looked this way and that. He was maybe realizing that a good cop can always call for backup, but a bad cop rides alone.

He decided that his cruiser was the best place to mull over the situation and quickly returned to it, holstering his sidearm. He moved too fast to see Maven hunched down behind the rear left fender. Maven grabbed his arm at the wrist and shoved the cop around, headfirst across the front seat of his cruiser. The cop smacked his head on his between-seats computer, and Maven relieved him of his sidearm. The cop tried to fight back, but he was facedown and powerless. Maven showed him his gun, then shoved him fully into the passenger seat.

The good thing about the harsh blue strobes was that they acted like an umbrella of distorting light. The lookout on the floor above the garage could not see clearly through them, looking down onto the light rack atop the roof of the cruiser.

Maven sat behind the wheel, breathing hard, watching the scared cop twist himself into a sitting position.

The cop said through deep sucks of air, "You know how many years you get for assaulting a cop?"

"Gimme the shirt."

"What?"

Maven yanked the cop's hat off his head, showing him the muzzle of the gun again. "The shirt."

The cop had this stung, pouting look, as if he had nothing else to lose and so wouldn't budge. Something about him reminded Maven of that Quincy cop coming into the City Oasis and buying skin mags every night. Maven hit him and the cop's nose broke open with blood.

"Gimme the fucking shirt!"

The cop took it off fast, having to unclip his radio handset from the shoulder. Maven took the shirt and then the cop's handcuffs, clasping one ring around the cop's near wrist.

"What are you doing?" wheezed the broken-nosed cop.

"Grab the wheel."

"What?"

Maven hit him again, this time on the ear.

"Fuck you!" yelled the cop. But he reached for the steering wheel.

Maven clasped the open cuff around his free wrist, shackling him to the wheel. Then he reached outside the still-open door and slid the cop's sidearm underneath the cruiser. He pulled the shirt on over his armored vest, buttoning every other button. He put on the hat.

The cop realized that this was his career right here. This was his life, his family's life. He yanked hard at the steering wheel, trying to get free. "You fucker. Give me a break here."

Maven found the cop's radio handset. He located the recessed orange button. The emergency button.

The cop said, "What the fuck . . . ?"

Maven pressed the panic button—then dropped the handset onto the seat and backed out of the cruiser.

The radio crackled immediately, a dispatcher broadcasting the cop's name and unit, asking if he was in trouble.

"You . . . you fuck . . ."

Maven locked eyes with the cop, letting him know what he thought of him—then hit the wailers a few times, the cruiser siren screaming short bursts into the night. Maven ducked out, running around the cruiser to the business entrance of the garage, the door opening as he arrived, the cop hat low over his eyes.

Termino rounded the corner, wielding an H&K MP5K with the folding stock extended at his shoulder, hitting the door at the same time Maven did. They went in hard, the dealers crumbling fast, going down onto their bellies, giving up weapons. They said nothing. They knew what was going down.

Termino braced the others while Maven hit a red button and the door rose on Glade and Suarez. Glade had a blade out, truck tires whining as he sliced them and they exhaled.

A police radio sat atop a tool cart, and the dispatcher's voice again called the cop's name and unit. The lookout must have had a radio too, because they heard footsteps above, then a sound like a window opening, and the grunt of a body dropping to the ground. Suarez went out to make sure the guy was running away.

The kilo packages and the cash were all set out on the floor near the emptied umbrella bases. Maven found a drum full of waste oil and cut open the kilos of powder and added them to the toxic waste. Termino bagged the cash, pausing to kick a guy who started crying and begging for his life. They heard sirens—probably every on-duty cop in Boston speeding to the garage to assist a comrade in trouble—and had to wind things up fast. Termino changed one detail at the last moment, deciding that it would be better to have multiple bodies fleeing the scene, and so got the dealers up and running.

Maven's last sight before fading into the escape route was the cop's cruiser parked in front, lights blazing, rocking with the effort of the officer trapped inside.

SPECIALISTS

THE TWO JAMAICANS DEPLANED AT T. F. GREEN AIRPORT IN WAR-
wick, Rhode Island, met their driver at the luggage carousel,
and claimed their leather travel bags. They watched the driver set
their bags into the trunk next to an identical third leather travel
bag before climbing into the backseat. They were large men, the
driver having to push his seat forward to accommodate the knees
of the one sitting behind him.

They stopped at a restaurant on Atwells Avenue for an order of
kingfish, fried plantains, and bottles of Bedroom Bully, an herbal
tonic said to promote sexual energy, and consumed the meal on
the drive up to Boston.

Ernesto Lockerty ran his drug-dom out of the second floor
of an old piano factory near Malone Park in Chelsea. He was
a half-Italian, half-Irish product of the neighborhood, who had
consolidated power through a combination of bare-knuckled
intimidation and Machiavellian savvy. While many street dealers in the Commonwealth of Massachusetts were aware of the

higher mandatory minimum penalty for Possession with Intent to Distribute within one thousand feet of a school, few were aware that this "school zone violation" included a hundred-foot radius around any park or playground. Lockerty's hallmark move was to draw his competition into zone-violation busts, sending them away for the minimum two-year first-offense felony stretch—whereupon Lockerty's people moved in to assume control of the newly vacated territory.

The Jamaicans, named Mr. Leroy and Mr. Moodle, carried the heavy third travel bag to the outer entrance of Lockerty's warehouse office, where they were expected. Lockerty's doorman made a friendly but firm attempt to frisk Mr. Leroy and found a grenade thrust into his hand, the striker lever compressed. The safety pin hung from the elongated nail of Mr. Leroy's left pinkie.

They pushed the doorman into the wide room. Lockerty did not rise from behind his table. A second man, named Fale, a brush cut in an old suit, looked at Lockerty to see if he should do something.

Lockerty remained still, alert. He said, "What the hell-o is this?"

Leroy stood the booby-trapped doorman in the center of the room and said to him, "You wan' end this anytime, jus' leggo, mon. We all blow."

Moodle set the travel bag down at his feet. Behind Lockerty hung shades as thick as mover's blankets, covering big windows set into the brick wall. Fale gripped his armrests, but followed Lockerty's lead.

Lockerty said, "What's the gimmick? I called you here."

"Like to make bonny first impression is all. You de big bout, yah?"

"Uh . . ."

"You Lockerty, you de top dog."

Fale turned to Lockerty. "Is this the guys?"

Moodle focused on Fale. "Whas' yer dance, mon? Feelin' feisty?"

"I just . . . I never seen . . ."

"Seen what, mon?"

Fale stammered it out: "You guys're white."

"Never seen white Jamaicans before, bra?" Moodle looked at Leroy, who was twiddling the keys of the only piano in the room, badly in need of tuning. "Alla time, we hear dis. You wan' dread bwoys comin' in smokin' ganja, dat it? You wan' Tosh and Marley inna here. Be my personal pleasure reeducatin' you bumbaklaat fools."

"Hold on, hold on," said Lockerty. "I think we're all here for the same thing."

Leroy came back to the travel bag. "Sure, dat. So give up what you know 'bout deese bandulus, sight?"

Lockerty shook his head after a moment, unable to understand. "About what?"

"Deese bandits, seen?"

"The bandits." Lockerty looked at Fale. "The bandits. Tell them what you saw."

Fale did. He was one of the sellers who had got ripped off in the Hyde Park auto shop job.

The Jamaicans asked no questions, as though listening to court testimony.

"Cho!" exulted Moodle, then sucked his teeth. "Dey knew fucken everyting."

Lockerty nodded enthusiastically. "They're like fuckin' . . . like fuckin' devils, they are."

"An' you lagga heads keep a-goin' on. Trustin' de beast now."

"The . . . ?"

"Da bumbaklaat police."

Lockerty was not used to being insulted, especially in his own crib. "Look. I am the one losing money here."

"You lose, every man lose."

"I put out a very healthy price on these clowns' heads. But nobody knows shit. Now, your boss wanted more involvement, to secure his investment, and so I welcome you here in that spirit."

"We got no boss, mon. We specialists, seen? We up onna *con-*

tract. Tek care dis problem you havin'. Make everyting cook and curry again, sight? We here to help."

"Okay. Yes." Lockerty thinking, *These two white Rastas couldn't find the corner store.* "How?"

"Ah, dat."

Moodle went into the bag on the floor, coming out with a knife with a short, hooked blade like something from a fisherman's kit. He sprang forth without any warning and, with tremendous force, struck Fale in the side of the head, upending his chair and knocking the man to the floor. Moodle knelt on top of Fale and went at him with the knife. Lockerty jumped to his feet, but Leroy's outstretched hand and tsk-tsk face held him in place.

Lockerty yelled, "What in the name of hell are you—!"

"Dis how you deal wit it, blood!" said Moodle, yelling over Fale's horrified screams. "You show what failure mean! Is *cru*cial!"

Lockerty saw a spray of blood hit the floor. He looked at his doorman, who stared in horror, the live grenade in his hand.

"This is my office!" Lockerty howled.

"You tink you workin' for you, but you work for de don. And de don—he not happy."

Leroy knelt down, removing a white, medical-looking box from the duffel. "You tink you can handle deese bandulus?"

"Yes!" Lockerty yelled over Fale's cries, thinking an affirmative answer might stop them. *"Yes!"*

"You wrong, mon. But we help you. Stop deese bag-o-wires. Do dis right."

Moodle stood, leaving Fale rolling on the floor, holding his bleeding face. The high-pitched moan coming out of Fale's mouth was an aria of insanity.

Moodle carried something small in his hand, like a baby onion with a bloody tail, over to Leroy. Leroy lifted the cover off the box, which breathed steam. Dry ice.

Into the box, Moodle deposited Fale's eyeball.

"We earn a bonus, every eye we brin' back." Leroy closed the box, a drip of red stuck to the styrofoam exterior. *"Every* eye."

Moodle turned back to Lockerty, the bloody fish knife still in his hand. "Feelin' us now?"

Lockerty stared at the white Jamaicans, two psychos he had invited into his office and his life. "Jesus Christ."

"Perk up, mon. Now we get us deese bloodclaat bandulus, sight? We got us a box to fill."

NESS

LASH COULDN'T SAY WHY THE FATHERLY IMPULSE HAD COME ON SO late in the game, or why it had come on so strong. It really is a love affair, your relationship with your kids. It's powerful and frustrating because there is no real consummation. No finish line. The closest you get are the moments when you can share in your child's triumphs—as when watching them on the field of play—though even those successes are tinged with sadness because every accomplishment only pulls them further away from you, toward an adulthood all their own.

He was fighting afternoon traffic out of the city because he had missed too many of Rosey's lacrosse matches to miss another. He liked to stand on the sidelines, apart from the other spectators, watching his boy play, this chunk of him that had broken away and grown whole into a man.

This was why, when Lash's phone buzzed in his cupholder, he answered it expecting to hear Rosey.

"What up, M.L.?" Tricky's serious voice.

"Everything good?"

"Breezy. Checking in."

Not true, but better that than trouble. "I heard some bullshit about somebody rounding up the bandits."

"Nonsense rumor," said Tricky. "Junkies trying to turn in their brothers for twenty-five long."

"They showed up that cop though, didn't they?"

"Everything but put a pink party dress on him. Pretty good, maybe edging toward showboating. Fifteen-yard penalty for dancing in the end zone."

"Could be they're getting cocky. Could be anger."

"You sounding sympathetic. You get anything from the cop?"

"If I did, I wouldn't tell you." But, no, Lash hadn't. The only people who lawyer up faster than dirty cops are dirty lawyers.

"Major haul, I heard."

Couldn't hurt to say. "Fifty-odd keys."

"Blow?" The ensuing silence was Tricky figuring out the wholesale amount in his head, with a dealer's facility for numbers. "Whoo, damn."

"Yeah."

"Maybe I'm in the wrong line of business."

Lash said, "You are in the wrong line of business."

"So lemme ask then. You want these guys because they're in your way? Or because that was your money?"

"*My* money? What's that mean?"

"Your task force's. These bandits are copping your style, Eliot Ness. Only cutting out the middleman—in this case, the U.S. gov."

"What's your point, Trey?"

"They eating all your pie, is what I'm saying. Can't feel good seeing that. Hell, we should go freelance, you and me. There's a team."

Lash said, "Maybe you're trying to be funny."

"Maybe, yeah. Maybe I'm just working my way up to telling you this." Tricky's pause wasn't meant to be dramatic. "I'm cooking up something for you. Something big. Real big."

"In terms of? Men or money?"

Tricky answered that with a question. "What percentage can I get of seized assets?"

"Percentage of product? Zero."

"I know that."

Tricky had never asked about money before. Never discussed a payment package. Everything he and Lash had was personal, one-to-one. "There is a contingency fee. Twenty percent commission is standard, with a quarter-mil cap."

"That's tax-free?"

"Afraid not."

Silence. "A cap, huh? Any give there? Cost of living increase, say?"

This discussion was making Lash's palms sweaty. "Out of my league."

"But you could ask."

"I could ask. You gonna give me something to chew on, or what?"

More silence, the moment weighing heavily on Tricky. "This could change a lot of things for me. Change everything. I'll hit you back when I can."

THE BREEZE

MAVEN HELD A SHEAF OF LISTINGS AND A RING OF KEYS GRABBED OFF one of the Realtor's desks. "I think you should take this one."

He was trying to sell Samara on a tiny sublet near St. Mary's Street, technically in Brookline but just three blocks outside Kenmore Square. She stood with her arms crossed, tapping a Puma sneaker on the refinished maple floor, looking out the window as a trolley passed. "Are the property fees included?"

"Property fees?" he said, flipping back through the listing sheet.

"You are the all-time worst Realtor." She stood at the kitchen sink, trying it out. "I kind of want to be more in the city though."

"At your price range?"

"Well, I plan on having a job."

"It's a sublet. It's small, it's clean. Very safe area. Available immediately."

She wide-eyed him. "Now you're a pressure salesman."

He wanted her out of her old place and away from Lash as soon as possible. The rest of it—what to do about her forwarding her mail, for instance—he would worry about later. Including breaking up with her. It was rotten, but he had dug himself into a ditch here, and the only way to protect both himself and Samara was to dump her.

When the time was right. First things first.

He said, "I just don't want you to miss out. Places like this, they go fast."

"What about my current lease?"

"You can get out early."

"Maybe if I had a roommate. Help with the rent . . ."

He was still searching the listing page for the property fees, so it was a while before he looked up to see her smiling.

She said, "Don't you think it's weird you still live with a bunch of guys?"

Maven stuttered out, "I don't know."

"My friends say it's too good to be true. Four successful single guys living together on Marlborough Street who aren't gay. They think you have to be drug dealers or something."

Maven smiled sickly and went back to the listing sheet.

LASH'S INTERCESSION HAD MAVEN LOOKING OVER HIS SHOULDER everywhere he went. He worked obsessively not to be traced or followed, feeling too conspicuous on his bike, taking alleys instead of streets if they were available. He stayed away from Marlborough Street whenever possible. He expected to see the DEA around every corner, and Maven's not having crossed paths with Lash again only made him more anxious.

Maven followed him one day, in a rented car, away from DEA headquarters in Government Center out into Somerville, to, of all things, a college lacrosse match. Maven never got out of his car, waiting in the parking lot, almost driving away a dozen times, knowing he was taking a great risk—until Lash reappeared, Maven trailing him to the driveway of a triple-decker on Rogers Avenue before pulling off. After, he couldn't fathom what he had thought he would gain by following the man who was trying to follow him, except maybe an ulcer.

He said nothing to Royce about the DEA. At first the choice tore at him, but soon he realized he needed to keep his distance from the man with whose girlfriend he was having an affair. Royce could sniff out the one lie at the bottom of a barrel full of truths. Maven felt twisted every which way, double- and triple-thinking his way through simple exchanges. No way could he tiptoe through this and come out okay at the end. Some sort of calamity was on its way—just as he had always known.

With a backpack on his shoulder, he walked into the Bank of America at the corner of Boylston and Exeter streets and was led down into the safe-deposit vault by the same assistant branch manager Royce had first taken him to. The man's fingernails glistened under a coat of clear polish as he and Maven inserted their keys in Maven's double-locked box door. Maven removed the three-by-ten-by-twenty-two-inch box, setting it down on the table next to a new, empty six-by-ten-by-twenty-two-inch box, whereupon the assistant manager left him alone in the examining room.

Maven opened the smaller box and transferred the stacks of cash into the larger one. He unzipped his backpack and added new bundles from the auto shop job.

Don't count it.

A lot of paper in there. A three-inch stack of hundreds equaled roughly $70,000, and he had just grown out of a ten-by-twenty-two-inch box.

Don't give it a number.

In his mind, it was his treasure, a glowing pile of wealth stowed deep inside a bank vault. In reality, it was a few pounds of paper tucked inside a metal box. He liked knowing he had it, but he didn't like handling it, getting the smell of decomposing paper on his hands.

Losing something.

Maven's answer to Royce's question "What is the one thing worse than having nothing?"

He'd been having dreams of getting called back to Iraq. Of having to leave in the middle of the night, no time to prepare. Of getting ambushed on his way back into the Green Zone from the airport, taking a sniper round in the neck, bleeding out on the sandy side of the road.

It wasn't dying that woke him up in a hot sweat. It was money unspent. It was the good life unlived.

HE WAITED A GOOD DISTANCE DOWN MARLBOROUGH STREET wearing a distressed trucker's cap and a medium-length, tan jacket bought off the rack at the military surplus store on Boylston.

Danielle stepped out of the building in a short jacket and heeled boots, and Maven went on full alert, watching other pedestrians and cars as he trailed her across Newbury to the Copley MBTA station. He was following Danielle to see if she was being followed. He had to know if Lash was onto her.

Underground, he hung way back until the subway arrived. Guys checked her out, but Maven didn't see anyone paying her anything more than passing attention.

He boarded the same inbound Green Line train she did, one car away. He could see her through two sets of windows when the jointed cars pivoted on the turns. She stood holding a strap near the door. At Boylston Station, she stepped out and switched cars, boarding his. A simple tail flip, maybe taught her by Royce. No one followed her from one car to the next. She was alone, or so she thought.

Maven sat head-down on a single seat near the center, looking like your typical subway psycho. He didn't dare look up, as she was standing right next to him. He stared at her brown leather boots and waited.

It was just one stop. She moved to the door at Park Street, and he waited to rise and follow her.

A guy boarded the car, and she received his arm around her waist, greeting him with a kiss. Maven watched from between his coat sleeve and his threadbare cap brim as the doors closed and they huddled close, whispering, smiling.

The guy was lanky, big-nosed, not much to look at. He wore a Dr. Who–length scarf with stripes of black, gray, and white, brown loafers, and a corduroy jacket.

Maven lowered his arm such that his face was fully revealed. If Danielle had eyes for anybody but this stiff, she would have seen Maven sitting not three seats away from her, glaring.

But she didn't. While the rest of the riders settled into their public-transit funk, she huddled close with Dr. Who, sliding her hand down the seam of his pleated pants, rubbing his cock. She said something more into his ear, and he grinned like a frog being kissed into a prince.

At North Station, they exited, and Maven stood and followed, completely exposed and not caring. He stopped after the turnstile, watching them go off, Danielle clutching the guy's arm as they disappeared into the swarm. Maven had seen enough. He didn't care to know any more.

BACK HOME, AFTER SITTING ON THE SOFA IN A DAZE, MAVEN WENT into his bedroom and started packing. Packing to leave, to walk away, emptying the contents of his bureau drawers onto his bed and stuffing them inside a canvas laundry bag.

He came to an old black hoodie and stopped. It was the sweatshirt he had worn on all those cold nights standing out at the parking lot, watching the city spin around him. He thought he had thrown the thing out. He sat down on the bed with the hoodie in his lap and tried to think through his distress.

MAVEN WAS LATE FOR THE MEET-UP AT THE PAD. SUAREZ WAS LEANING over the pool table trying a trick shot. Glade was watching *Team*

America: World Police for the umpteenth time on his media player. Termino was drinking a large protein shake.

"Look who decided to show," said Termino when Maven walked in.

Even after all these jobs over all these months, the Dynamo had never cottoned to Maven. It was a personality thing; Termino didn't share in Royce's high estimation of him. Termino thought Maven was too straight, too smart.

Royce's sunglasses hung from the collar of his expensive T-shirt. He singled out Maven in that way of his, a glance carrying the same weight as physically pulling Maven aside. "What's up?"

Maven shrugged, said, "What?"

Termino said, "Maven, you look like ass."

Suarez said, "Your ass or Milkshake's?"

"Looks like mine," said Termino. "Looks *at* Milkshake's."

Royce was still studying Maven. Waiting for an explanation.

Maven said, "Little under the weather."

Royce neither nodded nor shrugged, only looked away, letting him off the hook for the time being. "It's not just Maven," Royce said. "You're all fucking flat. This isn't nap time."

Glade closed his player. Suarez set aside his pool cue.

"Now that I have your attention," Royce said. "We're gonna switch it up a bit. Get you guys back feeling frosty and alert. This is something big, and it's come up suddenly."

The others moved closer, leaning around the table, except Maven, a sour taste in his mouth.

"It's a stash house. A currency drop. The wad one of the king-pins ships back to South America for payment. All his honey poured into one pot."

Termino said, "Sounds lucrative."

"Seven figures beginning with the number three."

Glade said, "Bullshit."

"I give you no guarantees, but that's the word. Three days from now."

Maven looked around for Royce's trademark envelope. "Where's the phones and intel?"

"This one's a little different, as I said. We can't go the usual route. I'm told there is some outside muscle being brought in to oversee this."

Maven said, "So—no intel?"

"I've got enough to get us going." Royce meant that to be the last word on the subject.

Maven said, "What about product?"

"Money cell is separate, you know that."

"So this is more of a straight-up heist."

"A raid," said Royce. "A takedown."

Maven said, "A robbery."

Royce turned fully toward him, responding to Maven's tone. "And what's so unusual about that?"

Maven didn't back down. "No product is a first."

"This is a backbreaking amount. This is going-out-of-business money. And do I have to do the math for you on what a one-sixth share will bring?"

Maven scowled. He didn't like having a cool half million dollars dangled in front of him. Plying them with easy money felt condescending.

"I don't like it," said Maven.

Royce looked at him, very cool. "You don't like it."

"I need to know more."

Royce kept staring. "I need to know what the fuck has crawled up your ass."

Maven took that, was braced for it, knowing it was coming. "You're sending us out there to do a straight-out stickup job with no tech, with no backgrounds, nothing." Maven looked at the others. "I think we need to know where this is coming from."

A smile flickered on Royce's face, energized by the anger aroused by Maven's blasphemy. "That is the question you don't ask."

"I just asked it."

The stillness of the others reflected the electricity in the room. They didn't want to move for fear of getting a shock.

Royce looked at them. "What is this? He speaks for any of you?"

Termino made a face as if he were about to spit on the pool table. Glade and Suarez shook their heads.

Maven said, "It's dangerous enough out there as it is. Now we're rushing into this thing, dicks in hand, three days? Why can't we know what you know?"

Royce was too flabbergasted to be furious. "Because I protect my sources. Is there some reason my word isn't good anymore?"

"Your word is good. It's just not enough."

"What is this? You want out? Is that what this is, Maven?"

"Maybe it is."

Royce looked at the others, registering their shock. "Well, you can't. Not without our blessing."

"Your . . . what?"

"Mutually assured destruction. Remember that? We've got a contract between all of us, written in crime. There's no revolving door here. This ends when we all decide to walk away, and not before. And I mean walk away for good. From the life and from each other." Royce looked at the others again. "You ready for that? I'm fucking not."

Termino said, low and menacing, "Maven, what the fuck?"

Suarez was too stunned to speak. Jimmy Glade said beseechingly, "It's half a million fucking dollars, Mave."

Royce was finally coming around to anger, bolstered by the others' support. "Why are you shitting all over my floor like this, Maven? What, I haven't done quite enough for you?"

Maven said, "Come on."

"You don't trust me now? That it? Me, who's held your hand and taken care of you every fucking step of the way?"

Maven was breathing hard, harder than he expected. It was the way Royce got inside you and figured out what mechanism needed to be pulled to make you work. That Maven's sequence was a little more complicated than the others' only energized Royce.

"Where'd you get your religion all of a sudden?" said Royce. "'A robbery.' You're awfully pure. You want to burn your share, that makes you feel better? Go ahead. But in the meantime, you will carry your fucking weight."

Maven stood there and showed Royce he could take it.

Royce said, "Milkshake, you back on the inside. Maven's losing his nerve."

"My nerve?" said Maven, knowing Royce was trying to get to him, and letting it happen anyway. "I don't see you out there with us."

Royce stared, furious as ever, but now trying to figure out the reason behind Maven's pushback. "What the fuck did I ever do to you? Except make your life *one thousand percent better*. All of a sudden, that's not good enough. Well, fuck you again. What are you without me, Maven? What are you?"

Maven didn't answer.

Royce looked at the others. "Where else could you guys live so well and make what you're making? Let me know your prospects."

No one spoke.

Back to Maven. "A guy makes some money and all of a sudden he's smart. He must be smart to have all this money, right? Must be a genius. Money doubles your IQ and triples the size of your cock. You know what?" Royce made a hand motion as if he were waving off a second cup of coffee. "I thought I'd built up some credit with you guys," said Royce. "Some goodwill—thought I'd earned that. Some respect, and some motherfucking courtesy. I even thought we were a unit. But there is a chain of command here, though I don't like to bring it up. Questions go top down, they don't come bottom up. I give the marching orders. And never have I sent you walking through a door 'dick in hand.' So fuck you."

Termino said, "Maven, you're being an asshole."

Maven didn't dispute that. He was acting out on his fury for Danielle, his guilt about screwing Royce's girl, his fear of Lash and the DEA—trying to blow up the crew rather than deal with these issues.

Royce said, "You know what? Walk if you want to. Go. Termino says you've been flaking off anyway. You're a fucking mess to look at, you're never around. Spending so much time with this girl, playing real estate agent. Go ahead."

Suarez said, "You going to ditch us now? You're leaving us a man down."

"Biggest haul of our young lives, Mave," said Glade. "Why you pick now to flake?"

Their words were nothing compared to what Maven saw in Royce's face. Maven had ruined what they'd had, and he wondered what it would look like from here.

BLACK FALCON

TRICKY SAT ALL THE WAY TO THE LEFT IN BACK, UP AGAINST THE tinted window so he couldn't be spied through the windshield—so far over that he disappeared out of Lash's rearview mirror altogether.

Lash took him down the street past the Black Falcon marine industrial park. The Edison plant was across the channel to the right, Logan Airport ahead of them across Boston Harbor. Lash said, "What about this blond guy here?"

The guy was well built, athletic, wearing a green tracksuit and jogging slowly with white speaker buds in his ears.

"Naw," said Tricky. "Don't know him."

"He's been hanging around. Did this loop three times yesterday."

"This is still Southie right here. Lotta fools dope up and go exercise. White guys, mostly."

Lash followed the road left around the turn. "We're gonna unplug this thing today."

"Today?" Tricky sat up a bit. "You sure?"

"Never sure. Never, ever sure."

The light, repetitive thumping was Tricky's fingers paradiddling on the back of Lash's headrest. "Damn."

"What?"

"Just . . . did I make the right decision, you know? For me."

"You made the right decision."

"If things go wrong, then what? Where am I then?"

"Nobody on my end knows about you yet. No one's known this whole time, and there's no point in bringing them in now. But people will know you after."

"Fuck," Tricky said. "That's dangerous shit. They gonna put me and my money on a beach somewhere?"

"Not likely. But someplace safe."

"Nowhere's safe for a snitch." Lash heard a sigh come out of Tricky. "I must be out of my Negro mind. You always said you wanted me out of the game."

"And you better stay out."

Foot tapping joined the thumping, a riff of nerves. "Where is this place anyway? I never been down here."

"Just passed it."

Tricky turned to look, his fingers stopping. "Bandits profit from inside info—why not me?"

"First smart thing you've done since I've known you. Just keep thinking about the money."

"Exactly right," said Tricky, his fingers resuming their patter. "You just read my damn horoscope."

GLADE CALLED IN. "MOVEMENT UP IN THE WINDOWS, BUT NOTHING by the door. Guess I'm in for another loop."

Maven thought that Glade's jogging around the Black Falcon in a tracksuit was way too obvious, but couldn't say anything to Termino and Suarez. They sat together inside a van in a lot at the head of the loop. They were having trouble getting their eyeballs on the stash house—the "house" in question being the office of a seafood importer sandwiched between freight terminals.

Maven said to Glade, "What about that Sequoia that went by?"

"Didn't see it."

"Silver. Tinted windows in back."

Glade said, "Lotta cars out here, Mave."

Maven hung up on him. Over on Dry Dock Avenue, an Edison crew worked their second day on a streetlight, with no cop detail. Maven mentioned it earlier, but Termino only thought he was looking for a way out.

Maven said, "This loop is essentially a dead end. Only one exit."

Suarez said, "We could go into the drink."

Termino said, "First of all, and come up where? We'd have to swim two miles—and they'd still find us. Second—I, for one, don't love that dirty water. Syphilis down there."

Maven said, "We don't even know how many doors we have to go through."

Termino said, "So we have to get fancy. We've done it before. Stop shitting on this, Maven, and man up."

The passing rumble was that of the Edison truck surging down the street, pulling up just out of sight—right about where the seafood importer's office was.

Two SUVs followed it at a high rate of speed.

They heard the loud banging of a door being rammed open.

Termino said, "What in the goddamn—"

Maven picked up the ringing phone. Glade said, "Shit, I'm fucking bailing."

Three gunshots—muffled, from inside the building—were followed by yelling.

"A setup," said Termino.

Maven broke apart the work phone and reached for his backpack.

More gunfire. Glade went jogging past them, toward Summer Street. Suarez jumped into the driver's seat and started the engine, but Maven pulled on his arm. "Leave it. Bail."

Termino was already out the side door and walking away. Maven went out the other door, then Suarez, heading off in different directions.

People exited the adjoining marine park buildings, fleeing toward Maven as he crossed onto Dry Dock Avenue. He saw the Edison truck and the SUVs with police lights flashing in their taillights.

Automatic gunfire blasted down from the second-floor windows, spraying the vehicles. Agents wearing body armor and DEA vests crouched behind them, pinned down.

Maven watched the action from behind a skinny, city-planted tree. The feds were taking heavy heat, outflanked and overmatched. Then he saw a long-limbed DEA agent ducking behind a vehicle's front end, yelling into a mobile phone.

Agent Lash. Calling in more backup. He evidently couldn't hear anything from his phone and took a chance, ducking and running behind a pickup truck.

It was a raid. It had gone wrong, and fast. This was an ambush.

Lash pulled a sidearm and peeked over the bed of the pickup, squeezing off shots at the building—ducking back when retaliatory rounds plunked the vehicle.

Maven dug into his backpack. He carried an all-black Beretta 92, an instrument of his paranoia. He slipped it out of its nylon bag and slid off the safety, holding it low against his leg, starting down the far side of the road, moving from car to car as more people fled past him.

One of the SUV's gas tanks exploded. Not a spectacular ball of flame, but a concussive burst that lifted the back of the vehicle and threw back the men behind it. No one was on fire, but they were hurt, rolling from side to side in the road.

Maven came up beside a black guy sitting with his back against a blue Honda, biting the neck of his navy blue Champion hoodie and saying over and over, "Shit, shit, shit."

Maven peeked through the cracked window glass and saw Lash reloading, the pickup not thirty yards away. He moved up one more car, not wanting to be seen.

In the second-floor window above, Maven saw a shirtless blond guy wearing a gun strap across his bare chest. The shooter aimed down at Lash. Maven straightened and fired over the Honda's roof—too far away to be accurate, but enough to break the glass and send the shooter ducking for cover.

Maven spun back down and wondered what sort of insanity had caused him to do that. His lack of judgment turned him ice-cold, and he ducked away to the previous car as a hail of rounds came whistling near.

LASH FLATTENED OUT AND SLID UNDERNEATH THE PICKUP. THEY were surrounded. Lash heard fire behind him.

He looked up at the undercarriage of the truck and remembered the exploding SUV, and that made him slide partly out, enough to see the shirtless shooter in the window firing down into the street.

Lash's first round cracked the rifle's stock. The second burst red over the shooter's neck. Shots three, four, and five struck the chest of the howling shooter, who was too dumb to fall.

Lash scrambled out from beneath the truck. Sirens in the distance, all the sounds combining in his head to form a machinelike roar.

The raid was a disaster. The bad guys had been waiting for them inside. Lash wondered if, in hoping to draw out the Sugar Bandits, maybe he had waited too long.

He remembered the gunfire behind him and looked across the street. He saw a body behind a car. Maybe the shooting from that side of the street was friendly fire, saving him from the assassin above.

Lash raced back there, one round chipping the tar at his feet. He dove over the trunk of the Honda, falling to the sidewalk near the man's boots.

The man lay on his side. No armor, nothing identifying him

as law. Lash crawled up on him, seeing broken glass from the car windows on his sweatshirt, blood soaking the neck of his hoodie.

Lash rolled him faceup. It was Tricky. His head was ringed as usual in a drawstring hood, and Lash reached inside, putting his bare hand over the neck wound, just as he had all those years before.

This gash was worse, obliterating his former scar.

"The fuck are you doing here, man?" said Lash.

Tricky tried to swallow, couldn't. His hand gripped Lash's wrist, holding him tight. "Protecting my investment," he coughed out, gritting his teeth.

"What are you talking about, Trick?"

"You. Something happened to you, I'm fucked."

"You goddamn fool," said Lash, which was not what he meant to say. Lash looked around for the gun. "Where's the piece?"

"Gotta save me again, man."

Lash looked up the road for ambulances, a cruiser, anything. "Shit, Tricky, hold on. Hold the fuck on."

Tricky stared, but no longer at Lash's face. His grip slackened, and the pressure of the blood pushing through Lash's fingers ebbed.

"Hold on!" said Lash.

ONE MORE

T HEY WERE WAITING FOR US," SUAREZ SAID. "THAT WHOLE THING. A trap. What else could it have been?"

Their placement around the pool table told the story: Glade and Suarez together on one long side, facing Royce; Termino on one short side, Maven across from him.

Glade said, "They were waiting to drop the hammer on us. We'd gone in there? Wipeout. Fucking massacre. Game over."

"The DEA," said Suarez. "Right there with us—Jesus."

Royce waited like a man paid to listen to complaints, letting them air their frustrations. "Point taken."

Glade said, "We're on borrowed time now. This thing has been beautiful, man. It's been beautiful."

Royce said, "Calm down."

"I will," said Glade. "In about a year. When I'm far away from here."

Royce was looked at Maven. This mutiny was his fault.

"Look," said Suarez. "Nobody wants to do this. At least this way, we end it on our own terms."

Royce's smile was tight like a seam about to burst. "Don't fucking let me down gently like I'm your girlfriend. Surveillance would have shown that this last one was a bad bet, and we would have pulled back, we would have walked away. Okay? It's our usual caution that kept us out of trouble. This isn't so fucking dire that we can't pull our pants back up and walk on."

The other two wouldn't look at him. Glade finally said, "If it's a vote, then it's three to—"

"It's not a vote." Royce pressed his knuckle into the cloth covering the rail. "It's not a vote. It's a decision we all make."

He walked to the table against the wall and brought over a thick mailing envelope. A new job.

"This one's back to basics." He tore it open and dumped the contents onto the table. Oversize index cards containing the marks' vitals, clipped to photographs. Prelabeled mobile phones, for work and snooping. "A civilian, a dermatologist piped in to pharmaceutical supplies. Opioids."

Termino said, "What the hell's that? Geometry?"

"OxyContin, morphine, fentanyl, methadone. Also some steroids and human growth hormones."

Termino studied a photograph. "Dude could use a cycle or two himself. He doesn't look like much."

Maven saw through Termino's role as Royce's straight man. It was about as subtle as the propaganda posters on the walls. He checked the other two, Glade and Suarez, who were listening.

Royce said, "Typical too-smart-for-himself frat boy with a taste for the dirty."

Termino passed the photograph and the index card to Suarez, who shared it with Glade.

Royce said, "I'm asking for one more. You owe me at least that. Let's not leave this job on the table."

Glade passed the photograph on to Maven. The standard surveillance shot was snapped from the same Bushnell binoculars they used, with a built-in camera. Maven glanced at the man in the picture—then stared at it. A long moment passed when everything else in the room disappeared.

It was Dr. Who. The guy with the long scarf, whom Danielle had met on the Green Line train.

Maven was bewildered a moment. Only a moment.

In a sickening moment of lucidity, everything became clear.

How Royce got so close to the marks.

How he got mobile phone access and personal information, setting the table for the bandits' takedown.

Danielle.

She was the advance team. Fucking their marks.

He stared at the picture, wondering how he could have been so stupid for so long.

Then he looked at Royce. Pimping his girlfriend? Was she really his girlfriend? Or was she another bandit, just like Maven?

His stomach went sour. He looked onto the table at the ripped envelope. It was as though Royce had torn Danielle open in front of him.

"Oh, Christ."

The words escaped him like a belch or a sob, something he couldn't hold back.

Royce looked at him. "Fuck is wrong now?"

Maven let the photograph fall onto the table. "Not feeling well," he said, the truth, the words tasting like throw-up.

Royce rolled his eyes, everything going to hell. "One more," he said to them. "All I'm asking. If this is truly over, you'll know it. You'll have your answer. Who knows? Maybe you'll regain your appetites."

Maven went to a chair and sat down. He heard footsteps and looked to the ceiling. Danielle. Overhead, right now.

"You take a vow of silence all of a sudden?" said Royce.

Suarez and Glade were leaning toward yes. Maven realized Royce was looking at him.

"Fine," said Maven. He felt like a boxer on the canvas being asked to count the referee's fingers. "One more."

THE OTHERS LEFT TO SCOUT THE ADDRESSES OF THE NEW JOB, PER the usual routine. Maven begged off, sick and not having to fake it. He lay down on his bed until they left, then dragged himself back up, pacing the condo in a lover's blind fury. A childlike feeling of betrayal, both by Danielle and by Royce.

He listened again for her footsteps. Maybe he had imagined them. Maybe she was out fucking their next prospective victim.

Maven pulled open the French doors and stepped out onto the balcony, looking up. He couldn't reach the bottom of the third-floor balcony until he stood on top of the black iron railing surrounding his.

He tried it, gripping the base of the upper balcony. For a moment his feet kicked free, Maven dangling high over Marlborough Street.

He swung himself up and got a foothold, and then in a burst of arm strength he climbed up over the top of the railing.

He stood on the soft rubber surface of the small balcony. Two wire chairs and a dirty, rain-wet ashtray. He looked across the street to the facing picture window, seeing the second-floor reflection and remembering the night he had seen Danielle standing where he stood now.

The twin doors were identical to the ones downstairs. The handles turned and the doors opened, unlocked.

Curtains swirled as he entered the room above the pool table. A king-size bed, built-in bureaus, a flat-screen TV over the fireplace. A small bar was wedged into the near corner, stocked with a few bottles and glasses. An air purifier whirred near the door.

He went out through the door into a short, angled hallway. A bathroom stood across from a spare bedroom. The spare bed was not a spare, however: it was unmade, slept-in. Maven slid open the mirrored closet doors to reveal women's clothing.

Danielle's clothing. Her dresses and a multitude of shoes.

Was this her bedroom? Separate from his? Or just a dressing room?

The only personal item he found was a small, framed photograph of Danielle's sister, Doreen—the sight of which stopped Maven, kicking him a little. But he could not be sympathetic. He had to know what he was to her.

He heard movement in the kitchen. Footsteps coming toward him. He went out, Danielle startled by the sight of him there.

The sight of her in the flesh took the stinger out just a bit. She looked like nothing special, wearing lounging shorts and a T-shirt, barefoot, her hair up in a twist.

"What the . . . ?" she said, looking behind her. "You shouldn't be . . ." She didn't understand. "Is Brad here?"

Maven shook his head. He couldn't find words yet.

"Are you crazy?" she said, smiling, misreading him. "Did you come up the balcony, like Romeo? I like the gesture, but we can't— not here."

"Bellson. Curt Bellson."

She answered with true bewilderment. "What?"

"I saw you with him. The guy in the scarf. We just got handed his folder downstairs, he's next on the list."

She closed her mouth, searching him, her eyes never leaving his face.

Maven said, "Don't pretend anymore that you don't know what we do."

She swallowed hard. "This is dangerous. This is crazy."

"What is? The truth?"

"We can't have this conversation." He saw it setting in now, the realization that Maven knew she'd been consorting with them.

He said, "Do you fuck anybody, or just the ones Royce tells you to?"

She didn't speak. She couldn't speak, she just looked at him, breathing through her mouth.

"Answer me."

Her voice came as thin as breath. "What were you doing fucking following me?"

"How do you do it? Copy down what they say in their sleep? Are you a pickpocket, what?"

"I get their phones. I give them to him. He does whatever he does, gives them back to me. I replace."

"Ghost phones. He builds in snoops. Or do you even know that? Maybe you're just a pretty pair of hands."

She said quietly, "You're as big a fraud as I am."

"Am I? Am I fucking around on somebody else's say-so?" He stared at her. He didn't want to see her shame, he wanted to *feel* it. "Where does he get his information? *Before* you come in, I mean. How does he know to point you to these guys?"

"I don't know."

"You just follow orders. You do as you're told. With anybody."

Now she started to push back. "I. Don't. Know. Or care."

"You should. Could be our necks, the way things are going."

"What does that mean?"

He couldn't tell her about the DEA. He couldn't trust her with anything now.

Maven said, "Is he having you do this with me . . . to keep me here?"

"Don't flatter yourself. He doesn't know jack shit about us."

"Why, then? Why us?"

"Why do you think?"

The pain on her face was real. Whatever they had—she needed something in him. That made this even harder for him.

"How much money do you have put aside?"

"Money?" she said, surprised. "None."

"He gives me everything I need. I don't do it for money, Neal."

The use of his given name stung him. "Then what do you do it for?"

"Why the fuck do you do it? Do you do it for the money?"

"No."

"But you get money. I don't. But you're not a whore, right? You're doing a good thing—right, Robin Hood? Mr. Innocent."

"I'm not saying I'm innocent."

"You're saying you're more innocent than me. The guy who's fucking his boss's girlfriend."

Maven was speechless.

"Do you really think you want to know where he gets his information? *Really?* Even if you find out it's something you don't like?"

"Tell me what you know."

"What do you care? And why now, all of a sudden? You're out past your curfew on this one. It's too late."

"You're wrong there. It's over. We're ending it. One last gig, then—out."

She said, "Bullshit."

"Look at me. I mean it. Everybody. Splitsville."

"He said that?"

"He doesn't have final say anymore."

"Who does? You?"

Maven didn't answer, leaving the question open.

"I don't like this," she said. "I don't like change."

"So here it is. If there's anything left between you and him—"

"Oh, Jesus, don't do this—"

"I'm doing it. I can't be taking you from him. That's not me. Even if it is me . . . I'm not going out on him like that. I'm not. It has to be your decision. I can get you out of this. But you need to make the move."

She looked away, closed her eyes. He had dropped too much on her.

"I don't want an answer now," he told her. "I want you to be sure."

A car horn in the street got their attention, opened her eyes.

"You need to get out of here," she said. "Before he comes back."

The stairs were too risky. Danielle opened a door off the kitchen that led up six steps to the roof. Maven went out into the sun-light, shoes crunching stones. Instead of moving straight to the fire escape, he stood and took in the city from above.

He wasn't sorry to leave it. He had no choice now. Instead of feeling depressed—at the ruination of his relationship with Royce, and the truth about Danielle—he felt strangely, cautiously elated. All the strings were cut. The lack of a choice made his path clear.

LOOSE ENDS

THE MOVERS WERE GONE. MAVEN REASSEMBLED SAMARA'S BED AND hooked up her wireless router and screwed in her curtain rods. At her insistence he checked the bathroom for landlord cameras and helped her test the intercom. While she unloaded her kitchen glassware, he walked to Chef Chang's for takeout, rehearsing what he was going to say when he got back. He returned and, over orange-flavored chicken eaten off paper plates on a cardboard box, he broke up with her.

He said all the things you say, about how great she was and how sorry he felt, and he meant every word.

She sat there stunned, staring at the open boxes and empty walls. "This isn't happening. How can I live here now? This place you got me. Everywhere I look . . . every time I walk in that door . . ." She looked at him as though he had morphed into someone else. "There's something wrong. I've felt it."

"No. Well—one thing. This client. Long story, but . . . see, I'm being sued. It's a bullshit case, but they're trying to serve me, you know, and they don't have my address, so . . ."

"They don't have the address of your office?"

"No, they have that. They don't know that I live upstairs from there. So—remember my motorcycle registration? I'm just saying, if a guy comes around, a tall guy, black, older, pretty smooth—he might even try to show you a badge or claim he's law enforcement or something—just know that you don't have to tell him anything, okay? You don't know me. I don't want to see you dragged into this."

She stared at him in such a way that he wasn't sure she'd heard a word he'd said.

"Okay?" he said.

"Did you take money from someone?"

"What? No."

"My dad, I didn't tell you this, I don't tell anyone, but he took some money from some clients, there was a scandal. He went to jail, I mean prison, for almost a year . . . and we had to move. But he paid it all back, and so I know how it is to fall behind sometimes and maybe get desperate . . ."

"Jesus—no, it's nothing like that. I just . . . I just want to tie up all our loose ends."

She stared, openmouthed. "God, that's an ugly phrase."

"I'm sorry."

He had unpacked the contents of her desk with an eye out for anything linking him to her. His number was still in her phone, but he was going to dump that mobile. And with the bandits disbanding, there soon would be nothing to trace.

She stared at him, darkening, actively trying to read his mind. "Is it your boss's girlfriend?"

Maven was stunned. He thought about lying, then blurted out, "Yes."

"*What?*" She was more stunned than he had been. "What do you mean, *yes*? What the hell does that mean?"

"You just said—"

"I wasn't *serious*. Oh my God . . ."

And on it went for another hour, Samara vacillating between sadness and anger, between self-examination and self-righteousness, the argument running its course until it ended as only it could, with her ordering him to get out.

He lingered at the stoop outside, letting the night air get at him. Knowing he had acted in her own best interest didn't stop him from feeling like a shit. But if this was the worst of it, then he would be lucky.

THEY WATCHED THE DR. WHO GUY, CURT BELLSON, HIS COMINGS and goings. They listened to calls he made and received. The usual drill, but executed with more care this time. A bit more respect for the process.

They staked out his South End condo. They double-tailed his Saab 9-3 convertible all around town, keeping an eye out for other tails: bounty hunters, or DEA. They even played "flat tire" outside a rambling old farmhouse in the rural suburb of Easton, surrounded by acres of cranberry bog, where the deal was set to go down.

Things fell into place quickly as Bellson moved up the timetable. This busy Boston dermatologist was on the verge of financial ruin, needing the proceeds from this deal to pay off partners in a real estate venture that had gone bust in the recession.

Maven focused on the work, pouring all his extra energy into hating this guy. Taking him down was going to be a pleasure.

SPANKING

THE WINDOWS OF THE CORNER OFFICE OVERLOOKED GOVERNMENT Center and Downtown Crossing. Lora Jeffers, the special agent in charge, came around from her desk and gave his hand a good shake, called him Marcus. Lash knew what was coming. She sat down and closed her laptop to see him better.

She started by listing his procedural lapses. Never registering his confidential source with the DEA. Using an informant with whom he had a personal connection. No Form 356 payment authorizations.

"I never paid him a cent," said Lash. "He never asked, until this. Yes, we had a personal connection. He owed me his life."

"No Form 512, the CS Establishment Report? No prints on file?"

"I knew who he was."

"That's not the point, Marcus, and you know it. No 473 Cooperation Agreement? Not one DEA-6 report? Nothing memorializing any of your contacts with him?"

"No paper whatsoever. He was too highly placed to go on the registry."

"Not so far as the DEA is concerned. Not so far as I am concerned." She placed her palm flat on top of her desk. "We use interdiction and eradication, Marcus. Title Three intercepts, surveillance . . ."

Lash tuned her out, looking over at the M. C. Escher prints on her wall. The hand drawing the hand; the stairs rising up and leading down at the same time.

When he came back, she was telling him, "You've got plenty of years in, enough to know the consequences. Nothing will happen officially until things settle. When it is to be done, it will be done quietly, out of respect for you. You'll just have to dangle until events run their course."

"You're shutting it down. Just say it. The machine needs to run the way it's always run. Someone will come in with orders to drive it into the ground until it can be called a failure and taken apart for good. Windfall is kaput."

"Marcus, I do believe we have a case here where the old ways, the accepted ways, the proven ways, bear out. You lost a very valuable informant, and we have three agents in the hospital. You should count yourself lucky they will all survive."

"What went wrong at the Black Falcon terminal had nothing to do with tradecraft. We walked into an ambush. That Jamaican wasn't waiting for us. He wasn't looking for cops to shoot. He was lying in wait for these Sugar Bandits who've been raising hell all over town."

"These so-called Sugar Bandits are as much myth as they are substance. There is a turf battle going on—"

"If you're going to make me eat crow here, then you're going to listen to me talk with my mouth full. What I am saying is that there are big changes afoot. A sea change coming to the local scene. It is fully within your power to smack me down, but Windfall or no Windfall, something has to be done out there."

Jeffers was just waiting for him to finish. "Be that as it may—"

"Oh, fucking Christ. Can I go?"

"What did you say?"

"I've taken my spanking. Am I excused?"

She fixed her eyes on him a moment, then reopened her laptop. "You are."

Lash pulled up to the gated driveway on Brush Hill Road in Milton and turned off his car. He scaled the stone wall and dropped down onto the other side, pulling out his badge in anticipation, heading straight up the driveway of crunchy gray stones.

Two gunmen came out of the trees near the circular arrival court at the head of the driveway. They carried AKs and wore inexpensive dark suits. The best-dressed gunmen in all of Milton, Massachusetts.

"I'm DEA, motherfuckers," said Lash. "I'm here to talk to Crassion."

"This is a private residence," said one.

Lash showed them the badge again. "Shoot me or get the fuck out of my way."

The house was a Victorian with a Boston flavor, three gables with deeply overhanging eaves, just short of a BBC-miniseries mansion. Lash counted five chimneys. The carriage house to the right was the size of a normal suburban residence, with room for more than four vehicles and living quarters above. Gardens and footpaths began behind.

The arched front door was unlocked, and he let himself into the foyer, under armed escort, getting angrier by the minute. Busting up one of the gunmen was a temptation, but it wouldn't make him feel any better in the long run. He kept himself on simmer instead. Tricky's death weighed heavily on him.

"Whatever happened to protocol, Agent Lash?"

John Crassion, a portly gent in his sixties, entered from the living room to the left, wearing a merlot-colored robe and slippers, a thin newspaper tucked beneath his arm. His gruff voice was the only indication of the South Boston boy he'd tried so desperately to leave behind.

Lash said, "Tell these two boys to go play."

Crassion nodded to his men, and they stepped back. "At least let them frisk you."

Lash shook his head. Not today.

Crassion shrugged. "This is criminal trespass anyway, so any recording you might be making, legally it would be about as admissible as a drawing of a gun. In here." He pointed at his library with the newspaper.

He closed the twin doors behind them. Lash looked at the books lining the walls. "These come with the house?" Crassion sat in one of the tall-backed, leather chairs, but Lash remained on his feet. "Who is it you're trying to fool with all this?"

"I am a person who never expected to breathe a day past age thirty. When I did, I looked around me and I smartened up. A man matures, Agent Lash. Not you?"

"You're the regular American dream."

Crassion frowned, realizing that Lash wasn't in the mood for bullshitting. "What do you want?"

"I'm here to let a little light in. About these fucking bandits."

Crassion nodded. "Heard of them."

"Think I can't read a fucking pattern? Who's getting hit, who's not? Broadhouse is out there arming himself to the teeth for a war. Lockerty brought in some crazy, fucked-up Jamaican to try and collect his own bounty."

"The Jamaican who died at the Black Falcon terminal. I hear he has a half brother. I hope you're going to visit Lockerty as well."

"I am here to say that I am onto you. *And* these fucking bandits. I'm not going anywhere, is what I want you to know. I am not going to stop."

Crassion digested that. "They've taken Windfall away from you, haven't they?"

Lash weighed the pros and cons of taking apart Crassion right here in his study. But Lash needed to stay out of trouble in order to stay out on the street—to give himself a chance to put this fuck away.

Lash said, "I wouldn't worry about my survival. I'd worry about your own."

AFTER LASH WAS GONE, CRASSION WALKED CIRCLES INSIDE HIS library, hands deep inside the pockets of his robe. He knelt at a lower row of books, dumping gilt-edged antiquarian volumes of Hawthorne to the floor until he found the door to a small safe.

Inside was a mobile telephone, nothing else. He swapped in the battery from the wall charger and dialed the only number stored in the memory. The call went straight to voice mail, aggravating Crassion. He left a stern message before slipping the phone into his pocket, awaiting a call back.

THE BOG

MAVEN CREPT TOWARD THE FARMHOUSE THROUGH THE FLOODED cranberry bog. A late-afternoon fog rolling in from the surrounding trees, smoking the surface of the eight-inch-deep water, helped obscure him.

The slow drag through an acre of floating berries gave him time to think. About this, their last job; about the chill in the early-fall air; about all the changes the coming weeks would bring. He and Royce had had a reconciliation of sorts during the weapons check back at the pad, Royce admitting that Maven had been correct to question the Black Falcon job. Maven was more optimistic about the prospects for an honorable separation, with no bad feelings. This whole thing might end with handshakes and respect, as it should.

Closing in on the house, Maven saw vehicles parked at the end of the long dirt driveway in front, angled in from the country road. No movement anywhere: no birds, nothing. He reached the edge of the bed and slithered onto the muddy field. He crawled behind a large piece of harvesting equipment, stopping there to undo the strap on his wet bag. As Maven pulled out a Heckler & Koch MP5 submachine gun and three full magazines, Glade emerged from the bog, ruby traces of water streaking his vest and mask like blood. Suarez came out last, wide right, setting up with Glade behind irrigation equipment and fitting in his earpiece.

Termino was the point. Maven checked his Oris watch, waiting one minute past go time, squatting there, shivering in the mud. Then he turned on his radio. They were conservative about unsecured broadcasts.

Maven said, "Big Dog, read? Over."

Nothing.

"Big Dog, do you read? Over."

Nothing. Not a click.

Suarez said, "No one out in front."

Glade said, "Fuckin' freezing here."

Maven said, "I'll go around front. Wait for my go."

Maven curled out. The lawn up to the house was on a slight grade. He rushed to the underside of the wraparound farmer's porch, along a cord of stacked wood. The closer he was to the structure, the better.

Three vehicles out in front: a boxy blue Honda SUV, a small, white conversion van, and Bellson's silver Saab 9-3 convertible. The rear of the backed-in van was windowless, so Maven came up on the blind side, using the mirror to check the cab, make sure it was empty. The SUV had plenty of glass and was also empty. Maven came up low and fast on the front seat of the Saab, also unoccupied.

He scanned the trees, watching for some sign of Termino. Could be that he was inside already, forced to take a different position. Could be a radio malfunction, a broken watch.

It could have been any of those things, but it wasn't. As Maven turned back to the farmhouse, he noticed something on the floor in the back of the Saab. A curled-up body, facedown, with Bellson's telltale Dr. Who scarf wound around its neck.

Maven dropped low again, scanning the trees. He retreated to the broad side of the van, checking the house, then going to the back of the vehicle, trying the door.

It opened on three dead bodies facedown in a slick of blood.

Maven started running. Up the stairs to the front door. He didn't bother with the radio. He was yelling, *"Get out! GET OUT!"*

A volley of gunshots. An abrupt yell in Maven's ear.

Then return gunfire, and a howl.

Maven's heel crushed the frame plate, the front door cracking inward.

ONE TIME, BACK IN EDEN, WHILE ON PATROL AT A TRAFFIC-CONTROL point in urban Samarra, a buddy of Maven's loaned him his new Oakleys. The sunglasses had a built-in music player, making Maven's headspace an oasis in that desert hell. Maven was giving Cal, his buddy, some shit for listening to opera when a sniper round ripped through Cal's neck. Cal dropped to the sidewalk, dead before he hit the ground.

Maven spotted two fedayeen hustling away from an idling Opal, tucking something under their robes. With Verdi soaring in his head, he chased them through a curtain of smoke, into and out of a marketplace slaughterhouse, ending in a close-quarters firefight in a courtyard.

He heard that same music now as he crashed inside the farmhouse. Time sped up, became fractured into gunfirelike bursts.

Splintering rounds spun him back from the bottom of the stairs. He raced down a narrow hallway, elbows bouncing off the walls.

Glade lay on the kitchen floor, straight out. Head shot.

A barrage from his left drove Maven back into the hall. He returned fire blindly, rounds pummeling his armor like iron knuckles.

He tumbled into a side room and sat back against the dividing wall. The MP5 was hot, smoking. Not empty, but he reloaded anyway, needing a full whack.

He listened. An old house, full of creaks. One loose floorboard groaned on the other side of the wall.

Maven pushed off and spun, firing through the old plaster and wood. He heard a cry and a heavy fall. Return fire rained splinters and dust into the room, and Maven covered his head and ran for the other door. More rounds pelted his back—one penetrating the armor, a hot needle thrust under his shoulder.

Suarez. Termino.

Maven cut out from the wall, riding his open gun across the hallway, galumphing up the carpeted stairs. His left foot was better than his right.

He came upon Suarez at the top landing—slumped against the corner, talking blood.

Rounds stitched Maven's back, pitching him forward. He turned and fired back down the stairs, clearing some room. From the floor, he ejected his empty and reloaded, grabbing Suarez's semiauto and slinging it over his shoulder.

Suarez's eyes followed him. "Get 'em," he gurgled. "Get 'em."

With a rush of energy, Maven slid headfirst down the stairs, firing off his right shoulder through the banister. He hit the bottom landing and tumbled away. His gun clicked empty and he reached for his third clip, but it was gone, so he tossed away the MP5 and readied Suarez's. He could feel warm blood pulsing from his side, running into his underwear. With his free hand, he pushed himself up onto one leg and lurched through the room, firing, circling back to the kitchen.

He looked for Glade's weapon but it was gone. Another volley erupted, and Maven spun and fired, yelling, slowed by pain. Suarez's gun jammed, and he dumped it and went into a one-legged run-crawl—hitting the door, finding himself outside on the side porch. Not where he wanted to be.

He dragged his right leg, bumping past an old-fashioned porch swing to the rear. Beyond the railing and the short yard lay the acre of bog shrouded under fog. No way he could make it to the trees, but he had to try.

He pitched himself over the porch railing, dropping to the ground. From his leg strap, he drew his backup, a 9 mm Sig Sauer, and waited.

Blood dripped down the heel of his hand over the textured grip. His right leg was going cold.

Termino carried the out phone for calling Royce. Maven's only hope. But where was Termino?

One stepped onto the porch. Coming out in a crouch. Maven balanced on his good leg.

Two shots turned the gunman around. Two more shots finished him.

Maven dropped back, counting rounds. Four down, eleven to go. Thinking, *Save one for me.*

Another gunman edged around the corner, behind the slow-moving porch swing. Maven fired through the railing, pushing him back.

Then two more shots cracked out of a window, and Maven had to retreat.

He dragged himself to the harvesting equipment, stopping behind it, where he had left his empty wet bag. He fell back, dizzy. Too much pain, but he kept going.

He splashed into the bog. He had the crazy idea of submerging himself under the berries, but it was too shallow to hide him. He frogged it out a few yards before falling over.

He turned and saw the gunmen coming for him. His pistol against two full auto fire-barkers.

Maven turned back toward the trees, the floating acre of undulating berries and fog. Looking out at that dreamscape in this last moment, his thoughts went to Danielle. It had all been worth it. Every minute.

He pulled his gun hand from the water, the 9 mm dripping as he pressed it to his temple and squeezed the trigger.

The pistol clicked. Nothing happened. He shook out the wet gun and tried again.

Nothing. He slumped and dropped the weapon into the bog. He turned back to face them as the gunmen advanced to the berm at the edge of the water.

For a moment they hesitated, unsure which one should take the kill.

They looked like soldiers. They looked like him.

Then, an explosion of gunfire, but not from them. From the side of the house, ripping into them from behind. Shredding them before they could even fire back. The gunmen pitched forward, dead.

Maven's first thought was *Termino*. But two men came swimming into his vision, advancing to the berm.

Men in street clothes. Two new killers.

Maven slipped back, below the surface of the water. Berries clouded in over his murky vision—then darkness.

REIGN'S END

ELEVEN TOTAL HOMICIDES, FIVE INSIDE, SIX OUTSIDE.

A detective lieutenant of the Massachusetts State Police told Lash, "The homeowners came back a day early from a family wedding down in North Carolina. Found this."

Lash looked out at the floating berries from the side of the porch, near the swing. "They don't know these guys? These cars?"

"Only the stiff in the Saab. Their nephew. Saw him twice a year, Thanksgiving and Easter. Quite a shock. He had been invited to the wedding, but declined."

"Borrowed their house instead." Geese honked overhead, a phalanx of five flapping toward the trees. "So can you piece together any sort of timeline here?"

"Unofficially, it looks like the guys in the vehicles were done first. No armor on them, and only two pistols, both still with the guys in the van, neither one discharged. Body-armor guys, we're still sorting that out. Robbery gone bad? Got pills in the back of the Honda, cash in the van." The detective's phone beeped, and he silenced it. "We got two guys in masks, the rest without. No ID on anyone. One thing I do know, that sticks out, is that the two down by the bog there, they were killed by different ammo than the others. Found shells there, in the grass, that don't match any of the recovered weapons. Of which there are plenty."

"High-action pieces," said Lash.

"So, what do you think? These your guys?"

Lash looked out at the two staties in hip waders, doing a grid search of the bog. "Two in masks?"

"One upstairs, one downstairs."

"Let's take a look."

Ballistics, Criminalistics, and Crime Scene Services officers · were all over the inside. Lash viewed the faces of all the deceased, lingering over the two masked men.

One was a blond. The other Latino.

Neither one was Neal Maven.

Maybe the guy had been clean after all. Either way, this sure looked to Lash like the end of the Sugar Bandits' reign.

He went back and checked the faces of the other armored corpses. It was speculation, but the haircuts and builds said military. "Bound to happen," said Lash.

"You seem disappointed."

"I wanted them for myself. When you run the prints, try military first."

"You think?"

"These aren't cons. These guys are soldiers."

HE PARKED OUTSIDE CRASSION'S GATE, THIS TIME PRESSING THE CALL button on the keypad. He pressed it a few times and got nothing back. So he went over the wall again.

He walked up the drive to the circular court, looking for the bodyguards. He reached the front door without being accosted. He tried the handle and the door opened.

Lash didn't go inside at first. He brought out his cell and dialed 911. He identified himself to the dispatcher and asked to be put through to Milton PD. From them, he requested backup.

He drew his Browning Hi-Power 9 mm, readying the pistol with both hands. The foyer inside was empty and quiet. More than quiet. Lash listened, standing still.

A smell reached his nose. A tinge of cordite.

Then it was only a matter of finding the body. Which he did in the book-lined study where he had met with Crassion a few days before. The kingpin lay dead from a head shot that had blasted back part of his skull. The body wasn't more than a day old.

Lash backed out and made his way through the house, room by room, door by door. No one else, and no sign of a struggle.

Crassion's muscle had vanished. Lash wondered about that.

The Milton cops arrived and he badged himself and explained the situation. He then dialed the state police detective at the cranberry bog and told him to have his team grab lunch on the way over to Milton as soon as they were through.

Before he could hang up, he received a call from his office telling him of a shoot-out up in Fort Hill, at Broadhouse's place. The news turned Lash's chest cold.

Two Pins down, one to go.

Lockerty.

Whoever got the bandits didn't seem all that interested in collecting their bounty.

The Shore

MAVEN STRUGGLED TO CONSCIOUSNESS.
Amber clouds floating above him came into focus as water stains on an old plaster ceiling.

He was in a bed. Mattress springs creaked as he turned his head. He made out a chair. He made out a window.

He tried to sit up but could not lift his head.

He looked to the other side and saw a bag suspended from an inverted coat hanger nailed to the wall. An IV bag.

He was on a drip inside someone's house.

He tried to sit up again and kept trying until the room swirled and he fell into darkness.

HEY. HEY.

A voice, only.

You are mine now. Understand? Mine.

*   *   *

THE ANESTHESIOLOGIST WET HIS LIPS AS HE PICKED THROUGH VIALS
inside the messenger bag, looking for a twenty-milliliter ampoule
of propofol. He shook it, warming the sedative in his hand. He
noted that they had replaced the hydromorphone and Demerol,
exactly as he had requested. He was alone in the bedroom but for
the man in the bed, who was deeply unconscious.

He checked the IV lines in the manner of the doctor he had
once been. He had learned to work with the shakes. He checked
the closed door behind him, always afraid of being watched, then
pocketed a syringe of midazolam for later.

He picked out a vial of vecuronium, an intravenous muscle
relaxant more accurately defined as a paralyzing agent. Too high
a dose would shut down the body's respiratory system in minutes, leading to sudden death. The last time he had held a vial
of vecuronium in his hand was inside the surgery bathroom of
Mt. Auburn Hospital. When the police finally broke through the
door, they found him dressed in blue surgery scrubs, sitting on
the floor with a handful of stolen syringes in his lap, injecting
propofol into the femoral artery of his left leg. He was an authority on the chemistry, pharmacology, and therapeutic consider-
ations of the most potent and addictive medications available to
humankind. And his one need in life now was to have access to
these powerful narcotics. He had a significant court date coming
up that would prohibit his access indefinitely, an eventuality that
demanded its own solution, to be acted upon at the appropriate
time. In his mind, he was drawing up an anesthesiologist's dream
last meal, a feast of opioids and sedatives for his central nervous
system.

He administered the vecuronium in advance of the patient's
surgery, pocketing the rest. He watched the man in the bed,
recognizing subtle changes in expression as the medicines took
effect. The anesthesiologist would have traded places with him in
a second, regardless of the man's bullet wounds. He envied his

patient—lying there, submerged within himself—and wished he could somehow split himself in two, administering to himself as patient while simultaneously riding out his own ministrations in blissfully schizophrenic codependence.

A SEAGULL CRIED.

Maven opened his eyes. He watched the amber clouds until they were still.

The bed. The bedroom. A new bag hanging on the wall.

A man in a chair.

"You don't know me?"

The man was older.

"You don't recognize the face of the man you stole from?"

The face was that of a man you might sit next to in a coffee shop, flipping through a newspaper, never looking up.

Maven looked at the window. A seagull bobbed on a tree branch.

"I don't know your name. I don't know where you're from. But I know you stole from me. And that is all I need to know."

Another man stood behind the man in the chair. Maven could not see him.

"Why we waitin'? Dis bumbaklaat fool. He got my blood smoked. Be my personal pleasure reeducatin' him."

"This wounded animal? Too damn easy." The older man stood over him now. "We're gonna fix you up. Give you time to heal. Get you strong again. *So we can break you.*"

THE SURGEON EXAMINED HIS WORK AND WAS FRANK ABOUT ITS shortcomings. He had many excuses available: the lack of assisting nurses; the unprofessional bedroom setting in this seaside house; the inferior surgical equipment. But he saw no sign of infection, which was itself a small miracle.

Obviously the patient was some sort of criminal, like the rest of these gangsters. Although they did not appear to regard the man as a comrade. In fact, quite the opposite.

Just fix him up.

Whenever the doctor edged toward asking why he was being paid to heal this man they appeared to detest—

Just fix him up.

The doctor warned them about the gas man, saying he had the patient under too deep.

Justfixhimup.

So, fine. He did. And if some carelessness crept into the surgeon's work as a result of his treatment by these thugs, well then, too bad. Because you do not talk to people that way. Not if you want their best.

HE HAD A WEIRD, SWIMMY MEMORY OF SOMETHING—A TUBE—BEING pulled out of his throat, like a stubborn carrot from the earth.

He was too stiff to stir. His brain was packed in cotton wadding.

An old man wearing shabby clothes and latex gloves leaned over Maven to check the IV bag. He lifted back the sheet with trembling hands, and Maven felt a vague sense of blunted pain, as an apple might feel a bruise.

The man, a doctor, was checking Maven's wounds.

"I did my best," he said, to no one in particular.

Maven tried to speak but his tongue would not work. He focused on the drip-drip of the IV feed, his eyelids drooping in sync.

"YOUR BOSS. ROYCE."

Maven floated like a bubble suspended in molasses. Someone overturned the jar and he slowly rose to the top.

"That name sure opens your eyes."

Maven had to check himself. Had he given up Royce's name?

He tried to fix on the voice of his interrogator, but felt his eyes lolling in their sockets.

"I'm figuring things out about you. Things just coming to me through the air. You can speak, can't you?"

The other man, the one with the accent, was over Maven now, pressing down on his wounded thigh. Maven's vision went blazing red. He grunted.

"Good. Gotta make sure I'm not fucking throwing darts at a board that doesn't have a bull's-eye."

THE SEAGULL SAT ON THE BACK OF THE CHAIR. LOOKING AT MAVEN for a long time.

He tried to talk to it. The bird opened its wings and alighted on his thigh.

It stared awhile, then began picking at his surgical wound.

It flew away with stitching trailing from its beak.

"I'M STARTING TO WONDER IF YOU EVEN KNOW."

Maven knew that his only power here was his silence.

"Remember the cranberry bog? What do you think happened there? You got ambushed, didn't you? Somebody got tipped off. They were waiting for you."

The cranberries. Maven felt like one of them now, floating on the surface of consciousness, waiting to be picked and crushed for his juice.

"Who do you think did that? It wasn't me. My guys came in at the end, on a late tip from one of the buyers, who used to deal with us. Losing business to you punks was bad enough, I couldn't have this fuck freelancing all around. Honestly I didn't expect much. Mr. Leroy insisted on going. You see, his partner was killed at that Black Falcon clusterfuck. And he's none too happy about it."

Maven's head was pulled up by his hair, and he was looking into the other man's eyes.

"You remembering any better now?"

HE TRIED. WHEN HE WAS ALONE. HE TRIED TO REMEMBER.

He ran his hands over his body, searching out his wounds. His lower back, his shoulder, his thigh. Tracing the surgical scars was like piecing together the sequence of the farmhouse shooting.

Glade and Suarez inside. They never had a chance.

And Termino?

"HOTSHOTS, RIGHT? THOUGHT YOU HAD IT ALL. YOU WERE SMARTER than everyone else."

Maven's arms were tied to the bed now. Strapped down at his sides.

"This silence of yours, what is it? Loyalty? It's your dumb loyalty, isn't it. That's the key. See—I'm learning to listen. Here I thought I was going to be the one ripping info out of you. But it's me sitting here with the hammer of knowledge. Waiting to beat the truth into you."

HE WAS NEAR THE OCEAN. HE COULD SMELL IT SOMETIMES. HE COULD hear the surf roaring. Like a beast calling for him.

The seagull was back in the tree. He wanted to come back in. He wanted Maven's eyes.

MAVEN AWOKE PROPPED UP ON A FEW PILLOWS. A NOTEBOOK COMputer was set on his chest.

"Because I know you wouldn't take my word for it."

The man was in his chair, legs crossed. The other man, the white Jamaican, was behind him.

Maven's right arm was unstrapped. He looked at the computer screen. This was some kind of trick.

"Go ahead. I put up some recent articles from the paper. You don't have all day."

On the screen were half a dozen windows open one on top of another. He had trouble reading the type and had to keep blinking and looking away, regaining his focus. So he could not read sequentially and instead had to absorb the writing in static chunks.

Massacre in Easton.

Cranberry Farmers Arrive Home to Bloodbath.

Nephew among dead in reputed drug deal gone bad.

Recent spate of Hub-area drug violence.

Maven scanned the print for names.

Curt Bellson.

James Glade.

Carlito Suarez.

The article noted the number of dead Iraq War veterans on the list. Three besides Glade and Suarez.

Sidebar: *Veterans and Crime.*

Another window, another article.

Gangland Slaying in Fort Hill.

Broadhouse, one of the kingpins, had been murdered in his home along with three associates.

Another window.

Milton Mansion Sees Night of Deadly Violence.

Crassion, another kingpin, dead. A so-called mob hit.

Sidebar: *Recession brings consolidation, contraction in urban drug trade.*

Another window.

Chelsea Piano Factory Shootout Claims Four.

Local Drug Baron Disappears.

A surveillance photograph showed a tough guy walking into a bar, a younger version of the man sitting in the chair. The caption gave his name as Lockerty.

The third kingpin.

"He hit us all. Bing, bang, boom. Only missed me because— guess what?—I was out here at the shore. With you."

Maven let his head fall back. He was dizzy from reading and from the information gleaned.

"You still don't get it, do you? It's like I kidnapped a retarded kid nobody wants back."

Maven lifted his head again to look at Lockerty.

"It's Royce, you fuck. You did his bidding for months, knocking over the competition, cutting deep into mine and Broadhouse's distribution. Yeah—Royce was Crassion's boy. Until he turned on him a few weeks ago. I figured all this out. Crassion's plan was to use his secret soldier Royce to jack his competition and, in doing so, squeeze street supply down to a dribble, raising prices all over town. You were Royce's hit squad. I guess he needed you out of the way, cleaning his own house before he went scorched-earth. Set you up at that berry farm to end the bandit phase of the plan. A citywide coup. Crassion got what was coming to him, that fucking phony—and now Royce is king. Running everything single-handedly. An empire you helped him build."

Maven looked again at the laptop on his chest. Was it real?

"You dumb fucking slug. See for yourself. Not like we're setting you up a home office here. One more minute. Clock's ticking."

Maven didn't know what to do. He looked at the keyboard, wondering how to prove Lockerty wrong. He tried opening up a search engine, but had difficulty getting his stiff hand to work. So he reread the articles he had.

In the "Related Articles" sidebar, he read:

Drug War Link to B.U. Grad's Murder?

Maven stopped breathing. He moved his finger over the

trackpad, trying to get the tiny arrow cursor on the highlighted article.

He finally clicked it and waited for the page to load.

He didn't read any of it. He just stared at the photograph of Samara Bahaar, dressed in her cap and gown.

Hard Truth

THE BLOODLETTING AROUND TOWN IN PART VINDICATED LASH. This didn't mean that his overseas transfer wasn't still going through: it was. Or that Windfall wasn't going to die a slow death in someone else's hands: it would. But at least he was able to stay out on the street, keeping active, making moves.

He saw Samara Bahaar's parents at the police station but never spoke to them. The father wore a suit and the mother a yellow patterned sari. The father carried a fraud conviction from a few years back, and a ten-month bid. But nothing tied the murdered college graduate to the bandits. Her friends said that she had met Maven at Club Precipice some months before. They knew that his name was Neal, that he rode a motorcycle, and that he was a real estate agent. They thought he lived on Marlborough Street, though one friend insisted it was Commonwealth Avenue. The parents knew nothing of him, though her younger sister, a high school senior, confirmed that Samara had confided in her about a boyfriend named Neal, a Realtor who was not Indian, who had helped her find her new apartment.

The killer had entered her apartment by key, no sign of a break-in, the girl smothered in her sleep. No agency was listed on the real estate agreement, so Lash visited every office in the Back Bay area, to no avail. Lash did not pursue it any further.

Because Maven was dead. The Sugar Bandits were dead. Maven's motorcycle had been found in an alley in Cambridge, stripped down for parts. Two identical bikes registered to the other two masked men from the bog massacre, Suarez and Glade, had also been recovered around town.

Lash wished that he had pushed Maven harder. Specifically, he regretted not having intervened directly with Samara Bahaar. Tricky's death still walked with him, part of his permanent shadow now. What kept Lash moving ahead was the hard truth, long-ago learned, that good people get hurt sometimes. That he controlled nothing in this world. He only policed it.

VOODOO DOLL

As Maven's body healed, his mind deteriorated.

Left alone in the room, tied to the bed with nothing to occupy him, his brain began to feed upon itself. Eating away the better parts of him.

They let up on his sedation, though the straps remained. With no reason to interrogate Maven, Lockerty had taken to taunting, telling Maven what he and the Jamaican were going to do to him once he was fully healed. Lockerty thought he was mind-fucking Maven, but Maven was already well around the bend.

Royce visited one night. Standing back in the shadows, his arms folded, watching Maven lying in the bed.

"Danielle," said Maven. "What did you do to her?"

Royce never answered, never moved.

"I try to put myself in that bed, you lying there helpless, knowing what's coming. Knowing you will never see the outside of this room. And you don't say anything. I want to know, how is it you're not begging me for mercy? For *anything*?" Lockerty was up and walking around the chair, hiking up his pants. "At least give me the common courtesy of turning you down flat. Or—wait a minute. Are you dumb enough to still have hope? I want to know what keeps you going."

Lockerty was turned away from Maven, stretching his back, when Maven said, "Revenge."

Lockerty stopped. He turned. "It speaks." Lockerty went back to the chair and sat down, newly engaged. He looked at his captive in the bed. "Go on."

"You want to hurt me?" said Maven, his voice hoarse from disuse. "Get on with it. I've earned a beating. I deserve it. Not for ripping you off. For being a patsy. I'll take whatever you give."

Lockerty grinned. "Your tough talk is making me hard, soldier."

"I'm gonna get through it. Whatever you got. It's the only way."

"Only way to what?"

Maven laid his head back upon the pillow. "To escape. And go after Royce."

MAVEN WAS SITTING UP, MORE PILLOWS BEHIND HIS SHOULDERS AND head. The Jamaican stood behind Lockerty eating from a styrofoam take-out carton, something fishy.

Maven noticed the watch on the Jamaican's wrist. Maven looked at his own bare wrist. It was his Oris.

"*Admire* is too strong a word, but I like your fortitude," Lockerty was saying. "It makes me smile. Your fantasies of retribution. It's pretty fucking funny, you down here making plans."

"It's no fantasy."

"No? You're going to will it to happen?"

"What else do I have?"

"I love the spirit. You are a true American, kid. A dreamer and a fool." Lockerty looked outside the window, the first time

Maven had seen him do that. "What you don't know is, my entire organization, everything I built, is gone, kaput. Me? I'm fine, I'm out here now. I got my head and my balls. I got fire still. You?" Lockerty shrugged. "Even say you did somehow magically escape. The game has changed out there. Royce has all the muscle now. He pulled in Crassion's organization and added some of his own. Nobody knows where he coops because that's how he wants it. Otherwise I'd be out there now, instead of here with you. So what makes you think you could succeed before I would?"

"You're afraid of him," said Maven. "I'm not."

A flicker of a smile passed over Lockerty's face, masking his anger. The words hit a little too close to home. "Is that what it is?"

"That's why you keep me here like a voodoo doll against him, sticking pins and needles in me."

Lockerty forced a smile, to prove that he was still enjoying himself. "You shoulda started talking a long time ago."

"I WAS AMUSING MYSELF WITH THESE THOUGHTS TODAY, THESE scenarios." Lockerty stood by the window now, leaning against the frame. "I was thinking how funny it would be, how fitting, if I did turn you loose after all. Sent you off on your merry errand."

Maven's eyes betrayed nothing, no hope or desire. His future did not hinge on Lockerty's charity because Maven could no longer be deceived into believing that such a thing existed. No one could ever break his heart again because he no longer had a heart to break.

"His own soldier going after him. Good sport, right? Good opera. In theory."

Maven said, "You don't want to do that."

Lockerty knit his brow, flicking at his ear to show that he didn't think he had heard Maven right. "Not let you go?" He was more intrigued than before. "Why is that?"

"Because after I get through with Royce, I'm coming back for you."

Lockerty's hard stare eventually dawned into a smile.

Maven woke up to find someone sitting at the edge of his bed. Not a man but a kid, a teenager, his back to Maven, doing something with his hands. Making a repetitive *flip-flip-flip* noise that Maven recognized, but not right away. Not until the kid turned and Maven saw his face.

It was Maven himself. The adolescent time bomb, obsessively practicing the flicked-wrist opening of a butterfly knife.

Maven startled awake. Pain in his arm as he thrashed about.

The white Jamaican was pulling away from him—an empty syringe in his hand.

Maven tried to get up, forgetting the straps. "What did you do to me?"

"It's time, soldier," said Lockerty. "You know nothing, you are nothing. Even as an object of my wrath, you failed. That's epic emptiness, pal."

Maven's arm throbbed. Something working its way through his veins into his heart, then his entire body beyond.

"Time to cut my losses and move on. But first—Mr. Leroy here needs to get something from you."

The Jamaican came at him, smiling, with something in his hand. A knife with a small, curved blade—and he set upon Maven, carving into his face.

MAKE SURE

TWO BLACK KIDS, NINE-YEAR-OLDS, CROSSED THE FROZEN GROUND behind the park, turning right by the wall of cracked white cement between the two boulevards.

The box stopped them. This was the way they always went and it had never been there before. A refrigerator carton of sagging cardboard, lying on its side, the top flaps folded shut.

One of them kicked it lightly. The other kid pulled the flaps.

They heard something stir inside. They backed off, looking at each other. One silently dared the other to complete the task. The folds bent apart easily.

They saw a pair of legs inside. Worn blue work pants and work boots. The smell out of the box put them off. The guy had pissed himself and maybe puked sometime in the past few hours.

One kid grabbed a stick off the ground, the longest he could find. He poked the guy's shin. He got no response and poked it again, harder.

The guy groaned and shifted. He sat up. He shielded his face from the harsh winter sun. His eye, and almost half of his face, were thickly bandaged. He fell back, dizzy.

He wasn't wrinkled like the old-time junkies, but the kids knew high when they saw it.

"Hey." Maven reached out from the box, dazed and trying to see. "Hey, fellas . . ."

He received a smack on the top of his wrist and pulled back. He looked again, each of the boys wielding a fallen branch.

Maven said, "Hey, I—"

A whack across his chest. Another against his shoulder. A crack against the crown of his head, and he rolled into a defensive ball.

The blows rained down, barely felt on the surface, only their reverberation throughout his muscles and his bones.

MAVEN CAME TO FIGHTING OFF THE STICK KIDS, BUT NOW IT WAS TWO blue-gloved EMTs, working by the light of a cop's flashlight in the park.

"What did you take, sir?"

Maven tried to sit up. They pushed him back down.

"How long have you been out on the streets?"

They put a penlight in his one eye, flicking it back and forth.

"Nothing," the EMT muttered to himself. "Sir? Hello? What happened to your eye?"

Maven tried to respond, but could not put any words together.

Next thing he knew, he was wide-awake in a sickening surge of full consciousness. It looked like an emergency room, but the walls were rocking, streetlights and upper-story apartment windows rushed past the windows. He was inside an ambulance, strapped to a stretcher.

The EMT had boosted him with Narcan, the opiate antidote. All of Maven's claustrophobia from being confined at Lockerty's came roaring back, and he thrashed and tore at the single strap across his waist, loosening it enough to slide out onto the floor.

The EMT first banged on the partition for help, then held his arms out toward Maven as though he were trapped with a bear.

Maven stood inside the rocking vehicle. He was still alive. He was free somehow. He was back in Boston.

The driver slid open her window and Maven reached through and grabbed her throat. She cut the wheel, supplies spilling from the side of the ambulance. The impact with the telephone pole sent the stretcher into the partition, then back against the doors, popping them open. Maven stumbled out and fell to the curb, hurrying away, half-blind, from the gathering people and the lights.

MAVEN ENTERED THE VERIZON STORE, THE FIRST CUSTOMER OF THE day. The red-shirted greeter welcomed him, Maven pushing past her to the demo phones, all working models.

He squinted at the phone, his vision blurred, his head splitting. He dialed information, asking for Gridley, Massachusetts, a listing for Vetti. The automated system gave him a number and connected him.

While the phone rang, Maven was aware of the salesmen talking about him, trying to figure out what to do about this bandaged bum using the free service in their store.

Danielle's mother picked up. Maven told her that he was a friend of her daughter's, trying to track her down.

"I don't give out that information," said Mrs. Vetti.

"A phone number, an address. Anything. It's critical."

"I just don't give out that kind of information."

"Do you . . . can you tell me, is she all right? Is Danielle okay?" A long pause made him fear the worst. "Who is this?"

"A friend. I was at your house for your other daughter's birthday."

Another pause. Her hand over the receiver. "She needs a name."

"She—?" Maven straightened. "Is she there? It's Neal Maven."

Mrs. Vetti repeated the name. After some muffled back and forth, the phone was handed to a different person.

"Who is this?" Danielle's voice.

"Danny?"

A breathless pause. "Neal?"

"You're all right," he said, suddenly near tears. "You're okay."

"Neal Maven . . . you're alive? He said . . . he said you were . . ."

"I'm at a phone store, downtown. What are you . . . what are you doing at your parents'?"

"Brad . . . he dumped me. Dumped me flat. Threw me out, left me with nothing."

"You're lucky he didn't . . . he had Glade and Suarez rubbed out. Did you know that?"

"I knew they were . . . gone."

"I need you. To see you. I need your help."

MAVEN LURKED AROUND THE BOSTON FLOWER EXCHANGE ON ALBANY Street, a long, low, fully enclosed, warehouse-style wholesale flower market. Trucks off-loaded flowers from the port and backed them into the exchange, where they were sold to New England retailers. The sign said it was closed on Sundays, and while a few cars dotted the parking lot, the area itself was quiet.

He leaned against the outside wall, hacking into his hand, still sick from whatever shit they'd put in him. It was wearing off now, the pain in the back of his eye as intense as it was unreachable. He was jittery when he should have been hungry. The constant drip of anesthetics and painkillers had turned him halfway into a junkie.

A black Highlander pulled into the lot. Maven remained in the doorway, hidden yet hopeful, having forgotten to ask Danielle what kind of car she would be driving. The SUV pulled near, coming in at an angle, and he stepped out into view.

The tinted windows made Maven stop, but too late. The passenger's door opened, and a bald guy with a tribal tattoo on the side of his neck stood out, brandishing a MAC-10 with a muzzle suppressor.

The other doors opened and more men emerged, and Maven's heart dropped through a gallows trapdoor. He was grabbed and pushed inside the flower exchange. He tried to fight, but he was dizzy and weak and didn't have much more in him.

He was pulled past empty stalls and shuttered kiosks offering ribbons, silks, and baskets. They stopped at an open spot formed by the intersection of two aisles and kicked Maven to his knees. He slumped there, head down and throbbing, the building spinning around him.

A voice said, "Straighten him up. I want a good look."

Maven's head was pulled back to raise his face. A blurry figure appeared from behind the gunmen arranged in a half-circle. Termino.

"I thought the bitch was delusional. Truly, I did. Coke bugs or some such. But damn." He stopped right in front of Maven. "Back from the grave."

Maven stared, Termino swimming in his vision. "She called you?"

Termino grinned, working down the webs of his black leather gloves. "To get back in the boss's good graces? Junkie hookers'll do anything for the pure."

Maven's chest was empty. No air for speech.

"Forgot," said Termino. "You were sweet on her, weren't you?"

Maven stared, waiting for Termino to break character. "It was all bullshit?"

Termino shrugged. "Just the stuff that mattered."

"You ran on us. At the bog."

"I never even showed." Big smile as Termino walked a full circle around Maven. "It was over already. You'd served your purpose. You wanted out—so we arranged to take you out."

Maven looked at the others around him. He was looking for Royce. "He couldn't come himself."

"Oh, he's here." One of the goons passed Termino a notebook computer, and he opened it, speaking directly to the screen. "You ready for this?"

A familiar voice said, "Let me see."

Termino turned the laptop around so that the screen faced Maven. The video-over-Internet connection showed Royce seated behind a desk, before a window. Black collar, clean haircut.

"I always said it," said Royce. "Always, I said—this one, he's different."

"Told you he was trouble," said Termino. "I want to know where the fuck he's been all this time."

Royce said, "His eye. The Jamaican. Lockerty's still out there. And evidently still pissed."

Maven burned, staring at Royce on the computer.

Royce said, "See, Maven, if you were dead now, as you're supposed to be . . . well, then, there'd be no hard feelings."

Maven said, "Suarez. Glade."

"You were done with those guys, especially Glade. Look, if I could have kept anybody on, it would have been you. But you wouldn't go for it. You told me as much."

Maven said, "Samara."

"The girlfriend. Maybe you talk in your sleep, how do I know? She'd been up to the pad. She could make Termino and myself. She knew things, Maven. I'm not a guy who leaves things to chance."

"You didn't have to do it."

"And you didn't have to bring her around."

Somebody grabbed Maven's arms behind him.

Royce said, "So I am going to watch this now and make sure it's done right this time, and when it's over, one of us is gonna be dead, and the other one's gonna feel a lot better."

Maven struggled against the goon holding his arms, but he lacked both strength and leverage. A strip of duct tape was ripped off a fat roll, binding Maven's wrists behind him.

A goon brought over a wooden stool, and Termino set the computer on top of it so that Royce could watch. Another handed Termino a clear plastic bag.

Termino shook it open. He said, "Less mess this way."

He thrust the bag over Maven's head. Another screech of tape, and Termino sealed the bag around Maven's neck.

Maven shook his head as though he could throw off the bag. He tried holding his breath, but quickly realized that was a losing strategy.

Maven opened his mouth and inhaled deeply, sucking some of the bag into his lips. He caught the plastic with his tongue and began chewing it.

Termino smiled. Maven heard him say, his voice muffled through the sealed bag, "This guy won't ever just lie down."

Gunfire ripped the air then. Maven thought he was being executed and fell forward, twisting and landing on his side. The goons around him scattered, the bald one firing his MAC-10 full auto, the suppressor making a sound like chattering teeth.

Someone else was here. Rounds zipped overhead, and Maven's head screamed panic and pain, his lungs bursting as he chewed on the bag in his mouth.

He tasted a thin sip of cool air. His tongue found the hole and worked to make it bigger, Maven rolling onto his back and sliding across the glazed floor to the nearest counter. Through the clear plastic, he saw low shelves cluttered with supplies. He kicked at them with his boots, spilling the contents to the floor. Elastic bands and packets of flower food and blank note cards— and scissors.

TERMINO WAS AT THE EXIT WHEN HE SAW HIS GUY KELVIN COMING UP behind him.

"What happened?" said Kelvin, an Irishman with a tribal tattoo up the side of his neck to the back of his shaved head.

Termino pushed him back toward the shooting. "Find Maven. Shoot him in the fucking head. Make sure."

Kelvin nodded and started back as Termino went out the exit.

Maven sliced the tape off his wrists. Before he could rip off his plastic hood, he saw a shadow on the floor.

He stood and vaulted off the counter, the tattoo making for a nice target as he buried one blade of the scissors in the base of the goon's bald skull. He locked up the guy's gun arm, the shooter squeezing off chattering MAC-10 rounds until Maven wrested it from his grip.

The goon fell, and Maven took cover behind a cluster of potted trees. He was ripping the plastic off his face when he saw the notebook computer on the floor, knocked onto its side.

"Maven," Royce said, staring out of the screen in utter disbelief.

Maven opened up the MAC on Royce's image, blasting the computer across the floor.

Maven stumbled outside, hoping to find the Highlander, but the vehicle was gone.

Sporadic gunfire continued inside as Maven hurried away, turning toward a weeded lot, dumping the gun once he was safely underneath the expressway.

The Papa Gino's men's room was a single bathroom with a door that locked. Maven first washed the bald goon's blood off his hands, then stared at his bandaged face in the mirror. His own image drifted in the vision of his one good eye.

He started with his clothes, removing his shirt and pants, checking socks and underwear, running every inch of fabric between his fingers. Someone knocked, and Maven froze as though he had been followed. But when he said, "Go away!"—they did.

He viewed his surgical scars in the mirror, tracing the stitch marks over his side and arm, the hem of his flesh raised and rugged. Butcher work. Had they sewn something in there, under his skin?

He resumed checking his clothes, then his boots. He noticed a fine slice along the rubber side of his heel and went after it, banging the tread on the edge of the sink until the heel piece dislodged and a battery-size gizmo fell out.

A tracking device.

That was why Lockerty had let him go. So that Maven could lead him to Royce. Only—Lockerty's hired hands had jumped too soon.

He dropped the device into the toilet and hit the handle, watching it circle the drain before being sucked away.

Maven returned to the mirror: naked, dope sick, half-blind— but truly free. He felt the tape along the edges of the dirtied bandage, then slowly, and with great pain, began peeling it back from his face.

GOING BACK

HE WAS OUTSIDE THE BANK OF AMERICA AT BOYLSTON AND EXETER when it opened Monday morning. He had no key or identification and so asked for the manager who had assisted him on his previous visits.

"Oh," said the woman, stout with a pincushion face, lowering her voice. "Are you a friend of his?"

Maven caught the word *no* before it left his lips. "I am."

"He . . . he won't be coming back. For health reasons."

She widened her eyes to stress the word *health,* and Maven knew she meant drugs. He answered questions based on his original safe-deposit-box application—the one Royce had taken him to—and passed a handwriting comparison. He was then led to the vault and his box door was unlocked and brought to the examining table. They left him alone and he opened the long lid, and it was exactly as he had feared.

Wiped out. As empty as his eye socket. He sat holding his throbbing head in his hands.

*   *   *

THE MARLBOROUGH STREET BUILDING WAS LOCKED UP, ROOF DECK
Properties and Management abandoned. Even the carriage-house
garage was padlocked.

Maven was hungry and cold. He tried the Veterans Administration building on Causeway Street, but could not get past the front
desk—again, lacking any form of identification. An administrator
took pity on him however, offering him a flannel jacket with a
ripped quilted lining out of the donation bin. She gave him a clinic
pass, and the doctor cleaned out his orbit, redressed the wound,
and gave him something for the pain.

Outside the clinic, Maven was throwing the sample pills in
the trash when he saw a vet working cars at a traffic light. The
guy's cardboard sign said that he was disabled and hungry. Maven
reacted more to the patrol cap on his head.

Maven started walking. He did 8.2 miles on his broken
bootheel—the same route he used to run after his parking-lot
shift—arriving in Quincy just before dark.

The pea green Parisienne left little space for the other tenants'
beaters in the cracked driveway. Maven climbed the rear steps to
the top-floor entrance of the triple-decker. He thumped on the
curtain-covered glass with a cold hand and waited while a light
came on inside.

The door pulled open. "Hey, you're early—"

The words died in Ricky's open mouth as he recognized Maven.

"Neal?" he said, unable to hide his shock at Maven's appearance.

Inside the kitchen, boxes of sugary cereal stood in the center of
a Formica table. The house apartment hadn't been updated since
the late 1970s. Evidently the utilities were included in the rent
because it was like a sauna inside and the radiator kept hissing.

Ricky looked drawn, purple under the eyes. A shaving cut
under his chin had scabbed. He wore baggy, pajama-type shorts
and a V-necked T-shirt with yellow underarm stains.

"You okay?" said Ricky. "You want something?"

Maven pulled a chair out from the kitchen table and sat, his feet burning.

Ricky seemed agitated, not knowing how to act or even how to stand still. "What happened to your . . . your face?"

"I fell down a flight of stairs."

"Must have been one hell of a flight of stairs." Ricky moved to the counter, opening cabinets fast. "Something to eat, maybe?"

"Yeah. I think so."

"Uh . . . how about Campbell's Chunky soup? Date's okay."

Maven rested an arm on the table. "Anything."

Ricky plugged in an electric can opener, which made a whirring sound Maven hadn't heard since he was a boy. Then a grinding noise, the can jumping off the blade halfway around. Ricky swore and fumbled for something in a drawer. He jimmied the can top with a long screwdriver in his good hand. "So. What brings you by?"

"I've got nowhere else to go. No money. No home. No clothes. Literally nothing."

Ricky glanced back, still struggling with the can. "How can that be? What about your buddies?"

"They're dead."

Ricky's screwdriver jimmying stopped. Then someone rapped at the door.

"Shit. Hey, that's just a friend of mine . . . hang on, I'll have him come back." Ricky wiped his hands on his shorts and went out, closing the first door behind him before opening the second.

Maven got to his feet. He stood by the wall, listening, unable to make out anything. Hearing voices but not words.

Something came over him, and he rushed through the doors to the exterior landing.

The guy Ricky stood close to wore a parka and a knit cap. "Oh, hi," said the guy, before Maven grabbed him by the front of his coat, spinning and throwing him inside through the two open doors, propelling him backward through the kitchen and into a living-room easy chair.

Ricky came rushing in behind them. "Neal—what in the hell?"

Maven held the guy by his collar, his other fist cocked. "Who are you! Who sent you!"

The guy in the chair couldn't get out any words.

Ricky said, "Neal, that's Greg, my buddy Greg . . ."

Greg looked freaked-out as Maven patted him down, going through his coat pockets, searching him hard. "Who sent you here?"

Ricky put a hand on Neal's arm. "Neal, hey, come on—"

Maven shoved Ricky backward, and Ricky hit the TV table, knocking over one of his cheap speakers.

Maven found a couple of bucks in the guy's jeans pocket and threw it into his lap. Then he found a medical vial inside the phone pocket of his coat. Maven yelled, "What the fuck is this?" Greg said nothing, looking to Ricky for help, not receiving any. Maven tossed the vial onto the sofa. "Who's your supplier? *Talk!*"

Greg realized he was about to get hit. "I . . . a guy I work with." "Who?"

"Just a guy. I work at a managed-care facility." Greg was teary. "A goddamn nursing home. He gives it to me, I bring it to Ricky. Ricky's my friend. He's sick."

Maven caught his breath. He straightened, releasing Greg.

Greg was hyperventilating. "What are you? Some kind of cop?"

Maven reached down for him again, and Greg flinched as if he were going to get beat up, but Maven only pulled him to his feet. Maven fixed his coat somewhat, then stepped back. "Get out of here. Don't ever come back."

Greg looked at Ricky a moment, waiting for a contradictory word. Then he stuffed his money back inside his coat pockets and walked out the doors.

Maven stared at the floor, knowing he had lost it, knowing he wasn't fully in control of himself yet.

When he looked up, the vial was gone from the sofa. Ricky stood with his head down.

Maven walked to the kitchen. He bent back the cover of the hacked-open can and gobbled down the cold soup. Lumpy, gelatinous paste, but he barely tasted it, the food landing in his stomach like a fist.

He slid the long-shaft screwdriver into his belt. He found Ricky's car keys hanging on a peg near the door, next to Ricky's patrol cap. Maven took both.

Maven said, "I need to borrow your car."

Dark Energy

He drove the Parisienne back into Boston, cruising a gas station sharing a parking lot with a McDonald's just two blocks from a Topeka Street methadone clinic. He parked and walked over to the gated trash pen beside the gas station, away from the brightest lights. He waited with his hands in his pockets, Ricky's cap brim low over his eye bandage, until a guy in a black-and-gold Bruins hoodie sauntered past.

"Don't be so fucking obvious, man."

Maven let the guy cross the parking lot before following him. A row of trash-strewn evergreens lined a fence.

The runner doubled back, hands in his front pouch pockets. "Well?"

"I want it," said Maven.

The runner looked him over, sniffling. "You don't look cop."

"You neither."

He decided. "Front me ten, see what I can do."

"I'm trusting you?"

"That's how it works. Where the fuck you been?"

Maven said, "Iraq."

"Huh." The runner hunched his shoulders against the cold. "That's fucked-up." He snuffled deep, swallowing snot. "So, welcome back. Now pay to play."

Maven made as if he were going to do so, then grabbed the runner by his neck, spinning him around and putting the screwdriver to his throat, the point poised at his carotid artery.

He reached inside the runner's pouch and took from him a flip knife and a phone. "Where's the holder?"

"The who?"

Maven pressed the point harder against the runner's throat, enough to feel the artery pulsing through the handle.

"You crazy?"

"Wanna find out?" said Maven.

AROUND THE CORNER ON ATKINSON, A WIRE-TOPPED CHAIN-LINK fence ran to a shorter wooden fence abutting a stone wall. The holder emerged from his nook, seeing the figure jogging toward him under the weak, yellow streetlights in a Bruins sweatshirt, hood up.

Maven shocked him, grabbing him by the throat. The holder bore a little chin growth trimmed into a diamond, and Maven stuck the point of the runner's flip knife blade just below it.

He frisked the holder, coming away with another phone and knife, pocketing them, then bracing the holder's throat with his forearm. He used the knife blade to slice through the fabric beneath the guy's bulging cargo pants pocket and removed a folded wad of cash.

The holder couldn't talk because of the Baggies of crack cocaine tucked under his tongue. Maven chopped him below his diamond-bearded chin, covering his mouth until the guy had no choice but to choke them down.

Maven said, "Whose corner is this?"

"My fucking corner."

"Who you front for?"

The holder said, "You crazy."

Maven took out the holder's phone and opened it, snapping a photograph of the guy. "Everyone in your contact list gets this, with a message saying you're five-oh and you flipped—"

"Okay!" said the guy with the knife at his throat.

MAVEN ENTERED THE SHADOW OF THE TREES FRONTING THE SMALL house on a quiet Forest Hills side street. He waited out a bout of dizziness, then looked inside the window, seeing the back of a sofa in a darkened room.

He opened up the holder's phone and selected the dealer's digits from the list. He thumbed him a text message that read, *5-0 coming—ditch phones and split.*

Then he waited.

The room brightened and footsteps clumped around inside. Maven heard jingling keys, then the front door opened and sneaker soles tapped flagstones. The Jeep next to Maven chirped, the locks disengaging, the dealer rounding the corner with a backpack on his shoulder, wearing two sweatshirts under a coat.

When he opened the driver's door, Maven ran at him from behind, shoving him across the driver's seat into the passenger side, the dealer's head striking the door.

Maven ran his hands up inside the guy's sweatshirts, finding a pistol. The dealer squealed, trapped and unable to see, thinking this was it.

"Don't," he said. "Don't do me like this."

Maven grabbed the keys out of his hand and closed the door, saying, "Cut the meek act, sit up."

He did. The multiple layers bulked him out, but the dealer had good size to begin with. He was surprisingly clean-cut. He looked at Maven and the pistol and said, "You're fucking crazy."

"You shitbags keep telling me that." Maven stuck the key in the ignition, starting up the Jeep. Then he unzipped the backpack.

Phones, another handgun, and cash below.

Lots of cash.

Maven stuck the backpack under his legs, on the floor against his calves. "I want to see Royce."

The dealer stared, hiding his trembling under a constant nodding. "And?"

"You telling me you don't know the name?"

"I know the president's name too. Doesn't mean I met the man."

Maven threw the Jeep in reverse and banged out over the curb, riding fast down the street. "What other names you know?"

RICKY WOKE UP DEHYDRATED, HAVING SWEATED THROUGH HIS clothes. He changed into boxers and stumbled out to the fridge for some Mountain Dew and found Maven sitting at the kitchen table.

Instead of food in front of him, there were two guns, two ejected clips, a handful of phones, two knives, seven or eight thick bundles of cash, and a folded white take-out bag scribbled all over with a checklist of names and addresses.

Maven, all dark energy, looked up at Ricky. "I'm gonna be here a couple of days, maybe a week. Maybe longer."

KOOL

Lash showed up late at the shoot house in Mattapan. This one was full service. You go in through the front door and choose door A or door B. Door B was unlocked and led to a warren of rooms inside, each one worse than the next. That was the shooting gallery, where you shot, snorted, or smoked whatever you bought through the pay hole in door A. That door had been reinforced with a cage soldered into a steel frame, two hinged slots cut into the backing wood, one at eye level, the other at hand level.

Door A was open and warped now and wouldn't close. A table inside had been knocked over, a bag of Doritos spilled on the floor, along with Baggies and cellophane and powder. All this amid a drying pool of urine.

DEA agent Novack was inside waiting for him. "Still here, huh?"

Lash nodded. "Still got me bouncing."

"How long?"

"Any day now."

Novack said, "Hope you like tortillas."

Lash nodded. Mexico was the current hotspot. Also Afghanistan. The War on Terror had rejuvenated the Golden Crescent—Afghanistan, Pakistan, and Iran—now producing 90 percent of the world's opium.

Lash said, "The issue is—do I want to go back overseas, leave my boy? Or maybe it's time to just walk away?"

Novack was surprised. "I can't remember life without the shield."

"You and me both, brother."

Paramedics were attending to the only guy left inside, bleeding lazily from a gunshot to the thigh. Whiskers jutted out from his parched brown skin, too tired to grow anymore. He smoked a Kool.

The guy was already under arrest. He was more offended than anything. "You gotta get this freak, barging into my house."

"Your house?" Lash said.

The guy shrugged. Another abandoned property colonized by zombies. A neighbor had buttonholed Lash on his way in. "People going in and out all night and day."

Lash told her, "Why you neighbors always wait until the police show up to drop a dime?"

He looked at the blood being photographed on the floor. "Anyone shoot back at him?"

"No chance, no time," said the Kool smoker. "Dude efficient."

"You get a good look?"

"White-ass mutherfucka. Came in, did a buy first. Feeling it out. People don't respect nothing no more, not a locked door, nothing."

"I need more than skin color."

"Wore an eye patch. Silly-ass pirate disguise. And an army-type cap. Camouflage on it. Dude was circumcised."

Lash said, "Come again?"

"Whipped out his dick and pissed on my stash. You gotta get this freak."

"He took money, but not product?"

The Kool guy pointed to the mess on the floor.

Lash said, "You said an army cap?"

Ladder

MAVEN CROUCHED BEHIND A BURLAP-WRAPPED SHRUB, WAITING for a buyer to pull up. He closed his eye when he could, resting it, easing the strain. He was still getting used to the eye patch he had purchased at CVS.

A blue Camaro arrived, and Maven grabbed the guy on the front steps, hair-walking him up to the door, ringing the bell. The homeowner tried to slam it shut when he saw Maven behind the buyer, so Maven used the buyer's head as a battering ram.

Inside, he held a Glock 19 to the head of the homeowner as the guy worked the combination on a closet safe. He dumped the cash and two guns into Maven's backpack and pulled out two cellophane-wrapped half-kilo bricks of cocaine.

Maven asked him where the rest was.

The homeowner said there was no more. Maven hit him in the face.

The homeowner showed him a brownie pan in the kitchen refrigerator containing a full kilo wrapped in wax paper.

Maven sat both men at the table where he could see them. He found a roll of aluminum foil and wrapped it around the cocaine, then placed the shiny bundle into the range-top microwave and punched in five minutes on HIGH.

A bout of dizziness made him reach for the counter. He sensed them growing bold, and turned fast, the room listing a bit in his vision. "Where is Royce?"

The homeowner shook his head, staring at his microwave. "I don't know."

Maven pressed START. The foil started to crackle and spark.

"Where's Royce?"

"I don't know!"

The rotating package glowed, then burst into bright silver flame. White smoke leaked out of the edges of the door.

"Royce!" said Maven.

"I don't—nobody knows!"

The microwave popped as though bursting, the smoke turning an ominous gray. The homeowner started to get to his feet, but Maven gun-pointed him back into his chair. He couldn't get anything out of him about Royce and had to settle for information on the homeowner's supplier—the next highest rung on this interminable ladder.

The smoke detector went shrieking as the microwave door melted and the oven burst into flames, the fire going into the wall. Maven found a kitchen telephone and dialed 911. He said, to the dispatcher who answered, "I am a drug dealer and my house is on fire." Then he tossed the telephone into the owner's lap and walked out.

SOME NIGHTS, PARKED ACROSS THE STREET IN THE PARISIENNE, HE watched the hopefuls milling around the roped-off entrance to Club Precipice. But Royce never showed.

One morning he drove out to Gridley and knocked on Danielle's parents' door, but she had moved out again. They didn't know where.

MAVEN SAT AT THE USUAL ROUND CORNER TABLE INSIDE THE BERKELEY Grill, Ricky his only companion. They had a new waiter Maven didn't recognize. He did the Royce thing, ordering their Budweisers and steaks and a few appetizers, then asked if the headwaiter could come to the table when he had a chance.

Maven looked at Ricky, who had probably never had a good steak in his life. He didn't know why he had brought him, except that he didn't want to be sitting at this big table all alone. Ricky picked at the appetizers with his good hand, chewing an asparagus spear, the first vegetable he'd eaten all year.

Sebastian, the headwaiter, with the server in tow, slowed when he recognized Maven. Sebastian covered his surprise with a quick smile and approached the table.

"Mr. Maven," he said, tanned and tailored as always. "I'm sorry, I didn't . . . no one told me you were here."

Maven nodded, chewing. "This is my friend Ricky."

Ricky didn't wear his hat inside the restaurant, his head dent visible for all to see. Ricky waved his Bud bottle. "Hey."

Sebastian nodded back, the barest minimum of courtesy. "I trust everything is prepared . . ."

"Perfect as always, Sebastian. I notice you changed the broccoli marinade."

"In fact we did."

Maven nodded, eating as he talked. "Business good?"

"Well, the recession, you know. People still appreciate a good meal."

Maven nodded again, making Sebastian wait. "Tell me, does Mr. Royce still come in?"

"Only occasionally. Not as often as he once did."

"If you see him before I do, would you give him a message?"

"Certainly."

Maven worked with his notched tongue at some bit of meat stuck in his teeth. "Tell him I am going to kill him."

Sebastian went apron white. He stood very still, as though awaiting further instructions. "Very good, then . . . ," he said finally, begging off, making his way back to the kitchen.

HECTOR, WHO WENT BY THE STREET NAME HEX, WAS EXAMINED BY A guy with an audio scanner. Royce entered the foyer wearing dress pants and a sweater of warm yellow cashmere.

The audio guy pulled down his headphones. "He's okay."

Hex said, "You think I'd come here wired?"

Royce said, "Maybe without your knowledge."

Hex followed Royce into a solarium overlooking a backyard sloping to trees. Another of Royce's guys was out there, walking under a black umbrella in the rain. Termino muted the television.

Royce said, "So you saw him."

Hex said, "I saw him."

"How'd you get away without saying anything?"

"I was there to pick up a payment. He thought I was just another buyer. My guy didn't dime me out because he knows what's good for him. But, Christ, he put him through the wringer. Set his fucking house on fire."

"He took money that was yours. And therefore partly mine. And you let him."

Hex smiled away the attempted insult. "He had the drop on me. I know when I'm beat. This guy's on a mission."

"Who's he working with?"

"I didn't see anyone. All by his lonesome."

"Not for Lockerty, then."

"I think that last gambit at the Flower Exchange chewed up the rest of Lockerty's beaten ass."

"No. He's out there waiting. Watching. Hoping Maven can succeed where he failed."

"Who the fuck is this Maven, anyway?"

Royce looked out at the rain. "Trouble."

"Well, he's got armor now. He was wearing a Kevlar vest."

Royce sighed.

"He scotched the product and took the money and guns, but what he really wanted was you."

"And you're sure you didn't tell him anything?"

"I wouldn't be here if I did. He would."

Royce accepted that.

Hex said, "What the hell did you do to this guy?"

"I stole his money, killed his girlfriend, and tried to kill him. Twice."

Termino said, "I'm sick of sitting here talking about this. I say we flush him out. Get him to stick out his neck a bit, so we can cut his throat and end this fucking thing once and for all."

ROYCE HAD HIS HAUNTS AND HABITS, AND MAVEN KNEW THAT IF HE worked hard enough, their paths would once again cross.

Maven was watching Sonsie—the site of his and Royce's first sit-down—from a shoe store on Newbury Street when a black SUV pulled up at the valet station. The vehicle obstructed Maven's view of the first two people entering the restaurant, but two other occupants emerged, large guys in bulky North Face parkas, remaining out on the sidewalk in front of the restaurant's front windows.

One of them was Termino. Maven started right out of the store, stopping once he reached the sidewalk. Too many civilians. By the time he fought his way inside past Termino and friend, Royce would be gone.

Two beat cops came along the sidewalk on foot patrol. Maven took a chance, sliding the Beretta from the back of his waist into a curbside trash container, then approaching the cops.

"Hey, excuse me. Yeah, it's none of my business, but those two guys over there, who just got out of that SUV? I saw them zip up, and they're both carrying guns."

The cops thanked Maven and started across the street. They approached Termino and the other guy, starting an inquiry. Maven walked around them toward the entrance to Sonsie. Termino saw him coming and lunged—the cops grabbing Termino and shoving him hard up against the glass.

Maven walked inside, right past the hostess, straight at Royce's corner table. Royce saw him and stiffened, looking to the front windows.

Termino was being frisked by the cops in plain sight of everyone inside the restaurant.

Maven stopped before the table. Royce sported a tan wool blazer over an open-collared shirt, Maven wearing a work shirt of lined flannel, carpenter pants, black Timberland boots.

The silence between them was like a battle of wills, until Royce's server appeared. "Another for lunch?" she asked.

Maven pulled out a chair and sat down. His eyes never left Royce. "Mr. Royce will start with the iced market oysters."

The server departed. Royce again checked on the shakedown at the front windows. He knew he was on his own here. He looked back at Maven and said, "You must feel very clever."

Maven said nothing.

Royce relaxed a bit when he saw that Maven wasn't going to come right at him over the table. "Iced market oysters. We first sat here, you couldn't even read a fucking menu."

"You taught me a lot."

"Congratulations on being such a nuisance. Using my own game against me. I didn't think you believed in karma."

"I do when it carries a gun."

Royce checked Maven's hands, both of them resting on the table. Royce's were just out of sight, in his lap.

Maven said, "I'm not interested in any big explanation of your master plan. You can save that tale for the suckers working for you now. I just want to know—why?"

"Why?"

"Me and Milkshake and Suarez. Why lead us along so much? Why fuck around with us and make us believe, if you were going to off us in the end anyway? Why make it so fucking personal?"

Royce grinned as though it were the simplest question in the world. "To keep you loyal."

"It was all bullshit, then. All those hours spent together. All the jobs, all the talk. All the steaks and the late nights."

"Not all of it. Part of it was me feeling you out. The other two— they were good soldiers, period. You were the only one with any real ability. But no cold-bloodedness. The military had infected you with this thing known as 'honor.'"

"So you're just a sociopath."

"When did that become such a bad word? People use that term like it's a disease. Think about it. It brings me no harm. Only power. That's not a disease, that's a gift."

The shock of seeing Maven had worn off, Royce getting some of his bravado back.

"You think this is it for me? Kingpin of this shitty town—you think this is the top? This is just the beginning, Maven. I have ambition like you can't even fathom. Kings in exile—remember? You'll always be a peasant. A dangerous peasant, but a peasant nonetheless."

Royce's voice fell away as Maven picked up the knife at his table setting. Maven turned it point-down against the table, the end of the handle against his open palm, slowly rotating his flat hand, cutting a tiny hole in the table linen.

Maven said, "I figured I'd end up getting screwed by the army. The government—I expected that. But never by a fellow vet."

Royce glanced again at the front window. "You try anything here, you'll be dead before you reach the door.

"Not as dead as you'll be."

As Maven pressed down harder on the knife handle, linen threads snapped, widening the cut. It was going to happen—right here, right now. Nothing could stop it. Maven realized, for the first time, that nothing existed beyond this moment. His life had no meaning beyond this final act of vengeance. He was looking at a big door marked EXIT with nothing—nothing—beyond.

A woman appeared at the table near Royce. Maven thought it was the server and did not look up at first, his eyes staying hard on Royce. When nothing was said, and no food was set down on the table, Maven glanced up at the interloper.

Danielle stood there in a loose top and jeans, carrying a clutch, back from a long trip to the bathroom. Maven did not need to look into her eyes to know that she was high—but look into her eyes he did.

Danielle appeared run-down, shrunken. The spark had gone out of her attractiveness. She could have been anyone now.

Her stare back at him was one of horror.

"This must come as a surprise to you," said Royce. He stood, aping gentlemanly manners, pulling Danielle down into her chair. "When she called me to dime you out, I guess I realized how much I missed her. How valuable she is to me."

Seated, she continued to stare at Maven, his eye patch, his one good eye.

Maven thought he had died all of his deaths already. He was wrong.

Royce continued, "This is a reunion I never thought I'd see. Anyone feel like champagne?"

The oysters arrived on a platter with an artful assortment of condiments. The knife was still under Maven's hand, and he gripped the handle, slipping the blade point inside the oyster shell, twisting until he heard the pop. He slid the oyster into his mouth and swallowed, tasting nothing.

In this way he was no different from Danielle. All the flavor had gone out of their lives. They were both dead inside.

Royce said, "And here I thought you two would have more to say to each other."

Maven said to her, "Why?"

Her gaze fell to the table.

"You knew what he would do."

She could not look at him.

"Between you and me, Maven"—Royce sipped his Pellegrino—"I think she's smoking it now."

Danielle's eyes flashed up at Maven. Trying to tell him something. Admitting she was in the grip of a thing she hated. Drugs, or Royce. Both.

"The weak exist to be exploited, Maven." Royce sat back, one arm firmly on Danielle's leg. "And what with you running all around town, opening fire hydrants, acting recklessly—I figure she's safest with me for now. I know you wouldn't want anything to happen to her. Not like that other girl . . ."

A killer calm spread through Maven. Royce had pushed him to the edge. To a place beyond insult. Where the only recourse was direct action.

For the first time since leaving the military, Maven saw that his mission was evident and clear. He was a soldier again.

At the front windows, the cops appeared satisfied with Termino and the other gunman, their licenses and permits. Maven wished he hadn't dumped his Beretta.

He swiped his lips with his napkin, dropping it onto his plate. Royce kept Danielle close as Maven got to his feet, standing over the table. Pain seared in his missing eye, but the rest of him was at peace. Maven took one last look at both of them—Danielle looking away, unable to meet his one good eye—then turned and started out of the restaurant.

"Now don't go away angry," said Royce to his back.

Maven reached the sidewalk as the cops were starting away. He made certain Termino saw him, the direction in which he was headed, then he walked the short distance to the Parisienne.

STANDOFF

MAVEN DROVE STRAIGHT BACK TO QUINCY. HIS HEAD START wouldn't last long. He left the Parisienne in the driveway and moved quickly up the back steps. Inside, he jammed a chair underneath the second doorknob, then used his key in the lock he had installed on the spare bedroom. He unzipped one of the two duffel bags there and pulled a Glock 19 from the bag of weapons. He double-checked the load on his way out across the apartment to the street-facing windows.

He saw no one below. Not yet.

He lowered the torn shades and kept a vigil through one of the open flaps.

Twenty minutes later, a dark blue minivan turned the corner, signaling a turn in the middle of the street. A sedan pulled out from the curb, opening up a space that the minivan then took.

Ricky emerged from his bedroom. He saw Maven at the window with the Glock in his hand, and then the chair propped up against the back door. Through the open door to the always locked spare room, Ricky saw the oversize duffel bag full of stolen guns and rifles, and the regular-size duffel bag zipped shut next to it.

Ricky said nothing. He returned to his bedroom and shut the door.

Maven sat down in the easy chair facing the back entrance and waited.

MINUTES BECAME HOURS, AND MAVEN'S ANXIETY TURNED INTO annoyance. His head still throbbed, all that adrenaline gone to waste. He checked the street again, and another car looked suspicious, but it was parked on his side of the street and he did not have the angle to see anyone sitting inside.

When night fell, he turned out all the lights, giving his sore eye a break as he sat in darkness.

Ricky emerged one hour before midnight. The light from his room was the only glow inside the apartment. "Um . . . I'm heading out."

Maven, seated in the easy chair with the Glock on the table next to him, shook his head.

"Can I turn on a light in here?"

"No."

Ricky swiped his nose on the sleeve of his T-shirt. "What's up, what's going on?"

"Outside. Some guys waiting for me to leave."

Ricky saw duct tape patching holes in the drawn shades. "Okay." He went into the bathroom to take a leak. When he came back out, he said, "So why can't I go then?"

"They might think you are me."

"And?"

"And shoot you dead."

Ricky stood there a moment, formulating a comeback. He then returned to his room and closed the door.

Less than an hour later, they heard harsh thumping and muffled yells from the floor below. Ricky came out into the living room where Maven was standing in the dark, gun in hand.

"What the hell?" hissed Ricky.

Maven held out his hand to silence Ricky. "They just moved in on your neighbors downstairs."

WHAT MAVEN THOUGHT WOULD END QUICKLY AND VIOLENTLY turned into a slow-boiling standoff. He checked the street occasionally, watching cars pull up and switch off. Royce had his men working six-hour shifts.

Ricky came out of his room midmorning, dressed to leave. "Okay. I'm going now."

Maven opened the refrigerator freezer. "I wouldn't."

"It's daylight. They'll see I'm not you."

"They won't care."

"I'll go with my hands up."

"Where is it you need to go so badly?"

Ricky looked at the tipped-back chair beneath the doorknob. "You don't understand . . . I need my medicine. I got a lot of pain."

Maven closed the freezer with a frozen pizza in his hand. Ricky eventually retreated to his room again.

He reemerged twenty minutes later, this time with a coat on. "Look, this is bullshit." He launched into a prepared speech. "I can't take being locked in here, I just can't. This is my place, and I need to go, so I'm going. You hear me? I'm going to go."

He walked to the door, expecting Maven to stop him. Maven just kept chewing his pizza, his gun on the table next to a napkin.

Ricky stood before the front legs of the tipped-back chair, not getting the reaction he wanted. "If you knew they were following you, why'd you lead them back here? To my home?"

"I needed a gun."

"So now you're trapped here. Me too. Brilliant. That's fucking great."

Maven said nothing.

Ricky said, "Okay, if they want you so bad, why aren't they coming in?"

"Because no one wants to be first."

Ricky gripped the legs and removed the chair from beneath the knob. He opened it to the outside door.

"They will take you, Ricky. They will use you to try to get to me. But I will not bargain, and I will not bend."

Ricky stood before the second door, his chest rising and falling with anxiety.

MAVEN TOOK CATNAPS IN THE EASY CHAIR, RESTING HIS EYE AND TAK-ing the edge off his exhaustion. He kept waking from a dream of them coming up the back steps and rushing inside.

Ricky lay on the living room sofa halfheartedly playing *Grand Theft Auto* to pass the time. He was shot in an attempted carjacking, then threw aside his controller, speckled with beads of sweat. He jumped to his feet and walked twice around the room, disappearing into the bathroom, starting up the shower yet again.

Maven checked the Weather Channel forecast every few hours. He went to the window to check the street.

At the corner bus stop, three men waited inside the transparent plastic kiosk. The bus came and went, and only two of them had boarded.

The heat had been turned off a few hours ago. Ricky hadn't yet noticed. He kept taking showers because he was sweating through his clothes. Maven was disgusted by how short fentanyl's leash was on Ricky. When he emerged from the bathroom, Ricky wandered the rooms patting at the skin on his face, smoothing down his wet hair.

*   *   *

OVERNIGHT, RICKY WAS WATCHING *The Tyra Banks Show* WITH HIS arms crossed when the power went out.

Maven reached for his Glock and stepped silently into the kitchen. He watched the door and waited, listening.

He heard footsteps on the roof. He positioned himself in the shadows beneath the ceiling's only skylight as a shadow appeared on the slanting rectangle of moonlight on the floor. Ricky had fallen back into a fitful sleep on the sofa, where the man on the roof could not see him.

Maven readied the Glock. He watched the man cup his eyes to the glass and peer inside. Seeing nothing, he straightened and went away.

The apartment was quiet for the rest of the night.

RICKY KNELT AT THE TOILET BOWL, HIS DRY HEAVES BRINGING UP nothing. The water had been turned off, the interior of the bowl disgusting. Ricky muttering into it, "I gotta get outta here, I gotta get outta here."

He stumbled into the living room wrapped in a blanket as the lights flickered on again. The wall phone rang almost immediately.

Maven stood but did not approach the phone. The machine answered.

Royce said, "Not man enough to come out? You disappoint me, Maven. But don't worry. It won't be long now. Some guys, when they're cornered like this, they decide to tap out rather than face the end. I know you won't deprive me like that."

Royce hung up, and Maven stood still a moment longer before returning to his project, laid out on the floor: a yellow rain slicker covered with duct tape.

"What is that?" said Ricky.

Maven said, "It's going to rain."

Ricky turned the TV on, but a few moments later the power went out again.

MAVEN SHOOK RICKY AWAKE AFTER SUNDOWN. RICKY STARTLED AT the sight, Maven bulked up in vest armor beneath the tape-dulled slicker. A roar of falling water disoriented Ricky, who looked over and saw that it was pouring rain in his living room.

The easy chair had been set beneath the removed skylight, absorbing the water and most of the sound. The two duffel bags were zipped shut and waiting near the chair, as was a heavy coat for Ricky.

"Pass me up the bags," said Maven, who sprang from the easy-chair armrest to the lip of the skylight, hauling himself up.

The gun bag was heavy. Ricky pushed it up to Maven's hand with great effort. Then the money, which was lighter. Then Maven reached down his empty hand.

Ricky shrugged on the coat and let Maven pull him up over the edge, dragging him onto the roof.

The fresh, wet air was a shock. Maven laid the skylight back over the opening, then carried both bags to the edge. He tossed them onto the roof of the neighboring house, a few yards across a three-story drop. Then he went back for Ricky, sitting on the roof near the skylight.

"No way. Not jumping."

Maven pulled on him. "Get up."

"No." Ricky shook him off with more vehemence than Maven thought possible, whacking his arm away. "Leave me here."

"Come on."

He reached for Ricky again, and Ricky went at him with his fists. "Leave me!" he yelled. "Just leave me, like you did before. You don't care. Just go." Ricky sat in the rain as if he were never going to move again. "You were my only friend."

Maven stared at him a moment, feeling Ricky's words, weighing his options—then he knelt and took Ricky's wrist, getting him up and pulling him across his shoulders in a fireman's carry. Ricky did not fight him. Maven hauled him in that way to the edge of the roof, then paced back from it to measure out a running start.

The leap was ugly, but they made it, falling hard onto the lower roof.

Maven carried the bags, and Ricky followed, down the rear stairs past interior lights coming on. They reached the ground and went around the far side of the next house, up to the corner nearest the street.

A bus came along, moving right to left. Maven slung the money bag over his shoulder, grasping Ricky's coat with his free hand, and as the bus passed, he ran them across the street behind it, obscured by its bulk and bright headlights.

Maven ducked and went from parked car to parked car along the sidewalk until he was two away from the only idling vehicle. The driver's head was tipped back.

The dealer known as Hex jerked awake at the knock on the window, opening the door in an obedient daze. Maven went in hard, releasing the seat back and dragging Hex into the rear seat. Ricky dropped into the driver's seat, and Maven, beating on Hex, told Ricky to drive to the beach.

The tide was in, the water moving with the slow lubricity of freezer-chilled vodka. Maven dragged Hex onto the sand. He held Hex's phone and pistol.

"Where is Royce?" said Maven.

Hex wiped his bloody nose. One eye was swollen shut and he was missing a shoe. "Go to hell you mother—"

Maven shot him in the leg.

Hex howled and rolled in the sand.

Maven said, "Let's try that again."

SNOWFLAKES

MAVEN CRUISED PAST THE GRANITE MARKER EMBEDDED IN THE stone wall next to an electronic gate. The driveway curled into the trees, the house a mystery from the road. Royce renting an unsold mansion in the down real estate market.

Maven pulled over some fifty yards past the gate. Adrenaline was sending weird panic impulses to his head, his deep oxygenating breathing fogging the windshield.

Ricky lay against the passenger door, his head against the cool window. The rain was fading, and the faint shadow of it sliding down the glass made Ricky appear to be melting. Maven's aunt had once taken him to a wax museum when he was a kid, and Ricky resembled those figures now—neither truly alive, nor quite dead either.

Maven went over the thin stone wall with the gun bag, ducking through wet hemlock trees to the edge of the lawn. He was wide left of the driveway, the big house shining brightly before him, every window lit as though for a party. The rain was turning to light snow, lit brilliantly by prowler lights glaring down from the high corners and up onto the house from the ground. Even the drive was ringed by low accent lights.

The man standing outside the front steps was a clear silhouette, hands in his pockets, smoking a cigar. Maven slid the rifle out of the gun bag. No wind, but the falling snow played with his one-eyed perception, giving him a sensation of rising.

No sound cover either. Maven relaxed his shoulders and sighted the target. He did not want to fire twice. He squeezed the trigger and the rifle cracked and the silhouette went down. Cigar smoke hung in the air a moment before dissipating.

Maven exchanged the rifle for a Colt and started out from the tree cover at a jog. He was twenty yards from the corner of the house when a figure appeared in a second-floor window. Danielle, dressed plainly in sweatpants and a T-shirt, looked down at him without any shock or scream.

Maven slowed but did not stop, continuing along the side of the house, down wet stone steps. He came out in back to a courtyard centered on a pedestal birdbath, bordered by low shrubs, angled off a protruding addition. No other gunmen lurked on the grounds that night: they were back in Quincy, in the apartment below Ricky's.

Through tall French doors, he saw a library. A college football game played on a wall screen; a gunman wearing a shoulder holster was eating a sandwich.

Maven unzipped his slicker and tucked the Colt inside the front of his waistband. From the gun bag, he lifted the Benelli 12-gauge, a beauty he had taken off a Vietnamese guy outside Codman Square. Maven pumped and fired, pumped and fired—blowing out both door hinges with slug loads, kicking his way inside.

The gunman knocked over his sandwich trying to clear his holster, Maven drawing his Colt and shooting first, neck and shoulder.

ROYCE WAS IN THE FIRST-FLOOR STUDY CHANGING HIS INTERNET radio-station preferences when he heard the shotgun blasts. He stood, knocking his chair over. He looked around for his Beretta, and, realizing he had left it upstairs, grabbed his cell phone and went to the door.

Termino opened it, looking for him. Termino had a wire in his ear. "Your little possum slipped his trap."

Royce swallowed. Quincy was a good twenty minutes away. "Stupid fucks."

"Good help is hard to find," said Termino, pulling his pistol out of his belt, doing a brass check. "He's all mine now."

MAVEN HEARD GUNMEN COMING AND GRABBED THE GUN BAG AND ran to the kitchen, stopping at the door to the hall. One gunman had gone to the library, another remained at the stairs. Trying to hold him down here, maybe drive him back outside.

Maven slid the bag out into the foyer, and the gunman turned and opened up his tiny, full-auto Steyr on the decoy. Maven rushed out, cutting down the gunman at the stairs, then firing down the side hallway to push back the gunman returning from the library.

Then he grabbed his bag and took to the stairs. He leapt up onto the oak handrail to get a look at what awaited him on the second-floor landing.

One gunman. Maven held the bag in front of him like a shield, firing, diving into the first room on the right.

ROYCE DROPPED THE ARMORED VEST OVER HIS HEAD, TIGHTENING the Velcro fasteners one-handedly as he slid off the Beretta's safety, rushing into Danielle's bedroom.

He found her seated before a three-part table mirror in the far corner. She was adjusting the straps of one of the new dresses he had bought her, running her fingertips along her décolletage, as though getting ready to go out.

"What the hell are you—"

More gunfire. Danielle just looked at him, all three of her in the mirrors.

Royce grabbed her by the arm, pulling her out of the room toward the servants' stairs.

MAVEN CUT THROUGH AN ADJOINING BATH INTO A LARGE, FURNISHED bedroom. He paused there to switch guns, and the lights went out. A few rooms at a time—Royce's goons switching off circuit breakers—everything going dark and silent, the heat going off in the floor registers.

Maven dropped to a crouch. The exterior security lights still worked, shining in the windows from below, throwing dramatic shadows onto the ceilings. Maven loaded up from the bag, knowing he had to leave it. His empty eye ached. He shed his slicker, revealing twin holsters and extra magazines taped to his vest.

Maven went low around the corner, back toward the head of the hallway. He heard footsteps on the stairs, and some in the wide hallway.

"Maven," said Termino, calling out from somewhere nearby. "Why don't you—"

Maven didn't wait, he darted out and started firing, striking the body on the stairs. Someone opened up on him from the other end of the hall, and Maven returned, holding him off long enough to duck through another door.

Maven bumped up against a wall and smelled cedar. He realized he was inside a broad, empty closet. He rushed back out, taking rounds in the side and back, his vest repelling them as he folded inside the next doorway.

Another bedroom. This one smelling of perfume. *Danielle,* he thought, though he was alone there—for the moment. He waited behind the door, ears ringing, unable to hear footsteps.

Flashlights now. In the hallway. Going door-to-door.

Maven got low and stayed that way.

Two flashlights and submachine guns pushed inside, scanning the room. Their beams picked up a three-part mirror in the far corner, bouncing their light and movement around the room. They opened fire on the perceived ambush, shooting wildly, everything staccato and strobed in the room. Another gunman rushed in to join them, and Maven fired low from behind, dropping all three.

The flashlights fell, throwing odd slants of light across the floor. The gunmen groaned, gasped. Maven stayed where he was.

Termino moved inside. His flashlight playing over the faces of his wounded men, looking for Maven.

By the time his beam found the shattered mirrors, Termino understood what had happened. He never turned. He didn't bother.

He saw his reflection in the glass fragments remaining in one side of the mirror. Maven standing behind him, gun out.

"Fine," said Termino. "Whatever."

A SINGLE GUNSHOT PUNCTUATED THE BARRAGE OF AUTOMATIC FIRE on the floor below. *They got him,* Royce thought, belt-tucking his Beretta, keeping hold of Danielle's arm as he dug out his phone.

"Termino," he said, using the push-to-talk function. "Lew. Lew?"

Maven's voice answered, "He's unable to take your call right now."

Royce hardly believed it. Danielle squirmed under his grip, he was squeezing her biceps so tight.

He recovered, reasserting himself, a note of command in his voice. "You listen here, Maven. I've got Danielle with me, so be very fucking careful where you—"

Ponk! Ponk! Ponk!

Three chips cracked open in the floor around Royce's feet. Maven, firing blindly up at them. Royce staggered backward, unhit.

He had only three guys left upstairs with him. He grabbed a submachine gun off the nearest and shoved the guy toward the stairs.

"Hold him off!" said Royce, pushing Danielle toward the bedroom door at the end of the darkened hall.

MAVEN LOCATED THE SIDE STAIRWAY, RUSHING UP TO THE THIRD floor. He exited the alcove and entered the middle of the hall, behind the gunmen watching the main stairs. Maven had the drop on them.

Then a three-round burst from behind ripped up the back of his vest. Maven twisted, went down, fired behind him.

It was Royce, spitting flame from a door at the end of the hall.

The gunmen, alerted by Royce's volley, spun and opened up on the end of the hall, half-blind.

Maven rolled to face them, firing from the floor, shins and knees, dropping them.

He rolled back to face Royce, who had closed the door by then.

Maven rolled back again, finishing off two gunmen, a third alligator-crawling into a doorway to die.

Maven crabbed into a room to reload.

ROYCE DUMPED HIS PHONE AND THE BERETTA ONTO THE DRESSER, needing both hands free for the Steyr. It carried a thirty-round magazine, but he had no time to check how many were left.

He went to the east-facing window and looked down into the security light shining upward. A lower corner of the roof was near enough, but then what? A long fall onto the courtyard and two broken legs.

Barricading the door would be an idiot's play. He wanted Maven blundering inside, didn't he? Walking right into the chain saw.

So he set up along the shadows of the side wall, ten feet laterally from the door. He gripped the Steyr, ready to open up on the first person to walk inside. All he had to do now was to provoke Maven into making one final mistake.

Royce looked to Danielle, standing at the dresser with her back to him, her eyes catching some of the window light, teary, glowering.

"Call him," hissed Royce, crouching against the wall with a tight smile. "Call to him!"

MAVEN WAS SORE FROM THE ARMOR HITS, BUT STILL NOT CARRYING any lead. His breath was short and shallow, coming from high in his chest. He couldn't get enough air.

He had finished reloading when he heard Danielle's voice.

"Neal! Neal . . ."

Like stabs from a knife. Driven by thoughts of Samara, he rushed into the hallway. A thin strip of silver light lay at the bottom of the door at the end, small fingers of light reaching out from bullet holes in the wood.

Royce was behind that door. Maven didn't hesitate, starting toward it, pistols up.

Bang! Bang-bang!

The reports stopped him. He expected more holes in the door, but the shots had remained inside the room.

He ran at the door, striking the knob square with the heel of his boot and busting it open, crashing inside.

The barrage he had expected—the one he was relying upon to tell him the source and direction of his target—did not occur.

Instead, he found Royce on the floor at the base of the shadowed side wall. A puddle of darkness was expanding beneath his neck. The Steyr was inches from his hand, though he showed no interest in it.

Maven turned. Danielle stood in the shadow of a dresser, smoke rising from a Beretta pistol cradled in her hands.

Maven looked back to Royce. He kneeled on his chest. Royce's mouth was open, but he made no attempt to talk. His eyes were full, staring up at the snowy shadows drifting against the ceiling.

Maven waited. He waited for Royce to look at him.

Royce never did. His eyes stayed on the ceiling, amazed by the tumbling black flakes. He died watching them.

Maven stood after a while. Danielle came up behind him.

"He was going to kill you," she said.

The emptiness Maven felt was acute, like the hole in his head where his left eye used to be. He said, "We were going to kill each other."

Danielle reached out to him one-handedly, like a child uncertain whether the thing she wanted to touch was hot or cold. "I did it for you."

Maven took the murder weapon from her other hand and dropped it onto Royce's chest. Then he turned and started back through the broken door. He was walking away.

"Neal?" she said, a note of panic in her voice.

Maven kept walking.

RETREAT

MAVEN DROVE THE PARISIENNE NORTH INTO THE VERMONT mountains, Ricky sleeping fitfully next to him. No radio, no conversation, no stops. The stillness of the frozen terrain suited his mind-set.

The sign read MOUNTAINSCAPE RETREAT. The main building looked like a small ski lodge. The branches of the surrounding trees were coated with sun-reflecting ice, like trees made of glass.

The inside was alpine, peaceful. The admitting director's lips appeared very pink within his salt-and-pepper beard. "The VA has its own residential detox and recovery," he said.

Maven said, "They're not top five in the country. I looked you up."

"There is currently a three-month waiting list for a bed, and even then, his insurance would cover very little of it."

Maven lifted the duffel bag onto the counter. He ran the zippers down each end.

The admitting director looked at the cash inside.

"Enough for a full six-month program," said Maven. "He's a disabled army veteran. You can move him to the front of the line."

OUTSIDE, MAVEN HELPED LOAD RICKY OUT OF THE CAR AND INTO A wheelchair. Ricky looked over at the admitting director, watching them from the building.

"You can do this," said Maven, kneeling in front of Ricky. "You have to."

Ricky winced, the thought of a six-month stay worsening his headache. "You'll take care of my car?"

"I will."

"You gonna visit?"

"Yeah. I'm gonna visit."

Ricky looked down into his lap.

Maven said, "Ricky. I know I fucked up a hundred different ways. I'll carry that with me forever."

Ricky looked at him—really looked at him—and said, "What about you? What do you do now?"

Maven straightened. "One more thing I gotta do. One last guy I gotta see."

Burning Window

LOCKERTY WAS IN HIS UNDERWEAR EATING PASTA AT THE KITCHEN table. He was a messy eater and didn't like to feel self-conscious, so he always ate alone. And if the meal involved a red sauce, he ate without too many stainable clothes on.

The television was on next to the refrigerator, but he had the *Boston Phoenix* personals open in front of him, and he was more interested in scanning for some action. By chance, he looked up as the photograph of a young, black boxer was shown on the screen. The words below read, "Brockton Fight Legend in Grisly Discovery."

The Dynamo. Lewis Termino. Royce's pit bull.

A grisly discovery?

Lockerty said to the TV, "Are you shitting me?"

The story ended fast. He had come to it too late.

"Mr. Leroy!" he called.

He tried changing stations, but he kept pressing the wrong buttons. He couldn't find out anything more.

"Mr. Leroy!"

The house was awfully quiet. Nothing more than the sound of water running through the pipes. Lockerty stood, leaving his napkin on the table, downplaying his concern. He moved to the window and looked outside, where dusk was turning to night.

He arrived just in time to see the end of a long shadow running across the yard below.

"Mr. Leroy!"

He took a knife off the table and went to the back stairs, calling for him. The upstairs bathroom door was shut. Lockerty rushed inside with the knife, just as Mr. Leroy was stepping out of the shower.

Mr. Leroy looked at the knife, looked at Lockerty.

Lockerty said, "I think he's here."

Mr. Leroy squeezed his blond dreadlocks with a towel, then reached for his pants. "Bringin' me his other eye."

MAVEN WAITED BENEATH THE FRONT PORCH AS LOCKERTY'S WATCH-man came to the head of the stairs, looking toward the cars, investigating the noise. When he turned to go back to his padded chair, Maven grasped his ankle from the side, upending him hard. Maven jumped onto the porch in a flash, but the fall had done the job, the watchman out cold.

Inside, Carlo heard Lockerty calling him from upstairs. "A minute!" he yelled back, moving out the front door onto the porch, checking on the bang he had heard and felt. He saw a man lying half on his side at the top of the steps. "Jimmy!" he said, rushing to him.

But it was not Jimmy. It was Maven, and he lifted his hand and shot Carlo twice in the chest.

Mr. Leroy arrived thirty seconds later. He stopped at the threshold of the wide-open front door, seeing Carlo dead on the porch.

Mr. Leroy smiled and started back inside, going to the stairs, gun first.

Maven found the bedroom at the end of the upstairs hallway. The bed he had been strapped to was still there, the lumpy mattress stained and bare. He looked to the window, saw the same leafless tree branches he used to stare at. He went to the window and for the first time saw the ocean beyond, the shore lapping at a narrow beach underneath the low, swelling moon.

He pulled out a knife and slashed open the top of the mattress, exposing springs and old filler. He pulled out a squeeze bottle of lighter fluid and doused the mattress, flipping a lit match at it.

The white Jamaican entered the room barefoot and bare-chested. The flaming mattress compelled his attention, leaving Maven just the extra moment he needed to come at him hard from the side.

He drove Mr. Leroy against the wall, rattling the old window. Mr. Leroy's gun discharged, the round firing into the floor, the shock of it causing him to take his finger off the trigger. Maven slammed his arm against the wall and the gun popped free. Maven reached for it and quickly tossed it onto the flaming bed.

Mr. Leroy pulled a knife from his pocket, flipped it open, and—before Maven turned back—buried it in Maven's thigh. His leg screamed, and Mr. Leroy went after Maven's gun arm and neck, locking up his elbow, forcing Maven toward the flames. Maven pushed back, the knife in his leg weakening and yet hardening him at the same time. The Jamaican had a hand around Maven's throat, and Maven saw a timepiece around the man's wrist, and something about it commanded his attention.

An Oris timepiece. Maven's watch. Seeing it changed everything. Maven pivoted on the painful leg, shifting his weight with a wrathful yell, spinning Mr. Leroy around. He backed the Jamaican toward the flames—near enough that the Jamaican's dreads began to smolder.

Mr. Leroy let up on Maven's throat, and Maven shoved away from him, the Jamaican just avoiding the flames. Maven looked down at the knife handle jutting from his thigh and yanked it out in one swift motion. It hurt more coming out than going in. The blade was slick with his blood, and in a moment of madness, staring at Mr. Leroy, Maven licked the silver clean.

Mr. Leroy's fire-brightened eyes went wide, seeing this. His hair was smoking. Maven advanced, backing him up to the window, not with his gun but with the knife.

MR. LEROY'S HOWLING CHASED LOCKERTY FROM HIS HIDING PLACE inside the house. He rushed out the still-open front door, past Carlo's dead eyes and down the stairs, past Jimmy lying on the grass, rounding the corner toward the cars with keys in hand.

The cars were all burning inside, the upholstery torn up and flaming.

Lockerty panicked. He thought about running for the road in his underwear. Then he went back up the porch stairs to Carlo, looking for his gun. He grabbed it and ran down to the grass, this time heading around the house toward the back, toward the shore.

He stopped when he saw flames coming from the second-floor of his house. At that precise moment a shirtless body smashed through the window and fell, dreadlocks over bare feet, to the ground.

Lockerty saw one-eyed Maven standing in the window, framed by fire, looking down. Lockerty popped two caps in his direction, running across the grass to the wood steps leading to the moonlit beach. Wind ripped through him, running too fast, breathing too hard. The sand was harder closer to the water, so he ran with the edge of the tide lapping at him, out past the edge of his property, hoping to find some hiding place beyond.

The first gun crack he barely heard. The second kicked up a bit of sand in front of him. He turned and fired behind him while still running. The third skipped up some water, again a miss. Lockerty turned to shoot again and was struck, middle left between two ribs, and the sudden pain brought him down.

He fired twice more in anger at Maven's distant figure, and the gun clicked dry. Lockerty dropped it and tried crawling, but it was no good. He lay down to rest a moment and found it impossible to sit up again.

The water at his feet made bearable the heat building up inside his chest. All he could do was watch Maven limp toward him across the sand, a gun low at his side.

MAVEN SAT A FEW YARDS AWAY FROM LOCKERTY, FEELING NOTHING for him now. The older man was dying and there was nothing to say.

He looked out at the water coming in, cold as moonlight, dark as oil. His thigh muscle twitched, the knife wound like a little mouth crying out in blood and pain.

When he looked back at Lockerty after a while, Lockerty was dead.

Maven detected movement to his right. A seagull, picking through the night sand. Maven hadn't expected to see this: he hadn't expected to see the end. He'd envisioned himself somehow fading away as the job was completed. Expiring in the process. Dying in the attempt.

Maven sighted the gull, believing it to be the same one that had visited his sickbed dreams. But eventually he lowered the gun, knowing he was done.

THE CYCLE

THE MORNING SUN ROSE COLD OVER THE NEIGHBORHOOD, LIGHT coming in at a hard slant. Maven waited after ringing the bell, and the door was pulled open by a young, brown-skinned man wearing a Tufts crewneck over a collared shirt.

Maven said, "Looking for Agent Lash."

Rosey Lash sized up the caller, cautious. "Hold on."

Inside, Rosey stepped back into the kitchen where Lash was clearing their breakfast dishes. "Some guy here for you, Dad. Looks pretty out of it."

Lash went to his jacket hanging over a chair and slid his sidearm out from the holster beneath it. He tucked it into the back of his pants and went to the door.

It was Maven, though it took Lash many moments to be certain. The eye patch was legit, he could see the edge of a scar showing off one corner. Maven's face looked as if someone had got at it with a potter's tool. He wore a loose-fitting army jacket, a large duffel bag at his feet.

"Well." Lash backed away from the door, inviting Maven inside.

Maven carried the heavy bag with a painful limp. He set it down next to the kitchen table with a clunk and lowered himself into one of the chairs, one leg outstretched.

Lash stood for another moment, then sat down across from him, such that Maven could not see the gun tucked into the small of his back.

"Rosey, why don't you hit your room for a bit, all right?"

Rosey looked at his father. "You sure?"

Lash said to Maven, "We're fine here, right?"

Maven nodded.

Rosey didn't leave yet. "You sure you're okay?"

Lash wanted to pull his bighearted boy into a hug. He did care about the old man after all.

"We'll be fine," Lash said, and Rosey backed off, retreating down the hall.

Lash relaxed a bit, now that they were alone. "What'd you do—follow me here some day?"

Maven nodded.

Lash pointed to the floor with his chin. "What's in the bag?"

"Guns."

Maven's hand trembled on the table. Not nerves, more like muscle fatigue. The wristwatch was the only part of him that clicked with the put-together guy Lash first met. But there was blood on the strap, a smudge of dried red on the side of Maven's palm and on his shirt cuff visible below the coat sleeve.

Lash made as if he were adjusting his shirt for comfort, sliding the gun from the back of his pants to the underside of his thigh. "So."

Maven took in the open boxes on the counter and the two sealed cartons near the door. He was acutely aware of the blind spot behind him.

"I gave you up for dead," said Lash. "Bottom of a lake somewhere. Or parceled out into Dumpsters around the city. But then I started hearing things. People saying the bandits were back—only, one guy this time. Wearing an eye patch. And a patrol cap."

Maven reached up, feeling his unwashed hair. "Lost the cap somewhere along the way."

"And the eye?"

"Same thing."

Maven's intonation was flat, as though he had suffered a concussion or some other trauma. Lash noticed more blood now, flecks on the side of his neck, a spot on his earlobe.

"So you brought guns. What about the money?"

"Gone," said Maven. "All gone."

Lash thought he was telling the truth. "So what brings you to my crib this chilly winter morning?"

"I thought it was obvious. I'm turning myself in."

Lash's mobile rang in his belt clip. His eyes stayed on Maven, but he had to let go of his sidearm under his leg to free his phone. He pressed SEND. "Lash."

He listened, watching Maven staring at the table, the guy gingerly touching the bone around his eye patch, his mind somewhere else.

"Let me hit you back in a bit," he said, hanging up, placing the phone on the table in front of him. Lash was excited and trying not to show it. "Cops are at a house in Swampscott right now. They found Ernesto Lockerty down by the water, shot dead, his house half-burned down."

Maven nodded, looking up.

Lash said, "A similar thing happened to this new cat, an upstart, kind of a mystery man. Name of Brad Royce."

Maven's eye glanced away, came back.

Lash let all this settle over him gently, like a fresh sheet upon an old mattress. "Let me see if I got this straight. You just wiped out the drug trade in all of Greater Boston. Single-handedly. You tore it all down."

Maven shrugged. "It won't even last a day. Bad guys looking to fill in the void as we speak."

"But they have some fear in them now. That's a start."

Maven looked around. He would remember this room. In

prison, on long days in his cell, he would picture the old, imperfect glass of the cabinets, smell the congealed syrup and toaster crumbs, the tired white paint of the apartment walls. He would never forget the room he surrendered his life in.

The bruises in his back had fused into a brace of pain. He had done something to his shoulder that didn't start hurting until now. Even his teeth felt loose as he pushed at them with his notched tongue. But his blood felt clean for the first time in a long time. He was impatient, ready to go.

"So how do we do this?" he said.

Lash had never got a decent read on Maven until now. "Black Falcon Terminal. The mess that went down. You bandits were there, weren't you?"

Maven nodded.

"You came down and saved my ass. Why?"

Maven shrugged. "I don't even know."

Lash liked that answer. He let go of his sidearm and leaned forward, folding his hands on the table.

"Okay, here's the thing. You come to me at an awkward time. I don't want to say you went and turned yourself in to the wrong guy, but . . . see, you wouldn't know this, but I got my task force taken away from me. After that clusterfuck at Black Falcon, the one that was meant for you. Yeah. So they offered me reassignment overseas. And I was all set to walk, I even had this letter, this pretty little thing, all typed out. Had my boy proofread it for me—that's what I'm paying his tuition for, right?" Lash smiled at himself. "But I couldn't do it. I don't know. Couldn't go out like that. And that's when it occurred to me. See, overseas means less oversight. More wiggle room. The game we're playing here, the street game—it's just a cycle. A carousel going round and round. And the cycle is endless, you know that. All a man can hope to do is define himself in it. And you did that, you made it to the center, flipped the off switch. Stopped the fucker dead. Even for just a day."

Maven straightened a bit. He sensed something coming, something he hadn't expected at all. What was it Danielle had said to him that day in Gridley, against the flat edge of a painted rock by the side of the railroad tracks? *Don't you know by now that nothing ever happens the way you think it will?*

"This is my last chance to truly impact this game," said Lash. "I don't see anything left for me but to go all in. And to go all out. And if they don't like it? Hell, in my mind, I'm already gone. Like you."

Lash hesitated a moment. It was reckless, what he was about to do—but recklessness was exactly what the situation required.

This guy had something. Something Lash could channel and use.

"Long windup, but here's the pitch." Lash laid a hand flat on the table, calling for a new card from the dealer. "What if, instead of turning you in—I was to offer you a job instead?"

ABOUT THE AUTHOR

CHUCK HOGAN IS THE BESTSELLING AUTHOR OF *The Standoff, The Blood Artists, The Killing Moon,* and *Prince of Thieves,* which was awarded the Hammett Prize for excellence in crime writing and is being made into a major motion picture by Warner Bros. He is also the author, with Academy Award–winning *Pan's Labyrinth* filmmaker Guillermo del Toro, of *The Strain* trilogy. He lives with his family outside Boston.